Praise for APPREH

"Excellent debut from Mark Bergin. He writes with authenticity because he lived the life and truly knows what it's like to be a cop. That's what makes *Apprehension* such a great read and draws you in from the start."
— David Swinson, author of *Crime Song* and *The Second Girl*

". . . A great read written by a real cop. It delves into the contemporary workings of policing from the inside out. The book succeeds in capturing the emotion, humor, ambiguity, fear, complexity and excitement of being a police officer by telling real-life stories thinly layered in veiled fiction to protect the innocent. I enjoyed reading *Apprehension* very much, and you will too."
— David P. Baker, Retired Chief of Police, Alexandria, VA

"A terrific first novel that combines non-stop action, an authentic gritty world, and a hero to restore your faith in heroes. Crime fiction has a terrific new voice in Mark Bergin, a former Alexandria, Virginia, police officer, who knows what he's writing about."
— Christina Kovac, author of *The Cutaway*

"A masterful writer. Pick this up and enjoy the read from an author who has been there and writes from experience and context that is virtually unmatched since the Joseph Wambaugh days."
— Hassan Aden, Retired Chief of Police, Greenville, NC

"An exciting journey replete with interesting and engaging characters in a police adventure where the city's drug-infested streets come to life. It is a must read."
—Ken Howard, Retired Captain, Alexandria Police Department and first commander of the Jump-Out Boys narcotics unit

"An authentic and gripping cop story. Through the lens of retired police lieutenant Mark Bergin, the reader is provided with a unique insight into the inner workings of the criminal justice system. The plot twists are intriguing and keep you guessing." —David Nye, Chief of Police, Fredericksburg, VA

"Compelling. . . . Bergin, a former reporter and a policeman, writes with authority and empathy about cops. A gritty and authentic new voice in police fiction." —*Kirkus Reviews*

"Set in the shadows of Washington, D.C., Mark Bergin's *Apprehension* tells the story of wounded, weary police officers trying to keep their city safe and their lives as normal as possible. A police procedural that extends beyond daily practice and detail to get to the heart of its conflicted characters, *Apprehension* is also a timely testament to the courage of police officers and the complexity of the obstacles they face. A must-read for anyone curious to know the true intricacies of the men and women who serve in law enforcement."
—E.A. Aymar, coeditor and contributor to *The Night of the Flood!*

Published by Inkshares, Inc., Oakland, California
www.inkshares.com

Edited by Christopher Murray
Cover design by and author photo by Jim Craige Photography
Interior design by Kevin G. Summers

ISBN: 9781947848849
e-ISBN: 9781947848726
LCCN: 2018967131

First edition

Printed in the United States of America

APPREHENSION

MARK BERGIN

"Complaints are what lieutenants are for. Got a case number yet?"

"871019-145," the patrol officer read from his notebook.

Kelly pulled out his own notebook and took down the case number, which began with the year, 1987, and date of October 19 in four digits and ended with the sequence listing of the call as it came in. "One forty-five? That's a lot of cases today."

"Yeah, the TAC unit was out in the hoods after midnight, got a lot of drug stuff. Like they do."

Kelly nodded toward the apartment. "What's his name? How's he look?"

"They got it inside," he said, and smiled oddly.

Kelly slipped his sunglasses into his blazer pocket as he entered the dark apartment stairwell, jogged up the stairs, and began prepping himself for the case. Shoes shined, creases sharp, haircut tight. He was ready. He thought he was having a good day. He was wrong.

He hurried because of excitement, not requirement: the stiff was old and ripe, his sergeant had told him back at headquarters, so no real need for speed. But he loved his job, the importance of being a cop and the challenge of a new case, though as a Youth Services detective, he would hand this death case off to the first real homicide detective who showed up. Kelly didn't mind the relatively lowly assignment to Youth. He got to protect kids.

The unit door was propped open to air out the smell. A patrol sergeant stood just inside with two other officers markedly old and young, and Kelly looked to them for a quick rundown. The sergeant looked at the older patrolman, who nodded to the youngster next to him.

The youngster, a recruit in training, stammered a moment and began. "On Wednesday, October 19, 1987, at four thirt—er, sixteen-thirty hours, we received a call for a suspicious

CHAPTER 1

Dead Right There

ON THE SECOND-WORST day of his life, Detective John Kelly drove fast into the parking lot and stopped his green unmarked sedan outside the dead man's apartment, almost skidding but not quite. He unfolded his long legs and levered himself out of the car. Several marked cruisers were parked crookedly near the door, and Kelly had to turn his wide shoulders to pass between them.

It was a sunny October afternoon, an Indian summer in Alexandria, Virginia, and surprisingly warm, not a good thing where bodies are concerned, and he said as much to Peterson, the uniformed officer taking names at the door. Kelly checked the names listed on Peterson's clipboard.

"No EMTs came in? I see they're here," Kelly said, jerking his head toward an idling ambulance out front.

"Nah. Sarge got here before them, checked in, and told 'em they weren't needed. They were pissed, though. Wanted in. Might complain."

For Ruth, Anna, and John, the three-starred constellation at the center of my universe. Beloved, snarky, and vital all three, all three.

To the men and women of the Alexandria, Virginia, Police Department. Get home safe tonight.

death. Original call to 9-1-1 was at 1626, first unit on the scene was Peterson at 1631. Neighbors from the apartment upstairs smelled something and called management, so they came and knocked. Used the master key but found the chain on. The smell made it pretty obvious, so they called us." The recruit checked his notes. "We kicked the chain off and entered at 1639. Found him, called for an ambulance and . . ." He trailed off, unsure of what else he knew worth sharing.

Kelly looked at the older cop, obviously the recruit's field training officer and well-known to Kelly. The FTO said, "We secured the apartment. No one else was here. Quick look will tell you what this is about, though I'm sure the A-Team will give it a good go." The A-Team was the group of senior detectives usually assigned to death investigations. Little Alexandria did not have enough murders to warrant a full-time dedicated homicide squad.

"Did you touch him?" Kelly asked, pulling on latex gloves as the officers led him through a door to the source of the smell. "Do any CPR or first aid?"

"What for? He was very DRT." Kelly nodded, but the young recruit looked puzzled.

"DRT," the FTO said. "Dead right there. No reason to go near him, plenty not to."

Kelly could see why. The room was one of two bedrooms in the second-floor unit, at the back with no balcony. No furnishings except a weight bench consisting of a padded, adjustable seat with two welded arms rising at each side and ending in V-shaped flanges designed to cradle a laden bar for bench presses. The body lay on the bench, belly up and distended, with the head hanging down off the top of the pad. A man's dress belt was buckled around its neck to drape down near the body's left hand. The bench faced a large mirror that sat on the floor, leaning against a wall, and a wheeled stand with a small television and VCR, from which a tape protruded. Large handcuffs secured the body's thick ankles to the legs of the bench, heavy steel handcuffs, not the padded or furry shackles sometimes found in sex events like these. No pants, and what Kelly first thought was a frayed T-shirt turned out to be a silk teddy with lace trim.

Ain't self-love grand, he thought.

The body was male, white—*mostly*, Kelly thought ruefully—in his forties or fifties and nude, except for seventeen clothespins clipped to various parts of his anatomy. A circle of clips ran around his navel like a little picket fence, pinched to his once-flabby skin with gaps where some had fallen away. The hot apartment had contributed to the body's decomposition, and puffy, greenish bloat stretched the skin and popped the clothespins off, leaving dark marks. These matched the purple of the dead man's feet, hands, and buttocks, now filled with drained, dead blood in a process called postmortem lividity.

"Where's the key?" Kelly asked the FTO.

"Bottle on the floor on the other side of him. String to the key inside is attached to his left wrist. Floor's dry now, but discolored from the water that was in it. Looks like he never tried to pull it. Maybe died of a heart attack before the ice melted." Kelly knew some thrill seekers restrained themselves for kicks, but what's the fun in getting free whenever you wanted? It had to hurt, to last, to be inescapable at least for a while, so the vic secured the key in a bottle of water, then froze it. The time it took to melt was the time to play. The belt would be pulled to cinch around the neck and cut circulation in a way—urban legend had it—that would amplify orgasm. Or accidentally kill. As Kelly peered around the corpse, another clothespin pinged away, joining others on the floor.

"Got his name?" Kelly asked.

The recruit said, "Yes, his ID was in his wallet, in the other bedroom. We found it during the initial check. Waiting for a detective to get a warrant for the rest of the search." He stared at Kelly, trying to stifle a look between amusement and horror. Kelly thought the recruit must have a rather vanilla sex life to be surprised at this.

"Guess that's me, unless one of the other guys gets here," Kelly said. He stepped back from the room with the body toward the living room and leaned to put down his heavy, portable radio. In detective's clothes, he had nowhere to carry it other than a jacket pocket, and it ruined the lines. As he placed it on a table, it squawked with his call number, Unit 60. Headquarters was calling him. He brought it back up and keyed the mic.

"Unit 60, back."

"Per the watch commander, break from your call and respond to 1241 Airedale Drive for a missing person, juvenile. Code 2."

Annoyed, Kelly began to respond. "Headquarters, confirm? Break from a sudden death for—"

Kelly stopped, then ran from the apartment and the surprised uniformed officers there. His tires squealed before he closed the door as he responded to the address he knew well. His brother's house.

The call had gone out thirty minutes before. An eight-year-old hadn't gotten off the school bus at home at the end of the day. Two officers and a sergeant were dispatched at first, standard procedure.

There was little to no worry at this point. The first cop on the scene would search the family house: a surprising number of "missing" kids were in fact at home, hiding or just over-looked by a panicked parent. The majority of the rest (read: all) of the kids reported missing in Alexandria were found within minutes or at most a few hours later, wandering home from forgotten or unplanned play dates or late school programs.

Not this time.

When the check of the house was negative, the sergeant requested more officers to search and a response from CID, the Criminal Investigations Division. The mom was asked more and better questions, and better descriptions were broadcast citywide. An officer checked in at Emma's elementary school to question teachers and administrators while another responded to the bus barn to check with drivers for unrecognized kids who maybe got on, and thus off, the wrong bus in the wrong place. Officers were sent to specific homes of the child's friends, and other units began knocking door-to-door. Classic police foot-work. Slow and steady, by the book (there really isn't a book, but . . .). All normal, until Mom asked the reporting officer to call Detective John Kelly. Kelly specifically. Her brother-in-law. Emma's uncle.

Kelly drove Code 3 to Brenda and Patrick Kelly's home. Full lights and siren—not authorized, but he would deal with that later if anybody called him on it. All the parking spaces in the block were filled with marked cruisers, so he drove up on the grass in the yard. Kelly ran through the familiar front door and hugged Brenda, who burst into tears against his chest. Brenda had kept the baby weight these eight years since Emma, now missing, was born, but still had a pretty, round face and happy eyes. Kelly always felt happy for his little brother, Patrick, happy for a happy wife and two happy kids, kids like Kelly and his own wife, Janet, had never got around to having. And now Kelly would be the all-powerful big brother again to Patrick and bring home his wandering child, Emma.

They always came home. Almost always.

Kelly held Brenda for a full minute and whispered softly to her while raising a finger to stop the sergeant's report. Her wailing began to abate, and she gained control. Kelly spoke softly. "Bren, where's Kate?" He hadn't seen their ten-year-old.

"Reading program. She'll be on the late bus. Can someone get her? I want Kate here. Now!"

"We'll take care of that, Bren. Don't you worry. Did you call Pat? Yes? Good."

As she calmed, he stepped back and waved to the sergeant to begin. Kelly stood silently, absorbing the action report. Then Kelly turned it on.

"Okay. Door-to-door from the school. Four officers, one in each direction. Not just one to eventually cover each side. Is the watch commander en route?" Meaning, get the lieutenant assigned as today's watch commander here. Right now.

At the sergeant's nod, Kelly continued. "PIO, for a press release?" Again, telling the sergeant to bring the public information officer to the scene. Kelly lacked the authority to do this, but no one would argue with him right now. There were certain other things Kelly couldn't do, but the lieutenant could. And he did, when he arrived five minutes later. After a briefing, the lieutenant got on the radio.

"Unit 10 to Headquarters, call Fairfax or U.S. Park Police to get us a helicopter with FLIR." Forward-looking infrared could find a suspect hiding under a parked car from a thousand feet up, so it could easily pick out a child in a park or alley, even in the approaching darkness. "Unit 10 to the CID supervisor?"

"Unit 23," the detective sergeant piped up.

"10 to 23, let me have all available CID units respond to this address." A heavy response so early, but it was Kelly's niece, after all. "Also, Headquarters, hold over the daylight shift." A big step, costly in overtime to keep Days on duty after their normal end time, but missing person searches were staff-intensive.

Emma was eight years old, four-foot-eight in the black-and-white sneakers she was said to wear. She had red hair in a thick braid and round, brown eyeglasses. Her mother was fairly sure she was wearing a blue button-down shirt and dark pants and carrying her pink backpack when she left for the bus stop that morning. School administrators were called, and they confirmed she had been at school all day and was not in any after school activities. The driver of her bus route said he did not notice her on the bus that afternoon but wasn't sure, as there were about nine kids that got off at her stop. Her teacher, reached at home by telephone, reported nothing unusual in her behavior that day.

No progress was made making contact with Emma's friends. None had seen her after school, but two remarked that she had not been on the bus going home. She wasn't at the rec center, or at any toy, book, candy or other shop on the Avenue. Units continued to circulate, because she could pop out of any house at any unexpected time. She'd get home, they always did, but it would be nice to allay Brenda's fears as instantaneously as possible. And Kelly's. And now Patrick's, too. Kelly's brother came home before dinnertime, pushing past the uniform at the door with a blurted, "I live here!" and bursting in the door with panicked eyes.

"She's gone. She's—I don't know . . ." Brenda moaned into his shoulder. "She didn't come home off the bus. We don't—they . . ." And her control ran out, words melding into a long, low wail. Patrick looked up from nuzzling her collar into Kelly's eyes.

"What do we do, John? Is this serious? What's going on?" Kelly's brother's eyes burned with dozens of questions.

Kelly closed up behind Brenda, put his hands on her shoulders to wrap her in family, and murmured to Patrick. "We run it as dangerous, but it isn't. I know it's scary. We always find them. You're here now, so I'm going out to work on it. I'll bring her back. Trust me." Kelly spoke with the confidence of a big brother and a trained cop and with the glibness of an experienced liar. Patrick nodded, and Kelly broke away.

As Kelly strode out of the house to personally check that the officers were canvassing, he was hailed by Mike Burgess, the *Gazette* newspaper reporter. Kelly started to ignore him, but stopped and breathed in, then approached where Burgess stood at the curb. There was no crime scene tape to keep him back, but Burgess stayed on the sidewalk in front of the house. Kelly walked over.

"Hope the citizen doesn't complain about you on their lawn, John. Is this bigger than it sounds?" Burgess waved a small handheld police radio scanner.

"I'm related to the family, Mike. But you can't use that right now. What I need now is someone I can call at the TV news. I want to get something on the air now and not wait till the news at eleven. You got any contacts?"

"Sure, John. Let me make sure the stations totally scoop us by giving them the story before I go to print tomorrow. Related how?"

"My niece is the one's missing. Like I said, you can't use that. You have to have friends at Channel Four, or Seven, or Nine? Or that new one, Fox, what's it, Five?"

"Let me make some calls. Can I come in to use the phone in there?"

"No, we need that line open in case the kid or someone with her calls in to Mom." Kelly looked around. "Come over here with me."

Kelly walked across the lawn to the house next door and knocked hard. The woman who answered said she was a friend of Brenda and often babysat Emma and her sister. "I already told the other officer that she isn't here. Is there anything I can do?

"Yes. Let this man use your phone. It's police business—it will help us." Without waiting, Kelly stepped past the woman into her living room and picked up the phone receiver on the hall table. He handed it to Burgess and said, "Come back next door when you're done."

Burgess made calls and walked back to Patrick and Brenda's house. Kelly had warned the officer at the door to let him through. Kelly was speaking low with the trembling, wired parents, and the sergeant was taking information from a parade of officers. Burgess held himself back in the hall outside the kitchen, making himself invisible to absorb the atmosphere and pick up details and quotes he usually couldn't get at crime scenes. Officers continued their canvass, spreading outward from both the school and the family home. Others continued to circulate and to divert to specific locations as public calls of sightings came in—almost always inaccurate, but all had to be checked. The lieutenant asked to confirm a helicopter was on the way, and Headquarters said Park Police were available. Eagle One was overhead shortly thereafter, the intrusive whumping rattle of a Bell UH1 reminiscent of every Vietnam movie or, for some officers, their own real-life memories. The radio babbled.

"Unit 223, respond to 3800 Executive. Report of missing person seen entering the lobby there. Caller refused to be seen," said the dispatcher.

"223 direct, any apartment?"

"Negative, 323. Unit 242, respond to 509 East Monroe for a report of the missing person in the courtyard. See Mrs. Hernandez in apartment 101."

"Ten-four."

Numerous other sightings were broadcast. As each came in, it was noted by the sergeant on a big, white dry-erase board the watch commander kept in his trunk for such large-scale calls and had brought into the kitchen, which now served as a command post. Each officer working the call was listed, their current location or area of search plotted on a rough map sketched out in several colors. A column at one side listed each sighting by time and location. No need to note the results for each sighting. All were negative. The board would be closed out and wiped clean with a positive sighting. It was forgotten entirely in the scramble when Emma was finally found.

"Shots fired, shots fired! Unit 241, at 1211 North Quaker Lane, shots fired from inside the apartment. I'm . . . I'm okay. Gimme some units."

Brenda's house emptied as John quickly hugged Brenda and told Patrick, "Stay here. Stay calm," like commands to a pet, but Kelly's mind was already on North Quaker Lane with the patrol officer. Kelly's car was closest to the door, and the lieutenant jumped in with him as he accelerated backward across the lawn, throwing muddy grass and leaves and banging his back bumper into a parked civilian car before lurching forward and racing toward North Quaker, taillight glass sprinkling as he fishtailed away. Leaving the scene of an accident was a violation, but the lieutenant waved, *Go.*

The radio crackled. "I'm in the hall. Shots fired from inside through the door when I knocked. I'm not hit." Unit 241, updating for the responding units and breathing hard. "I got the hallway. Next unit cover the rear. Somebody cover the front, outside where my cruiser is. The apartment's one level up, windows face the front. Apartment 201." 241 paused, mic button held down, his excited panting audible. "No sounds from inside. Wait. Wait. I hear a girl screaming."

Kelly and the lieutenant were the third car on the scene. He ignored the lieutenant's order to stay outside and ran into the open entryway. There, staircases diverged, with one set leading up to the apartments and another, where 241 had taken cover, going down to the laundry and storage rooms. Kelly ducked next to the officer. He knew he should have gone to the rear and entered safely through the basement level to come up the stairs under cover, but that would have taken twenty more seconds.

241, a senior officer named Powers, was bleeding from a cut above his left eye, wiping it away regularly with his left sleeve while pointing his revolver at the apartment door with his right. The sleeve was sodden.

"When's the last time you heard screaming?"

"About a minute ago," Powers said. "Short. Sounded like, 'No.' Little girl's voice. Then a male voice. Nothing since."

Kelly heard more units skidding up, heard the lieutenant direct them on the radio. Heard him call for an SOT callout to activate the special operations team, members of which served in various duties throughout the department and came together when emergency calls required. This required. And for the hostage negotiation team. Kelly was HNT but knew he wouldn't be used to negotiate for his niece's life. Though he would do it best. "You talk with them?"

Powers shook his head, winced. "Nah, I just knocked. We had a call. Complainant said she saw a girl matching go into the building with a male. Said maybe this apartment 'cause the lights went on. White male or Hispanic, dark jacket, no further. I knock. Male said, 'Who's there?' I said, 'Police.' Three shots through the door. I was off to the side, but I got hit with

something, fragment maybe or part of the door. I'm all right."
Powers had to shout now over the roar of the hovering Eagle
One, whose spotlight brought daylight to the courtyard but
left the entryway and stairs in relative gloom.

"Go get yourself fixed up. Go out the back door."

"Nah, I'm fine. Staying," Powers said, wiping his eye clear
again.

Kelly tried to get the lieutenant on the radio, but too many
units were responding, confirming locations, getting repeats
on the description. "Shots fired" brought everyone, even officers from Headquarters or officers who had been operating on
other channels and uninformed of the focus of this call. After
a minute of jumbled transmissions blocked his own, Kelly told
Powers, "Get out of here, tell the LT what we have, and get
yourself patched up." Kelly yelled over the roar of the orbiting
helicopter. "Tell the LT where I am and what I can see and
what I can cover from here. Go now." Powers acquiesced to
the tactical need and scuttled away down toward the rear exit,
telling Kelly he'd send a backup or come back himself.

All but one of the bulbs were out in the stairway, and the
shifting helicopter spotlight alternately lit the courtyard, leaving Kelly in comparative darkness, or shone partway under the
overhang onto the stairs and caught Kelly in its scattered glare.
Kelly hunkered down more when spotlit and rose again to
cover the door, but his patience ran out. He had to get close to
the door to hear if the guy was talking or Emma was screaming
or worse. Maybe he'd just go through the door, not wait, go
right now. Take action. Save her. Not wait.

More cruisers pulled up on the edge of the parking lot
away from the front-facing windows of the target unit, and a
car alarm began bleating. As the spotlight shifted away from
Kelly again and he heard officers clattering in through the back
lower-level apartment entrance, Kelly stood erect, climbed the

stairs fast, and walked slowly to approach the door, gun out at eye level. He took a step and saw the bullet holes, rims shiny and sharp and splayed outward jaggedly, about heart high. He took another step forward and the door opened in front of him, inward, and a small leg in pink jeans and a black-and-white sneaker began to slide out into view.

Kelly stopped dead. Reflexively he had pointed his revolver at the leg, but it was Emma's leg, so he aimed away. Her arm, then her other leg, then her full body edged out. She faced back into the apartment, one little eye obscured and cheeks wrinkled in the hand of a man who reached around her with his arm under hers and up her chest. He looked down, not at Kelly. His right hand held a chrome revolver, its barrel in Emma's mouth, pointing straight in, and she coughed around it. She was panting, gasping, breathing hard around the horrid thing in her mouth that glinted in the shifting light. Her eye was locked up on the man, and she never saw Kelly till he spoke her name, softly not to startle but loud enough to carry over the clatter.

"Emma. Emma, it's gonna be all right. Emma, it's Uncle John right here. It'll be okay." Only the side of her face was visible, but her eye reacted to Kelly's words. Reacted with maybe more fear. Bewildered at a friendly voice within all this terror. Her body twitched and her head tried to turn, but it was held even tighter by the clenching hand of the suspect, her pudgy cheeks puffing out around the gun barrel. Kelly the cop, the negotiator, had to study the suspect, but Kelly the man, the uncle, could not break his gaze from Emma's confused and frightened eye. Safety so close, she had to think, but danger still there—why?

"Shut up. Shut up, *Uncle* John," the man said. The sneer in his voice was soft, oddly flat, almost inaudible. Mean eyes. "Stop there." Hard to hear with the helicopter, the shouts of the other cops now in the stairwell. The suspect walked Emma forward in front of him, his arms up and elbows out. He was a small man, white skin with thin blond hair. Jeans and a dark jacket that looked dirty. His face was dirty, too. Brown cowboy boots. One of Emma's sneakers was missing, and her sock was torn at the ball of her foot. As the suspect spoke, he gestured with his arms, raising them slightly in cadence with his words, and the gun barrel lifted Emma's face, pressing hard up against her front teeth.

Kelly was just fifteen feet from them, aiming his pistol at the furrow between the suspect's eyebrows. He could take the shot. He knew he could make that shot, five yards, the shortest distance they fired from at the police range, straight through the suspect's nose to the top of the spinal column, cut his strings before he could pull the trigger but even a tiny miss, an inch off with the weapon in Emma's mouth, any involuntary dying muscle spasm could trigger, a shot and end her. And Kelly knew the moment he fired, the uniforms in the stairwell would open up in sympathetic fire, maybe taking Emma out with the suspect. No. No no no no no.

"Get back, get back, get back," the suspect hissed. He ground the pistol deeper into Emma and stepped forward. Emma gagged and sobbed.

"Okay, okay. It's gonna be okay. We're all calm, it's all good," Kelly shouted at the man. "What do I call you?"

Kelly stepped backward to maintain a distance, toward the stairs leading down from the apartment landing to the courtyard. Orders from the lieutenant on a cruiser PA loudspeaker and shouts from officers outside the building and in the stairwell now were unintelligible under the pounding clatter of the helicopter. Dozens of officers, he knew, would be arrayed outside the building, fanned out around the entryway, behind cars, and at corners. *Let him come out*, Kelly thought as he stepped backward, matching their pace.

"I'm Pickett," the man said, almost unheard in the roar, finally looking up at Kelly.

Emma moaned unintelligible words, muted by the gun barrel in her face and drowned out by the noise of the scene. Kelly thought she screamed, "Uncle John."

"Uncle John," Pickett said, unheard in the roar but Kelly read his lips. The suspect's mouth clenched, his face low near Emma's terrified eyes. Kelly took another step back. Pickett slid his left hand up the front of Emma's chest to cup her chin and force two dirty fingers into her mouth around the barrel of the gun, which slid out to bring the muzzle clear of her lips. Pickett yanked down on her chin and her mouth opened in a dark moan behind the shiny gun barrel, now pointing almost straight up, maybe away from her now.

Pickett and Emma shuffled forward toward the handrail above the stairs leading down, and a shotgun barrel entered Kelly's view, trained upward on the suspect from the stairwell below. Before Kelly reached the end of the landing, he stopped and raised both hands wide, pistol now palmed and aimed away, pointed up in a big gesture to keep Pickett's eyes on him and not down on Emma or the cops below.

Kelly holstered his gun, spreading his arms wide again.

The kidnapper slowly raised his gaze at Kelly's supplication. The helicopter swooped low, almost stopped at a point over the courtyard and behind Kelly, at its loudest so far. Pickett fixed Kelly with a stare, flat then suddenly furious. Kelly focused closely on the gun, and it became massive in his sight. Time lengthened, stopped.

"We can work . . ." said Kelly, shouting over the copter engine's clatter and percussive hammering of its rotor, each blade's passage now distinct, *whap . . . whap . . . whap . . .*

His eyes, fixed down on the gun, missed the suspect's sudden, crooked smile. All he saw was his own face reflected in the chrome, then the twitch of Pickett's finger triggering the hammer, which seemed to move with preternatural slowness, falling with an audible click and, after an eternity, the gun roaring. The orange muzzle flash burst across the front of Emma's face as the bullet flew unseen. Before Kelly or any cop could react, Pickett threw the gun down and kneed Emma in the back to push her toward Kelly, then spun to face the wall.

Kelly dove forward and caught Emma as she collapsed straight down onto loose knees. He grabbed her head as she fell face-first toward the concrete landing, mindless to the crashing impact on his elbows, cradling her with his muscled forearm then scuttling to cover her still body with his bulk and shield her from the shotguns now fully extended up through the railing at the suspect. Officers from the stairwell jumped over Kelly and swarmed the suspect, hitting him hard, denied the chance to shoot when he disarmed himself, ramming him into the wall and pulling him down.

As the scrum of cops and suspect crashed to the floor, Kelly and Emma huddled motionless. Kelly moved his face closer to Emma's ear and told her, "It's all right now, hon. It's all right, Emma. I got you. You're okay. Emma, you're okay." He whispered despite the copter's roar, face tight to her hair. After a moment, Kelly looked up, away from her, and saw the suspect was handcuffed, his gun pushed away and locked down under a cop's boot.

"Get him out of here. Check the apartment," Kelly shouted. He turned to Emma, covering her, and his lips felt wet in her hair. "You're okay now, hon."

A minute later, with the suspect gone and the apartment cleared of any other potential threat, the lieutenant knelt beside Kelly, still prone and protective over Emma on the hallway floor, and clasped his shoulder. Kelly felt safe and looked up, but saw the lieutenant flinch back. Kelly began to lift himself clear of Emma's small form, gently lifting her face toward his as his forearm came off the concrete. Her little head flopped back, and a gout of blood pushed out of her mouth and splashed warmly on his arm, shiny and black in the shifting glare.

The shot hadn't missed. Her eyes were still open, locked on Kelly's but fading, not shiny anymore, not reflecting the strobing lights all around the stairwell. As he looked, her left eye wandered and a tiny line of blood formed on her eyelid. She was shot right in front of them. In front of him.

Unprotected by him. Her blood was on his arm and had drenched her face and his while he whispered to her, whispered comfort and reassurance, both untrue. Lies she may have heard as she faded and died in front of them all. She was dead in his arms.

Dead right there.

CHAPTER 2

Prepare
Tuesday, November 1, 1988
One Year Later
1300–1400 HRS

UNTIL DETECTIVE JOHN Kelly's partner told him they were digging up the body, Kelly had kept himself under control. Or so he'd thought.

Kelly rubbed his eyes, bloodshot but not bleary. He was hunched over his desk, reading an interview transcript and talking on the telephone with the mother of a victim. His partner, Larry Ashby, strode into the office, threw his radio on the desk, and slammed his thin frame down into a wheeled desk chair. Kelly, trained observer, knew Ashby was angry because of Ashby's thin-pressed lips and the agitated rocking of the desk chair. Ashby glared at Kelly and barked, "I am so fucking pissed off." Which was another clue.

Kelly had spent the early afternoon at Headquarters, prepping for a pretrial meeting with the prosecutor on a parental abduction case he had closed by arrest two months ago. It was a slam dunk, but you never knew what little thing the defense attorney might pick apart to create reasonable doubt and kill the case. *Especially this defense attorney*, Kelly thought wistfully. At his desk and surrounded by his fellow busybodies, Kelly suppressed a smile.

The office was quiet. Prepping for his pretrial, Kelly had double-checked his case file for copies of pertinent court orders, divorce contracts, and custody agreements that formed the basis of the charge—that the suspect had failed to return his child to his ex-wife after a month-long visitation per order of the chief judge of the Juvenile and Domestic Relations Court. But little Jumari, eight, was back and safe now and Dad was going to prison, Kelly hoped. J&DR court judges weren't known for long sentences, so maybe that was why the prosecutor didn't object to the defense attorney's odd request to move the case to a higher, adult court. Normally, a kid coming home even days late was not dangerous, but this particular dad was bad news.

Ashby didn't even hang his suit jacket on the fancy wire hanger device he had nailed to the cubicle divider. Ashby wore suits well. Kelly looked lumpy in his, unable to easily find jackets and shirts that fit his thick neck and shoulders without tenting out at the waist or pants that rode easily over bulging calves. Ashby kept punching his cupped left palm with his right fist, muttering. Kelly ended the phone call so that Ashby could unload.

"I can't believe fucking Sarge had the balls to tell me I screwed up. He reviewed the case, the lieutenant reviewed it, the prosecutor reviewed it. Now . . . now they're reopening it," Ashby said. His voice was forceful but low so it wouldn't carry to where the higher-ups' offices were clustered around the exit hall.

"Reopening? They said new info. But after two years?" Kelly leaned back precariously in the spindly wheeled chair, but experience had taught him its limits. He put his feet up on his desk, and mud cracked off his shoes onto a file. Kelly didn't notice. Ashby pulled some photographs from a file on his desk, wincing momentarily at the bruises shown in them.

"Nobody noticed this. Not the ID tech who took them, not the ER doctors or the kid's own pediatrician. You can't see the marks unless you know they're there." Ashby removed a photograph from the file, stared at it, and clenched his teeth. "Even now, it's hard. So they're writing me up. Those fuckers . . . Come in every day and do your job then these mother . . ." Ashby went on cursing for a minute or two.

"Writing you up for something from two years ago? They couldn't find anything you did bad this year?" Kelly said to keep Ashby on topic.

"Fuck this year. Fuck 1988," Ashby said, his usual high spirits flattened. Sometimes experience doesn't prepare you for experiences. He pushed the case file across at Kelly. "Fuck this case. Her case. Jeez, now I guess my case again."

Ashby ground down to a stop as Kelly opened the file and took out a different photograph. Kelly grimaced too, then masked it. The photo was labeled with a date two years ago. He poked at the file, read the name *Burke, Allison* upside down on the tab, and looked up at Ashby.

"And so I get a '67 for missing it. For not acting on what Sarge now says is clear enough and available evidence to confirm an offense and identify a suspect. I'm the one in trouble," Ashby grumbled. An APD-67 was the department's Complaint/Commendation Form, although nobody could remember the last time it was used for a commendation.

"Run it down for me again. I don't remember Allison Burke."

"Why would you? Simple, but we couldn't close it. Ugly. We thought—I thought—her brother did it to her. Allison was barely a year old. One of my first big cases up here, after we came up. You weren't working that day.

"So I'm on Days, and there is . . ." Ashby started but paused as the portable radio on his desk emitted a short squeal, the warning that a hot call was coming. Kelly's radio lay silent on his desk. He hadn't turned it on. The alert tone was for a fight near the high school, and the call was dispatched Code 3—lights and sirens. Because they were detectives, neither Ashby nor Kelly was required to respond. Because they were good cops, they wanted to go. Because they were experienced, they knew the uniforms would clear the call long before they even got out of CID—which they did, and the detectives came back to Ashby's story.

That morning two years ago, a trembling teenage boy opened the door for responding officers who found Mrs. Dawn Burke upstairs cradling her screaming infant in her lap. Baby Allison was wrapped in a blanket but reportedly had been found half naked on a pile of bedding next to her crib in her second-floor bedroom. Medics were already on the scene and trying to get the sobbing mother to relinquish the child for examination. When she did, they found severe bruising to the child's upper thighs, groin, and abdomen and blood traces on the groin and belly. While medics transported the child, the patrol sergeant called for a detective to assist in what appeared to be a sexual assault and for an evidence technician to process the scene. There were no signs of forced entry in the house, and no one in the family had seen or heard an intruder. The family's fifteen-year-old son Brian was the only other person in the house. Mom was a Fed, an assistant director in the Treasury Department in Washington, D.C., just across the river. Dad was traveling. Ashby turned to stare at Kelly, suppressing a shiver and went on.

"The little kid, Allison, was messed up. Didn't die, but it was a near thing. She'd about been crushed. But no penetration, no evidence of sexual assault. We had nothing to go on. We figured the brother lifted her out of the crib and onto the floor, then lay down on her. That morning, Mom wakes up, goes to check the baby . . ." As he spoke, Detective Ashby pulled a particular photo out of the file pile and handed it to Kelly. "She finds Allison with her diaper off, her legs open, blood coming out, and freaks. Uniforms get there, and brother Brian is in the corner—he's freaked too. He'd screamed but he's quiet now. So, he's my obvious suspect right away, right? I get him downstairs and he says nothing, offers nothing, but he looks wrong, right? I figured he was good for it, but he wouldn't open up right then. I knew I'd interview him more later and he'd break. We took his clothes, did a Physical Evidence Recovery Kit on him but it turned out negative." Ashby handed Kelly the tech's report on the PERK, which showed that no hairs, fibers, or fluids of significance were found on the suspect or his clothing.

Kelly handed it back and looked again at the photograph in his hand, noting the 1986 case number on it. There was a surprising lack of blood on the tiny body depicted in the glossy 8-by-10. Extensive mottled bruising started pink at her knees and darkened to a vicious purple and black across her hips. One leg puffed out, grotesquely swollen.

"He never broke. I tried and tried."

At the hospital, doctors found extensive crush injury to Allison Burke's lower abdomen. Her hips were dislocated and one femur was snapped in two. Her uterus was crushed and ruptured from exterior pressure, and there were crush injuries to the colon. These resulted in the observed bleeding. There were no signs of penetration or evidence of semen, and no hairs, pubic or otherwise, were found on her body, other than several of the mother's long blonde head hairs. These were expected and insignificant.

Ashby named a common household product. "It's probably in every house in America, in the bathroom or the hall closet, but there was a lot on her. And now we learn it can cover up semen or saliva, ruin it for sampling so we can't get DNA, and maybe not even tell if evidence was ever there. Did the brother know this? Did Brian know he could cover evidence with it? How could a fifteen-year-old know this? Did he use it on her because that was his thing? He didn't have any on him but he had all night to wash up. Baby was silent till mom checked on her in the morning, probably unconscious from pain." Ashby had to stop, as anyone would, contemplating this horror, living in it again there at his desk, the dim sun trying to glow through broken November clouds and snow showers outside the second-floor office windows but not enough to lighten the pall. Kelly moved the photo back to Ashby's desk, his fingers exaggerated pincers, and Ashby sneered.

As Ashby talked, he continued to rock back and forth in the little desk chair, first small oscillations, then bigger till he alternated between lifting wheels off the ground and almost banging his face on the desk divider. Finally he stopped and held his chin in his cupped hands, elbows on the cubby desk pressing down on the remaining crime scene photos. He looked away, but Kelly could see anguish on the visible half of his face.

"I always thought the brother did it. I followed up and met with all of them, a bunch of times. Mom and Dad, they never said they believed Brian did it. They got real angry about it, but what other explanation was there? I think maybe they did suspect him, but to their credit, the P's never accused him, at least not out loud, not in front of me. But they did, you know. They looked at him and it was in their eyes, their body language. They worried, but they didn't want to know. Can you imagine—your daughter is attacked and you think your son did it?" Ashby shook his head and stared down, vibrating with building, bottled fury and tension.

"Wart Lip," Kelly said.

"Huh?" But Kelly knew Ashby had heard him.

"Wart Lip."

Wart Lip was their best story together, and they used it as an ice breaker, a tension breaker, and a test. Kelly remembered the last time he'd told the story of the Lady with the Wart on Her Lip, at a bar and grill in the West End of the city. He'd gone with coworkers after Commonwealth Day, the big all-day stream of trials, motions, hearings and evidentiary reviews every Thursday in Circuit Court, the felony court for the city. Uniforms, detectives, and narcs might testify in as many as five cases in a row. It was difficult to keep details straight from arrests that took place months prior, so it was not uncommon to see trained investigators on the stand reduced to reading aloud from reports, not the best way to instill confidence in their testimony but better than risking mixing up details between cases. Read: inaccurate or untruthful. Read: perjury.

Commonwealth Day was harrowing, so downing a few afterward was a common stress relief. And the lawyers were similarly interested in liquid relaxation, both prosecutors and defense attorneys. Kelly remembered telling the Wart Lip story to Rachel Cohen, then just a new public defender. Telling Wart Lip was a reliable way to test the listener. If she laughed, she was cool. If she was grossed out, she failed, and she might complain about your insensitivity, and you might get a '67. Fights, shootings, chases, hitting bad people with nightsticks, er, batons—all were good stories to tell. But Wart Lip was the best. So he told her:

"My partner Ashby and I show up at this duplex in Del Ray, what passes for middle class in this town. Call was for a domestic, sounds of a woman screaming. It's 2020, er, ten o'clock at night, dead quiet, no sound from the address and no answer at the door. I radio to ask Communications to call the complainant back to get further, but all of a sudden we hear a woman shrieking her head off upstairs and something like glass or a plate breaking. She's dying, I know it. I look at Ashby, tell him to get Code 5 so no one else will talk on the radio for a minute, and I kick the door in.

"Inside, run up the stairs, into a bedroom, and there is the lady. She has blood on the corner of her mouth. There's a broken mirror on the floor. Seven years of bad luck for someone. And there is the guy. He is a man-mountain, as big as Ashby and I put together. He's just standing there, fists clenched but down at his sides. He's not even looking at us—he's talking to her, saying, 'Baby, I love you, you know I do. I love you, I'ma treat you right. Why you doin' this to me?'

"It's too small a room to hit him with my baton. Sirens are coming but they're too far away, so I pull my gun and stick it in his ear and I say, 'You are too big to fight, so I will kill you if you do anything but put your hands behind your back right now.' Damn if he doesn't just do that. I was so glad 'cause I really couldn'a shot him for that, but I was planning to.

"We get him cuffed and separate them. I talk with him, and he tells me how she is his girlfriend, she loves him, they were fighting, and he wanted to show her he loves her, so he kissed her. But the way he tells it, he didn't just kiss her. He put his tongue down her throat so she could feel the love, 'cause that's just what he does, you know? He's saying, 'That's how I does it, that's just my way. I'ma show her I loves her.' He's got blood on his face too, so I knew somebody hit somebody—we just had to work out who, or who first. I call for an ambulance, get one of the other guys who just got there to watch him, and I go where Ashby is talking with her down the hall.

"Just one light in the room, by the bed, so it's hard to see. Ashby is just staring at her while she is talking. And when I get next to Ashby, I see why. Beautiful girl, beautiful big eyes, and her hair is done, but she's got this enormous pink wart on the center of her lower lip. You can't not stare at it. It's huge, big, and pink. I'm thinking I don't know how she can eat things with that in the way. She has some blood on her lip, and as we are staring at her, she tucks the lower lip under her upper lip and mashes them together, like to wipe the blood away, and when she's done, it's gone. The wart is gone.

"It wasn't a wart. It was the tip of his tongue, and she'd bit it off when he kissed her. She swallowed it in front of us."

And that's when Rachel the public defender laughed and stole his soul. He said something else to her, something kinder and softer. And they went for ice cream.

Kelly sipped his coffee and redirected Ashby, now calmer.

"So how did we get here?"

"We got here"—Ashby sighed—"because Mommy and Daddy have a Bat-Phone to the city manager, like all the important, rich folks do in that neighborhood. They got city hall to get us to reopen it, and goddammit, a new lab tech just took one look at the pics of Allison's legs and saw bite marks in the bruises. Just took a new set of eyes. And if I told you the truth, you can see them. I can see them, now that I know exactly what to look for. Dad was hoping something would turn up to clear the kid, or maybe to clobber the kid so they'd know, you know? They don't appear to match the brother. Close, kinda. So basically Mom and Dad are trying to get him cleared. And get me clobbered 'cause I missed it. They might even send me back to Patrol." Ashby pressed the arms of the chair and lifted himself, trying to overcome the anguish with a physical effort, straining, stretching his chin up as if distancing his brain from the file.

Then he slumped back down and gave Kelly a funny look.

"Oh, my God, Kelly I didn't think about, um, you don't know the half of this. The bite marks on the pics, now they think it may be Pickett, the guy who . . . your niece's guy. He was a biter, but nobody made him for this till now, till we found the bite marks on her thighs. Jeez, Kelly, we should have told you it was Pickett. Because you . . ."

"Pickett? He's dead." Kelly rose without realizing and squared off on Ashby as if facing a threat. Kelly was remembering, his eyes hardening, gut sucking away from his loose beltline.

"We should have told you, Kell, first thing. You had a right to know it. It appears Pickett could be good for it, for the little girl. He was in town around that time. We know it's his thing, from what we know now. We just never put it together. But we're looking at him, so if we can put it on him, we can clear the brother. That would be good." Ashby looked up at Kelly, concerned at his reaction and wary of his aggressive stance.

"What do you mean, put it on him? We can't question him. He's dead. He died in jail." *And*, Kelly thought, *I was the happiest man in America when the son of a bitch died. Even though it meant no trial. I danced on his grave.*

And more.

"The pictures. When you know what to look for, they're perfectly clear. We can make dental comparisons with them," Ashby said.

"Dental comparisons?" Kelly froze to the core.

"Yeah. They can compare his bite, his teeth to the pics."

"We have his dental records?" Kelly's face grayed and stiffened as he realized.

"No. None exist. So they're digging him up to check his teeth. Judge signed the exhumation order this morning. They're digging him up two days from now. They can take his skull . . ." Ashby stopped as Kelly, now red-faced and wide-eyed, ran out of CID toward the men's room down the hall.

Kelly clamped his lips down and made his tongue big in a failing attempt to dam the bile rising in his throat. He wasn't going to make the hall, much less the men's room, so he turned into the last office before the exit door and threw his guts up, his hand on the desktop next to an engraved pencil holder that read, *CAPTAIN*.

Kelly's accuracy during twice-yearly pistol qualification was usually around 98 percent. His accuracy in projecting a hot stream of vomit into the captain's wastebasket was less.

CHAPTER 3

Jump
Tuesday, November 1, 1988
1400–1530 HRS

OFFICER TERRENCE CHARLES Sharpe heard the new guy calling him on the radio but ignored him for the moment.

Sharpe was assigned to the tactical unit, an eight-person plainclothes squad tasked with street-level drug enforcement. They covertly observed, swooped in, and busted hand-to-hand transactions. Sharpe, Unit 511, was senior man on TAC and its most skilled spotter. Spotters watched drug deals go down and vectored other officers in to make arrests using a radio channel separate from that used by the rest of the department. His orders this afternoon included teaching a new member of the unit. Sharpe was already hiding in his spotting location when the new guy called.

"Unit 516 to 511 on Three?"

Sharpe concentrated on watching a deal. A kid he'd been watching for thirty minutes had made two likely crack deals and was making another right now, and maybe this time he'd see it clearly enough to call a jump. The dealer was now standing close to another male subject who'd waved, crossed the street, and reached his hands into his pockets. The dealer also put his hand into and out of a jacket pocket, and now both were looking at the hand. The hand. *Lemme see the hand. Almost . . .* Concentrating, willing the deal to happen. Thin snow complicated the sight picture.

"516 to 511, you copy?"

"Stand by, 516. Units for a jump." That would keep 516 quiet and off the air, because Sharpe believed he was about to get a clear glimpse of what he knew from his training and experience was hidden there: rocks of crack cocaine—small, light-colored objects visible in the palm of the dealer's hand, like little broken chunks of peanut. Hard, most times impossible to see in the flash that they lie out in the palm before the buyer picked them up. *Gotta see the rocks.* Then, guided by his radio call, unit members in civilian rental cars would drive in quickly but unobtrusively, no squealing tires or revving engines to alert the dealers or their lookouts. Get as close as possible, then jump out of the cars to make the arrests. Their street name was the Jump-Out Boys.

Spotting with binoculars or telescopes was the usual way to see deals. Sometimes at night you could sneak up close, crawling through bushes and around houses. Even be invisible—just walk up unobtrusively in the dark and stand there believing you were invisible. But however they watched, police had to actually see the rocks change hands. So this day, five blocks away from the projects and atop a nine-story luxury condominium, Unit 511 lay in the cold and intermittent snow behind a twenty-power spotting telescope on a short tripod, a handheld radio just below his mouth, waiting for that glimpse that would put everything in motion. He had just warned the Jump-Out Boys that they were about to get descriptions and locations of a buyer and seller of illegal narcotics and that they could move in for arrest. When he had the final view he needed. And . . . and . . .

And it didn't come. The buyer bought, the dealer took money, and they split apart without ever allowing Sharpe a clear view of any drugs. A crime had occurred, in sight of the cops, and nothing was done. No probable cause, no specific and articulable grounds to believe a crime had been permitted and a specific person—or two—had committed it. It was hard not to let frustration eat at you. He whistled softly through his teeth an Elvis Costello song, "Watching the Detectives," but changed the words in his mind to "Watching the drug dealers, they're so cute."

Sharpe keyed the mic. "511 to 516, come on up."

Sharpe had been an Alexandria police officer for seven years. Five had been in the Patrol Division and two in the Jump-Outs. He was known for accurate observation and clear court testimony. He had been certified as an expert witness in the Alexandria Circuit Court in street-level drug activity, meaning the judges had decided to give great weight to his testimony on observed street deals. And that was what he would begin teaching Officer Al Grbonscowizc, a.k.a. Unit 516, today.

He heard him come out of the stairwell next to the elevator header shaft and shouted without turning, "Stop. Right there. D'you see me? Now step over that rail and crawl to me. Keep yourself down." They were five blocks from the target area, but in daylight their shapes would be silhouetted against the sky atop the high condo building and their spotting location blown. He kept his eye on the eyepiece of the spotter scope.

"So think of it," he told the new guy as few minutes later, lying side by side, both squinting through spotter scopes at the drug corner below. "In an hour, we'll see three deals go down.

We may or may not be able to call a jump on them, but there were three, and you'll see them.

"There are five active drug neighborhoods in Alexandria right now, five areas you can buy crack that are as busy as this one. They go 'round the clock. Three deals an hour times five hoods times twenty-four hours a day, is three hundred and sixty deals a day.

"Now a good day, average, we make two good jumps. A good jump is where we arrest at least one person, the buyer or the seller. Generally, we gotta arrest the buyer, otherwise we got nothing on the seller. But sometimes the seller has crack still on him. We bust two deals a day. Out of three-sixty. That's like, what, point six percent. That's some success rate, huh? But it's what the bosses want us to do.

"So you gotta see the rock. Gotta see it in his hand. You can't tell the judge he acted like a dealer, 'cause what's that? But you see a small, light-colored object in his hands, plus all the actions consistent with a deal, that's enough. You don't get clever or poetic. It's a small, light-colored object. Always. Or several, but don't count them. You say four, we recover three, we lose the case. That's how our judges are."

"That makes no sense."

"Doesn't have to make sense. It just has to be what happens in our courts. Judges don't want to send these kids away for time just for small-scale dealing. Neither do we, really, but what else we can do? They are dealing, right there, out on the street. We can't ignore it." Sharpe waved behind them, where Washington, D.C., was visible across the Potomac River. "We'd be like D.C. is now, setting murder records because the kids fight over street corners for sales. So much cash there. Here, we kinda keep a lid on it. Haven't been able to stomp it out, but at least we take off enough of the dealers that they don't build up to a critical mass and fight over territory or carry guns so much.

But sometimes they do. So . . ." Sharpe said, nodding his head back toward the small end of his spotter scope and bidding 516 to do the same. "Tell me what you see."

"A kid in a T-shirt with a picture of a dog, like a collie. He has sneakers, Fila, I think, with . . ."

"No. Too much. You'll be describing him over the radio to the jump cars. Think about what you want the guys to see as they drive up. You can't give that kind of little detail because you're gonna be describing two guys at the same time, the buyer and the seller. Colors and location are all you're gonna give. So, your fella there, he's a black male in a gray jacket, a red shirt, black sweatpants, and white sneakers, and he's in front of 943 Madison Street. And you are going to be talking while they roll in because when they get close, all the kids on the block start yelling Five-Oh or Rolleray."

"Rolleray?"

"Yeah, I don't know what it means either, maybe 'roller raid' 'cause we're the rollers—we roll in to make arrests. Maybe it's pig latin but they're too stupid to leave off the first R. Anyway, they say it, and the dealers will all start to scatter like roaches in the kitchen light. So then you're going to update. 'He's westbound, he's at the corner, he's crossing Patrick Street.' Like that."

"What if I just memorize his face? We can scoop him later."

"No good. We got to get him right now. Most of the case is, we find dope in their pockets or their mouths. We don't find the dope, we can't make a case. I supposed we could, say, get the buyer and then find the dealer later, but it doesn't happen that way. We make too many cases to spend time going back for ones that are marginal.

"And besides, they all look alike to us." Sharpe gave a wry grin at the old, bitter joke about prejudice. Glancing at 516 to see how he, a black man, would take the racial reference from a white. Many people believe cops are bigoted and only arrest black people, target young black males, keep the brothers down. But cops worked so much in poor, busy, densely populated neighborhoods. Black neighborhoods. Who else was there?

Sharpe likened racist appearances to Willie Sutton.

"You know, the bank robber. Supposedly said, 'That's where the money is,' for why he robbed banks. He didn't actually say that, some reporter made it up. But here's the point. Where are drugs being sold, out in the open, right now? Right there." And Sharpe pointed west in front of them, at the drug corner in the neighborhood flanking Route One called the Northside.

"Or over there"—and he pointed south—"the Berg. And over there at Queen and Fayette. And those are just in Sector One. Then you go to Sector Two, there's The Hole and Lynhaven. There's none in Sector Three, no concentration worth us setting up on. So. Our five drug zones. And all five are heavily black neighborhoods. Is that a coincidence? Are black people dealers or criminals, more than white people? I don't think so. But there's not a white neighborhood where we could go watch drug deals go down like this. Do you fish? You don't go fishing in a parking lot. You go where the fish are." 511 pointed down the barrel of the telescope. "There's the fish."

516 looked at 511 like he was from Mars. *Who cared why? Let's just go bust some bad guys*, his expression clearly expressed. 511, five years older, considered himself sage.

"We're not racist. But we know our work has a racially biased effect. We arrest more black people for drugs than white people. Our narcs tell us there is more powder cocaine moving through the city than crack, but it is invisible, secret. It's in bars and houses and apartments, not out on the street. And powder cocaine doesn't make its dealers pull machine guns on each other, or on buyers, or on citizens walking around like this crack does. It brings lots of crime with it. All kinds of stuff goes on down there, doesn't get reported to us. We don't even know how many robberies happen down there. Buyers get ripped off all the time and they don't call us. Sometimes we see it, not always."

The first time Sharpe watched a robbery in progress, he'd had no idea what was going on. Even though it was a fellow cop who was robbed. He told 516 about it.

"Two months ago, we had an undercover come work with us for a week. She was with Manassas City PD, went to the academy with one of our guys, so they knew each other. We worked it out that Adrienne would come and make buys for us, wired her up, sent her in in an old car. The first guy she talks with—now, she's done this before so she wasn't a total tyro—she handled it right but the guy walks up to her and busts her in the nose. No warning, no words, just BAM and reached in and took the money out of her hands. Walked away laughing, saying don't come down here no more. I watched it happen, heard it on the wire, didn't know what it was, it was so fast. By the time Adrienne was able to talk, the kid got away. Shame, 'cause drug busts are dime a dozen but a robbery charge is a good pop. Good prison time. It would up my stats."

"Stats? Wait. Kid?"

"Yeah, Adrienne said kid. He was young. Most of them are young, under twenty or twenty-five. For lots of them it'll be their first arrest when we get them. And sometimes it's their only arrest, but not so often."

Sharpe moved his scope slightly to track a potential dealer moving up the block. "So you get one spotted, and he sells, and now you call in the Jump-Outs. That's the apprehension phase. That's where the fun begins. Cars sliding, cops jumping out, holding guns, running around, knocking heads. Real Starsky and Hutch stuff."

"Who's Starsky and Hutch?"

"Jeez, how old are you? How young are you? Think the last ten minutes of *Miami Vice*, any episode. So our guys, they pull up and you hope you gave them enough description to pick out the right knuckleheads in a block full of knuckleheads. You're trying to update as they roll but by now they're talking to each other, and you can't get on the radio. You just watch. You pull back and . . . wait. Stand by." Sharpe stopped, refocused on the street below. He concentrated a moment, then keyed the mic.

"Units for a jump, roll now, in front of 835 Madison, go now go now GO NOW. Buyer is a black male, twenties, bright blue coat with red designs on the front, acid-washed jeans, Philly, he's walking east toward Columbus, stopped at the corner. Dealer is a black male, thirties, black jacket, black shirt, jeans, black ballcap down over his face, still in front of 835. Saw the drugs. Go go go!"

Sharpe sat up and switched from the high-power scope to binoculars for a wider view. At the edges of his focus, he saw the jump cars moving into the area, saw one close on the corner where the buyer now moved farther east. "Angelo, right in front of you, that's him, blue jacket, white jeans, yeah, that's him." A flawless jump on the buyer as the officers in T-shirts and jeans stepped out of the rental car just as it pulled past the buyer, the front passenger pinning the buyer against the rear fender and proning his arms out across the trunk lid while the driver zipped around to quickly click on the cuffs.

"Dealer is moving west, now into the alley. Timmy, turn left, that alley there . . . He's running, dealer is running, 'cross the courtyard to Alfred Street. He crossed Alfred . . ."

"We got his stuff," radioed the officer with the buyer

"Timmy turn right, come out on the street . . . He, there's a tree in the way. He got, there's a car going north now, high rate of speed. I think he's in it. Timmy, you're close, it's a red

Toyota four-door, can't see the tag, out the end of the block and toward Washington. Headquarters, you copy us on Channel Three? Pursuit.

"Pursuit!"

CHAPTER 4

Apprehension
Tuesday, November 1, 1988
1500–1600 HRS

KELLY RUSHED OUT of Headquarters in a furious daze, getting in his unmarked and navigating away from the CID parking area without conscious effort. He drifted down Eisenhower Avenue in the cloudy afternoon gloom and thin snow through an area of new development rising from former farmland, junkyards, and swamps away from the new headquarters building, built on a landfill, its walls already cracking as its foundations sank. Two miles to the upscale waterfront neighborhoods and businesses of Old Town, the heart if not the geographic center of Alexandria, where the courthouse and city hall dominated the main business strip of King Street.

There was free parking for police cars in the lot under the courthouse building, but cops can park anywhere, so Kelly crammed the Chevrolet sedan into a corner space on a surface street, tail into the crosswalk. Who would give him a ticket?

Besides, something might happen and he'd need the car in a hurry. It never did, but it could, and you had to be ready. Cops are always apprehensive. They plan for a million emergencies that don't transpire, think through contingencies for violence that rarely occur, stay alert for threats that could present but mostly don't. Kelly had a bumper sticker on his personal car that read, "Be kind, be courteous, but have a plan to kill everybody you meet." It's why cops sit facing the door in restaurants. Seat four of them at a table, the junior guy stays back to the door and nervous.

Before he shut off the car, he keyed the mic. "Unit 60?"

"Go ahead, Unit 60," the dispatcher said in her professionally bored voice.

"Hold me out at the courthouse for a conference, I'll be off the air." He would carry his radio, but he turned it off in the office out of professional courtesy. Today, that courtesy would be misplaced.

"Copy, 60, out at the courthouse at 1540 hours."

Up to the third floor with a brightly dressed couple en route to the Circuit Court Clerk's office to get a marriage license. They went happily in the opposite direction as he entered the Commonwealth Attorney's Office, a suite housing the city's elected top prosecutor and fourteen deputies. He walked past the large gun locker on the wall behind the receptionist's desk, not needing to lock up his handgun since he was not entering a courtroom today. Detectives didn't wait to be announced, so he walked toward the office of Assistant Commonwealth's Attorney Myron Duckworth, but stopped for coffee.

Above the coffee machine in the supply room was a bulletin board. On the board, among the official postings and detritus of any bureaucracy was a clipboard with a signup sheet on it. The sheet was titled, "D.C. HOMICIDE POOL 1988." Prosecutors, secretaries, and cops had listed their names next to guesses between one and six hundred, with a cluster around the three hundred mark. Alexandria, with between six and twelve killings a year, didn't offer enough variance to let everyone in the CA's office and the police department each get a fair bet. His bet was two hundred, but that had been long surpassed.

He went to Duckworth's office and sat down unbidden. Myron Duckworth was two years out of law school and eighteen months into his service in the Alexandria Commonwealth Attorney's office, time enough to work his way past the entry-level grind of General District Court traffic and minor criminal cases and, just recently, into a specialized assignment in Youth Crimes.

Duckworth looked up at Kelly dully over the Selectric typewriter on his desk and the stack of files next to it, the top one open and spilling out. Ten seconds until Duckworth raised an eyebrow and leaned back, his head at the wall just below his college and law school diplomas, his Virginia State Bar certification to practice law, his admittance to the state and city bar associations, and a photograph of him meeting the president just above one of his wife and dog. Duckworth didn't know Kelly's educational background since Kelly's normal workplace, some street somewhere or a little cubby, didn't facilitate the hanging of an I-Love-Me wall. But Duckworth didn't care anyway since Kelly was just a cop.

"Stibble," Kelly said.

The eyebrow stayed up.

"The Stibble case, the parental abduction. Thursday's trial? We had an appointment today to prep?"

Duckworth finally got it. "Yeah. All I need you for is the apprehension, how he got picked up in California, how you brought him back after extradition. We mostly need the mom. She's subpoenaed, she gonna be here?"

"Mom? She's subpoenaed, so she better. I told her I was picking her up. I told her last week and I told her on the phone today."

"When did you last talk to her?" Duckworth had looked back down at the open file on his desk, which was not the Stibble case file.

"Today. I just said today. An hour ago."

"You go over what she's gonna be asked?" Duckworth had finally focused on this case and found the right file.

"We talked for twenty minutes. I went over the stuff we need her for. She said she remembered from our meeting with her last month before the prelim."

Thursday the trial of Cedric Stibble was set to begin. A bench trial, meaning no jury, just the Circuit Court judge to hear the case. Unusual to stage a full trial with civilian witnesses and victims on busy Commonwealth Day, but some sort of arrangement was made by Rachel Cohen, the public defender who was handling Stibble. Same deal that had moved the case up from Juvenile and Domestic Relations Court, a.k.a. Kiddie Court. *Public Defender Cohen.* Kelly let himself consider her full title, *Assistant Public Defender Rachel R. Cohen*, and then thought of some of the other names he knew her by, stifling a smile.

Duckworth looked at him, annoyed. "What about the kid? The kid's here, right?" Meaning here in the city, not off with a grandmother or sister in some other city.

"Yeah, and his name's Jumari. He's here. I'll make sure tomorrow. I'm meeting with them both. I'll bring him Thursday, too. Ashby and I."

"Jumari, huh?" The prosecutor rolled his eyes. *Don't be like that, you prick,* Kelly thought. *Like Myron is better?*

"And you'll sit with him?"

"While I can, *Myron.* We'll all be out of the room while the others testify. I can be with him while his mom is on the stand, then she can while I go on. Then she and I will sit while he goes on. Ashby will be with me to help, so when I'm not there, he will be. And Ashby can go into the courtroom and be near when Jumari goes on."

"I don't know if he is going on. Not yet."

"He's the victim, he's the kid who got snatched. The vic's gotta go on. How you gonna—"

"What he did, what he saw, doesn't really matter. He's eight. What's he gonna know about court orders and visitation rules? We need Mom to tell us his dad didn't bring the kid back when he was supposed to, and you to tell where you found them."

"In the other guy's house."

"No. In San Francisco. The house doesn't matter."

"Of course it matters. It's the fucking point. The kid was there so Stibble could take him to the guy's house. It's why all this happened. You can't not talk about the house. It leads to the pictures."

"We're not talking about the pictures. We're not using the pictures. We . . ." Duckworth rolled away in the chair as Kelly jumped up.

"He was gonna sell the kid to the guy in the house. He had a buyer, we've got the name. We've got the letter, we've got the kid's photo in the buyer's possession. It's the whole point of the case. We gotta show why it means so much. It's not just bringing Jumari home late—it's what was gonna happen to him. What his dad was gonna do to him!" Kelly's hands twitched at his side as he spoke, his voice rising on a steady climb to an unsteady tone.

"Look, it's not what that fag was gonna do. I don't care what fags do." Duckworth realized he had retreated and reasserted himself by sliding his chair back toward the desk and toward Kelly. Kelly glared and tried to settle down. He needed this twit.

"Fags? This case isn't about fags or who's gay. Stibble's not gay—he's a pedophile. He is pimping his own son, or was going to." Kelly's voice rose. "Yeah, to a male. A male pedophile. Who cares who's gay? That's why they went there. That's why they were in San Francisco, to meet the buyer. Maybe Stibble's gay, but he was straight enough at least one time to produce a son. I dunno. Gay or not's got nothing to do with it. Here, he is a dad in violation of a court order, and working with a molester."

Kelly shuffled side to side, unable to pace in the small office. "Fags aren't molesters. Molesters are molesters, and we're gonna tell the judge this so he gets put away max. Child parental abduction is only ten years. We gotta make sure he gets that as a max. Our judges never give the max on anything. We gotta stack the deck. We gotta show what he was doing to Jumari. That's the point."

"That's not the point."

"That's the whole fucking point."

"You're missing the point. The pictures don't come in, so the deal doesn't come in. They're inadmissible. I can't bring them in, even if I wanted to."

Kelly stopped moving, but his hands still twitched, fists opening and closing. He said, "Stibble took Jumari's picture, mailed it to Anders in San Francisco after they wrote to each other for weeks. We've got the letters the US Marshals and SFPD found in Anders's house. The letters show a conspiracy to rape Jumari, show intent to defile, show the plan was to never return Jumari to his mom at the end of the visitation month. The letters are the whole thing. I got Hoffmaster from the Marshal's Service and Schoenle from SFPD coming off a plane today for the trial tonight."

"No you don't. I cancelled them. They're not coming."

"You cancelled them? It's my fucking case. We need them."

"We can't use them. Hoffmaster can't testify to the letters, and Schoenle can't testify to the photos. We can't admit the photos or the letters; they were improperly seized."

"Bullshit!"

"Show me your law degree, Kelly! They got Stibble at Anders's door. The pics were in his car in the driveway. The marshals had no right to search the car. The letters were in Anders's house and they had no probable cause to search the house."

"Carroll Doctrine says they got a right to search a car anytime without a warrant, long as they've got probable cause to believe there's evidence in it."

"And your law degree tells us that Carroll applies here, Detective?"

"Bet your ass." Carroll was a Detroit bootlegger in 1930. The FBI had good information he was running booze and searched his car on a border crossing without a warrant, and the Supreme Court upheld the search because cars, being inherently movable, could easily be spirited away and evidence lost.

Duckworth shook his head. "No Carroll here. No PC for the car. You gotta have PC to search, warrantless or not."

"Yeah, okay. How about a search incident to arrest? We can search around a guy when we arrest him for weapons and contraband."

"Weak, Detective. The car was fifty feet away, in the driveway. I'm not taking that before a judge."

"Okay, but they got a warrant for the house after they arrested him. The warrant gives us the letters. They give us the conspiracy."

"The warrant was based on the pictures in the car. Bad search. Without the pictures, bad warrant."

"They're only bad if the defense objects and the objection wins. The warrant is prima facie that the search is good. And we got a warrant, so it's on the defense to prove it's bad

"It's a loser, Kelly. I'm not going forward with it. Defense can knock it down. Knock down part of it. The rest can look weak. The case has parts. We got the part where Mom divorced Stibble last year, we got the part where the divorce judge gave custody to Mom and one month visitations to Stibble, we got where Stibble didn't bring the kid back to . . ."

"Jumari."

"Jumari . . . back to Mom at the end of the court-ordered visitation, and that's parental abduction. That's all we need, that's strong. We go with the strong parts."

Kelly knew what the strong parts were, and Duckworth wasn't one of them. "You gutless fuck. Go with what we need to really put this guy away. You don't mention what they were doing out in Frisco, then you're not telling the truth."

"What in the world makes you think we tell the truth? Truth? In court? Are you some kind of child? Are you in Disney World? We don't tell the truth in court. We tell the little bits we are allowed to. We tell snippets that we can get away with, that are admissible, that are connected. We avoid things that are inflammatory or suggestive because they could be considered unfair. Is Stibble gay? Yes—arguably, you say now. Do we tell them that? No. Is it germane here? Arguable, but not germane, because I agree with you—gay is not the same as pedophile, even though most of any jury in this town would equate them. But does it connect Stibble to Anders in Frisco? Sure, kinda. But we can't even mention it because a defense attorney would scream bias. And we can't mention things we know, even if they are true, if we aren't allowed to know them. And we aren't allowed to know about the pictures and the letters because they were seized illegally."

"That's arguable."

"I'm not gonna argue it. We go with what we know we can get in. It's bits, but we got enough bits. It's the elephant and the blind men story. Blind men go into a room with an elephant, then tell each other what the elephant looks like. The elephant is like a wall. No, it's like a spear, or a tree, or a snake. Little pieces they could touch. They're not the whole story, but court rules prevent us from ever telling the whole story. So we tell what we can. This is basic stuff, Detective. Criminal Law 101. You should know this by now. How long you been on?" Duckworth sneered up at Kelly as he sat below his framed law school degree, dated three years ago.

Kelly was holding still now. He loomed over Duckworth, and his stare dropped to the pale green Selectric typewriter on the desk. Kelly had to stop his hands from grabbing the type-writer and smashing it on the head of the gutless, smart-assed prosecutor, and he was not sure if he stopped because he would have killed the guy or because he liked IBM Selectrics and didn't want to break one. He momentarily considered the charges he'd face and the loss of an eight-year career versus the visceral pleasure, the desperate need to pick it up and use it to smash this pissant into goo right here. As his gaze alternated between Duckworth's chinless face and the typewriter, Kelly gained control of his fury, but control mandated that he move to safety. He spun and left the office, ignoring Duckworth's shouted demand to get back in and finish prepping.

Kelly slowly walked past the receptionist desk and into the hallway toward the elevators. Maintaining control, he spoke to no one. He hoped the elevator would be empty so he could ride down alone. His mind knew his anger and disgust at Duckworth and the vagaries of the legal system were unreasonable and groundless, but his loud gut and twitching fingertips were committed to his emotions and to the protection of

Jumari, just a little kid. He rocked back and forth between head and heart, not too sure which would win if war broke out. One more thing could tip the scale. Either way.

An up elevator arrived and two deputies in brown uniforms got off. The courthouse was the jurisdiction of the Alexandria Office of the Sheriff. Sheriff's deputies were sworn law enforcement in Alexandria, same as he was, but they were tasked to courthouse and jail security, prisoner transport, and the service of civil papers, not road patrol, emergency response, or criminal investigation. They looked him over in amusement, and the one he knew said, "Sure, just walk out. No need to run now, it's all over."

Distracted, fuming, Kelly just looked his question at them.

"You missed it. Big pursuit with shots fired. Pammie Martinson."

Kelly's heart sped up. CID was always needed on a shooting scene to locate and interview witnesses or interrogate suspects. He turned on his forgotten, silent portable radio in time to hear a lieutenant on the scene advising that no more units or detectives were needed, and to clear Code 5. Kelly punched the down button six times before an elevator arrived. When the doors slid open, he stepped in so quickly he almost steamrollered Public Defender Rachel Cohen standing inside. He skipped sideways and she yelped, her face first pulling back in surprise, then widening in a smile, then compressing as she hid the smile from anyone around except Kelly. Her brown eyes widened, as did Kelly's green. His anger vanished, and he prodded the floor button but held his hand ready over the control panel as the doors closed.

"Oh, thank God, Kell. I really need—"

He hit the stop button and reached for her neck with his other hand.

CHAPTER 5

Pursuit
Tuesday, November 1, 1988
1530–1540 HRS

PATROL OFFICER PAMMIE Martinson was eating lunch in a restaurant on Washington Street when the TAC pursuit call came over the radio. Washington was the main north-south boulevard down the middle of Old Town. It changed names and connected the George Washington Parkway on the north side of town with the Mount Vernon Highway that ran south to—wait for it—Mount Vernon, home of our first President and source of much of Alexandria's historical identity. "Better that connection than the Confederacy," she had once remarked to her field training officer, an Alexandria native. She got a lesson in history from the losers' side that night. That was the first time she heard the term "The War of Northern Aggression," never uttered during her Pennsylvania public schooling but common here in the South. The winners write the textbooks.

Lunch, 10-7 in radio code, was what officers called any meal period—morning, noon, or after midnight. Or, as now, late afternoon. They got fifteen minutes to get there once Communications cleared them and thirty minutes to eat. The trick was to already be in the parking lot when you asked to be cleared for 10-7—it gave you more time to sit. Not to relax. You never really relaxed on duty, and padded restaurant booths don't accommodate gun belts well, with handcuffs and flashlight rings pressing the seat and your seat. 10-7 was just enough time to order, take off your coat, slurp coffee, and wolf down whatever. You ate fast in patrol to ensure you ate at all before you were called off for a hot call. Like tonight. Her radio bleeped.

"All units, especially Sector One units, TAC is in pursuit of a drug suspect on the North Side. They're on Channel Three. Suspect is a black male, black jacket, blue jeans, black cap, in a light-colored Toyota four-door, Virginia tag Edward Peter William Three One Two. They are northbound on North Alfred Street approaching First. Units 214, 215, Sector One Supervisor, acknowledge?"

She ran out the door of the restaurant into the cold parking lot before the acknowledgements began, so fast she'd left her thick nylon cruiser jacket behind, forgotten in the booth. She was Unit 213, not assigned to the call, but when it is a pursuit, you just go. She was on Washington Street, which ran parallel to North Alfred Street and two blocks east. They were two blocks from her, so she might get in on it.

Martinson's front-wheel drive Plymouth, white with black police letters and a light bar with red and blue lenses, ploughed out of the parking lot, front tires chirping as they fought for both acceleration and cornering. She headed north, toward the last location given, in time to see the Toyota fishtail onto Washington Street, just a block up heading north away from her, closely followed by two compact civilian-looking cars—TAC's jump cars. These were not authorized for pursuit, their only police gear being magnetic spinning blue lights stuck out the windows onto the roofs, called "Kojak lights" after the television detective show. She caught up, the jump cars fell back, and she leaned forward to shout over the siren into the mic still clipped to the dashboard. "Unit 213, in pursuit, northbound. TAC suspect car, tag matches. One occupant. Now passing Slaters Lane north onto the Parkway. Confirm charges?" This last question meaning: *Am I actually allowed to chase this guy?*

"Confirmed, drug charges. Saw a deal," came the clipped answer from a TAC unit. Good enough.

"Weapons?"

"None seen, but a drug deal. He's the seller; we got the buyer. Go get him, Pammie!" came the reply from TAC. Drug deals, any felony, implied the likelihood of weapons. Excitement excused the informality.

"Headquarters, give her Code 5," came the voice of Unit 511. Pammie recognized the voice of T.C. Sharpe, the senior TAC officer, cooler than most and able to remember to ask for special radio procedures that limited transmissions to only those directly involved in the pursuit. Units did as ordered, and Martinson had the air.

The pursuit lasted a minute and a mile, until early rush hour traffic clogged the road. Martinson held about three car lengths behind the bad guy, zig-zagging between lanes. It was near dusk in wispy snow, but not dark enough for the emergency lights on her cruiser to really stand out. The unmarked TAC units dropped out of the pursuit per official policy but were following as best they could despite being regularly blocked by commuters. Finally, passing Washington Reagan National Airport into Arlington County and just out of Alexandria's jurisdiction, the suspect's Toyota skidded to a stop in the right-hand lane, balked by stopped cars. There was perfectly good grass on either side of the blocked lanes to pass on, no buildings, no trees or bushes close, but the suspect had tunnel vision and could not envision driving anywhere but on the paved surface. *Or he was just stupid*, Martinson thought. *If crooks weren't stupid, our job would be harder.* She cut off her siren and thumbed the mic.

"213, Headquarters. Stopped just into Arlington, near the first airport entrance, one in the car. Stand by." Dozens of civilians in sight, but she was alone, having outrun the TAC cars, and the nearest cruiser to her was a ways out, judging by the distant, ascending howl of its siren. Martinson exited her car, drew her revolver with her right hand, and advanced on the suspect. She hoped to get to him and get him out before the traffic jam eased open and let him move forward and away. She got only as far as her own front bumper before he fired.

The blasts were deafening to the civilians in cars nearby, but Martinson never heard them. Stress closed her ears but sharpened her sight, and she watched slo-mo orange puffs of exploding gunpowder bloom like roses from the barrel of a pistol suddenly thrust out a window of the suspect's car. Just the gun, no face behind it. Unaimed but surprisingly accurate, and she heard the bullets hit. Her gun was out, but her subconscious made its own snap decision: flight, not fight. She threw herself to the right and crashed down to the ground onto her shoulder. She pointed her gun but held her fire, having no clear view of the shooter now. Shots continued over his trunk lid, muzzle flashes bright, and she rolled back under the bumper of her cruiser. She felt the fluid heat of blood on her left arm and neck and face. She'd felt no impact but guessed that pain would follow. No fear, yet. She was aware of engines revving and horns bleating from civilian cars around and behind her. She felt drenched in her own blood but could not tell where she was hit or why she wasn't dead. With bullets still coming in, she couldn't dwell.

Her arms and body still worked, so she scooted farther under the bumper as far as she could till she was wedged on her right side, gun hand out in front and braced by her left but lacking a target, so still unable to bring herself to fire. As the suspect vehicle finally moved away through a hole in the traffic, she heard one last shot, the almost simultaneous pop from the gun muzzle and whang of the bullet into the radiator of her cruiser above her.

As the other bullets had.

Releasing radiator fluid to flow onto her.

Not blood.

Just for that moment did she start pressing the trigger on her Smith and Wesson .38. Holding her breath. Heart pounding but sights steady. And stopped without firing as the suspect vehicle juked left in front of a car that blocked her aim. Another two seconds to take the strain off the trigger finger and lower the hammer, then another two for a deep gasping breath, and angry Officer Martinson rolled back out from under her shot-up Plymouth cruiser, got back in, and reentered pursuit mode.

She caught the suspect less than a mile farther north on the Parkway. No longer maintaining a safe gap, Pammie floored the gas pedal, and the K-Car cruiser rammed once, twice, into the back bumper of the Toyota as they veered right up the ramp from the Parkway onto the 14th Street Bridge that carried Interstate 395 from Arlington into downtown Washington D.C.

"213, back in pursuit, onto bridge into D.C. Shots fired, shots fired. He fired."

"Copy, 213. Shots fired. D.C. was advised. They're en route."

Flying up the ramp to merge onto the highway over the bridge, the suspect slowed to avoid a car on the main highway surface. Martinson jabbed the brakes, but her front tires slipped, slick with spewing radiator fluid. The cruiser crunched into the suspect's rear fender and spun it out like a stock car. The little sedan crossed four lanes and banged the center guardrail, its bumper, license tag, and grille pieces flying off in a splintery arc, lurching back into the traffic lane but skidding, slowing, stopping, leaning over on a broken front suspension.

Looking past the wreck, Martinson saw the D.C. police responding from their side of the river, multiple sets of oncoming emergency lights flashing in the late afternoon distance, the Jefferson Memorial shining off-pink as the setting sun peeked through a cloud gap and struck its marble dome.

Martinson had a long second to admire the tableau from the driver's seat of her cruiser. She had stopped behind the Toyota but offset to block the fast lane and the lane next to it, a safe zone between the suspect and the passing cars. She caught her breath and across her hood took in the perfect lineup of her hood ornament, the cockeyed suspect car, the clouds of blue tire smoke as the D.C. cops skidded to a halt on their side, the Memorial. All seen through a mist of steam rising from her damaged and overheated engine.

Then, with a distant orange flash and the *tink* of a bullet passing through her windshield, the shooting began again.

CHAPTER 6

Recordings
Tuesday, November 1, 1988
3 p.m.–5:30 p.m.

ASSISTANT PUBLIC DEFENDER Rachel Rene Cohen used to tape-record tricky cases only, but lately she recorded them all. Usually the tapes she made of testimony in General District Court were not very important, just a fallback for failed notes or missed quotes. Lately, however, she'd been noticing a similarity, almost a word-for-word consistency in the way certain police officers on the anti-drug unit called the Jump-Out Boys were testifying. And it made her mad.

As Rachel walked the two blocks from her office back to the courthouse, a walk made several times a day, she found her stride speeding in anger. Sometimes the testimony seemed identical between different cases with different defendants, like a loop that played over and over. A loop that wrapped around her clients' necks. She needed to check audio tapes of prior cases to catch them. And she didn't need this today. She needed to get to her boyfriend, John Kelly—how odd that quaint term sounded, how unexpected—and tell him the news, a special secret. Rachel generally kept her private business private and especially with this guy. She hadn't told even her mother, who would get emotional and slip into Yiddish, saying *khaver*—male friend—or more romantically *geliebter*—lover—at such talk, but her mother didn't know about this one. Yet. But Momma would have to know now, and soon. And that's when the Yiddish would really come out.

This morning, Rachel had argued one of those questionable cases and had suspicious testimony on tape in her briefcase right now. But if the *farkakt* tape recorder had failed again, she didn't know what she'd do. Maybe just *plotz*.

It had been the typical tactical unit case. *A spot-jump by the Jump-Out Boys*, she thought, bitterly shaking her head at the happy, friendly moniker for the roughest group of police thugs she'd ever seen freely operate in any city. They seemed to arrest everybody they saw, mostly blacks, for anything from drugs to trespassing in their own city projects to jaywalking. Alexandria had so far been spared the furious gunfire and common death that crack cocaine brought to cities like Washington, D.C., just across the river. But arrests had doubled in Alexandria since the inception of the TAC unit, which in fact had led to her hiring to support a short-staffed Alexandria Public Defender's Office stretched by the increases.

Her work anger battled some special after-work feelings she'd recently found growing in her heart. Anger disappeared when she thought of him, her guy, her *geliebter*. They hadn't been together long—they weren't "together" in the accepted sense. They didn't date openly, and she had told no one she was seeing him. Yet. But after she shared her news with him, today she hoped, that had to change.

As recounted in testimony this afternoon in General District Court, which on angry days was just called GD, her client had been standing on the sidewalk near his house one evening last month when tactical unit officers ran up and threw him onto the ground. One cop testified that he'd found three rocks of crack cocaine in her client's pockets and charged him with distribution of a controlled substance, to wit: cocaine, and with possession with intent to distribute a controlled substance, to wit, cocaine. Meaning he allegedly sold crack to someone and had more to sell. This was where the questionable testimonial loop began again. Word-for-word identical. Suspicious? Hell yes. Criminal? Probably perjury. She wanted to prove this to the court, to discredit TAC and get them off her clients' backs.

And she could not, because she never got them on tape.

Today, she had lost her case. *Of course*, she thought bitterly. She had failed to knock any holes in the police story, and her client was bound over for the grand jury. This meant that the judge in the General District Court had decided there was enough probable cause to believe that a specific crime had occurred and that a specific person had committed it. And that these beliefs were not based on evidence improperly seized or procedures that violated the civil rights of innocent citizens. And all of her clients were innocent. The courts said so; it was the bedrock principle of American jurisprudence—innocent until proven guilty. But their cases were always bound over, of course. Drug prelims were always stacked against defendants because officers' testimonies were almost impossible to counter. Public defenders like Rachel, and defense attorneys in general, also lost most prelims because the Commonwealth dropped loser arrests before they got to court, so only persuasive cases, slam dunks, made it to prelim. She and her cohorts muttered, "Off to GD court," as they walked out to cover the two blocks between their office and the court building, the double meaning of GD very clear to their knowing secretaries. This was a typical day for her. Leave her office for court, lose a case, go back to the office to prep for the next, back out in the snow to lose again. Like she was doing now

"Tell the court what you saw." Early in this morning's case, an open-ended question from the commonwealth's attorney started the Jump-Out officer down what she was calling "the perjury path."

"Using a pair of ten by fifty binoculars, I observed Mr. Woods in front of 954 First Street, standing about fifteen feet from a lighted street light. I observed him reach his right hand into his right front pocket and remove his hand clenched in a fist. He held the fist out in front of himself, opened his hand, and I saw several small, light-colored, irregularly shaped objects in his palm. Mr. Allen approached, reached his own right hand out, appeared to pick up one of the objects, put his hand into his own pants pocket, then handed Mr. Woods what appeared to be a bill of U.S. currency. At that point, I alerted members of the tactical unit to what I had seen, gave the descriptions of the subjects, and directed units to move in and make arrests. They did so, under my observation. I confirmed for Officer Berman that he had stopped the subject who had purchased the items, Mr. Allen. I also confirmed by radio that Officer Hall had caught the subject who sold the items, Mr. Woods. Officer Berman confirmed for me that he had recovered a small, light-colored object from Mr. Allen's right front pocket, which he subsequently field tested for—"

Rachel jumped up. "Objection, Your Honor. Hearsay as to the alleged statement about the alleged field test. We can—"

"Yes, Ms. Cohen. Objection overruled." The judge glanced at the prosecutor and made his counterargument for him. "Not introduced as to the truth of the statement but to illustrate the frame of mind of the officer involved. Proceed, Officer," said the judge, not bored but not hearing anything that stood out.

Frame of mind? thought Rachel. *Who cares about his frame of mind? He's up a tree in the dark with binoculars. Nothing he does changes with what they find or the test results. Come on, Judge, pay attention,* she wanted to say. "Yes, Your Honor," she said. *GD judge,* she thought.

And she thought of the matching words: "held his fist out in front of his body and opened it . . . bill of U.S. currency . . . saw several small, light-colored, irregularly shaped objects . . ." Sometimes the testimony was of "greenish-brown leafy substance" if the case involved marijuana or the more potent mixture of pot and PCP known as "loveboat." A "subject" was "secured on the ground and handcuffed, whereupon a search incident to arrest found several small, light-colored objects that subsequently tested positive for the presence of" whatever they decided would be found that night. *Not to mention* searches *don't find things,* searchers *do,* fumed the part of Rachel that had started as an English major before prelaw at the University of Richmond.

But always the same words, in the same phrases, spoken simply and quietly, the cops' faces turned to the judge or to the panel in a jury trial. Or maddeningly directly to her. The cops' bland but confident faces sometimes almost hidden by the stacks of evidence and reports they carried from case to case, court to court, and then piled in front of them on the edge of the witness stand. *They were working from a script and just plugged in different men each night,* Rachel thought. *Like a thriller novelist, reusing a story pattern that worked before.*

Wrapping up his case, the prosecutor asked, "And all of these events occurred in the city of Alexandria?" Rachel always imagined an outburst at this judicial boilerplate, the repetitive verbiage needed to dot Is and cross Ts. *Of course the case occurred in Alexandria—I'm an Alexandria cop, right?* But they never said that, trained seals that they were. Rachel drew no attention to this question today, though she soon would.

Her turn now. Rachel stood up and gave her all. Her closing argument was as strong as it could be in the face of uncontroverted testimony. No defense witnesses, and her client did not testify. It could be enough to lead a judge to rule "no probable cause" and stop the case from going forward. But it was like these TAC guys were magic. Rachel ran into battle with a short, dull sword but a pure and hopeful heart.

"Your Honor, it is clear even from the testimony of the officers that there was no basis for their illegal detention of my client, Mr. Woods. He was innocently standing at his own home, clearly minding his own business, when these officers selected him to be their arrest of the night. They accosted him for no reason, brutally threw him on the ground despite his offering no resistance, and say they found rocks of crack cocaine in his jacket pocket. They do not say that the rocks found matched those allegedly seen by the officer who was using a telescope. They cannot even prove that the jacket in which the alleged drugs were found belonged to my client." Even she had to gulp a little at that.

"My client has no record before the court. Other than the unsubstantiated testimony of these two officers, there is no evidence to support any charge against my client. I ask that you dismiss these charges."

How could something so complex and important as a criminal case, a felony conviction, a life altered, voting rights lost, job applications forever marred by "yes" boxes marked next to "Arrests or Convictions" come down to something so simple as two against one, two officers' testimonies outweighing one innocent person's? Since her client did not take the stand, as was his firm and clear right to refrain from doing, the system was stacked against him in terms of presenting evidence to exonerate himself. And it is hard to find witnesses to something that *didn't* happen, maybe harder when the events occurred at 4:00 a.m. in an ice storm. Maybe that's why TAC arrested the only two men on the street at that time, her client for one, the other being the man charged as the buyer and represented by other counsel to avoid a conflict of interest.

"The court is satisfied that the Commonwealth has met the burden of proof in this case. Mr. Woods, your case is bound over for the grand jury. Next case." The judge spoke only loud enough to be heard over the rustling of the cop gathering his evidence pile off the witness stand, the prosecutor switching one crime file for another in his briefcase, and Rachel closing up her briefcase to vacate the table for the next defense attorney. Some days that next attorney was her, and she might sit for four or five cases in a row without break. Without winning.

Discouraged, disgusted, disappointed at the loss? Not after months of this. She was resigned. Her transfer to this densely populated East Coast city from the Public Defender's Office in rural Harrisonburg switched her caseload from a mostly thefts, fights, and domestic assaults to a near totality of drug charges. And they were all the same.

Her client walked out with her. She told him to come see her in two weeks. He was still free on bond but now awaited indictment and trial sometime in the next month or two. Cases moved fast here. He left down the elevator.

Rachel paused in the lobby, waiting and looking up and down the hall, her mood if not her poker face brightening. It had become her habit to look for him here, and almost everywhere, despite knowing he was supposed to be waiting across the street. Him. The impossible love of her life, not her first love but the big one. The one she never saw coming, or planned for, or expected. She often saw him here, his bulk standing out even among the building full of burly cops and deputies. Broad and solidly built, he was a brick with black hair, and he hit her like a ton of himself. At her first sight of him, a visceral current ran through her like hot floodwaters, a sexual surge unique to her and him. She'd never had a physical reaction to anyone like she'd had to him, thrilling, immediate and erotic. She felt it every time she thought of him now, and it was dizzying. His big hands, guiding her out of a bar, offering an ice cream cone, grasping her neck and shoulder blades while they . . . *Damn, Rachel, stop it,* she shouted at herself silently, shivering. *You're in General District Court, not a love nest. And you have so much more to talk with him about now than just your next kiss. The stuff of our future, together,* she hoped. His first words to her, three months ago in a bar, of all places, after listening to some horrible story like all the cops told. "I'm thinking there are so many different, better, happier, shinier places to be than here, and if you name one, I'll take you there."

Take me now, dreamboat.

She stopped and reshuffled her head, falling back into work mode with a gentle shake of her thick, dark red hair. *Frizzy,* she always thought. *Wavy,* he would say when he ran his fingers through it with a slight and gentle pull, his nose and mouth deep and close in its curls to inhale her. She took the elevator down from Circuit Court on the fourth floor, where she had gone to hand some files to a fellow PD, then back down to the second floor where General District Court met, the lower court for lower, lesser cases like her next, a motion to suppress with a teenage client, though at nineteen, old enough for adult charges. He was always late. He didn't pay attention to the time or the seriousness of his charge. Antonio "I Be Called Stick" Planter. Another victim of the Jump-Out Boys.

And she needed to figure out what Stick meant by his phone message, left yesterday with her secretary. The case is taken care of? By Professor Vulture?

With voodoo?

The elevator stopped at three, and her dreamboat stood at the door. He looked excited, no, almost frantic, and more so when he saw Rachel inside.

"Oh, thank God, Kell. I really need—" He shushed her with a raised hand. His wicked grin growing, he stepped in and waited till the doors closed and the elevator began to drop. Then he hit the stop button and reached for her.

CHAPTER 7

Dealing
Tuesday in, like, November?
After School

ANTONIO PLANTER HAD been called Stick for so long that few remembered his real name was Antonio. No one called him Stick for the reason he wanted: that he was a stickup boy, a robber who did that job on that bitch just last summer. Bitch come up here on his turf but not acting with respect, buying on the Block but not from the Block, y'know what I'm sayin'.

Got to represent the hood.

But the stickup derivation was only in his head; he was Stick because he was six-foot-two and 140 pounds. Better Stick than Shew, his name from baby times, a contraction of Cashew based on his tiny, rounded shape and pale brown skin, given when his brothers first saw him as a premature baby. Early by four weeks, not too terribly short a gestation but an arrival early enough to leave him on the small side for his first three or four years. Hospital bills put them all in public housing, but his mom worked hard.

He'd caught up, got taller in middle school, and had, in fact, been pursued by football and rowing coaches in high school. *No chance of that*, Stick thought. It'd get in the way of his J-O-B, each letter pronounced like its own word. Jay Oh Bee. Not really a job at all, though Stick put enough effort, concentration, and time into it to match most young working men. Not the job that Stick had enjoyed that one time, robbing that bitch, but the regular income-producing activity he engaged in every day almost. This particular job was not recognized or studied by the Department of Labor, except as maybe a subset of sales. But drug dealers rarely filled out government forms or surveys. Stick didn't know his own Social Security number.

Stick would have been in college by now, had he paid any attention to school during the hours he was in it, if he did even a minute of homework, if he were a member of a socio economic class that considered college a goal, if he did not align himself with a subculture that placed negative value on self-sacrifice or legitimate effort, if he had a single book anywhere in his house other than the Yellow Pages. Or so his guidance counselor would have said, if Stick ever talked with her. But he did not.

Now he was walking to the courthouse in the light afternoon snow to meet his court-appointed public defender lawyer lady. Untied Timberlands slid on his feet, a size too big but when you street-buy whatever somebody jacked, you didn't get exact fits. He didn't pay the lawyer, so he didn't pay much attention to her, how important she said his case was or should be to him. He wasn't worried about his arrest—the crack cocaine that the police was sayin' they found on him, the charges against him. He walked on snowy sidewalks in front of rich folks' townhouses and subsidized housing units like his own. Sometimes rich and poor were just on either side of the street. Stick didn't think about this. He'd had to get his mom to write a note excusing him from afternoon classes to go see his public defender. He took the yellow bus to and from school, but leaving early meant he would take the city bus to court and then home. He had $460 in his pockets from his morning's deals, but it never occurred to him to get a cab. Outside of his experience.

In the dark that morning, Stick had left his townhouse on North Alfred Street in the Alexandria neighborhood labeled the Samuel Madden Homes by its overseer, the Alexandria Redevelopment and Housing Authority, but known by residents and cops alike as the North Side. Stick, his mother, and his two brothers still at home lived in an ARHA three-bedroom, 1,300-square-foot two-story townhouse, walking distance to the Metro stop (though Stick had only once ridden the D.C. area subway system). His circle of life was the hood, the school bus to T.C. Williams High School, and maybe walking a few blocks to the Hungry Pal restaurant for pizza. A small world, but Stick's life came to him. Usually in the early morning, before the bus came.

His customers drove into the neighborhood and identified him not by name but by demeanor, by look. Slouched in a hooded sweatshirt, dark jeans hanging low under a visible white strip of underpants, a style called "jailin'" on the street because that's how a fella looked in jail after the booking deputies took his belt away so he couldn't hang himself. A driver's hand raised at the doorsill, a finger or two up, answered by his own raised finger waving them in. A sauntering approach and quick verbal contract.

"You workin'?"

"You lookin'?"

Neither answered. Each was. Stick was working as a seller of crack cocaine. The buyer was looking for a dealer to sell him crack. Why else would either be out here at five a.m.? Stick usually didn't work at night, had had some bad experiences when he did. One time ended when he felt the urge and robbed that girl, a bad time 'cause the popo showed up and stayed for hours but didn't find him. He inside looking out the window of his house, laughin.' The other time was last month, when the Jump-Out Boys got him for possession.

Morning was a safe time for business. Stick knew the Jump-Outs didn't work this early, and the regular popo were easy to see coming in their shiny white cars. And the popo didn't get out of their cars to sneak around like the Jump-Outs did. Jump-Outs worked at night, and that was when they got him, finding a rock of crack in his pocket. Shit, all they did was walk up and ask him if he had one, and he did, and he said he did. He didn't know better, knew they'd know if he was lying and make it harder on him. So he stuck out his hand and handed over the rock. Possession. Still, not possession with intent to distribute. They didn't charge him as no dealer. He was, but they didn't charge that.

Stick would have two hours to sell before the school bus came. Stick worked the corner of Alfred and Madison Street and halfway up the block away from the recreation center. Another nigga called Peanut was working a block away at Alfred and Montgomery. Stick didn't talk to Peanut, but they got their rock from the same boys in a house in the next project.

Stick bought twenty rocks of crack cocaine a day from his suppliers, for two hundred bucks, depending. He sold it for twice that and kept what he might pinch off from the rock before each sale—no pinch if the buyer was local and consistent, a bigger pinch if the buyer seemed stupid or not from the Block or white. Or he would sell a beat rock, something that looked like crack but wasn't, if the buyer was white and scared, so unlikely to come back and complain. Crack was a black drug in Alexandria, but white folks sometimes screwed up their courage to enter the projects to score. Another car slowed.

"Workin'?"

"Pull up over there." Stick approached the car, leaned into a passenger window open despite the November cold, and sized up the buyer. Thin, sweaty, looking in the mirrors. Stick didn't know his name but had sold to him before.

"'Chu want?"

"Twenty-rock." A specific size that Stick could not quantify by weight or measured dimension but a known and recognized bulk. Stick reached into his jacket pocket and by feel selected an appropriate item from the pile. He held out his hand and took short, sidelong glances through the auto glass. Yeah, Jump-Outs didn't work mornings but you gotta keep an eye. He opened his palm and the buyer pinched the rock away and placed it in his mouth, then gave up the $20 bill. Crack was not water-soluble, so it could ride safe in the corners of a buyer's mouth, ready to be swallowed if Five-Oh approached.

Just ten minutes into his workday, Stick had made half of his profit. He worked six days a week, fifty-two weeks a year. He worked mornings because it was crazy at night, too many sellers, too many Five-Oh, too many stickup boys who would take his money. That one time a few months ago, he had been a stickup boy himself. Too much drama, and big-time jail if they caught you, so he'd only done it that one time. Most days Stick left his home predawn and walked fifty feet to his worksite, where he sold $124,000 gross last year. Not bad for a nineteen-year-old high school junior. Not legal, but not bad. Two hours later, Stick had sold out, at least all the product he was prepared to sell. And onto the bus to high school.

That afternoon, in the bathroom before he left for court, he took the pinches of crack he'd saved for himself and gathered them together on the flattened side of a partially squeezed soda can where he had punched a bunch of holes. Stick reached into his pocket for his lighter and found the note to the school from his mom. He was supposed to give it to somebody so he could get out of school today. He didn't think much about it. He didn't think much about court either. He was going there for something called a suppression hearing, but it wouldn't happen. His lawyer'd be surprised, but he wouldn't. *Kike bitch, she don't know nothing.* He would tell her all about how he seen Professor Vulture last week and Professor Vulture had put a root on it.

All done.

Stick held the can horizontal in front of his mouth. A squirt of flame onto the rocks while he drew air from the drinking hole, and hot crack cocaine vapor was drawn down from the flame through the holes and into his brain, where it exploded.

Like sometimes happened, he had an orgasm when it hit.

CHAPTER 8

Meeting
Tuesday, November 1, 1988
4 p.m.–5:30 p.m.

RACHEL TRIED HARD not to think about Kelly, his green eyes, his wide shoulders, twice-broken nose, his hard arms . . . those arms on her arms, around her hips, her . . . *Uhhh! Be professional,* she had to scream at herself, but silently so as not to startle the oblivious judge and the courtroom crowd around her. The room had white walls over colonial blue wainscoting and trim. The gated wooden rail at the front and the pews it separated from the judge's bench and attorneys' tables were dark wood, cheaply varnished and deeply scarred by years of impact by briefcases and cops' utility belts. Rachel's thoughts of Kelly were romantic, often randy, but today troubled. How do I tell him? What will he say when I tell him? How will he take it? So important. She'd left him in the elevator after a long and dangerous kiss with plans to meet in a nearby bagel shop.

She and Stick sat near each other on the right side of the courtroom, waiting for the judge to finish up another afternoon hearing. Defense attorneys and public defenders typically sat on the right, and uniformed police and detectives on the left—an unwritten rule. Witnesses and criminals sat anywhere. They were awaiting the start of Cohen's motion to suppress. Cohen would argue that the three twenty-rocks of crack cocaine police seized from Stick one night last month were illegally recovered and thus inadmissible. In Stick's mind, the motion didn't matter. His gramma had taken care of it.

"He put a root on it," Stick had told Cohen outside the courtroom a few minutes before. They talked in the hallway outside the courtroom, moving away from the crowds at the doorway for privacy. Cohen wore her court clothes; dark knee-length skirt and matching jacket over a modest white blouse with frill at the neck, low-heeled shoes. Stick wore his best too, a bright white Le Coque Sportif tracksuit with red piping and high-top white Reeboks, deliberately chosen to look his best today.

"Root . . . ?"

"Yes'm. Professor Vulture, he know roots and chickens and blood an' stuff. He tol' my gran'moms he would make 'em forget about it."

It was forgettable, a simple case, one of hundreds of nearly identical cases heard by the court since crack showed up in Alexandria. The facts were these: One hour past midnight on October 7, the defendant, Antonio DeJerolme Planter, a.k.a. Stick, was approached by two members of the Alexandria Police Department Tactical Unit, who during the course of their investigation located and seized three rocks of crack cocaine hydrochloride illegally in the possession of Mr. Planter and that said possession was with the intent to distribute, not simply to use, in violation of Virginia Criminal Code section 18.2-248.

"Are you talking about voodoo?" Cohen, product of modern scientific culture and Jewish faith, didn't believe in voodoo.

"Yes'm. My gramma says it works. Worked on me before. I was small, I was a baby. She saw Professor Vulture, he do somethin'. I think my gramma said he burned somethin' and I got big. When the popo took me for this, she went to Professor Vulture again. He say he remembered her, said he knew just what to do so she sent me to 'im."

"And what'll it do? She say just how this case won't go?" From any and all of her clients, Cohen had heard nothing but stories that had no bearing on the case, case law, or the legalities of the police actions. Not that she was expecting an answer of any value or help. Cohen had heard hundreds of stories from defendants, young like Stick or old, literate or uneducated, sober, stoned, rich, poor. None of them ever helped the case. Only a few resembled truth. Never once did a client state, simply, "I did it, I had them on me. I bought/took/shot up/ingested/sold/stole whatever was named on the court papers." A burglar with a television under his arm: "I found it." A kid on a stolen bicycle: "No one was using it." Drugs in your pants pocket: "They weren't my pants. It was dark when I put them on and I was not at my house." Most often Cohen and the other defense bar did not put their clients on the stand. Judges didn't want to hear this stuff.

The judge would not want to hear Stick's initial story either. Certainly not the Professor Vulture business, and not Stick's version of events either, with the police holding him and taking the drugs. Jump-Outs were aggressive and might be liars and connivers, but no one ever verified stories of forced searches and deliberate violations of rights. Like Stick was trying to tell her.

"They come up and held me."

"They touched you?"

"Naw, they didn't touch me! They held me."

"How did they hold you if they didn't touch you?" A conversation with Stick was often challenging, tracing straight lines with balls of twisted string. "What exactly did they do?"

"All a sudden they jumps out the cars, they all up on me. One up in front, that big burly one with the chains on his neck, others all around and they tellin' me what you doin' here, why you out here? I tells 'em I live here, and I shows 'em my house up the street. They say, why you out here, it rainin' and you standing out here? I say I can stand where I want to stand. They say, you got any drugs on you? I say I don' got no drugs. They say, well, okay if we search you then? I say, go ahead, search me, you won't find nothin.'"

"And?"

"They did."

"So why did you tell them to search you, Stick? You had crack on you?"

"Ain't can tell 'em no. Din' think I can tell 'em no. They all up on me and stuff, they might beat me I tell 'em no. 'Sides, I thinkin' I tell 'em yes, they might just let me go. Tryin' to be smart."

Yeah, you're all smart like that, Rachel thought. "They in uniform?

"Hell, no, they ain't in uniforms. They all in clothes an' stuff."

"How did you know they were police?"

"'Cause they the Jump-Outs. E'body knows the Jump-Outs. An' they had guns and stuff."

"Stuff?"

"Badges and stuff. Radios. Handcuffs, they holding they handcuffs and spinnin' them round on they fingers when they talkin' to me."

"They showed you handcuffs and then asked if they could search you?"

"Yeah."

Gotcha! Cohen finally had an argument she could use to demonstrate that Stick had not freely given consent to a search by police, that force was implied and arrest was threatened, making the seizure unlawful and leading the judge to suppress or bar the evidence from use.

Armed now with at least a lightweight stone to weakly throw at the case against Stick, Cohen stood when the clerk read from a list and called *Commonwealth v. Antonio Planter*. They walked forward together, through the gate in the fence-like rail dividing seats from the tables, witness stand, and judge's platform at the front of the room. They sat at a table to the right of the judge, facing the prosecutor on the judge's left. Rachel noticed the judge glaring more than judges usually do at defendants.

Stick sensed the glare, stood up, and raised his right hand like he'd seen others do that day. This was his first time in court, his first arrest, the first time he'd even seen a proceeding like this. The cops had not seen Stick much before this either, despite their constant coverage of his public housing neighborhood. His usual early-morning work hours kept him off the Jump-Outs' schedule, and he'd only got popped that night coming home from a girl's apartment with rocks he forgot he had.

"Put your hand down, not yet," the judge growled. "You are Antonio Planter?"

"Yes, sir." Almost yassuh boss, Stick was almost that confident from the start. From the root.

"You filed for and received a public defender based on indigence?"

"Indi, um. I gots a public defender. She right here." Cohen was standing next to Stick now, unsure where this was going.

"Indigence. Means you don't have enough money to hire your own attorney."

"I in school. I don't gots no job."

"That's a nice running suit. I wanted to buy that suit myself, but I couldn't afford it. Glad you could." Stick glanced down at the shiny satin jacket, spread his hands in a flourish, and looked back at the judge, who dismissed the topic with a small wave. "Clerk, please swear in the witnesses."

Cohen overcame her anger at the bullying of the judge and saw it gave her another stone to throw: judicial bias. Turned out, she didn't need it today.

The clerk, at a short desk in front of the judge, shuffled a stack of papers looking for the court file. She double-checked the computer list. She glanced up at the prosecutor, mouthed, "Planter," at him and continued shuffling. The prosecutor also began looking among his files for Planter. He asked the judge for permission to approach and retrieved the list from the clerk, then again looked around his table and piles.

"Your Honor, I, I'm sorry but we do not have the case file for Mr. Planter with us." *We* and *us* being deflective pronouns since he was alone at the prosecutor's table. "If you give me a moment, I can have one of the officers run down to my office and get it for me."

"Which officers would that be, Mr. Prosecutor? I don't see anyone standing up with you."

And the prosecutor, whose name was Billy Simmons and who was still fairly new in the office, looked up from the table at the judge, then around and behind him, finally noticing that no members of the police Jump-Out squad were present in court.

"Your Honor, they may be in the other courtroom. Can the deputy . . ."

"There is no other courtroom open at this time. This is not Commonwealth Day. Mine is the only working courtroom. And you are wasting my time. Do you have a motion, or should I just dismiss this case now?"

"Your Honor, ah, I would request a continuance until this Thursday, which is Commonwealth Day. I am sure I can have my witnesses present on short notice. They're usually here all day that day anyway."

Rachel threw her last stone of the day.

"Your Honor, I would object to a continuance. My client is present and we are prepared to go forward with the motion. It would be unfair to my client to require him to come back to court again and again on what is a relatively minor charge. Alternatively, I would ask the court to dismiss this case at this time, due to—"

"No, I won't dismiss it, Ms. Cohen. I will grant the Commonwealth's request for a continuance until Thursday. It will be Commonwealth Day, and I happen to remember that you will be here that day too. You have a trial set before me that morning, that you insisted be on that day, despite the involvement of a number of civilian witnesses."

"Yes, Your Honor. I do, and that will be fine for us."

In the hall, the prosecutor told Rachel he had no idea what happened to the case.

"I remember it, I think. We get so many of these Jump-Out cases. I'll get the file and you know we'll be ready for Thursday. Can I take a look at your file?"

"No way, Billy. Against attorney-client privilege for me to give you anything. You want some kind of reverse discovery? Uh-uh." She glared at him. "Prosecution gets all the breaks and makes the case. I'm not making it for you," she said. *That's meshuggah*, she thought. "That's crazy."

"I don't know where it is, I remember having it, I think." Simmons looked over Rachel's shoulder, distracted, maybe trying to find a Jump-Out to help explain the missing case.

"I'm sure you will, Billy." And she turned quickly to leave, before he thought too much and actually solved the mystery. Time and delays were the defendant's friend: more time between the arrest and court meant a greater likelihood that witnesses forgot or evidence soured. Or case files disappeared.

Outside the courthouse, Rachel hustled across busy King Street toward a bagel shop where she knew Kelly waited. She couldn't see him through the window glare but entered the bagel shop and found him filling a booth. He tended to take over and hold the space around him like a hill he was king of. He'd tried to explain once the need to keep an eye on the entrance, with a wall at his back to limit exposure. He'd tried to explain the constant worry but saw the worry transfer to her and stopped.

He had ordered for her, and her favorite cinnamon raisin with butter and coffee with cream and sugar sat between them. Not very Jewish, but she'd finally cured his thoughtful but misled habit of ordering her lox on onion. His poppy with cream cheese lay untouched as he waited for her.

She sat, wanting instead to yank off his tie, unbutton his shirt fast, and bury her face in the hair of his chest as she wrapped her arms around him and he pushed his lips down into the hair at the top of her head like he did, breathing in her essence just as she did his.

But that would not be appropriate here in the bagel shop.

Not appropriate anywhere, really, with their clashing allegiances. Their jobs and their lives contrasted sharply now, but maybe her news would change that. It would sure change something. So all she let herself do was push her hand across the tabletop, between and partially hidden by their food orders, and gently touched the cords of his thick wrist. He shivered. Her adoring gaze held his and was changed by his anxiety, shifting from coy to concerned. "I've got something to tell you, but you have something going on, don't you?"

"No, nothing," he lied.

"That's bullshit, John. I know you like your wife does." He flinched. "We don't have a lot of time here. I have to get back to work. You're upset already."

"Already? Something going to upset me now? You got something?" His voice was angry now, swiftly changed from his initial calm and his usual exuberant wit and radiant warmth that first drew her to him, the power of his person. Rachel adored John Kelly. It should have made it easy to be with him, but not always. His mercurial swings frightened her less than they used to when they first met.

Three months ago, in her first week at the Public Defenders' Office, a coworker invited her along for drinks and ushered her into a circle of men whose suits and jackets hung loose and lumpy on their large frames. As they moved to accommodate her and, as the evening went on, to "accidentally" brush against her in their less-than-subtle come-on way, she discovered each cop in their best court clothes was wearing a holstered pistol. A few in the group were women, their hands protectively draped over purses equally and identically lumpy. So much firepower, she worried. And so much machismo.

And even wearing guns, they needed to show their power, their ruling class separation from the commoners, of which she was one. Their stories were gross, angry, offensive in detail, and dismissive of basic dignity and human rights. She stood at the edge of the circle, sipping her second beer from a bottle, while one or another recited their grossest calls for service. She sensed this was a show for her or a test.

"So this kid on the moped, when the lady pulled out, he tries to cut around her but doesn't quite. She knocks him towards the curb, and he pulls up on the front tire but the back one hits the curb and bucks him up, off the moped and over the sidewalk. There was a sign there in the corner. He hits it flying sideways, right below the ribs on his right side. He wraps around the pole and pops like a sausage—you know, you bend it? His face was where his feet were, and all his insides came out. Looked like a butcher shop. They took the sign out, people kept tying balloons to it, blocked the view."

Or, "Stank so bad, we had to get Scott AirPaks from Fire to go in. He'd been dead in there so long he was just a pile of stuff. The neighbors had smelled something for about a week, but only called us when they saw the windows looked funny, kinda shimmery. They got up close and looked, and it was flies, millions of them, all buzzing, stuck inside."

Or, "She had a whole .357 up there. Only way deputies found it, she was sitting funny on the bench in Booking, kinda leaning one way like she was tender. She was. Hammerless, of course. Otherwise she couldn'a got it out, like it was a fishhook."

And so on.

After about a half hour, Rachel became aware of a man sitting at the bar at the edge of the circle, leaning his arms back against the rail, elbows out, taking up more space than the others. He was staring at her, and his eyes flared as he noticed her noticing him.

Her whole body noticed him, and she felt a flush of warmth flow up through her from her hips. *Oh, my God, Rachel,* she thought. *What is this?* She actually stopped herself after taking a step toward him. The flush hit her face then, and she redirected, fleeing to the ladies' room to regroup. *You're a grownup, you don't have that kind of reaction, like a teenager.* But she did.

When she emerged, she looked across the bar, and he was gone from his anchor position in the circle. She found him standing beside her then, his fingers gently brushing her elbow to turn her toward him. "Hi, I'm John Kelly." She liked that his gaze held hers and didn't wander down to the one-button-too-many-undone neck of her blouse, white under her dark blue best courtroom suit from Garfinckel's. And, oh, my God, how he spoke to her.

"I'm thinking there are so many different, better, happier, shinier places to be than here, and if you name one, I'll take you there." He smiled.

"There's an ice cream shop around the corner." Weak on clever, but strong on result and only took her a second. Cool!

They turned their backs to the circle of coworkers and went out the door to the ice cream shop. He liked vanilla, she chose whatever, based more on color than taste. With cups and little spoons, they walked down the block, away from the bar, and ended up in a churchyard, sitting on a swing set. Talking. For four hours.

But this day in the bagel shop, Rachel had no time for such a languorous talk. Kelly was more agitated than normal. She was, too. He continually wiped his mouth with the napkin, a mannerism she once thought betrayed excess fastidiousness but learned meant he was embarrassed that cream cheese from his bagel was hung up in his thick moustache. He looked over her shoulders every few seconds.

"How's your day been so far? You have good cases today? I know you can't talk much about them but—" and she interrupted. Or tried to.

"No. John, listen, it's . . . John, I'm . . ." She kept talking but he was glancing past her and didn't hear. He spoke over her next few words.

"Election's next week. Haven't missed one yet. Even the one when I was in the Academy, they let us out to vote." He prattled on, nervously, manically, until Rachel reached across and squeezed his wrist in a rare public contact, forbidden here right across from the courthouse, too visible to attentive and likely critical coworkers. Cops and public defenders can't date. Hang out and drink with? Okay. Fuck? Sure, why not. But date? Get involved with? The L word? Way over the line. Well, Rachel and John had been on both sides of the line. And with Rachel's home test last night, they were officially together on the wrong side. She felt herself blushing. She looked at him like a heart surgeon looks at an exposed chest. It all happens now. This is where we fail or succeed. Right now.

She said again, "I'm late."

CHAPTER 9

Coffee
Tuesday, November 1, 1988
1630–1800 HRS

HE'D SPOTTED HER the moment she cleared the courthouse down the block from the bagel shop. Big, bright red hair in thick waves, almost curly. Under her lined raincoat against the blowing snow, she was small framed but curvy, what he'd learned to call *zaftig* in Yiddish because he thought it meant curvy but unlearned quick when he found it meant plump. She had the beautiful, shapely legs and ugly, gnarled feet of the ballet dancer she'd been through high school. Her feet were shod now, of course, but he knew what her covered parts looked like, *all* the covered parts, images rushing through him like the first cigarette of the day used to, before he quit again.

He had been elated when he bumped into Rachel in the courthouse elevator, an unexpected, happy shot. He waited a moment until the box was between floors and hit the stop button. Rachel turned to face him in surprise when the elevator jolted, her body and wavy hair bouncing slightly upward. He met her eyes and they came together, almost thudding as their lips pressed together. His hands ran up her back, beneath her coat and suit jacket but outside her blouse to palm her shoulder blades, fingers stroking the forbidden clasp of her bra. She dropped her briefcase and reached her hands around his neck, pulling his face down to hers, her glasses smudging on his cheek. He clung to her as they both absorbed and radiated the quick rush of lust.

After only a minute, unsatisfied but knowing that was all they'd get, they restarted the elevator, rode down to the first floor, and got out. No chance for privacy in a courthouse. And no time to waste.

"I need to talk with you about something, John. Like now," Rachel said, playfully moving her face around to find a clear eyehole through the smudged glasses. She never wore lip gloss in court, thank goodness, so no betraying smudges on him. She was a foot shorter, but he never thought of her as small.

"Maybe tomorrow. I'll call you."

"Sooner. Now. Today. I need to . . . I need you. We need to talk."

Kelly couldn't decipher the flutter in her eyes. He named a shop across the street and she said thirty minutes, then turned away. "Be discreet," Kelly said, as if there were things they could do differently.

"Yeah. You're as discreet as a dump truck," Rachel said, with a grin below happy but hesitant eyes.

She found him in a booth facing the door, of course. She sat down across from him. "I've got something to tell you, but you have something going on, don't you?"

John thought Rachel looked scattered. He didn't recognize how scattered he was too. "No, nothing," he lied.

"That's bullshit, John. I know you like your wife does." He flinched. "We don't have a lot of time here. I have to get back to work. You're upset already."

"Already? Something going to upset me now? You got something?" His radio, on the table next, buzzed and popped unintelligibly. Kelly occasionally cocked an ear to catch and release whatever was being broadcast. He swallowed most of the bagel in four bites. Rachel used to nag that he needed to slow down when he ate, both hands shoveling in sandwiches and fries in haste to beat the radio, to finish before being called away. Anything can happen, he had once explained to her early on.

"We just don't know what will happen next, who will come up to us, what happens when we do such and such. You know how normal people get angry when we come up to their car with our hand on our gun? They say, 'You gonna shoot me? I didn't do anything. Why you treat me like a bank robber?' It's because to me, you are, till I know you aren't. Cops get blown away every year. They walk up to cars with bad guys they didn't know were bad guys. They just thought they ran a red light, no big deal. And the driver's some Jimmy Cagney, 'I'm not going back to the joint, Copper,' and bang.

"So everybody is a bad guy till I know they aren't. That's how we think. Anyplace we are, we think, what happens if . . . if a guy with a gun comes in to rob the place, or shoots somebody right here? Can I take him? Can I draw and get him now, or do I wait till he clears and chase him? How many folks are around, where will they move, where will I find cover? Anyplace we walk around, we're looking for cover." His eyes swung rapidly around, on her then past, taking in everything static and changing in his environment. Distracted. It used to always bother her. Lately only sometimes. Like now.

"What's cover?"

"There's cover and there's concealment. Concealment means we can hide behind it. Cover means it'll stop bullets. A car door is concealment. A car engine is cover."

"And you think that way all the time?" Rachel had asked.

"Every working minute. Every waking minute too," Kelly said. *Too many minutes and not enough down time*, he thought. Beer helps.

Today he kept small-talking. "How's your day been so far? Snow's not too bad. You have good cases today? I know you can't talk much about them but—"

She interrupted. Or tried to. "No. John, listen, it's . . . John, I'm . . ."

"Election's next week. Haven't missed one yet. Even the one eight years ago, when I was in the Academy, they let us out to vote."

She said again, "I'm late." And he finally heard her. "John. John! Listen. I'm late."

John misunderstood, shot his left arm out to let his wrist-watch clear the cuff, and checked the time. "Nah, you got—"

"I'm . . . late. Late, like my period's late." She felt herself blushing. "I'm, I might be pregnant, John," she said.

"That's . . ." And he stopped. His gaze still focused on her new. Door, crowds, and movement faded and his mind raced. His loving mind took in this beautiful woman, warm and vibrant and adoring and here with him. He wondered whether she would want to be with him—and his vision began to expand, years ahead in seconds, to a future with her that they had only recently, fleetingly begun considering in tentative whispers as anything more than a happy but unlikely fantasy. A baby. With her.

Unbidden, his automatic cop mind thought, *Is it mine?* He crushed that down.

"That's . . . great. Great! Rach, that's fantastic. Right?" His grin broke out wide but faded in the next moment as her tears began. "This is big news. It's, it's a good thing. It can be a good thing, right? I know we . . ." He leaned forward and widened his shoulders as if to give her the hug they both needed.

Her wet eyes overflowed and blinked. "It's good, John. I think it's good. It can be good. Or it can be bad. You and I, we haven't really talked about, well, anything more than what happens next . . ."

"Yeah, what happens next is big."

"No, I mean, we've only talked about next in terms of next like tonight or tomorrow or this weekend. Not next like the rest of our lives next. Not what something like this means," Rachel said.

Since their first date, when he had told her the Wart Lip story and talked her out of the bar for ice cream, their world had been hastily grabbed nights or afternoons when nobody was looking. She used the pager he carried as a member of the Hostage Negotiations Team to reach him without having to call his office and give her name. Or call him at his home, where someone else could answer. He remembered a particular midnight when she first paged, prearranged and on a dare with him. "You won't do it, you won't take the step," he had told her. "Yes I will," she'd said, playfully defiant. And she did, typing in "07734," a signal to get up and get dressed and drive to her townhouse. Turn it upside down, the glowing pager screen read "hELLO." A secret signal.

"This means . . . It means . . . everything. We haven't talked about this, not this specifically but us moving forward, um." He got tongue-tied, unusual for him. *Spit it out!* he told himself. "Together," he told her.

And it was her turn to wipe her face, too intimate an act for him here, even at this moment. Her cleared tears left a frown. "So this would be an okay thing?" she asked.

"More than okay. Rachel, this would be . . . wonderful. I know it means a lot of steps, but we've kinda talked about this before. We didn't really know if we could." Kelly paused as his mind raced.

His words ran to catch up. "And you never said you would. But I've been planning to change, to make it final, to tell . . . her, not because of this or anything like this, or just because of you." John paused. "Not directly because of you, but I have to do it anyway. It's been coming for a while, you know that. So it won't be your fault, but we, we benefit from it. Or I do." He trailed off.

"We do, John. We do, both of us. It's time for me too," Rachel said. She smiled, tears brimming again but good ones this time.

"You mean, you'd want to . . ." And he could not speak the rest. From zero to elation, he was overcome, numb, and almost dumb. To keep the baby, break free, get married, live happily ever after. Change everything right now for me, and become us. He could not speak it. Yet. He tried to say it with his eyes.

"We gotta talk more. I need to see you without all these people around," Kelly said.

"Come by tonight."

"I, I can't tonight. I got something." Kelly's heart hit a wall. He shook his head, almost forlornly at the lame sound of his excuse. "I gotta go by my folks' house tonight."

"Your folks?" Her shoulders slumped. "You, we . . . we have to . . . You said your dad was . . ."

"I mean, my mom's house. Not for her, but she . . . My brother . . . I haven't seen him in a year. He's gonna be there. My mom set it up." He stammered to a stop. His brother had avoided him for the full year since the night, since Emma was . . . Since her death.

That night, Kelly had driven back to his brother's house after Emma was killed. There, the lieutenant stopped him and took his blazer, sodden with Emma's blood. His shirt was reddened, too, so the lieutenant gave him his own nylon uniform jacket to cover up. Kelly forced himself through the door and into the living room where Patrick and Brenda sat, as-yet untold in words but clearly informed by the quiet cops and turned-down radios. And then by Kelly's ashen face.

Brenda began to wail before Kelly spoke, and Patrick trembled and tried to comfort her. Kelly knelt in front of them, failing to find any words at all, staring at them with his hands partly out but unable to reach across to them. Finally it was Patrick who spoke the only words between them that night, or since.

"You lied, John. You said she'd come back. You lied. You should have done something. You should have saved her. She should be here now. And she's not. We know she's dead," and Brenda gave a huge flinch in his arms.

"She's dead, and you failed."

Kelly physically shook at the memory, and Rachel stared at him in confusion. "You're going to your mom's?" Rachel's voice rose at the end. "I don't understand. You go see your mom tonight? John, we need . . ."

"I know you don't understand, but it's, well . . . My brother, I . . ." Rachel's face was blank. "There's some stuff I haven't told you. Yet. My brother, his daughter. We haven't spoken in a year. My niece, she, she was . . ."

Kelly's radio squealed, saving him.

CHAPTER 10

Hara Kiri
Tuesday, November 1, 1988
1800–2130 HRS

RECRUIT WILLIAM HIGGINS had driven a careful and controlled Code 3 to the call for a suicide-in-progress, even stopping midrun to double-check the map to find his way there, watched closely by his Field Training Officer Herbert Jackson. It was outside of their normal patrol area, but the dispatchers knew that FTO/recruit pairs needed "hot" calls for training, and knew that FTOs liked to subject their trainees to dead bodies to assess their ability to handle stressful things.

Higgins drove across the Monroe Street Bridge, willing the rush hour traffic to get out of his way in the left lane and not force him to slalom around it. FTO Jackson watched him begin to slow down, to read the signs at the cross streets without recognition. They worked and trained in Sector Two almost exclusively, a geographical third of the city that was primarily residential, apartments and homes with a spine of business along Mount Vernon Avenue. Now they were entering Sector One, and it was a mystery to the recruit. He started to tense up and glanced at the FTO in supplication, but the FTO said, "You don't know where you're going, you could be going away from the call. Check the map."

The recruit gave him a "you're kidding" look, but the FTO just stared back. So the recruit pulled to the curb and grabbed the laminated city map from over the visor. The FTO watched him find the street listing and cross-reference the location, then figure the correct turns to get him there. After half a minute, the FTO snapped off the siren and lights, still blasting on their motionless cruiser. Finally oriented, the recruit checked the mirror and pulled back into traffic, reactivating the emergency equipment with a sheepish glance at the FTO.

Two cruisers were parked crookedly near the front doors of the condo. An ambulance also stood by, its crew of two EMTs leaning against the back, out of the chill wind that curved around the high rise off the wide Potomac River. No urgency now.

The condominium was very upscale, which they would learn had been the deceased's problem. His wife had called the cops after she got home and found his note on the kitchen counter. Higgins obtained some basic information from the backup officer before they went to the sergeant's location. The backup looked grim, and Jackson pulled him away from the wife.

"DOA?" the FTO asked.

The backup tilted his head and shrugged. "DRT," he said.

"So, dead enough we don't have to worry about getting a doctor here to tell us he's dead. And we can keep the medics out," Jackson said to instruct his recruit. Medics, by dint of their unhesitating urgency to reach victims, often trampled evidence and altered crime scenes, cut apart cars, and bashed in doors. "Our crash investigators call the fire department the Evidence Eradication Team," Jackson said.

They read the note.

I'm sorry I couldn't get a job with a salary that would let you have everything you wanted.

The note sat on the kitchen counter in the fourth-floor waterfront condo unit with panoramic Potomac views, next to the keys to a year-old Jaguar convertible. She'd parked her Mercedes two-door next to it in their assigned spaces when she came home from work. He was gone, but with his car there, the sergeant decided to check if his mountain bike was still in the storage area. The family name was Chinese, so the cops knew suicide was less likely than for Occidentals, but not unheard of, so they had to move quickly to locate the man before he took final action.

Too late.

The sergeant had used the wife's magnetic entry card to open the storage room door and found the vic seated in a red pool of shiny fluid against a concrete support column. He had placed the barrel of a .410 shotgun in his mouth, the butt between his spread legs, and leaned back to look up as he pulled the trigger with his outstretched arms and hands. It vaporized his face and left lead markings and spattered blood rising in a perfect triangle up the column's white surface. The curvature of the forehead from the upper lip to past the hairline was gone, removed by thirty lead pellets moving at 960 feet per second. What skin hadn't been atomized by the blast had pulled tautly back away from the wounded bone edge like a sandwich wrapper. The long gun had dropped into his lap, where his right hand still gripped it, index finger broken in the trigger guard by the recoil. The bright red blood and clear cerebrospinal fluid mixed into a thick jelly that oozed a few feet in all directions from the body, mostly flowing along the slight downhill toward a floor drain. One eyeball, torn out perfect and round, sat like a fisherman's bobber in the river of blood; the other was gone. Death was recent enough that the thick fluid was unclotted and shiny.

"Mind your step, Will," the sergeant said when they came down from the condo to the storage room. Higgins already knew to. "Wifey told us they owned a .410 when we asked. Just the one. She has the papers on it. We can match the serial numbers to this one," the sergeant said, both to inform the recruit and to distract him, now going green, from the gore. Technically it was the recruit's scene and Higgins's responsibility to learn the details and brief the sergeant, but allowances were made. He looked a little pale but was holding up, Jackson noted.

"We have his photo," the sergeant said, "but, uh, that doesn't help much here. There's a wallet in his pants, see the bulge. ID is en route, we'll let them pull it out after they photograph him. But it's gonna be him. Has CID been called?" And the sergeant looked pointedly from the FTO to the recruit, meaning, *It's time for him to get under control and up to speed.* So Jackson gave Higgins a few concise steps to follow. Routine in the middle of carnage. Police work.

And as the FTO had hoped, it was Detective Kelly who responded to the recruit's radio message asking for a detective. The FTO shook his head no when Communications followed up with "Do you want the removal service to respond?"

"Not at this time, Headquarters, we'll advise." And the sergeant, whose name was Conner, nodded at the FTO in approval of the recruit's clear and correct radio response.

Higgins asked, "Do we tell the wife?"

"No, we leave that to the detectives. They'll want to watch her when they tell her, see how she reacts. This looks clear-cut, but she mighta done it. If it's murder, it's always the wife or the hubbie. I don't think so, but we just got here." The FTO looked at Sergeant Conner.

"I think this will work out to just suicide, but because it might go another way, we title the report 'Sudden Death,'" Conner said. "Covers everything. Detectives supplement it later, so they can change it."

"So we don't write *harry carry*?" The kid was getting a little less green around the gills, breathing deeper and recovering from only the third dead body he'd ever seen, the priors being his grandparents on his father's side, cleaned up and powdered in caskets at funeral homes, not steaming fresh and violently taken. Trying on the tough-cop act like a new hat. The FTO looked at him a moment.

The recruit made a cutting motion across his belly and said, "Because he's Japanese, or at least Asian, right?" And Jackson thought, *Good that he could try to joke, but the wrong way to go about it.*

"First, he's not Japanese, he is Chinese, and until you can tell the difference, don't remark on it. Second, don't remark on it, 'cause it's racist. Third, it's *hara kiri*, not harry carry. Fourth, ritual belly cutting is called *sepukku*. Fifth, what if the wife were here or right outside the door and she heard you. Pick your time." Spoken more sharply than he should have, but the FTO hated shotguns. He'd carried one in Vietnam in his prior life, and the smells of gunpowder and fresh blood brought overwhelming memories. He shook it off.

"It's Kelly who's coming for CID," the sergeant said. "Did you find him earlier, talk to him? You used to be his FTO. The LT said you were looking for him."

"No, so this is good, him coming here." Only cops could refer to a shotgun suicide as good. "I'll get with him in a few, after he's got this started. And I got a thing we need to do. I'll run it by you later."

"No, run it now."

"Okay. The lieutenant wants us to cover the dig-up thing."

"It's Thursday? Two days from now?"

"Yeah, but it's early afternoon, so it's on Day Shift. We usually don't come in till four."

"And you want the call?" Somebody from the police department had to attend the exhumation and accompany the casket to the Medical Examiner's Office to document chain of custody. "The lieutenant wants you both on the call?" He sounded more curious than offended.

"Well, me, but Higgins goes where I go. We can adjust hours, so we work Days that day. We can take the call as part of his training." Jackson cocked his head toward the recruit. "It's an interesting call, so I can justify it as FTO-related training."

"So what's the idea? What do you have in mind?"

"You don't want to know."

Kelly arrived coincident with the ID van. The identification technician thanked Kelly for carrying one of her two heavy toolboxes/camera cases/evidence kits into the building. The recruit met them in the lobby and showed them how to get to the body and told the condo manager to stand by in her office for a few. She didn't know yet that her tenant had been found.

Kelly found the sergeant and the FTO crouched at the edge of the blood lake. They were admiring the crispness of the spatter lines above the skull, the sharp delineation at the edges, the way the majority of the pellets had skipped up the column and blown through the ceiling acoustic tiles. Absorbing impressions and data that could help them interpret some other crime scene, some other day. The recruit wasn't ready to get this close, yet. Maybe in a year or two.

Kelly and the ID tech donned white latex gloves and did their thing. Processing the scene mostly involved photographing the body and the room. The first pics were taken outside the storage room with the door closed, then close-ups of the magnetic lock, then into the room with the door open. Further pictures were taken at ever-closer distances from the body, a progression that would tell the story if ever needed for court. After ending with multiple close-ups of the gun and wrecked face, the ID tech moved to evidence collection. Her gloved hands gently slid the charging handle of the shotgun back a tiny bit, enough only to confirm that a spent shell was still in the breech after firing, the primer clearly dimpled from the impact of the firing pin. This meant the gun was safe, could not go off again, and did not need to be unloaded here, so she quickly bagged it for transport to headquarters for fingerprinting, cleaning the gore off, and disassembly in the controlled environment of the ID lab. Finally, she changed gloves and removed the wallet from the blood-sodden pants pocket, and they confirmed that the body was, in fact, the missing man. Or at least bore identification indicating so. Proof would follow the comparison of the body's fingerprints to known latent prints of the still-officially missing man that the ID tech would lift from items in the condo upstairs. Facial recognition was not possible, so no need to subject the wife to the sort of lift-the-sheet identification popular on television. She'd have to see him eventually, would probably want to, but that could happen at a time without Kelly. He would make sure other family members were notified and brought to the home to care for the wife. "Kelly was thorough that way," the FTO explained to the recruit.

The wife's fingerprints would be taken, too. She would be told they were needed to differentiate hers from the latents recovered off the husband's personal items, but in reality they would be used if her prints were found on the shotgun. They were cops, after all.

An hour later, the body had been removed. FTO Jackson and Kelly stood down the hall from the dead man's apartment. Wailing could be heard from inside, and a procession of neighbors and relatives passed them to go inside. They looked down the hall to where Higgins stood listening to the condo manager rant while he began filling in blanks on report forms held by a metal clipboard.

"It's seven at night. We don't have custodians on duty now, and God knows how you clean that anyway. Do you guys do it?" She stared up at Higgins angrily. This was his fault, of course, since he was the one who had told her about the scene downstairs and escorted her to view it after the body had been picked up. The backup officer followed the removal service's unmarked van to Alexandria Hospital, where a doctor was called out of the emergency room to examine and pronounce death. A formality, but necessary for the case documentation.

"Do what, ma'am?" Higgins thought he knew, but couldn't believe she was asking.

Kelly stood with his back to the hallway wall, at a slight diagonal to the FTO against the facing wall. There was not room for them to stand directly facing, and neither could overcome the habitual need to keep their backs covered. The diagonal gap also allowed room for the procession to pass. The FTO watched his recruit distantly, trusting him even at this early stage in training to be able to handle the irate manager. The FTO and Kelly stood with knees bent and feet wide, with hands raised before them, as if praying or holding a notebook. The Field Interview Stance, from which police officers could instantly respond with a punch, a block, or a gun in the face of danger. A byproduct of training, an unconscious habit of all cops, an odd dance to keen observers. The FTO observed Kelly more closely.

"D'you really barf in CID? What was that about?" The FTO knew but wanted to hear Kelly talk.

"They're digging up Pickett. For an old sex case, not related to Emma. They want to do a comparison."

"Clean up the blood," the manager said in exasperation. "Somebody's gotta do it. Is it a biohazard? The police should be responsible." The recruit was barely successful in hiding his disgust at her. Kelly and the FTO watched him as they talked.

"Comparison of what?"

"His mouth. Bite pattern. Teeth. And you tell me what his teeth look like, right now." Kelly's furious whisper raised till it was almost audible to the pair down the hall, leading the FTO to make a shushing motion with his outspread hands. Kelly left his next thoughts unsaid: *You were there. You know what I did. You know what they'll do to me.*

"What will you do, Kell?" The FTO ignored Kelly's embarrassment. They were deep into conspiracy.

"Tell. Quit. Plead. Run. Die. It depends."

"On?"

"On you, for one thing," Kelly said, almost accusingly.

"You know better than that. I've told no one," FTO Jackson said stiffly, biting down on the lie.

"Well, yeah. You, I know. And no one else knows. But it might be better if I tell now, before they charge me." Kelly's look at Jackson made it a plea.

"You dumb Mick, you know who you sound like? You sound like you. You the detective. That's what you tell all the suspects you bring in, right? 'It'll go easier on you if you tell me all about it. You'll feel better.' So does it ever? No. It's always worse." Jackson shook his head. "If they confess? Judge never goes easier at sentencing. Not that sentencing ever makes sense."

Sentencing. One night, FTO Jackson had turned a corner in a housing project called the Berg as a young man beat down, kicked unconscious, and robbed an elderly man. He caught him, and the victim turned out to be a friend of the suspect's own father. A week later, Jackson watched a teenaged girl throw a flowerpot off an apartment balcony during a DEA search warrant. The robber pleaded guilty to twelve years, which the Alexandria Circuit Court judge reduced to five, which the "good behavior" system calculated as less than one to serve. The girl, whose case went to federal court, got ten years to serve, mandatory minimum with no parole because the flowerpot was full of her dealer boyfriend's crack and the DEA was coming through the front door.

"Confession is dumb. How dumb are you?" FTO Jackson watched Kelly almost inflate at the insult, beyond what their friendship and respect should have controlled. The FTO watched Kelly's mobile eyes, red behind his round, steel-framed glasses. They didn't settle on him or stay steady on anything for long. Attentiveness to surroundings was normal in a cop, a survival skill, but this was twitchy, way beyond usual. "No, you don't tell. You feel like talking, you talk to me. You don't tell the bosses. Not yet." Maybe never.

The FTO took in Kelly's red eyes, clenching fists and almost vibrating chest. "You got any sick leave?" Meaning, *Take it now, get out of here, stay home for a few days because you need it, you twitchy insomniac.* "If you're getting any sleep, you don't look it."

"I'm fine. What do you think—you would sleep, with this coming? I'll get charged, they can't ignore it if it means we can't prove some rich kid didn't try to rape his sister. Important parents, you know. I'll get fired. I could go to prison. What would I do? I got nothing else to do!" Jackson looked around to remind Kelly to keep his voice down, but the detective continued. "I can't take time off, I got the Stibble trial. Abduction case, parental, they were in San Francisco, dad's a perv, took the kid but he wants him back if he wins."

"Take the time off. Delay it. One case doesn't matter."

"It matters. Kid's almost a victim, dad's a mess and has bad friends, the kid would'a got used. We can put dad away. Trial's Thursday."

"Used?"

"Raped. Dad is a creep. Has friends are creeps. They were with a group when we got them, when the Marshals got them for me in California." Kelly paused to let a flamboyantly dressed older man pass. Tall and very thin, in a purple velvet suit, red satin shirt, and a black neck scarf, with big Jackie O sunglasses inside, he was impressive, or at least interesting. His thick curly beard was pale under his chin, glowing against his black skin like white neon, matching streaks in hair that by its thickness belied his age. The FTO smiled and nodded with him as he passed, and the man put his hand out to dap with the FTO. A slap, grasp, elbow bump, and he kept on, saying loudly, "Be safe, my brother!" He continued down the hall, past the suicide's apartment, and entered another.

Kelly looked at Jackson, surprised that he would let a man like that touch him, so flamboyant, so . . . out there. The FTO said, "Don't you know Professor Vulture? You never met him? You got to know Professor Vulture."

"What's he, a pimp?"

"Witch doctor."

"Yeah, right. Seriously?"

"Seriously. Folks seek him out all the time, do stuff for them. He uses voodoo and makes incantations. Herbs, plants, roots. Been here for years, all my life growing up. Maybe you should go see him, he deals with death. When do they dig up Pickett?"

"Thursday."

"Big day for you. I know it's part of Ashby's case, but the guy. And you . . . your niece. Emma." Kelly flinched. Hearing her name could still be hard. He used to talk with the FTO about her and other stuff. Not so much recently.

"You gonna be there, Kell?" FTO Jackson did not tell Kelly his plan, amorphous and unlikely as it was.

"What, at the cemetery? I can't be there. It's a trial. It's Commonwealth Day and they only do short trials, so Duckworth thinks it'll be short. But I still gotta shepherd the kid and his mom, so even if I testify and get out, I'm stuck with them."

"Somebody else can handle them."

"No, they're mine," Kelly almost yelled. He looked around, lowered his voice, and said, "They're spooked enough as it is, testifying against Dad. I'll not have them be off with someone else they don't know. I gotta do it."

The FTO took a half step toward Kelly and asked, "Did you ever tell your wife or your family, your brother . . . tell anyone? You got anyone to tell things to?"

"No!" Again, too loud, and too quick, but Kelly couldn't stop himself. He thought, *Does Jackson know about Rachel?* "I've never told anybody, at home, nowhere. I hope you haven't."

"No," the FTO said. "Not a soul." *Well, not since I told the lieutenant, and you don't know about that*, he thought. And since that was months ago, it was like he wasn't lying now. Or maybe he was lying for Kelly's benefit. Are cops' white lies blue?

The manager had wound down and walked away, and Higgins approached Kelly and Jackson, holding out the clipboard. The top form was an Assault/Injury Diagram, bearing front and back outlines of a human body on which an officer would note the placement of cuts, bruise, gunshots, or other wounds. Kelly took it from him, borrowed a bottle of whiteout from Jackson, and obliterated the top half of the form's head.

"Easy enough," Kelly said.

CHAPTER 11

Dinner
Tuesday, November 1, 1988
1930–2230 HRS

IRISH COOKING IS not known for delicacy. Filling, easy, and cheap described the food Kelly's mother had prepared growing up. They were a small brood for an Irish Catholic family. Kelly had a brother and sister. The sister lived a short distance outside Philadelphia where she taught special ed in a junior high school. She didn't come down much, "down" in that odd construction in which the South is located somehow "down" from Pennsylvania. His brother Patrick lived three miles from Kelly and a mile from their mother, and Kelly hadn't spoken with him since the night of her death.

Patrick was there when Kelly arrived at his mother's townhouse on the southern edge of Old Town at dinnertime, and Kelly hoped they would have their first talk in a year. Patrick couldn't avoid it in Mom's presence but was showing up anyway, so Kelly took this as a sign that Patrick had, if not forgiven him, in some way pushed past the horror and anger that blockaded them after Emma died. Whether tonight was a confrontation or an embrace depended on Patrick. Kelly wasn't taking bets.

Kelly drove three times around the block to find a legal space to park. Little Feat came on the radio on WHFS, a weak Maryland station that didn't always come through. The song was about being down but not like this before. *Not down tonight*, Kelly thought. Maybe I can tell Mom about Rachel. Big news. Leave the other big news about pregnancy till later. An important discussion, especially since Mom didn't know what was going on with his wife, Janet. Or rather, not going on anymore.

Parking was always tough in this crowded town. Had he driven his unmarked detective's car, he could have dumped it anywhere, but he had his personal car because he expected to be drinking tonight. One of the few things they could actually fire you for was driving a cop car while intoxicated. There were a lot of ways to get in trouble with the Department, *within* the Department, but it took directed effort to get fired.

With carnations he'd bought just now from the 7-Eleven in his left hand, he pulled open the screen door, knocked twice, and walked in without waiting. It was still his house, in a way, from a long time ago. And she was his mom, standing right there to hug him, luminous and happy.

"Oh, Johnnie. Glad you're here, son." Her voice muffled as she hugged him tight, face against his sport coat, her once-red hair at a level well below his chin. "Give me those, I'll find a vase. Sit down. Where, um . . . Are you alone, John Michael?" she said, looking beyond him off the porch and down the empty walkway to the street. Her use of two names showed disappointment. The full three flagged anger.

"Yeah, Mom. Just me tonight." Kelly was momentarily surprised. How could she know to ask about Rachel? Only a moment till Kelly realized she was looking for Janet, still Kelly's wife but separated and firmly moving toward divorce.

"Well, come in, let me look at you. You're not sleeping, are you? Yer lookin' like hell." Mom didn't waste time, words, or bacon fat, which he could smell from the kitchen. Bacon at seven at night? She wasn't the most adventurous of cooks, so this must be something his sister-in-law Brenda brought. Bacon?

"That's not for you, Johnnie. You don't need the fat."

Jeez, how did she know what he was thinking? "You callin' me fat, Ma?"

"I saw you looking that way. That's from Patrick, he's come. He's actually come tonight. He's here with Brenda and little . . . little Kate." A cloud brushed over Mom's face and dimmed her light. She saw Kelly blanch, stiffening his neck as if pulling away from a punch.

"I need a beer, Mom. Can I . . ." Kelly said.

"Go on, you know you always can. You're grown up. Pat is in there," she said, standing in the living room and waving past, toward the kitchen. *I know*, thought Kelly with a dry swallow.

Kelly had seen Patrick's car on the street near Mom's. He'd not looked for it specifically but had the cop habit of checking out parked vehicles. In Mom's small townhouse tonight, there were no signs of invasion by a family with youngsters, like diaper bags and toys and little shoes piled by the door. As there had been the last time the brood had gathered here. *One child fewer since then*, Kelly thought as he braced himself to enter the kitchen.

Kelly often thought about how cops have to walk into scary places. Into dark buildings on alarm calls, alleys for reports of shots fired, woods into which burglars had run. Into homes to arrest wife beaters or bank robbers or embezzlers. That's the challenge of the job, one that sometimes forces new officers out early. All their desire, all the wannabe imagination growing up can't prepare them for the hollow fear that tingles in the gut at the moment of a risky approach. To succeed, to remain on the job at all, cops learn to cope with the stress of fear, to tamp it down or push past, but sometimes it overwhelms. It can make a rookie leave in the first week on the street, or make a veteran hit the bottle or the spouse. It's hard to make yourself cross that threshold and face the very present danger of assault or ambush, and some can't summon the daily courage needed. Kelly and most cops could. They learned to go through the door. Not without considering the danger, but in spite of it. But no door he'd ever passed through was harder than his mom's kitchen door to meet with his brother this night.

John and his family had lived in this house growing up, four bedrooms with a fenced backyard, on the edge of what later became the trendy Old Town section of Alexandria but was then middle class. Alexandria used to be economically diverse, with some neighborhoods of hard-scrabble families and others of the elite of business and the federal government, D.C. only a bridge away. The middle was gone now, and the city only rich and poor with little in between. The boundary often was the painted yellow line in the street between a block of ARHA housing on one side and a row of antique or elite townhomes on the other. Residents might eye each other across this divide in the morning as the rich walked to the Metro and their jobs in D.C. and the poor exited to begin scratching out their existence at menial jobs. That the line also clearly separated black from white was not remarked on but felt in the gut.

Their narrow backyard had had a swing set and a shed and a small brick patio at the top of the steps that led down to the basement door. Kelly's dad always sat at the edge of the back patio, one night a year in the dusk of late summer, staring at a gap in the houses across the alley where the sun set that time of year, and silently drank a toast of Bushmills Irish whiskey that he had transferred into a Jameson bottle when no one was looking, because Bushmills was Protestant but better and Jameson was Catholic and acceptable, an Irish-American ritual as secret and senseless as a Druid prayer. Kelly's dad drank all the time, but the toast was always facing west on August 5, at 7:15 p.m. Kelly had learned when he was ten that this was the moment of the atomic bombing of Hiroshima. Dad was seventeen in 1945 and would have been drafted, more likely enlisted, the next year and in time for the expected invasion of the Japanese homeland in World War II. Dad, and thus Kelly and the family, believed to their core that the bomb saved him from going to war, though some historians disagreed that the bomb or invasion at all were really necessary. In high school, Kelly got the date of the bombing of Hiroshima wrong on a test and only then learned that while most historians, archivists, and commentators recorded the blast as August 6, local date and time in Japan, Dad marked the moment in American time, this side of the Date Line—the calendar date before but the correct moment. Dad did things his own way. He claimed to be Irish but was half German too, and he played up what he wanted to be the happier, dancing, and singing component of his heritage over the dour, atrocity-laced Holocaust history of his German side. But the dourness came through, and the Irish aren't always as happy as they'd like to pretend. So Dad would sit in a creaking, webbed lawn chair and hum "The Patriot Game" or "The Bold Fenian Men" until the bottle was empty.

Kelly had always hoped he would not be so moody and brooding as his dad when he finally had kids, and the loss of Patrick and Brenda's daughter Emma had made Kelly confront the looming inevitability of having kids with his wife, Janet. It was the likelihood of taking that logical next step that made Kelly end it when he did, two months ago. But he'd told no one. Not his family. Not even Rachel, not wanting to pressure her with a hard demonstration of his commitment to her.

But with Rachel pregnant now . . . Rachel with child. His child. Their baby. The sudden warm thought brought him up short.

Janet had burst into tears when he told her he wanted a divorce. Her flood of emotions released by his surprise declaration stunned her into immobility and silence, and she sat on their living room couch and began silently weeping, thick tears on her cheeks, wetting the collar of her blouse while she sat still, hands clenched between her thighs. He hadn't planned out that moment, but she'd rushed home from work that day with the news that friends of theirs were divorcing, and so the forbidden word had been released into the room. It wasn't because of Rachel, he'd convinced himself, but because the marriage had been loveless and lifeless for months, maybe years. Near the end, they'd made love but without making love happen. He felt no joy with her anymore. Rachel, though, was the catalyst for his hidden, growing but untrusted hope that there might be actual happiness for him somewhere outside.

Finally, Janet had looked up from her tear-spotted lap, focused over his shoulder, and said only, "Okay." Then she rose, silent again, and walked out the door, driving to her parents in New Jersey, only returning a week later to pick up clothes and move into a friend's house. She still came by on occasion for stuff, but not when he was around. He'd cried too, a little, after she left, unsure of why. They hadn't been happy for a long time, worse lately, but that had to be her fault. And his life was getting better now. Down or up, he could handle it.

God, I wish Dad were here, Kelly thought as he steeled himself, combed his fingers back through his short black hair, and entered the kitchen. He first saw Brenda, his sister-in-law. Saw with some surprise how heavily she'd aged, hair grayer, body thicker, cheeks plumper below watery eyes, which widened when they saw him. *Uh-oh.* But she moved to hug him without hesitation, and he felt a relief he hadn't expected. His arms met around her and his fingers drummed her back in the eternal brotherly *tap tap tap.* As he lifted his face from beside hers, over her shoulder, he finally looked at Patrick.

His brother's change was a bigger shock. Hair still red, but he'd lost so much weight. His neck and arms were sticks, his chest narrow above a round belly that pouched out against his green sport shirt. Patrick's face sought an expression it could settle on while he fought internally for the relief of one emotion he could hold. Forgiveness and love for his brother fought in deep water with anger and resentment, each side surfacing for a moment till pushed under by the other. Brenda disengaged from John's embrace, and she turned to touch Patrick gently on the elbow, then squeezed as he ignored her, his puffy eyes squinting, just holes in his face. Brenda finally stepped in front of Patrick, interrupting his gaze with her gentle face. "Pat, it's good we're all here."

Patrick sagged only a little more and after a moment grinned, in a way. Suddenly he almost looked glad to see his brother. "Johnnie. Good you've come to see Ma." He took an involuntary half step to bridge the gap, not yet ready to hug.

Kelly, too, was frozen a moment, knowing Patrick's battle and what it cost, what he had lost. Brenda too, but she had taken it well.

He sidestepped. "I'm for a beer. Paddy, you?"

"Nah, John. I'm good for now." He raised his glass of dark beer. Guinness, of course, but only out of loyalty to an Irish image. It tasted horrible out of bottles here in the States, flat and bitter. "You look tired, John. Sleeping?"

"Sure, just busy lately and working late," Kelly said. *Out with Rachel,* Kelly thought, and his mind flashed on the look of her. His favorite part—the flare above her hips. "Don't get me wrong, her tits are fantastic!" he might say to a friend, if he had a friend of the type to whom he might say such a thing. But he hadn't. Maybe Patrick once, before that night, but not tonight.

Tonight, Kelly motormouthed his way across the gap between them. "And I got a case coming up this week. Kid's dad snatched him and ran off from his mom. Took him to California. He was planning to . . ." Kelly realized what unexpected horror he was about to share with his unprepared and innocent family and censored himself. "We think something bad was going to happen there." Kelly was talking about the parental abduction trial this week, but his scattered mind suddenly thought instead of a body surfacing in the upcoming exhumation. Kelly shivered as he connected thoughts appropriate and inappropriate.

Patrick misunderstood when he saw John's face darken. "Now you're mad. What, at me, John? You don't have reason for that, do you?" Patrick looked at John, then at Brenda, who took his hand and tried to stop him. "You, in that case you protected that kid, huh. Glad you could do that." His fingers twitched on his empty hand. Bitterness rose in his voice. Brenda led him out of the kitchen, her voice distracting the brothers.

"Let's make room for Mom in here. She's got to get the dinner out. Can I help you, Mom?" Brenda called over her shoulder as she pulled Patrick clear, hoping for a *no* so she could stay and keep the peace. *Brenda, God bless her*, Kelly thought. Why she didn't hate John like Patrick tried to, Kelly didn't know.

Kelly took a bottle of Becks out of the fridge, his mother's nod to the other side of her family heritage. He popped it and downed half the bottle at once, noting his mother's rebuking glance. "Well, you bought it, didn't you? Besides, I'll have but one more with dinner." His lilt came back at home.

"You carry this out." She handed him a big pan of ham, letting him slip his big hands around hers to take the mitts and hold the pan. "Then go sit wi' your brother and them. Dinner in a few."

Mom still had a brogue, a gift from her parents both fresh off the boat in Philadelphia at the turn of the century. They were Irish whose families had scraped through the Famine but emigrated to the new country anyway. Like her new Southern neighbors, she restated vowels, none sounding like its true self. "She was bred and buttered in the County Fermagh," came out "brid and bottered." In a catastrophe, such as an arm off or a husband run away—something needing a priest—she would say, "Eel gaw en' fitch Fayther fer 'im." Not oddly, she and Dad fit in well here at the roof of the deep South: everybody talked slow. "Not loyk those Dagos 'n' Wops 'n' Spics in Philadelphia." Come on, Ma? "Ool royt. Not to mention the Chinks, least w' them ya can point at the menu." Not a spot of hate in her, but a sure knowledge of whom she was above. All.

Rachel loved his accent when it came out—she told him from the first night they'd talked after the bar. Like with his family, Kelly censored his conversations with Rachel, electing not to tell her one of the test stories he pulled out on unsuspecting women, as a trap or as amusement, a gauntlet that cops made citizens run sometimes. The tortilla chips story. Totally inappropriate to think of this now, but his mind had been drifting off center lately. Kelly remembered telling it to another girl another night as she ran the gauntlet, trying to get close to the cheery, virile, but dangerous and attractive crowd of cops in the corner of the bar. The tortilla chips story was a horror, and she failed the test, stepping away in disgust and acting like she despised him. So Kelly didn't tell Rachel that one—he didn't want her to fail. Didn't want risk her despising him. *I don't want that now*, he thought. God, he needed her right now. Kelly silently and instinctively prayed, *Dear God, get me through this dinner, this night, this week so I can be with Rachel*, but this was just a reflex from being around his preachy mother. He did not believe God did things for people, because he would have to believe God did things to people. Even putting aside the Nazis of his linear past, and the crooks and killers in his professional present, he could not abide a God who would do what had been done to his niece and his brother. That the atrocity had also been done to him was something Kelly never recognized.

By the middle of dinner, and what he thought was his third beer but was number five, Kelly was happy and settled. Full of a roast and mashed potatoes with bacon in them, a masterpiece for this table, he leaned back in the sturdy wood dining room chair and crossed his arms. Patrick held his youngster Kate as Brenda spooned macaroni and cheese into her. They'd danced gently and slowly on thin ice all night, and it had held without cracking. Kelly thought that tonight it might start to thicken and solidify back to a firm ground beneath his damaged family's feet. Become a foundation of love and a return of the trust lost last year. *Maybe*, he thought recklessly, *it was a time to bring in some good news.* Start with what to them would be bad, the expected divorce with Janet, a wide pit to jump with his Catholic mother but not so deep to the younger and less dogmatic Patrick and Brenda. Then he could share the news of Rachel and her condition, joyful, not-yet comprehended, but the start of Kelly's happy future. He needed the future, not the past. But his usually reliable gift of gab betrayed him tonight. He started poorly and didn't get far.

"I have news. I can talk about kids with you now," Kelly said. And stopped, stricken as he realized what he said.

"Kids. Kids, you'll talk of kids. Now you will," Patrick said as he jumped up. Unsteadily, for he'd matched Kelly bottle for bottle after an earlier start. He began to clench his fists again but recognized the soft form in his bulging arms and handed Katie off to Brenda.

"There is no news you can share with us, John. Not now. There is nothing new for us. You took her from us." Patrick was trembling as he failed to hold himself back. "Kids. You left us without our kid. You left us without Emma." Patrick leaned back and bumped the glass-front cabinet full of china. The plates and servers rattled, but none fell save the family pictures on its flat top, dropping facedown to hide the faces his mom always gazed at over her morning toast. The only picture left in the room of Emma, in a family portrait, was among the ones that now fell out of sight. Mom had cleared out the others, off the wall and the mantel, but left the one. She needed one.

"Your news, what? You and Janet finally? Well good on you, John. Good on you, you get a child." Patrick's eyes welled up, but he didn't care. "And d'you know what? I pray you don't know what it feels like when you lose one. We do, John. We know that. We do." He broke his stare with John to look down at Brenda and reached to wrap his fingers into Brenda's hair, forcing them, if not himself, to be gentle. Fighting for control.

"No, Pat. I . . . Janet and I . . ." Kelly stopped, floored by the flawed moment.

"Sure, John. Share it wi' us." Patrick almost sneered. "You and Janet are having a baby."

"Janet and I are not. We're not together anymore. She . . ." Kelly found a small way to hide. "She left me. It's been a little while. I've not seen you. I haven't been to tell you either, Mom," Kelly said, reacting to her sudden tears.

"Oh, John. We didn't know you were having troubles," Brenda said. "We've not seen you in a while, since . . ."

And they were right back to that.

"Well. So you have a loss in your life, John. But you can rebuild it. You can get her back, or not, or another. But we can't

get Emma back. That is what happened. And that is on you."
Patrick had built to a full fury, voice thickened by stout and
amplified by anger and sorrow. He faced off with Kelly, who sat
still across the table, unmoving as if to avoid attracting danger.
Kelly opened his mouth but did not speak.

"It was God's will, Patrick," their mother said. "God chose
to take our lovely, good Emma home to him. She is with the
angels now an' with your own sainted father, an' you must comfort yourself wi' that." Her crumpled linen napkin stretched
between her bony hands like a garrote. She waved it at them.
"Children, our gracious God in his mystery—"

But finally Kelly cut her off as he blew, outshouting Patrick.
"Ah, Mom. Stuff that. God, your God dinna have to bring
Emma home to him like that. Not like that." Kelly had never
spoken against his mother this way, and his rough voice tore
now against her core beliefs ignored or tolerated, but he had
finally had enough of her, enough of months of her drivel and
maybe all his life's worth of listening to her praise that dogma:
that God's will brought about all things. Kelly stood up now
across the table from Patrick, body vibrating tight to match his
brother's but with his agonized face toward his mother. How
could such a system be a comfort to her, her faith that God
made things happen as his own choice? How could God have
chosen this to happen, the ripping cruel death of a beautiful
child, the unending agony for her family? Right before Kelly's
eyes. All the other atrocities happening every day, across the
world and close to home?

All of this, Kelly thought. Some he even said aloud, inad-
vertently in the uncontrolled crash of his angry and happy day
into this joyous then drunken and sad night. None he should
ever have spoken.

Patrick was still. His diatribe stopped, he was spent like
a fired cannon. He stared, deciphering Kelly's words. Kelly

slowly backed from the table, his glance whipping back and forth between his shocked mother and his furious brother, and made for the other room. Brenda sat still, holding a whimpering Katie. But Patrick's boiling heart reloaded one last round and let fly.

"She's dead. You killed her, 'cause you let him kill her and you didn't kill him. He should be dead. You should have done something. You should kill yourself, you son of a bitch. You should be dead."

Patrick's fists were balled and trembling, and Kelly thought he was about to be punched hard. Hoped so. But Kelly fled out the door before he or Patrick could achieve that release. He *had* done something, later, but Patrick and the world could never know what. Kelly would lose his job, maybe go to jail should they ever find out what he did.

And now they were digging it up.

CHAPTER 12

Homecoming
Wednesday, November 2, 1988
0030 HRS–Dawn

AS HE WALKED in his apartment door well after midnight, all Lieutenant Walter—never "Wally"—Ramirez could think about were the twenty-eight little plastic evidence markers, yellow tented plastic cards, numbered, placed where shell casings fell after guns were reloaded on the bridge. Twenty-eight shots.

He tried to put it out of his mind, softly calling, "Honey, I'm home," to Tracy, his "significant other," police parlance for unmarried cohabitants, cops being too tough to say girlfriend or boyfriend or lover. Tracy came in with wide eyes, a beer, and a gentle kiss on his cheek. Proffering his cheek automatically and accepting the beer, the lieutenant dropped into the living room couch and looked blankly across the room. A television soundlessly showed images of flashing red lights on a bridge. His crime scene. Big news of the day, actually yesterday now, showing on the late local news. The lieutenant was home in body, but not yet in spirit.

Tracy knelt next to his feet to unlace his boots, quietly saying, "You're okay. I see that. Are they?" Meaning the officers. Walter had called to say he would be late, and Tracy knew from the news that a big event had happened. Tracy also knew by Walter's expression that he was still worrying about the officers. His officers.

But the lieutenant didn't answer. He hadn't even heard Tracy's question. He was hours away, earlier, pulling up to the 14th Street Bridge shortly after the pursuit and shootings ended and just as the ambulances showed up. They had been called by the first APD officers arriving after Pammie Martinson's crash with the suspect vehicle and the subsequent shooting. Maybe D.C. police had summoned ambulances too, but they operated on a different radio system, so who knew?

D.C. operated on a different level altogether, at least where firearms were concerned. Ramirez couldn't decide whether he would rather they were more accurate, or less. Of twenty-eight shots fired by D.C. at the suspect vehicle after it crashed, nine struck the Toyota. Four hit Martinson's APD cruiser. Twelve hit a total of seven civilian cars passing by during the shooting and downrange of the suspect. Thankfully, no persons were hit. Not Martinson or the civilian drivers. Nor the suspect now in custody. Where the other three shots went? Unknown.

As he slumped in his Baltimore living room, windows dark save for distant lights in higher buildings, the lieutenant finally noticed Tracy pulling off his boots. He reached down and caressed Tracy's auburn hair. They locked eyes, and he began describing the night.

"TAC called a jump, typical no sweat. Got the buyer right there, but the seller got to a car and took off. They pursued, and then a uniform got into it. Got shot at near the airport, then they both crashed on the 14th Street Bridge. There," he pointed at the TV screen, "that's the cruiser. All shot up. D.C. shot it. The bad guy too." Tracy gasped at the sight of bullet damage to a police car, eyes horrified, pupils wide and black as the bullet holes.

"Who was it, do I know him?" Tracy was thoughtful to ask but actually knew few of the lieutenant's coworkers.

"Her. Pammie Martinson, she's been on about six years. Has kids. Careless sexism, dear, assuming a male officer. Anyway, all D.C.'s shots went through the glass and she ducked. She's okay. So is the bad guy; they missed him too. D.C. just opened up because he had shot at our officer first, down on the Parkway, before the bridge." The lieutenant knew Tracy was imagining the same holes in the lieutenant's unmarked car, or in the lieutenant.

The sergeant had briefed him when he arrived on the bridge, walking the scene and pointing. The sergeant wore a dull gray uniform shirt with silver badge, collar trim, and belt buckle, while the lieutenant stood out in the white shirt of a commander, his trimmings gold.

"Pammie's okay, not shot, not hurt. Got a lotta glass in her hair and her uniform is a mess. Got radiator fluid all over her. Bad guy is in one of our cars. We're about to take him to HQ so CID can talk with them. Her car is shot up, gonna tow it out 'cause it can't run. Take it to the back lot at HQ so we can process it there."

"But photograph it here before you move it," the lieutenant had said.

"Of course. Also once D.C. is done with it. They'll have a lot more to photograph and measure."

"It was all their guys?"

"Yeah. About five of them opened up. They just shot when the guy started coming out of the car. The driver. Fired a full cylinder till reload and stopped then 'cause maybe they noticed no one was shooting back. He never shot at them or anyone up here. They shot because he'd shot at our guy, er, girl. Not a bad decision, but jeez, they can't shoot at all." With that, the sergeant had swept his arms in a half circle to denote the seven civilian cars stopped at various places on the bridge. Each car had bullet damage from the Metropolitan Police gunfire, small, .38-caliber holes in windshields, doors, tires, and fenders.

"But no people hit, LT, thank God. How, I don't know. But they missed them."

"And missed our suspect in the Toyota too." Not a question.

"Yeah. Which makes it easier. We can just take him back with us. If he'd been shot, he'd go to D.C. General, and who knows when he'd be released to us. Worse if he died, we never get death certificates from D.C. They're a mess."

"Where is he now?"

"That ambulance there. Getting fixed up."

"Thought you said he wasn't shot?"

"He wasn't. But Pammie got to him first after . . . well. He, um, it appears he was injured in the crash." He caught the lieutenant's glare. "In the crash. Um, facial injuries."

"Facial injuries? In the crash. Is that what he says?"

"Kinda, so far, but I'll be talking to him again later, after detectives are done. For the use-of-force investigation. But I don't see it going anywhere bad. I mean, he shot at her, LT," the sergeant said.

The lieutenant's glare softened but he kept his eyes locked to those of the sergeant and gave a short nod. The sergeant stared back, then turned away to begin directing the actions of the crime scene photographer

A mess. The lieutenant walked the scene, starting with Pammie Martinson's Plymouth cruiser, still lightly steaming around the hood. Chunks of the plastic grille were missing. An

Alexandria officer was assigned to walk back down the road to find car pieces or other evidence between the initial shooting point and here. The windshield showed at least three bullet holes, small perforations surrounded by spiderwebs of cracked glass radiating out and merging with other webs so the entire glass surface shone white and silver and reflected the dull red of the snowy sunset. The right front tire was flat, and the car listed to that side.

Just beyond was the wrecked Toyota getaway car. TAC officers had searched it and found two sandwich bags with about ten rocks of crack cocaine in each on the floor of the back seat. The Toyota had nine bullet holes in it, on every surface that faced the D.C. officers and some exit holes on the rear panels and glass. Thin snow sparkled as it built up on surfaces other than warm engine compartments and windows.

In the dwindling light, the lieutenant glanced toward a flash and saw a man with a camera on the far side of the scene near the D.C. cruisers. He was in a light blue shirt and dark blue jacket and pants. Maybe a D.C. evidence technician. With D.C. having caused most of the mayhem, the lieutenant would make sure they took the bulk of reporting, documenting, towing, and maybe eventual reimbursing for damage that they'd caused. That distribution of effort and responsibility would take hours. But that's what lieutenants were for, not real police work but the administrative detritus of the fun stuff the street officers got to do.

The lieutenant stopped at an ambulance parked near the wreckage, peeked first through the small window in the back door, then opened it. Pammie Martinson sat on a gurney while an Alexandria Fire Department paramedic in latex gloves picked glass out of her hair and mopped up dribbles of blood from cuts caused by the fragments. Her face was pale, and she grimaced at the touch of the alcohol swabs to each cut. Her gray polyester uniform shirt was damp and pink-tinged, especially across her chest where her badge should have been. There were red marks on her knuckles. She looked up at him, and her grimace of pain turned to nervous apprehension.

"It's okay, Pammie. Looks like you did well. You all right?" Obviously not, but it was what one asked. The lieutenant had been very fearful when he first saw the shot-up Alexandria cruiser.

"Yes, sir. Sorry about the car."

"We give it to you knowing it's going to get damaged sometimes. We just don't want you damaged. Good ducking." She needed a hug, but he couldn't give it. He did too, but would never admit it.

Pammie breathed out.

"Sure you didn't fire?"

"Never had a clear shot, sir. Wanted to but never was in a position to go without citizens in the way or downrange."

"Didn't seem to stop D.C. Anyway, I'm glad you are all right. Take your time, breathe, we'll get you back home and we'll start writing this up."

The lieutenant stepped back through the ambulance door and down to the street. He closed the door and walked to the sergeant. He looked past him for listeners, saw none, and asked, "Where's her badge?"

They walked toward the other ambulance, where the lieutenant, again, looked through the peephole in the back door to see the suspect. He was a male, twenties, with now-puffy eyes and fresh blood being wiped away from his nose. He didn't enter the ambulance.

"You noticed that, huh? On the seat at Hojo's, where she was 10-7. That's how she got on the pursuit so quick, she was right there. But she ran out without her cruiser jacket, on the back of the seat where she was eating. We got it. I sent one of the Sector One units to grab it."

The lieutenant stared at the sergeant a moment, then glanced around at the wrecked cruiser and the pair of ambulances. "Write her up."

"Bravery, yes, sir. Already writing it in my mind."

"No. Write her up for being out of uniform. A '67 for violation of Directive 10-23 Uniform and Equipment. And for reckless driving for ramming that car without authorization. She never radioed for permission to ram, did she? No. On second thought, no need for a '67 for the crash. You can give her a traffic summons right here. Amounts to the same thing, but easier, and you've got enough to do."

"Sir, I . . . A traffic summons? She's a hero. She could be dead. She could'a shot that kid dead, no question. She . . ."

"She fucked up, Sergeant. Maybe in lots of ways. But definitely in this way. I told you what to do. You gonna do it?"

The lieutenant turned away from the shocked sergeant to seek out his counterpart on the D.C. side, to see what they could do together to begin clearing this mess.

Later, back at HQ, he called the chief to outline the events and his command actions taken, called the Daylight Shift Commander for whom Martinson worked, and called the Special Operations Division commander whose TAC unit had started all this. He made calls to each of the three community group presidents whose neighborhoods had been crossed in the chase and whose residents were often outraged at the dangerous actions of the boys and girls in blue. Then he wrote the entry on the Watch Log, a single paragraph encapsulating the biggest event the Department had seen in months.

Then read the reports, for each separate part of the event. Distribution of Cocaine (for the initial TAC jump). Felonious Assault on Police (for shooting at Pammie). Possession with

Intent to Distribute Cocaine (for the two bags found in the car). State and city accident reports for the crash on the bridge. A City Property Damage report for the bullet holes in Martinson's cruiser inflicted by D.C. Police. An Officer Injury Report with four subsections (for Martinson's cuts.) A Pursuit Report (just for the driving around.) And two more. All written by others but requiring his review. Which took hours, well beyond his normal end of shift, before he could drive home to Baltimore.

He looked up from his beer bottle, barely sipped. Tracy was asleep on the couch across the living room, face pale in the silent, flickering television shine. He may have nodded off but wasn't sure. Dawn's early light was starting to lighten the windows overlooking the Baltimore skyline. Time to head back to work. A caffeine day.

The last two reports had taken the longest time. The internal investigation of Martinson's uniform violation—no badge in a shootout—and the Virginia Uniform Summons charging her with reckless driving. He had held these on his desk for hours before signing finally them and sending them up.

He stood and walked softly to where Tracy lay on the couch. He gently leaned to press his lips lightly against his lover's cheek, where Tracy was now showing the stubble of a long night. He awoke when Ramirez kissed him. "Tough night," Tracy said with warm eyes.

"Yeah, tough night. And now a tough day," Ramirez told his common-law husband and turned to walk down the hall to shave and transfer all his metal—badge, nameplate, pins, pens—to a fresh, white shirt.

Tough guy, he told the guy in the mirror. *Gotta be tough so nobody can say I'm not.*

CHAPTER 13

Hole
Wednesday, November 2, 1988
0030–0200 HRS

KELLY AWOKE WITH a start, sprawled across the front seat of his car. He had wandered twice around the block looking for it after leaving dinner and the pain there. That, and his difficulty in fitting the correct key properly in the door slot, got the message through that driving was contraindicated right now. But so was going back to his mother's house. So he had sat for a few, then lay down. Just for a minute.

He'd left, trying not to appear to be fleeing, walking wordlessly out of the room where his brother Patrick had flayed him. His mother sat, knocked speechless by Kelly's diatribe toward her and her God and by Patrick's searing but accurate attack on him. Kelly's attempt at a dignified withdrawal was ruined when he knocked over a table lamp in the hallway by the front door, which opened in and let him free of the acidic spray of anger in the house.

He'd placed his arms on the roof, crossing his wrists to hold his chin above the frosted steel as he faced across the street into the yard of a house where he'd played as a child. The name of his playmate was gone from memory. Cowboys had chased Indians here, and cops had chased robbers. He was usually the cop and got to enforce the rules and bring evil under control. It may have been more fun to play bad guys ungoverned by rules instead of having to be the big brother all the time, guiding, watching, and protecting his sibs. It was probably what attracted him to police work, getting to be the big brother to the city.

The moment against the car became a minute, and another, then twenty of them, till the late-night chill persuaded Kelly to try again and get in before someone called the cops on him. Kelly had no fear of arrest or departmental censure at being discovered in the grips of an alcoholic swoon, but didn't want to be braced by cops who might know him and not yet have formed a negative opinion. Sitting led to lying led to sleep, and when he awoke, he looked toward the garish glow of a convenience store a block away, as startlingly out of place among the houses as a road flare in a coat closet. But they sold beer, so Kelly walked in and bought a forty-ounce malt liquor bottle. Wrapped in a brown paper bag, the forty was the image of outdoor alcoholism found in most run-down urban neighborhoods, but rarely carried in this genteel part of Old Town. Out the door and away from the fluorescent lights, Kelly twisted off the bottle cap to access a sip that turned into a gulp or two. His thirst slaked, he walked back past the car, stretching the sips.

He headed toward fields where he used to play. Back then they had been sparsely spotted with tombstones and markers. Churches in the dense city center planted their dead in fenced-off cemeteries here and these were almost filled now, but some of the many trees he'd climbed still stood, and a dirty, fishless creek still bordered the far edge. Emma was not buried here—she was with Kelly's father and other family up King Street and over Shooters Hill, away from this poor spot. But Kelly still had a plot to visit.

He didn't stumble much as he passed wrought-iron gates and open entries through each section, some with high poles bearing crossbeams with the congregation names on signs like Western ranches have. The cemeteries were separated by rutted roadways, rough stones marking each tire track. The nearest streetlights in the adjacent neighborhood glowed dimly in the low clouds as Kelly made straight for a large but unmarked and untended area in between three well-cared-for meadows. This was what city hall referred to as Indigent Interment Section One. Old folks called it a potter's field.

Near the center of Section One—were there others?—a simple white concrete marker stood in sparse but high grass. The name was Pickett, and the date of death was seven months ago. Pickett's first name was Edward and, chiseled into the thin concrete, it always surprised Kelly. He had never thought of him as a person with a full name and in reports had used only Pickett, like an epithet.

Kelly never got to testify against him. Pickett had died before going to trial for killing Emma. A brain embolism killed him instantly in jail about two months after he shot Emma to death in front of Kelly. The medical examiner's report noted a cut to the back of Pickett's head, possibly sustained through impact of the skull against a hard surface, like the floor he would fall on after passing out. Or a wall if the head were deliberately banged backward in a certain way. Child murderers didn't tend to do well in lockup, but nothing malicious was ever discovered, if it was looked for at all. Innocent until proven guilty was a tortuous construct that existed only in courts of law, not in the street and not in jail. Autopsy X-rays of the skull were not at useful angles to map out bite patterns and make him for the job on the little girl. So Pickett would be disinterred in two days to see his teeth.

And Kelly's world would end.

Kelly stood wobbling in front of the marker. Kelly had been here the day of the burial. His old FTO, Herb Jackson, had been assigned to monitor the interment and document it, a final supplement to a Sudden Death—a homicide report with Emma Louise Kelly listed as victim. Pickett's body was listed as evidence on the supplement. "Could have been Property Seized," Kelly had joked, grim humor battling fury and winning for a moment. Kelly showed up that day. He hadn't behaved well. His FTO was there and got him out, but not before he did damage. No mourners for the creep, no family was ever located or came forward. No clergy, said to be running late according to the city worker who ran the backhoe. Its motor was still ticking as the coffin hung from the digger claw over the fresh hole. "Don't wait," Kelly had barked. "Drop him now." The worker shrugged, and Pickett was dropped, the bucket first lifting the dull, cheap coffin on canvas straps above the hole, perpendicular to the marker, feet away and head close. Kelly had drunkenly shoved it, made it spin till they stopped it, and lowered it into the hole. The bucket arm dropped till the straps went slack, then pulled them back out and they rasped and abraded the edges. Bits of wood were rubbed away and fell at the sides of the coffin, a careless abuse that would not have been tolerated in the service of anyone but this monster. Kelly had stared down into the hole that day and cursed. Then did something worse.

He looked down this night, fresh from his mother's dinner table, at the rough, tufted grass, black in the darkness, where the grave once gaped. The white concrete marker, only marginally lighter than the ground, picked up the distant street lights.

Bare dirt still surrounded the stone, as if grass and life could not come close.

Kelly needed one arm to steady himself on Pickett's marker while the other still held the beer bottle, nearly empty now. He raised the bottle in its brown bag and smashed it against the top of the stone, shards cutting through the paper and spreading behind the tombstone to tinkle against other bits of brown and green glass already there. Kelly, dizzy with anguish and anger and eyes closed against memories, needed both hands now to keep himself erect, drawing deep, shuddering gasps. He remembered Emma, remembered her crowded funeral and this piece of shit's dreary unremarked burial day. Kelly rocked back and forth in front of the marker, his cold hands gripping the thin concrete hard enough they whitened to match its marbled paleness. He hoped it would break away at its base, but it was no more fragile this night than any other.

Finally, he was able to stand unsupported. He swept open his topcoat, unzipped his slacks, and began to urinate on Pickett's name, an impotent attack, but all he was capable of this night. After releasing an improbable volume, he stopped and zipped up. The spread of urine softened the hard, exposed dirt, and he stepped back from the mud but began to wobble and slip. Too drunk to stand stable, Kelly spun and sat down hard in his fresh puddle. It wasn't his first time doing such. Once down, he drew his legs up, pressed his eyes tightly to his knees, and cried.

An hour later, near frozen but unaware of the cold, he was awakened by the chirp of his pager and its tickling buzzy vibration at his hip. The alerts stopped before he fully came out of his stupor, but he remembered their call and unsnapped the pager, holding it up to his face and pressing the button to illuminate the message. It read, "07734."

He thought of Rachel, her news, the new life within her and their coming life together and the unusual, undeserved blessing of her now-proven love for him, and his heart climbed out of a dark hole. Up and down so much lately, it was hard to keep track. He'd call her when he got home. He figured he was too drunk to risk driving into D.C. to her but okay to make the trip home here in Alexandria, surrounded by friendly cops who wouldn't have to bust him if they pulled him over. He needed her, or at least needed the image of himself he created when he was with her. She didn't know about all this, about Pickett and Emma, yet. About the coffin below him now. About him, who he really was. He was not a good guy, but she thought he was, so he could pretend.

As he stared down to slowly reclip the pager to his belt, he saw in its red glow a shiny yellow metal disk reflecting in the muddy slush he'd created. Thoughtless of the vile coating, he curled his fingertips around it but had to grasp tight and pry the item out of the hard dirt underneath the thin layer of mud. It turned out to be the butt end of a short cylinder. Brass for the first quarter of its length, then red plastic for the remainder and open at the other end. He recognized it as a shotgun shell.

It can't be here, Kelly thought. It's impossible, after all this time, and all the times he'd been here and not seen it. No way. Not after six months. Against logic that denied its presence, but in accordance with his years of training and experience, he seized the shell and secured it in a coat pocket. Might still have fingerprints, his cop mind said.

His fingerprints.

CHAPTER 14

Hero
Wednesday, November 2, 1988
0700–1100 HRS

THE DAY AFTER the pursuit, Alexandria Police Officer Pammie Martinson sat in morning roll call as her sergeant held up the front page of the *Washington Post*. Her picture was below the fold, walking the suspect straight toward the camera, a photograph large enough to show a trickle of blood from her hairline down her right temple to the corner of her mouth, smearing on her teeth in a grin or grimace. Hard to tell which. She was shown yanking the suspect past her shot-up cruiser, her fingers gripping the suspect by his shirt, leading to the story headline:

COLLARED

She had spent her morning telling and retelling the story in the hallway and sitting in the roll call room. The room was loud, and her raucous squadmates crowded around her, especially those who weren't able to get on the call, get to the bridge for her. If it weren't for the bulky Kevlar vest, her back would have been sore from congratulatory slaps. When the sergeants showed up with the day's assignment sheets, lists of BOLOs and other paperwork, it took several minutes before the rowdy crowd moved away from Pammie and settled down. The sergeants, sitting up front and facing the rows of tables and seats for the officers, wisely had not called for quiet, but their presence finally settled the room.

"Okay. Assignments first, then Pammie, you can tell us about it. When I call your name, gimme your cruiser number. Stull?

"1742, Sarge."

"Stull, you're Unit 224 today. Gittins?"

"1777."

And so it went, as thirteen officers on Day Shift received beat assignments. The crowd laughed when Unit 213, Martinson, answered with a cruiser number different than usual, a temporary replacement while her battered cruiser had a new radiator and windows installed. BOLOs—be on the lookout—for recently stolen cars or suspects in significant cases were read aloud and their information written into officers' notebooks. Other matters like new department directives, transfers, and vacation lists were announced at roll call, and detectives or narcs sometimes stopped in to share new crime trends or patterns. It was the only time each day that all the officers would be together in one place, though most would see each other regularly throughout the shift, assigned to handle calls together or meeting for meals, but today the room was filled with almost every cop in headquarters there to hear about yesterday's shootout. Despite common perception spread by television and movies, cops rarely shoot their guns or get shot at, so today's roll call was crowded with almost every cop in the building to wish her well and to see that she was okay.

The sergeant finished at the front of the room. "Bartlett, Torres, Sandoval? See me after roll call for a special assignment. Pammie, tell us about yesterday, but you got five minutes, 'cause you're needed in court like immediately. They want you for the advisement on this fuc—" He caught himself; there were extra brass in the room today, and you never knew what they got in a twist about. "—Joker, so head there right after we get done."

"Subpoena?" Pammie asked curtly, reaching out her hand.

"No subpoena. There wasn't time but the CA's Office called this morning. When you mark in, tell HQ you're out of service in court. I don't know how long you'll be."

"Since when do we testify at advisement? It's just picking lawyers and stuff."

"Dunno. Doesn't matter. You're wanted, you go."

Pammie looked at the sergeant a moment before she began to tell her tale. He met her gaze, and Pammie would never know how hard that was on him. Few in the room knew she had received a traffic summons for reckless driving from the sergeant for her actions yesterday. There was always so much going on around here that was secret. She had planned to tell roll call about the traffic charge against her, but the officers began applauding at the end, rising to a standing ovation, and she decided not to bring everybody down. Winding up, she noticed her old FTO, Herb Jackson. Odd for him to be here, not currently assigned to Day Shift. The FTO was in the back of the room whispering something to Lieutenant Ramirez, the same prick who'd had her written up last night. She wanted FTO Jackson to look angry about what happened to her, but maybe he didn't know about it, although he seemed to know everything, usually. The lieutenant, crisp uniform aside, looked like he hadn't slept all night, hollow-eyed. Good for him, the son of a bitch.

She parked in the city lot underneath the courthouse and walked to the bagel shop across the street to grab a little more coffee. She needed extra caffeine after the long night spent hugging and reassuring her daughters after they saw Mommy come home late with a dirty shirt, bloody hair, and gritted teeth. They were six and four, and she had needed time to quiet them before bed and in the morning to prepare them for school. Pammie knew her daughters' day would be filled with, "Is your mom okay? Did she get shot?" Like that was okay for her kids to hear. Pammie had considered keeping them home, but her husband couldn't take the day off to care for them any more than Pammie could. The lieutenant had almost put her on administrative leave, common practice for officers in shootings, but his bosses told him that since she hadn't fired her gun, she didn't need time off.

Pammie was twenty-nine, married seven years ago right after college, and had been an Alexandria police officer for five, coming on after realizing her English degree from a local college wouldn't get her much further than the retail jobs she was working and hating. Lack of law enforcement education didn't hamper her; most cops thought criminal justice degrees only a step beyond a Boy Scout merit badge. Her husband loved her and was strong enough himself to support such a radical career move. A major life adjustment too. Becoming a cop wasn't just adapting to a new job and challenging hours (new patrol officers always went to the midnight shift) but represented a change in outlook, experience, and self-image that some marriages didn't survive. It fostered a self-worth that might be beyond reality, in addition to a sense of responsibility that colored and changed most civilian habits. Pammie, like most cops, felt like a cop all the time and sometimes failed to take off the mantle of authority or the thick skin needed to survive the street when she unpinned the badge at shift's end. Her husband, like many cop spouses or lovers, sometimes found it hard to get close to a significantly changed significant other.

Pammie Martinson was lucky that her husband was cool with her choices and changes. But he still bit down on his fears when his wife walked out the door with a gun and a bullet-resistant vest and comforted kids who might not yet appreciate the danger but missed a mom whose workday might unpredictably extend hours past normal come-home-and-kiss-us time. And whose activities might leave her bloody and newsworthy, like yesterday. The kids didn't usually get up at five a.m. with her but had done so today, two pairs of wide eyes near tears as she left into the cold. Her husband crouched protectively behind their small forms, his hands on their shoulders bringing them in tight.

"You don't pay today, Officer,"

Pammie wasn't listening to the clerk. On autopilot and watching the customers seated in the bagel shop, standing in line around her and citizens parading past the shop's large windows, she looked back around at the little Latino clerk holding a steaming paper coffee cup. "Huh?"

"You don't have to pay, today, Officer."

Oh boy, here we go again. "I appreciate that, you know I do, but we talked before, Luis. You know I can't take free coffee. It's against the rules and it's not fair to all these other folks." The party line, but Pammie believed it. She took a half step back and waved her non gun hand to indicate the customers behind her, some of whom she knew without looking would clearly display their resentment when they realized a cop was getting free coffee. *On the arm,* it was called in some cities where gratuities were accepted. Not here. "Please, I gotta pay, I want to pay." Pammie began to reach forward with two dollar bills toward the Jerry's Kids jar on the counter, an acceptable alternate payment plan.

The short, Hispanic clerk put his hand over the jar. "No. I know you got to, but the guy in front of you, he paid for you. He said you're a hero. He showed me your picture, from the newspaper. He paid, you don't."

What could she say? She turned, but her benefactor had mixed into the crowd and was unidentifiable for thanks. If he'd been a crook, she would have noticed and remembered him, but as a law-abiding citizen, she'd given him no more notice than a leaf on a lawn. Embarrassed by the gesture, Pammie walked out of the shop red-faced but grinning.

The Alfred P. Bachus Alexandria Courthouse stood four stories tall two blocks from city hall in the central business district of Alexandria called Old Town. The first floor housed Juvenile and Domestic Relations Court. The second floor held the two courtrooms of the General District Court for traffic cases, minor criminal cases, and hearings, accessible by stairs that flanked the high-entry atrium. Elevators reached the third floor—crowded with prosecutors' offices and the massive file room of the Court Clerk—and the fourth floor with four courtrooms of the Circuit Court for felonies, two rooms off each side of a large foyer usually gray with cigarette smoke. Off the elevator on three, Pammie entered the Commonwealth Attorney's Office suite, passed two secretary-receptionists, and stopped at a large table with a dull, steel box full of small, keyed compartments. She drew her handgun and locked it in one of these vaults, disarming herself. An uncomfortable ritual, required by courthouse security protocol but alarming here in the one building in the whole city, other than the jail, guaranteed to hold criminals and others particularly hostile to police.

Pammie asked another cop and found out which CA was handling Criminal Court this morning. The answer led her to a prosecutor's office door where she lined up behind five other cops waiting to sit inside and go over their cases for today. The chairs were already occupied with officers going over cases with the prosecutor.

The prosecutor looked up from a seven-page printout of today's criminal docket and noticed Officer Martinson, squinted to read her name tag for confirmation, and said, "You're late. Advisements are already starting. They do them first, like right now. Get downstairs to Courtroom One. Myers is handling those."

"I don't know why I'm here. What do you—"

"Go now, they've started. Myers will get with you. Go straight to him so he knows you're there."

She entered crowded Courtroom One, gently edging between citizens standing behind the hard wooden pews filled with cops, suspects, victims, families, lawyers. She felt nakedly uncomfortable to be in such a crowd without her gun. No talking was allowed, but the room buzzed with whispers. She approached the railing between the filled rows of seats and the well where the prosecutor and defense tables were arrayed facing each other and edge-on to the judge's stand. That railing was called the bar. And usually, the only ones permitted to cross it other than witnesses and suspects had passed the bar exam. Judge Alexander Fish stared down at an officer from the bench, raised high over the witness stand, not more than a chair in the center of the room. Fourteen years on the bench, and Judge Fish had heard it all, over and over again. An officer was on the witness stand now, reciting from a notebook, counting out loud, sounding like a moron.

"Sixty-seven, sixty-six, sixty, fifty, forty-nine, forty-eight, forty-eight, um, forty-six . . ." As he droned on, Pammie stood by the bar and stared hard at the seated prosecutor, hoping by force of mind to turn his head toward her. It worked! Myers scanned her uniform shirt and motioned her forward. She slipped through a gate and stepped up softly to the prosecutor's table, trying to be unobtrusive up there in controlled territory, subtle as a tugboat in her full uniform, unbalanced gun belt, and lumpy protective vest.

"You were due here twenty minutes ago, when they called the case," he hissed from his seat, shielding his mouth from the judge with a manila folder. "Fish held it for you."

She glanced up at the judge. "I didn't know you needed me today until just—"

"Sit down. We'll call it next. Not long. Don't leave." Like she would. But officers sometimes had cases in both courts. Officers had been called for contempt for not being present when their name was called by one judge while they were on the stand in the other room. The officer on the stand continued to testify: "M, n, o, um . . . r, p . . . a, b, c, d, e, f, g . . ." He lapsed into singsong at the end. Martinson exited the well through the gate and squeezed into a four-seat pew with four officers already in it and waited.

Two hours she waited.

The judge ran through dozens of minor cases, short defense motions until, shaking square his loose pile of papers, he said to his clerk, "So, is that it, Valerie?"

"Sir, the advisement we passed before," clerk Valerie King said, passing up a file. Without turning his head, the judge swiveled his eyes toward the commonwealth's attorney and barked, "We ready now? Is she here?"

The prosecutor jumped up. "Yes, sir, Officer Martinson is here. She got here a little bit ago. We're ready to . . ."

"She got here a bit ago? How long ago, Mr. Myers?"

"Just a few . . ."

"So Mr. . . ." The judge looked down to read the name. "Goodell has been waiting in Holding for a *few*, while you handled drivel? Advisements come first, Mr. Myers. Citizens locked up and held deserve the most expeditious opportunity to seek their freedom. We've held Mr. Goodell since," a glance at his wristwatch, "nine a.m. for you, because you wanted Miss Martinson here." *Miss?* Pammie thought. *Uh-oh.*

Judge Fish continued. "Which should have been unnecessary. We don't usually entertain testimony at advisement, Mr. Myers, and we have delayed quite a bit for you to be ready to present it. Perhaps you are ready to explain why we need to hear from this officer?" The judge raised his eyes to the crowd, especially the gray-tinged uniform presence on the left side of the room. Not segregated officially, but cops always sat on one side, crooks on the other. She stood up. "Approach, Officer. Deputy, bring in Mr. Goodell."

As Martin passed the bar again and sat down on the witness stand, deputies brought Aaron Goodell into the room from a small door behind the defense table. Still in street clothes, jeans, and a white T-shirt spotted with blood at the collar and chest. His right eye was visibly black and swollen under his medium-brown skin. He walked through the door until he saw Pammie, then slowed and hunched forward slightly, as if aging a decade. He groaned loud enough for the judge to hear and slumped down in the defendant's chair like he knew where to go.

"Mr. Goodell, if you will stand," began the judge.

"I ain't stand."

"Mr. Goodell . . . What? Sir, you have to stand for this part."

"I ain't stand. All hurt. Gotta sit."

"You're hurt, Mr. Goodell?"

"Yeah, I hurt. You know," and raised himself upright to point at the officer.

Behind him the two sheriff's deputies adopted stone faces. The judge ran his gaze across Goodell, then Officer Martinson, then Commonwealth's Attorney Sandy Myers, and back to Goodell. Pammie unconsciously raised fingers to touch the prickly, raised scabs over the cuts under her hair and the red burned skin at her throat.

"Has he received medical treatment for his injuries?"

"Yes, Your Honor," a deputy said. "On the scene and in Booking."

"All right then. Mr. Goodell . . . you are Aaron Goodell? You have to answer aloud, Mr. Goodell. Don't nod."

"Yeah, I's Aaron Goodell."

"Mr. Goodell, you have been charged with attempted felonious assault on a law enforcement officer, distribution of cocaine, and possession with intent to distribute cocaine. You—"

"Not guilty, Judge. They put that charge on me. They—"

"Mr. Goodell, you are not entering a plea at this time. This is an advisement, solely for the purpose of telling you what the charge is against you. Mr. Myers, the prosecutor, told us earlier that he wanted the arresting officer here too. I don't know why yet, but that is why this was delayed from earlier. So, do you understand the charges that have been made against you?"

"I know what that bitch charged me with." His eyes flared at the judge, then at Martinson. The bailiffs, without seeming to move, were closer behind Goodell now.

"Mr. Goodell, this is not the time or place for your outbursts. I can see that you have reason to be angry at them." The judge cast his eyes toward Martinson and Myers. "But for now, all you need to do is listen to the charges against you and to tell me if you have a lawyer or wish one to be appointed for you."

"I wants a lawyer, right now. This is bullsh—" Goodell stopped when a bailiff's hand clapped down on his shoulder. "This wrong. I want a lawyer."

The judge stared at Goodell, then looked over, opposite the police side of the courtroom, at a clump of dark suits. "Miss Cohen, would you approach, please?

Public Defender Rachel Cohen, startled, looked up from her whispered client conference in the third pew and stood. "Judge?"

"Miss Cohen, Mr. Goodell here certainly needs counsel and will probably qualify for the services of your office once he fills out the forms. I wonder if you would step forward and assist him and us with this, I'm not sure what we will call it now, *advisement plus*, I think?"

Cohen carried her briefcase through the gate and sat next to Goodell at the defense table. "May I have just a moment, Judge?"

Pammie Martinson fidgeted. On the stand for she knew not what, parts of her scalp burning. She found a tiny dab of new blood on a probing finger. She held a copy of her police report in her lap but didn't need to refresh her memory. She was fairly clear on what had happened yesterday. Goodell had tried to kill her. And she had been professional enough not to kill him.

At the defense table, the public defender finished murmuring with the defendant and told the judge she was ready to proceed. So the judge did.

"Yes, Mr. Myers. Please tell us all why you are introducing testimony at this unusual time?"

Myers gathered himself up at the prosecutor's table and began. "Your Honor, one of the tasks we will address here will be the issue of setting bond for the defendant. And while his record to date indicates little matching the seriousness and scope of this current assault, it behooves the court to understand the savagery of the attack on Officer Martinson to ensure that Mr. Goodell is not released before trial. This case represents a terrible attack on a law enforcement—"

"Objection, Your Honor," Cohen stood to say. "Mr. Myers is not only going beyond the scope of the issues before the court, but he is in fact testifying as to the truth of the allegations made against my client. If he has information to present today, let it be introduced through proper testimony."

"Sustained. Mr. Myers, if you have a case to present, present it without your own testimony."

Was that a loss for us? Martinson wondered. She had been part of enough cases to know momentum swung back and forth with these objections, challenges, sometimes zingers. Zingers, hard questions on gray-area issues, worried her, especially since she had no time to work with the prosecutor before taking the stand. Oh well, another dangerous door to walk through.

They started with the typical boilerplate necessary to begin laying the foundation of a legal case. State your name for the court, how are you employed, were you so employed on the date of these events. Then step-by-step, Martinson laid out the events of the afternoon before: TAC pursued a drug suspect, she took up the chase, he shot at her by the airport, he crashed on the bridge and was arrested. The judge had some concerns about the injuries now evident on the defendant, but Officer Martinson testified that they were sustained in the crash on the bridge. "We will see how that plays out at trial, Mr. Myers," Judge Fish said.

At the end, one normally benign boilerplate question nearly zinged her: "Did all these events occur in the City of Alexandria?"

"Yes. Well . . . sort of."

The judge popped in his seat. "Did you say 'sort of,' Officer?"

"Yes, sir. Sort of, sir."

"You're aware, Officer Martinson, that 'sort of' is generally not precise enough for my courtroom?" Cohen stood to frame an objection based on this exchange, but the judge raised his hand. "Mr. Myers, please begin using this witness to tell the court exactly what it is you want me to know? Specifically? Not *sort of.*"

"Yes, sir. Miss, Officer Martinson, where exactly did these events occur?"

"Sir, they started with my pursuit of the suspect, Mr. Goodell, in the city. On Washington Street by Hojo's, er, in the 800 block of North Washington. We then proceeded in a northbound direction on Washington to where it becomes the George Washington Parkway. It's still the same street just gets called the George—"

"Yes, Officer. Proceed with the locations."

"We went north on the Parkway and he stopped on the Parkway where the entrance to National Airport is. That's where he shot at me. Then we got going again and he crashed on the 14th Street Bridge. And I got him."

"That is a greatly simplified version of what I am sure will be more complicated testimony, Officer," the judge said. "But let me ask this." He raised a copy of the *Washington Post*, a section with Pammie's bloody picture on it. He had been reading it during pauses in the morning docket. He folded it over to show the photo to the courtroom and said, "This is you?"

"Yes, Your Honor."

"Making the arrest?"

"Yes, Judge."

"On the 14th Street Bridge?"

Yeah, you fucking doofus. "Yes, sir."

"And in what jurisdiction is the 14th Street Bridge?" *Zing!*

"That's Arlington County, your honor, at the beginning, then it becomes D.C. But—"

She was interrupted by Cohen standing up. "Objection, motion to strike, Your Honor." Cohen raised her voice.

"These events occurred outside the jurisdiction of the City of Alexandria. I demand that charges against my client be dismissed."

Prosecutor Myers stood and began picking up the knocked-down pieces of his case. "Your Honor, while the events depicted in that photograph, the actual stop and arrest of Mr. Goodell, did occur in Arlington County, the shots were fired at Officer Martinson inside Alexandria's jurisdiction. Is that not true, Officer Martinson?"

"Well, sorta, sir," Martinson said. Laughter finally broke out among the cops and other knowledgeable observers in the pews, and the bailiffs bit down on quivering lips.

"Officer Martinson, if you say 'sorta' again in my courtroom, I will hold you in contempt. Where did the gunfire take place?"

"In Arlington County, Judge."

"There you have it, Judge." Pammie thought Rachel Cohen could get tired, all these calisthenics up and down to object and argue. Cohen stated her objection and was countered by Myers, and the judge raised his hands to try to slow the legal avalanche. Pammie stood and shouted.

"Eight-tenths of a mile from the city line, Your Honor. Where we still have jurisdictional authority to arrest!"

They stared at Pammie, who realized what she had done, and sat back down wide-eyed and blushing.

Myers caught up first. "Your Honor, the felonious assault occurred within the one-mile limit of a city police officer's authority under Virginia code 19.2-250. County police jurisdiction only extends a hundred yards into an adjoining city or county, but city jurisdiction is a full mile."

Pammie thought of the sergeant on the bridge yesterday. After he had written her the ticket, he arranged for another officer, much senior to her, to drive her back to Headquarters while her shot-up Plymouth was towed to the shop. En route, they stopped on the Parkway at the shooting scene. Evidence technicians were scooping glass and bullet fragments off the road. The senior officer set the trip odometer to zero, then continued on to the city limit sign. He stopped again and made Pammie look at the readout. "Point-eight miles. Note that in your report," he told her.

So she could tell the judge, she realized.

"I'm satisfied," the judge said, "that Alexandria Police have the authority to make an arrest based on events occurring where they have been testified to. Miss Cohen, your motion is denied. And Mr. Myers, I still haven't heard what it is you think will have influence over my decision on bond. Without shouting and without further histrionics, Officer Martinson, please proceed."

Myers spoke. "We've established that Mr. Goodell at the defense table is the person who shot at you, Officer. Please tell the court what he said to you after."

"Objection, Your Honor," Rachel wearily stood to say. "There has been no foundation given for this testimony, no mention of any rights waiver by my client, no introduction—"

Myers interrupted her. "This is not offered for the truth of the statements made but to demonstrate the state of mind of Mr. Goodell in terms of his relationship to the police and to authority. I—"

"Go ahead, Mr. Myers. This wasn't supposed to be a trial today, despite it now bearing all the trimmings of such. Officer, what did he say to you?"

Pammie didn't need notes. She glanced at Goodell and told the judge, "He said, 'Bitch, should'a blasted your bitch ass all the way back to Bitchville. Would'a jumped out and taken you and alla them down but those trigger happy cops would'a blasted my ass.'"

"Is that when you hit him?" Cohen said, out of turn, but she couldn't stop herself.

"No, I hit him when . . ." She stopped and looked at Myers.

"Objection, Your Honor," Myers said. "There has been no testimony about Officer Martinson or anyone hitting the defendant."

"Other than that of your officer, no, Mr. Myers. Miss Martinson," the judge said, the demotion in title deliberate. "Are you now telling the court that you did in fact strike Mr. Goodell?"

"Yes, sir."

"And you didn't before as part of your earlier testimony?"

"That was on the bridge, outside the city, and we didn't charge him with that."

Cohen jumped in, out of turn, but nobody cared by then. "Charge him with being hit by cops?"

"No, ma'am. With resisting arrest. He wouldn't get out of the car, then he wouldn't lie down to get cuffed."

"So you beat his face in." Cohen was on her feet.

"No, ma'am. He sustained all his facial injuries in the crash." Pammie glared at Cohen, who glared back at her for a long ten seconds. Then Cohen turned to the judge and asked for the newspaper he had shown.

"It's not evidence, Miss Cohen."

"You brought it in, Your Honor. Let me have a moment with it."

The judge handed it down to the deputy, who carried it across the well and handed it to Cohen. She spread it on the table, and said, "Officer Martinson, you are testifying to statements given to you while you were on duty?"

"Yes, ma'am."

"In uniform?"

"Yes, ma'am."

"Full uniform? Badge of authority displayed?"

"Yes. Um . . . sort . . ."

"Then where is it here?" And Cohen held out the front-page photo of Pammie holding Goodell's neck, her uniform shirt stained with fluid, her badge noticeably missing. It was clearly visible this day in court, having been retrieved from the restaurant where she left it at the beginning of the pursuit, pinned to her jacket she'd left in the booth.

"Judge, at this time I renew my motion to strike all of Officer Martinson's testimony based on her lack of legal authority to take police action under state code. She was not acting under color of law as she was not displaying her badge of authority. I therefore argue that her actions in detaining my client, wherever those actions occurred, were illegal and any statements made by my client, and his actions allegedly taken in connection with those statements, are inadmissible in trial." Cohen barely took a breath. "Statements made in Arlington County . . . My client should be released immediately."

All the cops in the pews were leaning forward. A voice from the right side of the room said, "You go, bitch!" And no one looked anywhere but forward, toward the judge, who slammed his hand down on the rostrum and said, "You win, Miss Cohen. Your client is free to go. No, bailiff, not back to Booking for processing, out the door now." More yells, less muffled now, rang out in the room.

"Setting this court up today," the judge continued, "to hear the most inflammatory of testimony, testimony not usually allowed at this early stage in proceedings, is unfair to Mr. Goodell and an embarrassment to the administration of justice. You, Mr. Myers, and you, Miss Martinson, should be ashamed of yourselves for trying it."

The battered cop looked away from the judge in uncomprehending shame. She turned in the witness seat to scan the increasingly unruly crowd, nervous about the anger she heard heating up. There were several cops around the room, and she noticed the lieutenant and FTO Jackson standing at the back, whispering to each other. The judge was now leaning forward on the bench, chin sticking out toward the loudness. As he spoke, the clamor rose steadily, almost covering his words even to those closest to him. But Pammie and Myers on one side and Cohen facing them across the room could just make out through the furor as the judge banged his flat hand on the bench in lieu of a gavel, then waved it toward the door and said, "You can walk out now, Mr. Goodell. The charge is . . ."

The rest was drowned in the sound of all in the room rising like baseball fans for a line drive, voices calling "No!" on the cop side of the room and "Yeah, baby!" on the other.

Pammie sat shocked, watching the young man who had shot at her, cursed her, fought with her, called her names, as he sauntered free through the gate. He joined apparent family members, chased by a man with a reporter's pad not unlike her own patrol officers' notebooks. She blinked back the tears a female cop could never show, looking at Myers in incomprehension. Myers glanced at her, caught her glare, and turned away. Pammie was a hero when she woke up today. Then she wasn't.

She took a deep breath, raising the thick coat of Kevlar over her chest and testing it, sensing its failure to blunt the knife of betrayal and unfairness stuck in her by the judge. And a tiny cut penetrated her heart, one she might not feel till thousands more joined it. Events, insults, injuries, challenges, resentments, and losses would add more scars, joining together in a deadening mass as she moved forward toward the end of her career.

Or her life.

CHAPTER 15

Evaluation
Wednesday, November 2, 1988
1000–1130 HRS

KELLY WALKED THROUGH the lobby of Police Headquarters two hours later than the morning shift start time. He had called his supervisor to ask for a few hours' leave.

"You're not calling in sick again, John? You know that's five times this year," the sergeant said on the phone.

"What, you got notes on me, Sarge? Right at hand?" *You prick*, Kelly thought, slurping his second coffee.

"Yeah, as a matter of fact. Today's your anniversary date, so I just did your annual evaluation. We'll go over it when you decide to come to work."

"I'll be in, just gotta take care of something." *My throbbing head, my muddy shoes, where I parked my car.* He hung up. *Enough coffee sloshing around*, Kelly thought, *so the three aspirin won't burn a hole in his belly.* He'd awakened drowning in his own blood, mouth full and blocking his breath, lungs desperate and pulling but unable to bring life back, impending death retreating but so real that he was surprised when he patted dry lips as he awoke from the dream to his phone's trill. Ashby. "You better get your ass up and in here, John. Sarge is pissed."

Kelly knew his unmarked was still in front of his house, where he'd left it to drive his personal car to Mom's. The POV's location now, after leaving the cemetery, he couldn't remember. Kelly spent ten minutes walking around his neighborhood before he found it, two tires up on a curb three blocks away from home. No dents, no blood or clothing fragments. Good. He repositioned it and took his city car to headquarters.

Walking through the lobby, he heard, "John? Detective? Detective Kelly?" He turned and recognized a reporter for the *Alexandria Gazette*, a small daily newspaper that was one of three that tried to compete with the *Washington Post*. The kid never knew whether to address him informally or professionally. Kelly owed him a favor since he'd helped on the day Emma . . . when Emma died. The kid wore a light blue shirt and dark pants, almost a uniform with him. The PIO had told Kelly the kid and other reporters dressed to blend in at crime scenes and sometimes get in closer than the police wanted. Same reason many of the television station remote units drove dark sedans instead of gaudy-marked vans; they could move through perimeters because cops often thought they were detectives.

"Why aren't you at the courthouse? The kid from the shooting should be advised today. Can't be anything better going on here."

"I was. He walked. Judge set him free because the officer fu—messed up." He peered at Kelly's red eyes but said nothing more.

Kelly, still befuddled from last night's indulgence, couldn't take in the idea that an attempted cop-killer would walk out of court. "And you're here for . . ."

"Hoping the chief will say something, or the PIO will. But he's busy, and PIO is out somewhere, and I got a question for you. Maybe."

"Not on that, not my case, but shoot." So to speak.

"There's an arrest sheet here for a girl. Arrested for burglary and GLA. She's nineteen. Is it a good story? She a badass?"

"Lemme look at the CCRE."

Central Criminal Records Exchange forms were filled out for every in-custody arrest. A copy was kept on a clipboard at the front desk, an open record for seventy-two hours. Kelly put his third cup of coffee down on the edge of the records service window and checked the clipboard. He stared at it for a minute, then asked the clerk for a copy of the original report.

While they waited, he said to the reporter, "Not a big story. She's a hooker, got greedy. This isn't going anywhere."

The reporter was shocked. "She's a hooker. How can you . . . Why, 'cause she's a black girl? That's a pretty big conclusion to jump to—her charge is grand larceny auto and burglary."

"Now who's jumping to conclusions? She's not a hooker 'cause she's black, and who are you to think I think such a thing?" Kelly's headache came back, and he was regretting stopping to talk to this foolish young kid.

"Here's a conclusion," Kelly said. "Young black girls don't do burglaries. So what else is going on here?" He held out the clipboard and pointed to blocks on the form. "Look. This shows her name, address, DOB, Social Security number. Here's her height and weight and race. She's nineteen, five-feet-two, a hundred fifty. Short but not small. These blocks show the charges and code sections. This is burglary, this is grand larceny auto. And these show her home address, the location of offense, and the location of arrest. That's where your story is, or isn't.

"Location of offense is 300 Wythe Street. That's the social services old folks home. We call it the elderly high rise, not 'cause it's old, but its folks are. That's also the victim's address. And look at the suspect's address, in the 300 block of Hopkins Court. ARHA project housing, a block away. That's also the arrest location, so she got picked up at home. Warrant was issued at time of arrest, means not through prior investigation, probably means we found her in the car. And she's black, living in Housing, a block from the vic. She's a hooker."

"Come on, she's a hooker 'cause she's black?"

"I dunno why she's a hooker, but black girls don't break into apartments to steal cars. Just doesn't happen. She was there to do the guy, and either took his car for fun or to cover the cost of doing business. Happens all the time in that building. Old folks need to get it on like the rest of us—y'all just don't wanna think about it. Vic either found the keys gone when he woke up or just decided she'd borrowed the car long enough and wanted it back, so he calls us and spins the burglary story so he won't look the fool."

"So I can write she's a hooker?"

"God no, she's just a visitor to his home who helped herself to the loan of his car, by the time this shakes out. Any public defender"—and Kelly paused a moment, a smile finally pushing the headache pain and thoughtful sadness off his face—"can knock this down in a minute. She threatens to put the vic on the stand and he'll cower. Most likely this will disappear before prelim. Just keep her name in mind and watch the indictments for the next month or two. Her name won't surface. The vic won't prosecute. He just wanted his car back."

"So you guys are just property recovery?"

"Yeah, and social services, financial advisors, life counselors, babysitters, limo drivers, trash men. I gotta go. Whatever you run with, you didn't get it from me, but PIO will give it to you officially if you need it, which you won't." Kelly left him in the lobby reevaluating his notes and took the elevator to the second floor, where the detective bureau was located. He stopped by his desk to hang his jacket, took two more aspirin with the remainder of his cold coffee, and went to his sergeant's office for the evaluation.

He came out thirty minutes later. Sweat darkened his sides and back, and he was pale. He walked but he could have staggered, so rocked by his sergeant's opinions of his performance and abilities. Opinions pared down to bureaucratic file-speak, almost like a checklist with all the bad blocks marked: fails to notify superiors of actions, regularly late for roll call and shift assignments, unable to commit to group activity, inattentive to detail, unresponsive to callback requests. Low opinions, damaging observations now documented in his squad file, the official permanent record of his capabilities.

Observers watched his progress across the CID office, as they had watched how he had regressed recently. Fellow detectives. Coworkers but not friends. Unlike Kelly himself, most could trace his altered path back a year, but like Kelly, few could think, much less say aloud, all the words that described what had happened, and could only refer to the event as "the thing with Emma." Few could offer support beyond an invitation to hoist a few after work, not a solution or much solace. When Kelly reached his desk and sat down, he was surprised he didn't lean over to one side, the side where his supervisor had chewed his ass.

"You know, John, how these things are supposed to go," Kelly's sergeant had said to begin their evaluation session. The sergeant held a four-page memorandum, to the Chief of Police through channels, in which he had documented Kelly's performance for the year in nine different categories: volume of work, quality of work, reliability, and so on. Each category got a rating: outstanding, very good, meets requirements, below requirements, and unacceptable. Nobody ever got unacceptable, because that meant the supervisor had failed to motivate or control the employee, and what supervisor would admit that? Few got outstanding. Kelly always got outstanding, until this year.

"We're supposed to start with a good thing, build you up, show we have confidence in you, then if we have to, lower the boom." The sergeant sighed and pushed the eval across his desk. "But, John, I got nothing . . ."

His sergeant, fifteen years on the job and five as a supervisor in CID, was embarrassed. Detective duty was slogging, often unrewarding, and tedious work, but not hard to do once you knew the ropes: read the reports when Patrol takes them, follow up to locate and interview witnesses, make connections between crimes, find patterns, identify and track down suspects, bring charges. Write supplements. Shepherd the whole mess through trial. It was a grind, but satisfying because it meant you were catching bad guys. The sarge ran it down.

"And you do that, John. You still do the basics and I really can see you are trying to work hard. But I need the little stuff. I need to know where you are, and when you'll be here. Tardiness is . . .,"

"Tardiness, Sarge? That's what you'll be dinging me for?"

"I gotta be able to trust you, John. Trust that you'll be here at work when you are supposed to. Trust that you will show up every day. If I can't, then how can I trust you to go out and do work alone without me checking on you every minute?"

"You know I . . ."

"I don't know nothing lately, John. You're a mess. I can't get you on the phone. You're subject to callback, you know. You're on the Hostage Negotiation Team and carry that pager. A big case, I gotta be able to call you and have you come in to work it. We all do."

"Maybe you should pay me standby pay, then. You're gonna ding me for not coming in when you call, that means I'm on standby. We don't get standby pay, so you can't write me down for not coming in."

"I'm not dinging you for not coming in, I'm dinging you for not being reachable when I call you to come in. You don't answer the phone, you got no answering machine. What did you do, tell your wife not to pick up the phone? I don't get her either." The sergeant stopped when he saw the slack look on Kelly's face, the quick droop of the chin. "What is it, John?"

"Janet and . . . I'm not with Janet anymore. We broke up." I kicked her out the door because we were never happy anymore. "She left. It's been like five or six or so months. We're getting a divorce, I think." When I get the balls to tell her so. "She moved out." But still comes back, sometimes.

"Aw, John. I'm sorry. Didn't know. You didn't tell me. You tell anybody? You got somebody to talk to?" *Here's where the sergeant goes into full manager mode,* Kelly thought. *Next thing, he'll offer me EAP.*

"You know there is the Employee Assistance Program. You can call and talk to someone, it can even be on duty. I don't, the Department doesn't have to know about it other than I clear you to go there. They don't report back to us."

"Sure, Sarge. Nobody'll know. Except you. And your boss 'cause you gotta account for me. And all the way up the chain. No way. No fuckin' way."

"It's not like that, John. EAP is a good program. Absolutely confidential. Nobody knows except me that you're going. Nobody counts it against you."

"Sure. No way it doesn't show up in my file."

"Hey, dumbass, who do you think writes your file? I do. It's right here. I put stuff in it, I decide what goes in it and what doesn't."

"Like this eval?" Kelly pushed the evaluation report back across the desk. "That the kind of bad news you gonna put in my file?"

"You think I want to, John? You think I get points for zapping you? You zapped yourself." The sergeant pushed the report back at John. "You did the work that goes in here, basic, and didn't do what should go in here, the good stuff. You should be a team player, like you used to be. You should be out with the new guys, backing them when they go on interviews or bringing them in to watch yours. Teaching them. You should have the highest clearance rate up here. You used to. Not anymore. I didn't include yours this time, I didn't want to calculate it, and I hope my boss doesn't ask for it 'cause it would suck. You gotta get a grip, John. Get Janet back, or get over her, or get a new one."

"What makes you think I don't now? Have a new one?"

"Well, shit, John. That didn't take very long. Is she why you broke up with Janet?"

Big question. "No," Kelly said. *Yes, maybe*, he thought. "We, we'd been drifting for a while, like a couple of years. I think it was gonna come, but when I met . . . the woman I'm, um, with now, I knew that I needed to not be with Janet anymore. It was like I suddenly figured out that I could, that it could be different with someone, not like it had always been with Jan. Better." Kelly shivered and found himself grinning at his sergeant in a way that he had not expected after the eval review went so far south. "I haven't really told . . . the new one that Janet moved out. Didn't want to scare her off."

My worst day with Rachel is better than my best day with Janet, Kelly thought but couldn't share, even though he'd just opened up more to his sergeant than he ever had, more than to anyone at all in fact. Maybe even more than to Rachel. Have to change that. He grinned at his sergeant, then stopped when he noticed how the sergeant was peering at him.

"John . . . John." The sergeant waved the report. "John, I can't change this now. It's accurate. It's you this past year. Your work has sucked. You've been short with me and the others up here. You haven't been the same. But this is just one year. You've been on, what, nine years? You can get out of this, easy. I'm gonna pay more attention to you and keep you in line, not to bust your ass but to keep you from wandering this way. We don't want you to have to go back to Patrol." *Or jail*, Kelly thought, thinking about Pickett's body coming up tomorrow.

"And I'm gonna talk with you more about EAP. I want that to happen. I can't make you go. Regs don't let me without it being a result of an II. And you haven't fucked up that bad, yet. But I want you to go."

Fuck EAP, Kelly thought. "I'll think about it," Kelly said.

Maybe he *could* talk to a counselor.

Maybe after a few beers.

CHAPTER 16

Delivery
Wednesday, November 2, 1988
1100–1300 HRS

WHEN THE NEW guy Grbonscowicz met with Officer Terrence Charles Sharpe at the Property Section service window, he didn't expect to become a mailman. It was a hassle.

This was Wednesday, the morning of the tactical unit's weekly drug lab run. All the drugs from all the cases they made in the past week had to go to the Virginia State Police crime lab in Merrifield, outside the city but not far. The hassle wasn't the distance; it was the loads of evidence and their attendant paperwork.

TAC had made fifteen felony arrests in the past five days. Each involved painstaking, detailed incident reports and evidence documentation. After each arrest, officers individually weighed each piece of drug or leaf or paraphernalia, then locked it in a plastic bag heat-sealed to melt it shut, then put the heat-seal in a heavier manila evidence envelope with

printed blocks for writing and metal locks on the flap. It took
hours of clerical effort that delayed their return to the street
after a jump, so sometimes members of the unit would do two
or three jumps before coming into Headquarters to complete
reports and commence bagging and tagging. On a good night,
a unit member might end up with crack from the first jump in
a shirt pocket, seized cash from the second in a front left pants
pocket, and "love boat"—marijuana laced with PCP—from
the third in whatever pocket was left that wasn't yet crowded
with bullets, spare handcuffs, drug field test kits, or latex gloves.
It was a wonder they didn't mix them up.

Honest, Judge, it never happens.

Unit 516, Grbonscowicz, and his trainer, Unit 511, T.C.
Sharpe, carried forty-seven evidence envelopes in two boxes
out to their very unmarked car, a used sedan chosen yesterday
off a Toyota lot belonging to a very civic-minded dealership
owner who supported the police department in general and
TAC in particular by providing new sets of wheels every week.
"New" meaning "it's new to you" and thus new to the dealers,
runners, hangers-on, and general street corner lounger population that, they hoped, wouldn't identify the car as full of burly
plainclothes cops until it squealed to a stop next to them.

"You didn't find nothin' on me," was muttered or shouted
a dozen times a month, and with great sincerity, from suspects
who seemed to truly believe that if the crack wasn't located in
their pockets during a search, then it could not be linked to
them in court. Getting written statements (read: confessions)
was hard from arrestees who by this twisted logic didn't consider themselves guilty of possessing drugs that twenty seconds
before TAC got there had been in their hand, or their pocket,
or their mouth.

So be it. Those arrested would have a strong case to argue
against, even if they didn't confess. "Judge, I drove up and saw

Mr. Fillintheblank throw several small, light-colored, irregularly shaped objects onto the sidewalk, and when I recovered them (after whatever struggle, foot pursuit, or gunplay) I tested them positive for the presence of cocaine hydrochloride." Or terms to that effect, although those were the terms generally used and precisely repeated.

516 carried the boxes of evidence envelopes like a serf, while 511 held the door. Each envelope bore the name of the recovering officer, the arresting or spotting officer, the suspect, and the location of recovery, not just the address but the spot on the body where the items were found: left front jeans pocket, hat, under the tongue (hence, latex gloves). Each also bore a short description of the contraband inside. Among forty-seven individual envelopes, forty-one contained suspected crack cocaine. And each of these bore the written description: "small, light-colored, irregularly shaped objects."

"You drive," said 511 to 516. Rare for a senior police officer to defer to one younger or newer, but 511 didn't feel like pushing a civilian car through Beltway traffic, even at 10:30 a.m. on a Wednesday. A cruiser, sure. Folks generally got out of your way, but in this three-year-old Camry, the plainclothes officers were just part of the herd.

516 pretended to massage his writing hand and said, "Haven't signed my name that many times since I bought a house."

"And you've got quite the name, Mr. Grbonscowicz." The younger officer smiled at the rare correct pronunciation, the added vowel sound at the start and the -ts ending. Sharpe went on. "You have a house? Where, not in the city, right?"

"Oh no, couldn't afford it here. In Manassas."

"How long's it take you to get home from here?"

"At night, after work, maybe twenty, thirty minutes. Mornings in for court, maybe an hour. More."

"You're screwed, then. You know how much we go to court, right?" 511 shook his head, invisible to 516, who was threading his way around slow cars on I-495, setting an aggressive weave through the gaps, outpacing traffic by five or ten miles per hour. Not enough to really stick out, although it was unlikely to impossible to get a traffic ticket as a cop. As he had been trained by his FTO to say, "Trooper, would it make any difference to you if I told you I am a police officer?" Always worked.

"Yeah, I heard about court. But it's overtime, right? Time and a half for hours spent outside the regular schedule."

"Lots of it. You'll make money in TAC, but you'll put in long days. Most of us end up in court a few times a week, not like in Patrol when you had one court day a month for all your traffic and criminal stuff. Big court, like Commonwealth Day tomorrow, every Thursday, we're all there, so we adjust our schedule so we're on the clock and not on OT. The money's good but you'll miss your wife. Family?"

"No kids yet."

Both men had put in long hours yesterday in the aftermath of Pammie Martinson's pursuit. It was a TAC spot-jump that led to the shooting, so 511 and 516 had responded to the scene to help secure any drugs and generally help out. With so much time spent among his fellow TAC members, the nom-de-police 511 now stuck more than T.C., his nickname. 516's real name was Aloisius James Reed Grbonscowicz, so everyone gratefully shortened it to 516.

"You're local, right? I heard that about you," 511 said conversationally, slumped down in the passenger seat like a king and trying not to notice the tight gaps between their car's fenders and the passed traffic. He knew the job was dangerous when he took it. He wouldn't remark on 516's apparent recklessness. Though only twenty-eight years old, Sharpe was senior enough on the department to know a junior officer had to sometimes show off to prove himself. *Better here than in an alley with twitchy suspects*, he thought. Drug work was generally synonymous with guns, but even an unarmed man can hurt you if he is quick or desperate. And there is no such thing as an unarmed man in a fight with a cop. If he knocks you out or otherwise takes control of your gun, you're dead.

"That's why you can shoot an unarmed subject," Sharpe's FTO had taught him five years ago when he was a recruit. "If he gets your gun, he can kill you. And if you don't want to worry about yourself, worry about the citizens now he has your gun. Or better yet, worry about me. Shoot him to save me. That's good."

Sharpe had planned to talk about deadly force with the new guy at some point in their training, but Grbonscowicz brought it up as he drove. He said, "You read in the paper a lot about cops killing young men, and it's mostly young black men. And most cops are white. So . . ."

"Glad you asked that. We spend most of our time in the black neighborhoods. That sucks. It probably sucks to be black, and maybe you'll tell me about that sometime. I've never been black. You, obviously, have. Even with that name. You don't meet many Polish blacks. And you grew up here. You're a homeboy, 516, certified. Where'd you live, growing up?"

"Hunter's Run."

"So, you were in an apartment in the West End. Not projects but not rich. Always something going on in there, like any apartment complex. High population density and low income. You saw cops there a lot while you were little?" Funny to say little. Grbonscowicz was six-feet-five and two hundred and forty pounds, one-third more man than skinny, pale Sharpe.

"Yeah. Lots of times. And I might go to my friends' houses, and there were never cops there."

"Friends lived in white parts of town?"

"Yeah."

"And you wonder why cops weren't there, when they all over your hood?" 516 gave that look that black folk do when white folk use black slang.

"You've been a cop now a year, right? In Patrol before you got transferred over to TAC?" 511 paused with a wince after a particularly close swerve. "Tell me, in Patrol, how many calls you get in the white neighborhoods? Beverley Hills, Seminary Valley, southern Old Town?

"I got calls in southern Old Town."

"Like what, suspicious persons, larceny from auto? Calls that came in 'cause there were youngsters walking through the white neighborhood to go to homes in the projects all around the edges down there? No, you got calls in the projects. In the low-income apartments. Where the poor people are."

"Where the black people are," Grbonscowicz said and glared at Sharpe, who forced himself not to snap at him to get his eyes back on the road. *You're not his FTO,* Sharpe thought with difficulty.

"Yeah, sometimes that's the same. Some poor are black. Some poor are crooks. Doesn't mean blacks are crooks, but it ends up seeming like that. Harder on you than me, but spend a few years where everybody you bust is black, makes you prejudiced."

"You saying you're prejudiced?" 516 was surprised that 511 would admit that to him.

"'Course I am. We are all prejudiced. Not bigoted, though that happens to some. But prejudiced. In the real meaning of prejudging things. Here is prejudice. You're in patrol and . . ." Another swerve, another pause. "Sarge says whoever gets a marijuana bust tonight goes home two hours early. Now, you want that, you just-got-married guy, you. Where you gonna go? To Beverley Hills, catch maybe a lawyer or banker toking up while he's washing his car or sitting on his patio? Or you gonna go to the Northside, or Arlandria, or Hunter's Run, where there's folks out smokin' up 'cause that's what they do out there, outside? You know where you'd go. And it's not because they're black, or necessarily because they're poor, or uneducated, or jobless. It's just what they do there. You prejudge the neighborhood based on what you know about the neighborhood."

"So white folks get a pass?"

Damn, Sharpe thought, *this kid will be good. Not afraid to confront.* "No. If someone, one of his neighbors, called 9-1-1 to complain about pot smokers in their cul-de-sac, we'd go. In fact, probably everybody'd go, rare call like that's gotta be a good call, not some typical bullshit called in by an old lady saying there's a hundred drug dealers in front of her house. There's maybe two or three, but we can't tell them from the other ninety-seven out there."

Sharpe went on. "So what could we do, prone 'em all out? Nah. But we get out and talk to some of them. And they get mad, saying, 'Why you always up in here, givin' us shit?' And you, new guy, you say, 'Well, sir, it's because one of your neighbors called to report illicit drug activity here on this block.' And he calls you an asshole. Me, I just say, 'Free country,' and stand there till the dealers walk away. They gonna go around the corner and deal? Yeah. Can I stop that, a uniformed officer? No. Can I go around the corner too and make them go around some other corner? Yeah, I could do that. I've done that all night sometimes. But now we got the tactical unit, and we watch them all night. And sometimes we can see them deal and take their drugs away. You hear our song yet?"

"Song?" Grbonscowicz was glad to get off a topic too close to home. Too close to racial challenge.

Sharpe turned down the music on the FM and sang: "*We the Jump-Out Boys, from the Ay Pee Dee. We jump out of our cars and take your P C P.*"

"You're kidding. Is there more?"

"Yeah, there's more. There's even a line about me. Wanna hear it?"

"No."

"*Well there's T C, don't he look nice. He got on TAC 'cause he couldn't go to Vice.*"

"Don't quit your day job," 516 said.

"So don't think about what we're doing in racial terms. Yeah, we bust a lot of black kids, kids being maybe even thirty or forty. We don't bust 'em 'cause they're black. We bust 'em 'cause they're just standing there, doing crimes right in front of us. And if we don't, then Alexandria looks like D.C. The homicide capital of the world. You know how many homicides they had last year. It's in the hundreds, every year for years. Highest was 572, in '87, just last year. Alexandria? We had five last year, and five this year. Know why? Us. TAC. Well, Patrol too, they run their asses off. But a lot of it is us, 'cause we might be anywhere, jump out anytime. Bad guys don't get settled." 511 gulped and puckered in his seat at another close call. "Hey, Darrell Waltrip, we gon' get there alive, right?

"Anyway, when we formed TAC back in '87, we about doubled the number of felony arrests APD was making. Totals are still high. But all that bustin' and chasin' means all that arrestin' and report writin' and testifyin' and runnin' to the lab. Which brings us here today."

"About that. Lab processing and testifying." 516 nodded his head toward the boxes in the back. "All the lock-seal envelopes say the same thing."

"No, they don't."

"Yeah, they do. They all say, well, all the crack ones, say, 'Small, light-colored, irregularly shaped objects.' The same thing."

"And . . . ?"

"And why are they all the same? They're not all the same, they can't be. I mean, yesterday we go out to where Pammie got that guy. He's got rocks in his two back pockets, and there's rocks in the car on the floor. And you wrote them all on the envelopes as 'small, light-colored, irregularly shaped objects.' So you wrote they're all the same."

"Yes, I did. But I also didn't."

"Don't fuck with me, T.C."

"Look. Crack is crack is crack. Sometimes there is a minor change in color, depends on what it was cut with, how fresh it is, how long it's been in Charlie's pocket or Mona's mouth. You gotta describe it some way. You gonna get out a color chart each seizure and compare so's you can say 'objects with a light-reflectant characteristic of blah-blah, and approximately twenty-two-one-hundreths of an inch in diameter?' No way. So crack is small and light-colored. So whatever it actually looks like, that's what it is on paper. And it's always true."

"Think about this," Sharpe said. "You get sent on a jump, I radio you to get the guy. You get the guy, find the drugs he just bought from the other guy. Now our other TAC guys get the other guy. All the drugs go to the lab, in those envelopes in that box right there, and two months from now we bring them back, and a month later we go to trial. Now, the chain of evidence means that anybody who touched that evidence has signed for it. You wrote your name forty-seven times just now, signing property forms. You're gonna do it again at the lab, transferring custody to them. You'll do it again in reverse when we bring it all back from the lab in a month or two. All to prove to the court, at trial, that the evidence in the lock-seal is in fact the evidence that you or whoever seized on whatever night it was."

Grbonscowicz shook his head silently.

"I grok you, man, to the fullness, but this is how it is. The lock-seal is individual. It has the suspect's name, the case number, the individual property number the records clerk gave it when you turned it in after the arrest. They're not all the same. But the way we describe the junk, yeah, it's the same, it's the way the court wants to hear it, or at least the way the defense can't go after it.

"We started it after Bergman got our first love boat bust last year. Broad daylight, on the sidewalk, guys selling boat. Easier than crack 'cause love boat is marijuana laced with PCP, and PCP is a liquid and it's skin-soluble, so they sold it in foil packets. Easy to see, easy to . . ." Swerve, pause. Sharpe was glad the snow had stopped. He went on.

"So the first trial we had? Bergman testifies to what was in the envelope. With love boat, the PCP makes the pot real green, like new grass on your lawn. So he reads that description off the lock-seal. Then he cuts open the envelope. He's on the stand, he's just told the jury it is green. And what comes out? Brown. Dried. Wrong color. We lost the case, just on that. Never mind all the lock-seal, evidence procedures, testimony. No, call it green and it's brown—we lose.

"So marijuana, love boat, it goes in the envelope and it's a greenish-brown leafy material. The same words, 'cause they work. No matter what it is when you put it in, it's greenish-brown. Crack is light-colored and irregular. Powder cocaine or heroin is whitish. Not white. Whitish. Money is bills of US currency. And that goes for the spotter too, that's how I'm gonna describe what I see, in my report and on the stand. I'm not lying, that's what I saw. And so we all testify the same."

516 looked over, the glance lingering a little too long for 511's comfort at seventy-five miles per hour. 511 said, "It's not

lying. Nothing we say is untrue. But it's the kind of truth we know works better than other versions."

"And nobody cares you, we, say the same shit over and over?"

"Nobody yet. Really hasn't come up as an issue. Only Circuit Court is taped, and nobody is comparing testimony there that I know. Machines are built-in in Circuit, but half of our cases go away before they get to Circuit Court anyway. A lot of suspects, they lose the prelim in General District, they plead to short time before it goes to the grand jury. Or they take a deal and plead to misdemeanor possession of drug paraphernalia, and the judge drops the felony drug charges if they agree to take drug counseling. And the paraphernalia deal means no jail time. So it comes up a lot in General District. Sometimes in GD we're on the stand case after case, and it's the same, it might stand out. General District doesn't have a central recording system, so sometimes the public defenders record us. They put a little tape recorder right up on the edge of the witness stand in front of us. They might notice we use the same words and make a complaint about it. So we'd look like we're perjuring ourselves, get in trouble, lose cases. But we got a way to deal with that."

"How many of them take the paraphernalia deal?" Grbonscowicz asked.

"Lots. Most, maybe," Sharpe answered.

"How many of them make it?"

"Huh? Make what?"

"Finish the deal, finish drug treatment."

"Oh, they all finish. Show up for meetings, take one piss test, but that's usually right after they got out of jail to take the deal, and they're clean in jail. But they don't make it *after* treatment." 511 sat up straight in the passenger seat. "We get them again." He blew air out, popping his cheeks, a hard sigh.

"How many again?"

"All of them. We call that job security. Turn in here, this is the lab."

Two hours later, they left the lab. Forty-seven signatures on evidence envelopes when delivered for processing. Fifty-two signatures on other envelopes being retrieved after testing. And fifty-two more when they dropped them off at Property.

Back in the tiny TAC office, 516 followed up on the earlier conversation.

"You said the public defenders record us and we have a way to deal with that. What did you mean?"

"Not a big deal. We only really do it to fuck with the defense, but we got so many cases going on, we, it's hard to keep them straight. Time they get to Circuit, they're pretty much weeded out and there's fewer of them. But in General District, we're on the stand all the time. Could we get something wrong, describe it the wrong way? Sure, maybe. Not so it would matter, we're always testifying from the evidence we've got, and it's in the reports or on the lock-seals. But what if we, one time, said something different between one case and the other? We lost that one I told you about, green stuff in the envelope and brown stuff out.

"We didn't want them to start pulling out tapes of our exact words from every time we ever testified." 511 bent down under the desk, removed a bulky, sturdily taped lock-seal and cut it open. An industrial-sized magnet slipped out of the envelope onto his desk with a thump. Paperclips and a pen jumped up off the desktop and flew to it.

"Carry this into court. Put it up on the stand next to your evidence, 'cause that's where they put their tape recorders. Magnet fuzzes out the tape. We've all got one. Here, wrap this one back up, and it'll be yours."

CHAPTER 17

Victims
Wednesday, November 2, 1988
1500–1600 HRS

DETECTIVE JOHN KELLY parked his dark green unmarked Chevrolet on the street outside the block-wide Alexandria Redevelopment and Housing Authority project and walked through a cut from the sidewalk into the interior courtyard. ARHA homes were two- and three-bedroom brick town-houses, built in banks of six-unit buildings. Three buildings flanked a courtyard, and three others faced these across narrow alleys and out to the city streets surrounding the project. These were officially named the Andrew Adkins Homes, but were known as the New Projects and, like the other three ARHA neighborhoods, were identified by police as a high drug area. The Jump-Outs routinely hit it several times a week. A jump the day before in a project three blocks east led to a pursuit and shoot-out and some heavy police attention, so few people were out and about. Afternoon school buses had just dropped children off. There was no snow this afternoon, so most stayed outside.

Ashby had ridden with him and stood by as Kelly knocked on the Stibbles' front door. Kelly needed his arrest partner to help shepherd Mom and the boy through trial tomorrow, to stand by with them while Kelly testified. So they could meet him before, Kelly had asked Ashby to accompany him today. Ashby had tried to get Kelly to talk about the evaluation he'd received hours earlier, but Kelly wouldn't discuss it. Which told Ashby what he needed to know.

"Fuckin' Sarge. He's so fulla shit. You know you do a great job." Ashby, who knew Kelly well and had watched him recently, said the reassuring words without much feeling.

Mrs. Stibble let them into a living room crowded with cheap furniture and a huge television on a stand. Kelly sat on one of a set of matching chairs with a faded brown pattern as she made them instant coffee. Kelly didn't need a fourth cup today but took it from the mother of his victim so she could feel useful. It was terrible, but she presented it proudly as she sat on the other chair. Ashby leaned against the wall in the opening between the living room and the kitchen.

Jumari sat on the arm of his mother's chair. He had his mother's large eyes, widened further by thick glasses, but the studious look contrasted with shoulders wide for a ten-year-old and big feet. He was already a star in the local Pee Wee football league and kept his grades high in third grade. He watched Kelly with interest and an accepting smile. Jumari's mom had told him Kelly helped with a problem with his dad, which he didn't understand but he listened to his mom. He glanced at Ashby with little interest. He didn't know what had happened, or almost happened, in San Francisco with his dad and Mr. Anders.

Mom hadn't known, either, until Kelly brought Jumari back, along with a letter found in Mr. Stibble's rental car and several photographs seized inside Anders's house. Kelly remembered her going quiet, sitting furious but silent in this house earlier that year, like an armed grenade thrown on a kitchen chair. But the only signs of her explosive anger, fear, confusion, and betrayal were tears that fauceted from her wide eyes into a growing pile of paper towels Kelly had pulled one by one from a roll he found on the kitchen counter.

"After we tracked them to California, I had the cops there arrest him on the warrant we got here." The PC for the warrant was simple in this case. Jumari Stibble was on a one-month court-ordered visitation with his estranged father Cedric, once a year in June of each year since his parents' divorce. When Cedric Stibble failed to return Jumari to his mother at midnight at the end of that visitation period, he was committing parental abduction as proscribed under Virginia criminal code.

Mom called police at three a.m. July 1. A midnight patrol took the missing person report, passed it to CID, and Kelly got it when he came in the next morning. It didn't appear to be a high-priority case, and Mrs. Stibble didn't answer the telephone that day, so they didn't meet till the next when she called furious at the lack of police response. Right after they hung up, he had driven to the New Projects and had two cups of horrible coffee with her while she spun her angry tale.

She and Stibble were married for a year before Jumari was born. They'd married solely so she could have a baby. Not a shotgun wedding, but by her plan to marry, then conceive and bear an honorable child by legal parents. This was hard for her for several reasons. One, she was dedicating her life to single parenthood since her plan called for a divorce from Stibble immediately upon the birth of the child. Two, she knew he was gay and had no interest in her sexually, which had actually made him more attractive to her as a life partner for reasons that took Kelly days to understand, and it took considerable effort for her to coax Stibble to their eventual mutual achievement. Cedric seemed to have agreed to the act, and the ongoing attached marital activity, almost as a lark. And three, she herself had no interest in sex whatsoever, because of what she referred to as her asexuality. Kelly had never heard the term and his police experience hadn't prepared him for a person who described herself as a homoromantic asexual, meaning she preferred the companionship of women but desired no physical or sexual intimacy. A direct and piercing interrogator, Kelly held himself back from probing at this, to him, unheard-of life path, but over days spent with her and developing rapport and respect for her and her hard work in raising a strong son in the projects, he finally couldn't stop one improper question from slipping out.

"And you don't think it is something that is, well, hormonal, like you, um . . . If you were to, if your system were off-kilter, kind of . . ." He ground to a halt as she, mercifully, rolled her eyes in amusement.

"You're asking, is something wrong with me? Let me ask you. You like women and you've got a wedding ring on, is that something that's right or wrong with you? No, that's just the way you are. And I am just that. Asexual. You could look it up. I didn't want anything to do with Cedric other than he could give me a baby. I told him he wouldn't owe me nothing, that's what I told the judge. It's nothing that's wrong with me. And I'll tell you, if you were a doctor and you said you could do something to change me to, well, to what y'all call normal? I don't think I would do it. I'm good with what I am. How about that?" And she sat and stared at him, hands on her knees, head canted to one side, eyes glinting.

How about that? Kelly thought. You really do learn something new every day. With this, he was done learning for a month.

"You want to tell me I'm a wrong way? What if somebody told you, John Kelly, tomorrow you gotta love men instead of women, just like that. Think you could do it? There's people tell gay people that all the time, say all you got to do is change. But you can't change. It's your way. It's what you are, and it ain't a bad thing. So's I thought, Cedric was that way, a gay way. And that's why he wasn't on me all the time, like most men. He didn't bring nothing home, he didn't talk about what he did, so I didn't know he were actually something worse. I didn't know nothing till you brought Jumari back to me, praise the Lord. He safe, 'cause of you. You want me to warm up your coffee?"

Interesting and forthright woman, Kelly had always thought.

Kelly had called a friend of his, a former cop who worked for a national credit card company. He quickly, without a warrant, pulled up Cedric Stibble's credit card history, tracking him across the country to California and to payments made at a gym where Stibble worked out regularly. Maybe not legal, but the location information would be attributed to an informant. Kelly faxed a copy of the parental abduction arrest warrant to the US Marshals, who had a simple time of staking out the gym and spotting Stibble. The boy wasn't with him, so they followed him to a man's house in the hills east of San Francisco. Stibble was arrested as he entered the front door, and the boy was found in a downstairs rec room, unhurt. The marshals searched Stibble's car for his identification and found a letter from the homeowner to Stibble dated a year prior, discussing in disgusting terms Stibble's offer of his son to the man in exchange for an unwritten amount of money. "But you will like him a lot, so I know you will show me that, a lot," he had written. Dollar specificity didn't matter, the clear contract did, and Kelly wanted that letter to be introduced in court so the judge could see that this was not simply a case of failing to meet a curfew, but was rape for sale.

There were photos, too, found by the marshals and San Francisco Police Department detectives who searched the house using a search warrant based on the rape contract letter. None of Jumari, thank God, but of other boys. Some clearly with Anders, the San Francisco homeowner, some with unidentifiable adult males. Some maybe of Stibble, Kelly hoped. He had planned on coordinating an ongoing investigation with SFPD and the marshals when they came out for the trial scheduled for tomorrow.

Which my prosecuting attorney nixed, Kelly thought, his bitterness bitten back and not shared with Jumari's mom in their trial planning. Which brought him to today.

"So, we're ready, right? Jumari is excused from school for the day, all day Thursday and maybe Friday too? I'll pick you up at nine. This is my partner, Larry Ashby. He's gonna be with us to help out. He didn't do the case, so he doesn't have to testify and he can hang around in case we need anything." He and Ashby donned identical good-guy grins to reassure her. Mrs. Stibble was a good woman in bad circumstances, fighting to raise a good son against bad influences, bad neighbors, a bad neighborhood, and a no-account freak of an ex-husband, keeping him safe, proud, strong, and unbent by the poverty and crime around them. Being a mother in this neighborhood was hard and ceaseless work, and when she failed, Kelly had rescued her son.

"I sent the note with him to school yesterday. They gave him extra homework today. He can do that tomorrow while we are waiting." She smiled proudly at Jumari, a studious kid in a neighborhood that didn't prize such effort, where some of his friends looked down on him for raising his hand in class and showing effort and enthusiasm. "Why don't you go get started on that right now, Jumy."

"Mom, I wanna stay. We can talk with Mr. Kelly." Jumari liked Kelly and had talked endlessly to him and the other cops during his rescue in California and the long flight home. Football, studies, school, even girls, a normalcy in contrast with his upbringing that relieved Kelly. Good kid, strong as his mom.

"You go ahead, Jumy. I'll see you tomorrow."

"Go now, Jumari. Homework or reading, go on." Meaning, *Get out of the room so I can talk with this man.*

After his feet thumped upstairs, Dora Stibble asked Kelly, "I know Cedric'll be there. That man Anders gonna be there too?" She bit down on the name.

"Yes. The defense gives us the names of people they will introduce as witnesses, and his name's on the list."

"What he got to say about this? We can ask him 'bout his plan?" Kelly had told her about the letter, the photos, the apparent plan Jumari's father had with Anders. Kelly didn't have the heart to tell her that. For tomorrow at least, Anders and Cedric Stibble would skate on their conspiracy to commit child rape. Kelly comforted himself with the knowledge that he wasn't supposed to discuss case testimony at all with witnesses and victims. He knew Duckworth was not going to introduce the letter or the photos. He hoped he could take advantage of some imprecise question, some door accidentally opened by Duckworth or the public defender, Rachel Cohen, to sneak them in himself. Duckworth might slip. *Cohen was too sharp,* he thought with hidden proprietary pride. Kelly drifted off a moment, thinking about Rachel and their future. *What would our child look like? Would she have red hair, like Rachel, or black like mine? Wait a minute, would she have to grow up Jewish? Her mom is Jewish, so that follows. I guess I'm not so strong a Catholic that it really matters to me. Does it? Could I convert? Would they take me?*

A crunching tap noise brought Kelly back from his reverie, coming from where Ashby had been standing near the kitchen. He saw that Dora Stibble was staring at him, and he apologized for momentarily zoning out.

"We let the prosecutor introduce information. About the plan or about the photographs. If he doesn't ask you, it will mean he asked me and doesn't have to ask you again." *Liar,* Kelly called himself, but he didn't want Mom getting all upset about this issue right now. Dad was going to jail, for whatever time he got here in Alexandria. The other stuff, maybe California, would go forward with charges. But the Alexandria case was classic open-and-shut. Did Dad have the kid? Yes. Was he supposed to return him at midnight on June 30, the last day of the month? Yes. Did he do that? No. So is he guilty? Yes.

Slam dunk.

"How come it's not gonna be downstairs in Juvenile Court?" Dora Stibble asked. "He's only ten. It's supposed to be there so juvenile cases don't get out in public, usually. Right?" *Jeez,* Kelly thought, surprised at her awareness of the court differences. *How'd she know that?*

"Yes, usually. In this case, they wanted it in the upstairs court. His attorney made a motion and got it moved. Honestly, probably better for us. Sometimes the judges in Juvie seem to want to make deals and let things go so families don't get too messed up. Upstairs, the judges might be harder on your hus—on Cedric than downstairs would." At least, that's what Kelly hoped. They were stricter in interpreting the law upstairs too. Less lenient, more prone to follow the exact letter of the law and not the spirit. Another *crunch-tap* sound from the kitchen, where Ashby was still out of sight. And another. What *was* that?

"Because I got my own photo of his dad from a while ago, while he was with me. I could show that too, show he always was wrong."

"Wrong? How's a photo show a man is wrong?" Kelly asked in all sincerity. This woman had surprised him once so far today. Twice?

"Found it cleaning." She reached into her purse, next to the chair, and took out a Polaroid picture. She handed it to Kelly and said, "Kind of man takes a picture of hisself with hisself like that?"

Kelly looked at the color instant photo. It depicted Cedric Stibble in a green sport shirt, only, in a mirror apparently taken by Stibble himself. His right hand was raised and held up the bulky Polaroid camera. His left hand was low and held something else bulky. Kelly was reminded of the line in Mel Brooks's movie *Blazing Saddles*, Madeline Kahn saying to Cleavon Little, "They say black men ah gifted. Oh, it's twue, it's twue." Kelly stifled his laugh, channeling it into a snort.

"I ask you, what kinda man does that an' takes a picture of it?"

"I don't know whether the judge will let that into evidence," Kelly recovered, "but we can show it to the prosecutor tomorrow and see if he wants to use it."

Crunch-tap, crunch-tap from the kitchen. Ashby twitched when he stepped into sight and said to Kelly, "Time we got on?"

Kelly didn't know why Ashby was interrupting, but he was done anyway. He told Mrs. Stibble again that they would see her at nine, and the detectives left. In the cruiser, rolling away from the project, Kelly looked at Ashby. "The fuck were you doing in the kitchen?"

Ashby looked at him and shivered. "Tell you later."

Kelly drove on but stopped as they passed through Old Town. He parked in a crosswalk near a florist, told Ashby to wait, and went inside. He asked the price to deliver a dozen red roses to an office near the courthouse. When he brushed back his jacket to retrieve his wallet, the clerk saw the gold badge clipped to his belt.

"You some kind of cop?"

"Some kind? The only kind."

"You works here in Alexandria?"

"That's right. But we don't get stuff cheap 'cause we're cops. You gotta charge me full price."

"Oh, that not why I'm asking. Just wanted to know." The kid took Kelly's credit card and asked Kelly what the note should say. After a moment, Kelly said, "An old life ends, and a new life begins."

The kid looked up from writing while Kelly spoke and watched him. "You a cop, huh? You ain't act like a cop."

"Yeah, cops don't send flowers? You get what I said?" Kelly inflated into tough-guy mode without thinking, squaring off on the kid and looking hard.

"Yeah, I gots it."

"And you can deliver it today?"

"That's extra."

"I want it sent today. You can do that?"

"Yeah, Mr. Police," the kid said, squaring right back at Kelly. "We can do that. We can do anything you want." He handed the slip over. Kelly signed it and left, wondering what the hostility was for, well beyond typical twenty-something dislike of authority.

Yeah, Mr. Police. We take care of you, the kid thought, and spiked the order on the bottom of the delivery list. *Fuckin' cops.*

Parking in back of headquarters, Kelly remembered. "What were you doing in the kitchen back there?"

"Huh?"

"You were banging something."

"Oh." Ashby paused, stopped walking across the lot. "She had roaches. All those units have 'em, nothing you can do. Clean or not, they come in from somewhere. Roaches. Ugh."

"So . . ."

"So I have my expandable baton, took it out, and I was using it to kill them on the wall across from me." He shuddered.

"And you just left them there, dead roaches?"

"Like I was gonna pick 'em up? Scrape 'em offa wall? Fuck that. Dead roaches. She a cleaning woman, she can clean them up. Looks like she cleans all the time anyway. Except for the roaches."

"She's not a cleaning woman. She's an office manager for a doctor. She works part-time so she can go home for Jumari after school." Kelly looked at his friend, who usually didn't display prejudice. Especially toward people of the same deep brown color as Ashby.

"Thirty-two of them," Ashby said, with another shiver.

"Thirty-two?" Kelly asked.

"Roaches." Ashby said.

"You counted?"

"I count things."

CHAPTER 18

File
Wednesday, November 2, 1988
1500–1600 HRS

LIEUTENANT WALTER RAMIREZ spent all afternoon chasing Kelly. The first time he missed him was when Kelly closed the door in the sergeant's office in CID. Ramirez had just tried Kelly's desk phone, but it went to voicemail so he left another message, his third that day.

Earlier today, Ramirez had been present during Officer Pammie Martinson's flaying. He'd come in earlier than his normal start time so he could be present at Pammie's roll call and her shooter's advisement. He and FTO Jackson watched the prick who shot at her walk out the courtroom door, the judge unable to quiet the shouting and chanting crowd, their shock only suppressed by their years of similar unfair experiences as police officers.

Charges dropped. Free to go.

But not if he could help it. He had an idea.

"Did you hear what the judge said at the end? No? Yeah, me neither. I saw something, I think. Let's talk." The lieutenant and Jackson stayed at the back of the courtroom till the bulk of the loud crowd flowed out the door. When Pammie started out, the lieutenant turned and preceded her through the door and down the hall, while the FTO waited till she cleared the court before following her. They walked along, flanking her, an escort unnoticed by the stunned and sullen young officer, shepherding her until she got on the elevator to return to the CA's office to retrieve her gun and sign out.

He couldn't act then because the clerk was still busy in the courtroom, so they too retrieved their guns and hit the street, the lieutenant to do whatever commanders did (*nothing*, most street cops thought) and the FTO to kill time till his recruit came in.

"There's only so much you can do," the lieutenant told Jackson, and he said, "So we do what we can."

Lieutenant Ramirez and FTO Jackson came back to the courthouse in the early afternoon. They went to the second floor and entered the "Employees Only" door next to the public service window, into the interior of the General District Court Clerk's Office. File cabinets along three walls held current traffic and minor criminal cases pending adjudication, and rooms down the hall held papers on completed cases. Desks for the clerks were in the center of the room, most with neat piles of manila folders, typed and printed documents, phones, and computers.

They walked to one of the desks, occupied by a thin, older woman in a neat dress. She looked up at him over half-rim glasses and smiled.

"Well, hello there, Walt," she said, her face shifting from bored to beaming as she took in the lieutenant and the FTO.

"Saw you in earlier with Herb. You don't get in here much anymore, do you?"

"No, Valerie. Lieutenants don't arrest people much."

"You used to, a lot," she told Ramirez, and looked at Jackson. "He led the Department in DUIs for three years before he went up the ladder. Must be what got him promoted."

"Nah, we don't promote for hard police work. We promote for being able to get other folks to do all the hard work." The lieutenant knew that Valerie King was the queen of hard work in the General District Court Clerk's office. Always capable of pulling off miracles like getting favorite cops' cases moved to first in line, or last if they were running late. He went on.

"Speaking of hard work, you were there for Officer Martinson's guy's advisement. When you saw me today was when Pammie was on the stand."

"Oy, what a mess. Poor kid. Going through all she did yesterday, and then all this today. She must be so upset." Valerie leaned forward. "I'm surprised the suspect only had a broken nose, with all that happened. Y'all are training them better now. Old days, Walter, he'd have fallen down the stairs a few times."

"We don't do that now, Valerie. We're a better place for it, but you know you can understand where that came from. But what's really the reason is . . ." And again, a glance around. Ramirez leaned in as Jackson took a step back. "How'd that case end?"

"How'd it end? You were there, you know how it ended. He walked. I've never . . . Judge Fish gets mad sometimes, but I've never seen him take it out on an officer like that before." Valerie paused, coloring slightly as she realized she was criticizing a judge. "He doesn't like when cops, oh, sorry, officers go old-school on defendants, even ones that deserve it. Not that I'm saying Mr. Goodell deserved it, innocent till proven guilty and all."

"Crap, Val. Innocent till proven guilty is for inside the courtroom, nowhere else. Out on the street, he's guilty as shit, and lucky he's not dead. Letting the guy go was . . . unusual." A lot of other things, too, but the LT wouldn't say them aloud in an office setting. He put both hands on the desk and leaned forward, lowering his voice. "No, what I'm getting at is, what did the judge say, at the end?"

"Well, he let Goodell walk out. He dropped the charges."

"Yeah, but how'd you write it? In the file. Did you write dismissed or nol prossed?"

She stared.

The lieutenant reminded her. "It got super loud, almost out of control. Judge Fish banging his hand on the front of the bench, folks yelling. To me, at the end, it didn't look like you wrote anything at all in the file."

Her stare squeezed into a frown at him.

"Herb and I were thinking, maybe you didn't write down what Judge Fish said, there at the end." Her frown led to pursed lips. "Maybe you didn't mark down the ruling. Yet."

And the furrows in her brow disappeared above a growing smile as Valerie caught on. She pulled a pile of folders out of a tray on her desk, rooted down a bit from the top, and removed one. She paused and looked up from it at the lieutenant and back down. The smile now faded into a worried look.

"I, I got to . . . You know how loud it was in there. Even with me sitting right by the bench, it got so loud at the end there that . . . It can only be one of two ways."

"Yeah," Lieutenant Ramirez said. "But one way means a bad thing, and the other way means not so bad. What'd you write down?"

She opened the file and displayed the top sheet of paper. It was green, as were all felony arrest warrants, the arrest warrant Pammie Martinson had sworn out before a magistrate last night after the pursuit and shooting. It bore the defendant's full name and identifiers, the full charge and code section on which he was arrested, and the name of the arresting officer. A large column on one side was left blank, eventually filled with notes documenting court proceedings. Today, recorded in her own penmanship, Valerie could read:

> *ADVISEMENT November 9, 1988.*
> *Judge: A. Fish.*
> *Def. Atty: PD R. Cohen*

It was writing she'd started at the calm beginning of the case when the courtroom was quiet and under control. And hadn't finished in the chaos at the end.

Valerie leaned back in her chair and looked at Ramirez, astonished. "It's blank. I didn't write anything. I don't know what he said."

"And what if I told you," murmured Ramirez, still leaning on her desk, "that I was sure that I read his lips, and I can tell you exactly which way the judge ruled." Jackson scanned the room. Valerie faced Ramirez full on.

"You know what you're saying?"

"I do."

"And you know what you're asking?"

"Val, I most certainly do. And you know why I'd ask. Can you imagine a favor on anything more important than this?" *As risky to ask as to do*, Ramirez thought. The transition from an idea to an act, now, through the dark door. "And not a word of this, or I'll hang you," he said with a wink.

A thousand words swirled behind her eyes. A full minute she looked at the file, and at the lieutenant and the FTO, and at the door to judges' chambers. Then she picked up a pen, discarded it for the one she had used in court, and began to write. Just two words.

CHAPTER 19

Doomed
Wednesday, November 2, 1988
4 p.m.–11 p.m.

AFTER HER THREE afternoon preliminary hearings, Public Defender Rachel Cohen stopped by the Circuit Court clerk's office. She was trying to find what was happening with the case against Stick. He was due for a motion to suppress tomorrow on busy Commonwealth Day, but the clerks had no copy of her filings, or the warrant, or any file altogether. The only official indication that he was ever in the system was Stick's name—his real name, Antonio Planter—on the computer printout of the Commonwealth Day docket, listing which cases were to be where in the three active courtrooms tomorrow. Odd.

She had lost two of the three prelims today. A loss meant the case proceeded to the grand jury, a win meant the judge had decided there was insufficient probable cause to proceed. She won one only because the complaining witness, a security guard at a department store, failed to appear to testify against an alleged shoplifter. As she walked out of the courthouse, behind two uniformed officers, one in a white shirt, one in gray, she shook her head over the two loser cases. Both were TAC arrests, and again she hoped her tape recorder had captured what her handwritten notes showed: identical words in identical testimony in separate drug jumps.

Done with the courthouse for the day, Rachel absently followed the broad-shouldered, uniformed black patrolman and the white-shirt commander, who appeared Hispanic, off the elevator and out the lobby door. The two cops talked quietly, looking around the way they all did but paying no attention to her. She was too close behind them, but they had already dismissed her as no threat—female, short, well-dressed, at least in her opinion. Attractive? She hoped but didn't think much about it. Lawyer-looking, professional, clean, so probably unlikely to pull a gun and shoot them without warning, the threat that her boyfriend Kelly said cops see everywhere. *Boyfriend.* She rolled that label around in her mind.

Her boyfriend. Lover, mmmmm. The father of her child? Yes. Yes! A new label and still hard to apply. Rachel had only had a night and a day to begin thinking of the new life inside her, or at least the indication of such life as was shown in a little pink cross on the plastic window of the pregnancy test she'd bought at a Rite Aid and used to test her urine (*yuck!*) last night. The positive test was shocking, though really not surprising in light of, well, their activity. And frequency. And careless urgency, as if the new child she now imagined she could feel growing inside her resulted not from thoughtless disregard but secret yearning toward something they both needed and wanted to make happen. They hadn't discussed it, but Rachel felt strongly that Kelly was right for her, right to be the father of her children, despite the short time they had been involved with each other. Or at least she willed her heart to make it right.

Six, no, seven months now. Kelly swore his marital failure greatly predated their dating and the split had been imminent and certain before Kelly even met Rachel at the bar and took her for ice cream. And met again at the coffee shop, and at another bar, and walking between her office and the courthouse—a favorite interception point for him, reluctant as he was to call and leave messages with her nosy secretary. She reached him via his pager.

So rapt was Rachel's reverie over Kelly and the growing evidence of their love that it took about a minute for her to recognize that the cops in front of her were saying his name. As she caught it again, her mind tried to play back the conversation that had just passed. *Are they talking about John Kelly? My Kelly?*

"So that's the thing we're coming in early again tomorrow for, Kelly's thing?" said the black one.

"Yeah, but it's not Kelly's thing," said the white shirt. "It's Ashby's case but it was Kell's guy. The guy who killed his niece. His name was Pickett, a bad guy but not a known sex offender before all this."

Rachel thought, *Kelly's niece was* KILLED? He'd never told her. She listened to the bulky black officer.

"Pickett died in jail before trial for killing her, aneurysm, his brain blew out. We thought somebody beat him down, and maybe they did but it never came out. Who's gonna look that close? Jail staff? They don't want to find a murder inside. Us? Fuck him, it's justice." The bulky cop kept looking forward and around as he walked but never directly backward where Rachel kept close and strained to listen. They stopped at a corner and waited for the light, no traffic but not jaywalking, no sir.

"But we still need his head," said the white shirt, and Rachel reeled at the imagery. "Will Kelly be there for the dig?"

"No, he's got a trial tomorrow, parental abduction." And
with that, Rachel knew for certain it was her Kelly about whom
they spoke. She had a bench trial tomorrow with Kelly. She was
going to win even though the cops had a tight case. She had a
secret weapon. It would hurt Kelly. Maybe even destroy him,
hurt him at work. He'd be crushed, and more than angry with
her. It could kill their, what should she call it, relationship?
Romance? Love? Parenting? *Oh, my God.* But to Rachel, she
had no choice, had to do it for her client despite the damage
it might do Kelly, or their connection of whatever name. But
now what she was hearing meant something else was going on.
She couldn't hear it all, traffic noises and bus rumbles covering
some of the cops' words. Some came clear.

"So, basically, he destroyed evidence."

WHAT? Rachel stretched her ears.

"Something like that. At least discharged a firearm in the
city limits. Broke written directives out the whazzoo." Rachel
heard the big officer sigh. "And now we probably can't clear
some apparently innocent kid of something heinous. It's evidence we didn't know we had, in a case that Ashby couldn't
close. That probably gets to Kelly as much as losing his job or
being charged will."

LOSING HIS JOB, Rachel shouted in her mind. *BEING
CHARGED. Oh, John.*

"So Kelly is doomed. He'll be lucky if he isn't indicted,"
the black one said. "He might end up in jail. Either way his
career's shot . . . What, you disagree?" The light changed and
they began to cross as the older one said something more about
a plan, but Rachel could no longer hear for the rushing in her
ears.

It hit her like a physical blow. *DOOMED.* A punch to the
abdomen hard enough to make her double over. And she did,
bending at the waist to seek relief from a shuddering, grabbing

pain suddenly tearing through her belly, like broken glass bursting in her. She dropped her briefcase in the roadway to clutch her middle and whimper. The two cops whirled as Rachel collapsed to her knees on the hard street, toes of her dark pumps scuffing as her slender ankles absently kept her feet moving despite her fall. The gray-shirted officer was next to her and held her shoulders as the white shirt stepped around to block her from car traffic and spoke into his radio.

"Do you need an ambulance?" said the cop holding her. "We can get one in a minute. Do you know what's wrong? Do you have a medical condition, miss? Do you need a doctor?" He repeated this over and over until his calming but demanding tone got through to her. She raised her head and looked at him without focus.

"No, I, my office is just right there."

"I know, miss. But I don't think you can wait. I want to call you an ambulance right now. No, I'm going to do that. Tell me your name, I'll call your office, or take your bags there, but you need a doctor. Right now."

"No, I'm just, it just hurts, it'll go away." Rachel told him her name and squinted past him at the clouds, oddly bright. She closed then clenched her eyes.

"Okay, it will. You'll be all right," said the large black officer, his voice trying to reassure her. "And a doctor will tell us both that it will go away. Now, sure it's the street but you can stay right here for now. It's our street, you'll be safe with us. Now, why don't you lean back a bit and lie down? I'm gonna put your feet up on your briefcase for a minute. You'll be okay."

He removed his stiff, dark blue jacket and draped it over her body against the November wind. As he did, his eyes flashed with worry. Rachel was paler now when she tried to speak with him. "I'm preg . . ." was as far as she could get.

"All right, Miss Cohen. It'll be all right." He squeezed her shoulder and her face tilted toward him. He let her chin rest against his bracing wrist and turned as if to speak with the other one, hiding his worried face from her for a moment until it reverted to a cool, professional mask. A siren was already audible. Jackson and Ramirez were grateful for the promptness: they had noticed but not remarked on the spreading dark stain on the back of her gray skirt. She was onto a gurney, into the ambulance, and en route to Alexandria Hospital within five minutes of going down.

She'd insisted on keeping her briefcase from the cops, full of information on defendants (crooks to them). She held it feebly on her lap as they lifted her in. The FTO recovered his jacket and put it on after checking for blood. He went to the Public Defender's Office and told the secretary that one of their attorneys had taken sick and was being hospitalized. When the secretary promised to inform her boss, the FTO left.

Seven hours later, Rachel was being driven home by her boss, Barbara Dodson. Rachel was a public defender: Dodson was *the* public defender, who had hired Rachel from the Harrisonburg PD's office less than a year ago. Dodson was a mother hen and beside herself with worry about her new attorney but didn't let on. She also didn't let on that she knew what had happened to Rachel, though Rachel herself hadn't revealed it. Dodson, once a candy striper, knew enough medical terminology muttered by staff or scribbled on charts left hanging on bed frames to know that Rachel had suffered a miscarriage. Dodson was unaware of the relationship Rachel had with whoever the father was. "Mrs. Cohen," the charge nurse had said at one point.

"Miss," Rachel corrected, and watched the nurse's eyes flash down to her ringless left hand and go flat.

Taking her home was not what Dodson wanted to do. She had wanted Rachel to stay at the hospital, at least one night.

The emergency room staff was on Dodson's side on this but bowed to Rachel's insistence that she be released.

Rachel gave no reason but felt she had a good one, even though she wouldn't tell her own boss. She couldn't miss court the next day. She knew Dodson would insist on either taking on Rachel's Commonwealth Day case load herself or going before the judges to request continuances that they would surely grant for such a medical emergency. But Rachel couldn't risk a continuance of even one week on the Stibble case, her main case tomorrow. If she waited, everything changed. And she'd lose one of the few cases where things were lining up for a win. Not that her client was innocent, far from it. Just that this week, the law would find him not guilty. And next week the law would change and he'd go to jail. She knew from a friend working as a staffer at the state capitol that an amendment to rewrite the law was scheduled to come up for a vote in the Senate. Whether it passed, just the fact of a vote would alert the prosecutor and Kelly of a case weakness and he could reopen the investigation and plug the hole.

So she gritted her teeth, hardened her heart, pretended to ignore her loss, and wished that Kelly were with her. Once home, settled on her couch with tea Dodson had brewed and new bottles of antibiotics, painkillers and anti-inflammatories on a tray next to her, she was free to call Kelly's pager with a "hELLO" message. Their secret code, a request for him to call her if he could.

She followed up with five more "hELLOs." And finally, driven past caution by physical and emotional pain, she began telephoning his cell and his home. *Kelly, I need you*, she thought, but without a machine at the other end, she couldn't leave the message. Calling over and over. To no avail.

Oh, Kelly.

CHAPTER 20

Street
Wednesday in, like, November, Right?
After Dinner

STICK PLANTER'S MOTHER told him not to go out, like she always did, but he ignored her like he always did because he had business to do.

Nine p.m. and it was sleeting, in the thirties, unusually cold for November in Alexandria. Stick didn't own a coat; rather, he no longer had the coat his mom bought him last winter. He had left it in somebody's car, or somebody's house or on the Metro that one time he took it to a hip-hop show at the D.C. Armory. Chuck Brown. Stick just knew he could do that sound like that, if he wanted to. *Boogie Get Down.* He just had other stuff going on, other business to do. That man Chuck had talent, though.

Stick's business to do was the same he hadn't finished doing that morning. He hadn't sold out before school, had to get on the bus with three rocks, and had to carry them through classes. He held up all day to the mental pressure, the rocks calling to him to smoke down in the boy's room sometime but he held off. He was proud of that. Showed he wasn't addicted. He would come home after school and help his sister with her babies till his mom got home from work. Mom brought home her dinner from the cafeteria at her office. Stick was on his own for dinner, not that he'd cook anything. He would get some chicken while he was out or get some punk to run get him some. He might spend fifty dollars to get a bucket. It was through such poor economy that most of his money was wasted. But he looked good throwing out the fifties.

When he went out the door now, in the evening, it was not his usual time to work, but crackheads didn't keep a schedule. "They awake, they out of rock, they be coming by" is what he told Skeeter and Go-Go Hop and Beebo. They were out front of his house, looking at him, talking like, "Wha'chu doin' out now, nigga?"

"Working, what you doing?"

"Nothin', just hangin. Watchin' the fool popo crashin' they cars."

They were looking at a car wreck, lots of cops around for not much damage. It was one of the little cars that the Jump-Outs drove, different ones all the time, smaller than normal cop cars and the big old sedans that the gangsters called hoopdies. He didn't know much from cars, he just knew that they'd crashed one, and it got them all upset. Stick didn't have a license, so he didn't know what all the fuss was about. There were cops talking and writing in little notebooks. Other cops in white shirts came and pointed at stuff.

He stood down the block and watched the flashing red lights of the tow truck as it backed up to pull the cop car off a fence. As he told a friend later: "Popo told us, Beebo 'n' me, to go away. The man be sayin', 'Clear the sidewalk.' Beebo be like, 'Sidewalks free to walk on in America, right?' I be like, 'You right, nig. Popo ain't tellin' us we got to go places. Fuck that shit. Givin' us orders. We goin' 'cause we gots business to attend to.'"

Stick gave a Nazi salute to the last officer giving orders to clear bystanders away, because he'd seen a movie once in which an actor had said "order" when he raised his right hand, out at head level, fingers up and palm down. Stick could not have described what a Nazi was or picked Adolf Hitler out of a photo lineup. He didn't know about history or the Holocaust or persecution of the Jews. He knew he didn't like Jews, wasn't sure why and had never knowingly met one other than his lawyer Miss Cohen.

He had called her Mizz Kike last week when he met with Professor Vulture to discuss him putting a hex on the criminal case against him, smiling like he was tough-guy funny. Professor Vulture looked down at Stick and said, "That's hate. That's bad juju. You knock it off." *Huh?*

Stick had gone to see Professor Vulture at the instruction of his grandmother, who knew the voodoo witch doctor from years before, when he first came to Alexandria from coastal South Carolina, but he was originally from some place called Belize. She called him and set up an appointment. Stick found the professor's real name in a display case in the lobby by the elevator. Amato Higgenbotham. Stick had to say that one three times to himself. He'd never heard another like it.

"Professor gon' make it go away for you, but you got to pay him some of that bad money you makin' off that crack," Gramma said. "He gon' put a hex on it."

Two weeks ago, Stick had ridden the bus south on Washington Street through the heart of Old Town. There were high-rise apartments on one side, low garden apartments on the other, and a luxury condo was the last building in town.

That was Professor Vulture's address. Stick had started to tell what he was going through, but the witch doctor stopped him. "I know what they say, and I know what you say. And I know what you need, to send it away. You don't need a hex, boy. Nah, I'll put a root on it for you,"

"How you know about my case? What'chu do with it?"

Stick had never been down this way before, the southern end of the city. There was nothing there or beyond but the George Washington Parkway, a wide road going through parkland along the riverbank. Nothing that would bring Stick or his friends this way. No recreation center, no parked cars with other people's stuff in them, no buyers driving in from the burbs and signaling and pulling over. In nineteen years, Stick had never gone anyplace just for fun or for beauty. His parent had not shown him how or why to do that.

"Hex be to make things bad. You don't need nothing to go bad. You just need something be forgotten. You're small, he he, you're *still* small, they'll forget you when I put a root on you."

Stick paid the two hundred dollars his granmom had given him, and Professor Vulture, taller, thinner, and darker than Stick and maybe sixty years older, sat him down at a large, dark brown dining room table near a window overlooking the Potomac River nine stories below. It was a spectacular view, one that Stick had never seen, but which the nineteen-year-old failed to even glance at, so engrossed he was at Professor Vulture's look and demeanor. The professor reached into a chest of drawers in his dining room and took out some jars. There were markings in paint on the jars and Stick read them as the startling man worked. The witch doctor, in a green velvet jacket over black tuxedo pants, wore tinted eyeglasses even though he was inside. They held his thick braids, tinted light brown, away from his face. He took what looked like an old french fry, tan and brown and stiff, out of one jar marked "Creek Bank."

"This a root. It's from my homeland. It's got powers."

He took dirt out of another jar marked "Cimitiere" and made a small pile of it on the scarred dining room table. Stick read the label and pronounced, "Cemetery," because he couldn't spell. Accidentally right. Professor Vulture left the room and returned with a short length of rusty chain and arranged this in a circle around the dirt, then placed some french fry–looking things on the pile. He then went to the refrigerator and removed a shoebox. He opened the box at the table and removed a sandwich bag with a brown, dried sticky thing in it. He waved this over the pile and placed it carefully atop the root, then sat at a chair across from Stick with the pile between them. He placed his hands flat on the table on either side and hummed a minute, then spoke.

"Pigeon heart. Almost as good as owl, but we don't have owls here I can catch. I'm an old man," he told Stick, the glint in his eyes imperceptible through the shades, two-color beard bristling out from his jaw. He sat quietly and stared just over Stick's head and out the window for five minutes before Stick gave up and spoke.

"Now what we do?"

"Now we are done, boy. The roots got what you need. You gots three. You take them roots there, you pick them up now. Take one and when you go into the court, you at the door, you break it in half. And you eat the one half. Then you go inside and you look at the judge. You got to look at him for an hour."

"While I'm eatin' it?"

"Nope. You got to chew it, and it's hard. You chew it before you go inside. Then you go and look at him. For one hour. Then you leave, because you can leave. And when you get out of the court, you eat the other half. You got to eat that other half right then or bad juju comes. Then you're done."

The huge witch doctor leaned forward across the table, tilting his head down till his eyes rose above the tops of his Jackie O glasses like pale yellow suns, dreadlocks swinging forward. "An' maybe you'll be stayin' out that court building from now on, and you don't get yourself arrested anymore. You find some other way to make your money."

Stick wanted out, wanted to get away from the crazy man wanting him to eat some root. But he wanted to get away from the charges too, and that bad juju stuff, so he planned to do what Professor Vulture said.

"Get outta here, I'm calling my sister now on the telephone," Vulture said. Stick got out. As to getting out of drug selling, he'd have to think more on that. Do his voodoo in the court, then he'd think about his next steps.

So tonight, after he'd sold his last three rocks by just going around the block, he came back and watched the police looking foolish around their crashed cop car. He and Beebo took to trying to listen to them. Popo kept telling folks to walk away, but Stick and Beebo just turned their backs on the uniformed patrol officers and, step by slow step, backed up till they were close enough to hear them. Like they were invisible.

Stick and Beebo got twenty feet from a clump of Jump-Outs in normal-people clothing, closer still to a mad cop in a gray uniform shirt and full utility belt and another in a white shirt who looked maddest. The white shirt said, "Distracted? You're going with distracted? That's what he told you?"

"He was, he did," the gray shirt said. "He said thought he saw the kid who robbed Adrienne last summer, so he was trying to pull over quick. He misjudged the distance to the curb and . . ."

"Misjudged? He drove straight over the curb and into a fence in a yard. That's a big misjudgment. How does he say he recognized the robber?" *White shirt man's words were calm*, Stick thought, *but his voice was angry.*

"I dunno. He says the kid just looked right for it."

"He get him?"

"Nah, boofer skipped when the car got stuck in the fence and got away. Anyways they all look alike." Stick and Beebo didn't see the white shirt give the gray shirt a stink-eye for the way he was talking. Didn't see their expressions to recognize that the gray shirt was putting on a front.

"This was when we had whatsername from Manassas buying for us? When she got hit that time?"

"Yeah, a stickup boy punched her in the face." Stick's ears tingled. "Grabbed her buy money and laughed. Busted her lip good."

Damn, Stick thought, *there's more than me out here bustin' 'em up. Maybe I get back into that. That some easy money.*

"He lying? Sounds like a good story to tell to get your ass out of trouble for wrecking a car. How could he recognize the robber's face, he never saw him, only our girl from Manassas saw him."

"Lying? No, he's not a liar. No, really. He'd just take his lumps for the crash. He's had 'em before, we all have. Drive a car for ten hours a day, you're gonna have a crash."

"Did you?" the white shirt asked the gray.

"Well, no, but I was a pussy. I never did any real police work, just sucked up to the command structure. You know how we sergeants are, we don't do nothing."

At this, Stick turned to watch, cops talking funny, and saw the one with the white shirt reach up and touch some metal pinned to the front of the one in the gray shirt. "I wrote you up for these two commendations. They're not nothing."

"You know what I mean. He saw something. It's not a real big deal. Scrapes on the car, and we can bend the fence back.

We found the owner, well, not the owner, but the lady who rents this unit. Getting a counseling letter for his squad file's about all that has to happen in the end."

"I can make that happen."

"I know. Thanks, LT."

CHAPTER 21

Sleep
Wednesday, November 2, 1988
2300 HRS–Midnight

DETECTIVE JOHN KELLY was dead to the world. He was asleep on the hardwood floor inside his front door, the woven doormat clumped up beyond his feet. It had slipped out from under him as he leaned on the doorframe, fumbling with the knob on his way back out. He'd been leaving to drive to Rachel's apartment but ran afoul of the law of gravity, aided and abetted by a blood alcohol content of about .25 percent. The legal limit was .08 but he was a cop so . . .

He lay on his gun side, and the squared-off lump of his holstered revolver hard on his hip should have been uncomfortable. The open bottle of Jameson near his left hand would have spilled but it was empty. The phone's persistent, then inconsistent, rings could have awakened him but failed. A decorative clock on a living room mantel was about to bong midnight, but Kelly wouldn't hear that, either.

He'd been home for two hours. He would stand by the phone and think of Rachel, then walk by the door and think of his car and driving to her apartment, then look for his keys but find a drink in his hand instead. His quest turned into pace laps around his house, living room to kitchen to dining room, orbiting the central staircase to the upstairs bedrooms.

For what had become a bachelor pad seven months ago, Kelly's three-bedroom home was surprisingly clean. Despite the absence of a woman's touch, the bathrooms were not filthy, the kitchen not overrun with dishes and dirt. Laundry was picked up, washed, folded, and put away. Kelly kept it clean.

But no longer neat, not this week. Since Tuesday, Kelly had let things go. Only two days, but two six-packs' worth of beer bottles lay in various corners, on tables, in the bathtub. Yesterday's muddy clothes, brown at the knees and elbows, maybe a vomit spot on the shirt front, were clumped at the foot of the bed where he'd shrugged them off when he awoke this morning. Matching mud stained the bedsheets where he'd slept without undressing that night, home and depressed and drinking.

Tonight he'd come home elated and had a drink or two to note some old-fashioned real police work that he got into for a short moment on the way from Headquarters to his small three-bedroom in Alexandria's quiet West End. After meeting with the Stibble family, he and Ashby had gone back to HQ, he to complete a supplement on the Stibble interview, his partner to do something similar. A few hours later, beyond his normal end time but making up for coming in late, he left HQ and got into his unmarked for the ride home. The car's radio came on with the ignition, and Kelly heard an officer nearby report that he was making a felony traffic stop. Kelly's tires, and those of another patrol officer starting a night shift, splashed slush squealing out of the lot.

In ramping up attention and response, calling in a felony stop was the equivalent of a pilot declaring an emergency landing. It meant officers thought there was a likelihood of weaponry in the target car, so its occupants would be treated as armed and dangerous. That was fun, and fun brings cops out of the woodwork. After less than a minute, Kelly and the uniformed officer from Headquarters skidded up behind the car originating the call and scrambled out, Kelly with his handgun drawn, the uniform arming his shotgun with a loud *clack-caclack*. Sleet bounced off the shiny black brim of the uniform's eight-point hat.

Kelly stepped to the rear of the first cruiser. It was properly pulled behind a green minivan, properly meaning the cruiser was not in line but was offset by about half a car's width to the left, protruding into traffic to afford an officer a safe space free of close-passing cars.

The primary officer had his driver's side door open, though he was still sitting behind the wheel. A car door didn't stop bullets, so it was considered concealment. Cover was a car engine block that did. His spotlight, mounted on the windshield post, was on and aimed at the back of the target's head, ideally catching both his mirrors and blinding him. Kelly had positioned his car even farther left to completely block traffic in the curb lane, switching on his emergency lights in the back window and turning off his headlights so as not to backlight himself and the primary officer. The secondary officer with the shotgun had pulled his cruiser to the right behind the target, half onto the sidewalk, and lit the target car up with his own lights.

Other sirens closing in the distance, Kelly spoke to the primary officer. "What's up?"

"Tag shows reported stolen out of Fairfax County. Suspects listed as two black males. There's two in there. They got squirrely when I passed them on Duke, made a quick cut down here. You ready?"

"I'm good," Kelly said, as did the backup with the shotgun. And the dance began.

"Driver of the green minivan," bellowed the primary over the cruiser public address loudspeaker, using a different microphone not connected to the radio, "this is the Alexandria Police Department. You are under arrest at this time. Do not make any movement until I tell you what to do." The primary glanced back at Kelly and Kelly nodded. Their minds were matched: okay, legal requirements covered, if the subjects do anything stupid now, it's their fault. As Kelly's FTO, Herbert Jackson, had taught him: cops don't shoot people, people get themselves shot by doing stupid things.

"You are considered armed and dangerous, and you will be shot if you do not do exactly what I tell you." The young cop sounded calm. Kelly had been through dozens of felony vehicle stops but still felt the shiver of excitement up his back and the hollow in his belly of, not fear, but realistic expectation of violence.

"Driver, when I tell you, reach your left hand over and open the window next to you. Do it now." After a moment, a cloud of steam showed the officers that the window had opened to the cold. "Driver, when I tell you to, use your right hand to turn off the car, remove the keys, and throw them out the window. Do it now." They never did that, first time. Throw my keys away? Second time, the target gently tossed them onto his own roof. Good enough.

"Driver, when I tell you to, reach your left hand out the window and open your car door. Then step out of the car and face away from me. Do it now." Other cruisers arrived, other officers arraying themselves around next to Kelly, behind the two cruisers closest to the action.

It was the action that thrilled Kelly. And the simplicity. All of his job was pared down to this simple moment: I'm a cop, this is my gun, there's the bad guy. I'm in control. Little was so simple anymore.

"Driver, when I tell you to, begin walking backward toward me and stop when you get to the back of your car. Don't turn around, just walk. Do it now."

I'm ready, Kelly thought. *I know what to do here, and so do my partners.* Gratifying confidence.

"Driver, stop there. Now, when I tell you to, reach your hands down and pull up your jacket and your shirt so I can see your belly. Then turn around all the way, one time, and face away from me. Do it now."

We got him. If he has a gun in his beltline, we got him, Kelly thought. *If he spins and shoots, he will naturally aim toward the spotlights, they all do. That's why we're not right behind them.*

"Got a gun." They could all see what looked like the dark brown butt of a handgun over the top of the suspect's pants, a lump at the center of his torso under his belly button. Another cop shotgun was racked, but the only speaker was the primary officer. Kelly's heart pounded unnoticed. Vision tunneled.

"Driver, put your hands on top of your head and interlace your fingers. Do it now. Put your fingers together. If you reach down, we will kill you. Hands together. Do it." Voice just as calm, but more intense, and the driver could tell. His movements became very deliberate. His fingers first spread over his head like he was catching a basketball, then fitted together and down tight on top of his head.

"Driver, keep your hands like that, and begin walking backward toward the sound of my voice. Do not turn around. Keep walking backward till I tell you to stop. Do it now. Slowly."

Kelly holstered his revolver and moved up next to the primary. A sergeant sent a newly arrived officer up, and he positioned himself next to Kelly, and when the primary ordered the driver to stop, they moved forward in tandem. The uniform grabbed the suspect's left hand and cuffed it while Kelly brought down the right hand to be cuffed. Then Kelly reached around the suspect's waist to get the gun. Which turned out to be a wallet.

Nonetheless, still a suspect, with another in the van. So Kelly and the uniform walked backward with the suspect between them and whoever was still in the van. As cover. They took him farther back, through several layers of parked cop cars, and searched him while the primary and another arrest team corralled and cuffed the van's passenger. And uncuffed them a few minutes later.

Investigation revealed the following: The driver was the owner of the green 1984 Dodge Caravan. He lived in Washington, D.C., but worked in Fairfax. Four days ago he had reported the van stolen to the Fairfax County Police Department. When he found it two days later, he neglected to notify FCPD, so the stolen listing was never removed from NCIC, the National Crime Information Computer.

"I forgot where I parked it, man. All this 'cause I forgot?" said the driver. His passenger had turned out to be short-haired female. They were on a first date.

"No second date ever again," guessed the primary officer as it all broke down.

"Dunno," Kelly said. "Kinda exciting date. All these pretty lights. Getting on toward Christmas season."

The driver couldn't explain why he carried his wallet folded over and half tucked into his beltline and wouldn't accept that it looked like a gun.

"Ended up all right," the primary said. "We mighta' smoked him if he reached for it wrong."

"Well, you told him what to do. If he does something else, he's stupid. Stupid people are job security too."

"I thought the passenger was a guy."

"Looked like a guy from the rear," Kelly agreed. "Once I stopped a guy, he was sitting in front of me at a light in a Mustang. I could see he wasn't using seat belts, neither was the little kid in the front seat, they were hanging free. He peeled out, I lit him up right then. I get his license and reg, and say, 'Is this your son in the car with you?' I'm thinking, I'm gonna write him for no seat belt on a minor. He says, 'That's my date.' I look closer. She's a girl with short hair. Skinny, no boobs. I couldn't write the guy anything. Figure he didn't get any that night, so that was punishment enough."

Kelly felt good on the way home. That had gone well. He stopped en route to pick up a six-pack of good bottled beer to supplement the cheaper cans in his refrigerator. He felt pumped by the action. At its core, police work was fun. "Don't let anybody kid you," he'd once told his wife when the job was good, back when he and Janet were good. "Driving fast, skidding around, this is why we become cops." He felt positive and strong, like he was supposed to feel. And tried to stay feeling that way all night, but failed.

He'd tried once or twice to explain to Rachel what it felt like to be on your game in police work, to be effective, to make a difference. To handle things that others wouldn't or couldn't. To be tough. Janet had never understood what it meant to him to become an officer, though she had been with him through his transition from salesman to academy recruit to field trainee and finally a cut-loose cop. Rachel didn't get it yet, but he remained hopeful. Most times she got quiet, but at least didn't roll her eyes, didn't reject him outright. In fact, she gave as good as she got, challenging him.

Like the tortilla chips story. They had a conversation one night where he brought up tortilla chips: "Brains look like deli-sliced ham in a clear ziplock sandwich bag, if you were to step on the bag with the ball of your foot and spin."

"You put a lot of thought into that description. You don't have anything better to think about?"

"I wanted to be able to describe it to you."

"Why? Why would you describe that to me?" She pushed her thick red hair out of her eyes and looked up. She was reading on the couch with her head in his lap.

"I want to communicate with you. I want to describe things to you, my things. I want to describe me to you."

"And this is how you see yourself, your center, in things like these?"

"Yes, this is what I do. This is what we do. It's what we are paid to do," and she heard pride in his voice.

"We pay you to do that, to deal with that?"

"We're not paid for what we do, we're paid for what we might have to do. Sometimes we just write tickets or reports, or direct traffic, or just drive around. It isn't all the time we have to deal with the good stuff." What Rachel or any normal person would call the bad stuff.

"And you deal with this good stuff by, what, you make brains into ham? Is that a deliberate thought process? Do you do it naturally or learn how?"

"You have to learn it, Rach. You survive by learning it."

"Then what do you do?"

"You finish up and you go eat."

"Eat?"

"Yeah, eat. Like a ham sandwich. So you know you can. So you can do it next time. You have to be able to know you can handle it, go to the call, and get the call done, help people. Do the job."

Silence for a while, then . . .

"You know, skull pieces, if a head got broken up, if it were run over by a semi on 395, they look like tortilla chips. How about that?"

She didn't leave him that night, which he considered a success. But she didn't kiss him, either. He wished he could share tonight's good feeling with Rachel but hadn't been smart enough or strong enough to avoid drinking so many beers. He should have gone straight to her apartment, but he had stopped off at the cemetery again. He could probably get to her, if he drove slowly and maybe held a hand over one eye—one eye doesn't give double vision.

But double vision caused the pause at the door that let gravity take over. Then sleep. Then the pager bleeped and the phone rang. And Kelly slept some more. Twenty rings. Then a long pause, several minutes of quiet. Another twenty before a shorter pause. Then constant rings for nearly an hour. And Kelly heard nothing.

CHAPTER 22

Exits
Thursday November 3, 1988
7 a.m.–8 a.m.

THE NEXT MORNING, Janet Paulson Kelly hit her husband with the door when she entered their house, not hard enough to wake him initially, though he moaned. She stopped and stared in disgust, her lips pressed and her chin dimpled. The force of her contempt cut through the foggy sleep and brought him the rest of the way to consciousness.

Kelly opened the eye closest to Janet as she stepped over his body from the narrow door opening, her heel clicking down on the hardwood floor a foot from his nose. She still had nice ankles, the unsought thought slipping from the automatic male part of his sub-brain as he slowly surfaced. His pager peeped quietly, once a minute to indicate an unchecked message. Ten messages, actually, according to the little glowing screen once Kelly could focus well enough to read it. He moaned.

Janet Kelly walked away down the hall, carrying two empty cardboard boxes toward the kitchen. She turned out of sight toward the counter, and Kelly began trying to get up. After a few minutes of her clinking things and him thumping and bumping toward standing, they met in the hallway. She put a box filled with cooking gear—pans, pots, plates, utensils—down by the open front door, winter's chill seeping in under the aluminum storm door where glass panes had been slid on over summer screens. He had to move aside as she passed.

"I can carry that out for you. In a minute. Lemme get my shoes . . ."

"No need, I've got . . . Tony's with me." Janet's eyes dropped out of submissive habit at her revelation of a personal fact, but the habit had been broken recently, so she looked back up again, slowly passing her eyes up Kelly, floor to face. "You've got your shoes on, John."

"Tony." Kelly lowered his voice on the last syllable and made it not a question, although Kelly had never heard of Tony before. He caught her challenging gaze and said, "So, you've got a *Tony* now, do you?"

"What if I do? I certainly don't have you. And thank God for that!" The promise Janet had made to herself to keep it cool broke like an ice dam in a winter creek. She looked around what had been their home, trying to place herself and to distance herself. Months of avoidance after the breakup and her shamed and bewildered departure had led to a rigorously applied if self-deceiving facade of anger. There followed a deliberate coldness she had hoped would carry her past the limited but inevitable contacts with this man whom she had wooed as a teen, seduced as a coed and captured as a young wife. But she had lost him in their shared and delayed transition to adulthood, one that only kicked in when Kelly joined the force. Janet had watched him grow away, then she grew too.

"I've got someone, John. I've got a man who cares for me. I . . . Oh, fuck it, John. Why do I try to get you to get it?" Janet's eyes welled with tears she would not let fall. She pointed at him, holding him at bay.

"You gave up on us. You're not a husband, you stopped being a husband. You don't care about me, I'm not gonna care about you." The flare in Janet's eyes, the sparks of anger and emotion at the start of her tirade burned out fast as she drew herself back under control. She saw Kelly straighten up under her fury, bleary eyes seeming to focus into her like they used to. Now she had his attention. But didn't want it anymore.

"Gave up. Gave up? You think I gave up on you?" Kelly asked.

"Gave up on us, John. Gave up on our being together, on what we used to mean to each other. On our marriage, or just to marriage itself. You just stopped being one of *us*, you and me, part of something to be called *us*—don't do that," Janet interrupted herself as she watched John raise his chin and start lifting his arms to put his hands on his hips. Superman pose, an old habit and not one she'd missed. Gathering himself to counterattack. And Janet would have none of it.

"Don't you dare try to say you didn't change, John. Don't even try." She waved her hand in front of John's face as he clearly formulated the response of *Who, me? Not my fault, not me who changed, you didn't change with me, you never wanted me to become a cop*, all the crap he retorted when she tried to explain her feelings and resorted to whenever they met. Maybe theirs hadn't been the strongest of marriages, but they'd committed to each other from the start, from high school on. And held on till John graduated from the Police Academy, hit the street, and started to harden. He became aloof and arrogant. Janet knew things were bad even before Emma died. Kelly denied it affected him and bulled on like the tough guy he'd become under the badge. Her death made him angry, or angrier, and he brought that home every night, often under a skin thickened or numbed by alcohol.

Only one time, at the beginning of their end, right after she fled to a friend's apartment, did John's litany end with a promise, a commitment. An "I can change, I can be better, we can go back to us, I can go back to how I was." But even on that day, Janet saw the light in his eyes, the momentary conviction with which John had delivered that last hopeful plea, dim as words even he recognized as empty fell on the floor between them. Janet had watched his reddened eyes as something John forgot, then remembered in a rush, flooded his face. He went up and down, on and off, light and dark. He'd pushed her off his rollercoaster, but she'd survived the fall. She wouldn't get back on.

"I've got another box to fill. Some spices and cooking stuff if you're sure not using it. I'll leave the bottle openers." He missed the jab.

"To cook? I cook. Sure. What, are you having some sort of party or something? Cooking for *Tony*?" She turned from him and walked back into the kitchen and opened a cabinet. She wouldn't rise to it. *She wouldn't*, she thought, but she did anyway.

"Yeah, cooking for Tony. For the building. For the entire fuckin' Seventh Fleet. Dammit, John, none of your fucking business, not anymore. You wanted out, you wanted me out, I'm out. Okay?"

"Five months, all it took for you to move on, huh?" he said to her, but she saw his eyes wander as he looked inside at his own thoughts. *Hmmm.*

"Move on, move out, move up, John. You will too. You will." Janet held the second cardboard box, now containing spices and a set of matching coffee cups, and walked directly toward John in the hallway, toward the front door. He stood still until the loaded box she carried nearly made contact with his chest. She stopped moving, he stepped backward away down the hall, and she widened her view of him. Shirt tail out and flapping, but not obscuring the badge clipped to his belt just in front of the gun holster. Mud encrusted at the knees of his tan corduroy pants. Thick black hair, short but cowlicked up on the right side by sleep. He needed help, but she was done.

"It's just as well I'm out, John. And I am out. This is it. We can file the papers. I want that. I won't have to be the one to pick you out of the gutter. Or bury you." She stepped around him in the entry hall and pushed open the storm door, carrying the box to a car double parked out front.

A tall, skinny man leaned against the curbside fender, the casual lean of a smoker but without a cigarette. Straight brown hair, longish, over a black shiny rain jacket that glistened in the thin sleet. His hands were back against the fender as if ready to push off toward Kelly's door. Tony, huh. He smiled as she approached and took the box as she turned back to get the last one. Wordlessly, she did, and they left.

CHAPTER 23

Killing
Thursday, November 3, 1988
0900–0940 HRS

DETECTIVE JOHN KELLY found himself out of clothes suitable for court and had to pull last week's suit off the dry-cleaning pile. He ironed it and brushed dried mud from the pant cuffs and washed off a pair of lace-up dress shoes in the kitchen sink, uncaring about the shine. He telephoned Ashby at the CID office to have him pick up the Stibbles.

As he circled the courthouse block for parking, he caught a glimpse of a person who attracted him. Something in the countenance, the shape, the radiance pinged, and when he glanced back, he saw with happy surprise it was Rachel. Funny, he would tell her later, how his heart picked her out even before his brain recognized her. Why wait, he decided, and jammed the unmarked into reverse, chirping the tires and chasing her back up the street till he drew even and blipped the siren to attract her attention. He called through the open window, "Hey, baby, wanna ride?"

Assistant Public Defender Rachel Cohen started at the siren. She looked at him for a minute, long enough that he had to turn on his emergency lights and wave traffic around before she walked stiffly toward his stopped car. She got in and stared ahead without speaking and he drove off, glancing at her, curious about her stiffness and silence. Yeah, he hadn't returned her page, but that had happened before. She noticed him peeking at her but didn't remark on it.

This was Rachel's first time in his police car, a seat she'd avoided to prevent exposure of their, what, connection? Affair? Hard to say exactly what they had, and after her crisis last night, Rachel was even more unsure. She blankly scanned the unusual switches, the microphone hanging on a clip next to the AM radio. After a short drive, Kelly parked outside a small restaurant he knew had quiet booths. As they went in, Kelly took her elbow to steady her uncertain steps.

"Coffee, decaf for her and two waters."

"Regular for me," Rachel said, and Kelly was surprised.

"Don't they say decaf is better for babies?"

"Where were you last night?"

Kelly reached his hands across the booth, but Rachel kept hers in her lap, pressed tight to her belly. "I got your messages but it was kinda late for calling. I'd had a few. I was gonna come over but I, I . . ."

"What, John? You what?" Rachel hissed, and it lashed Kelly like a scream. "You got my beeps but you what? You decided you didn't want to bother calling me? You were going to come over but, what? You decided, nah, I think I'll do something better?" Just for a moment, Rachel paused, then her fury pushed her further.

"Did you have another drink, John? Two, ten? You couldn't make time for me, John? I needed . . ." Rachel couldn't know that she needed sobriety from John. She knew he drank, but in their time together, he'd never been drunk. At least, she'd never seen him drunk.

The coffee arrived. Kelly pushed the little plastic creamer containers toward Rachel. She opened them and poured them into her cup, then poured in powder from pink packets and began sipping, holding the cup above tabled elbows. The steam rose in front of her face as she asked, "Where were you?"

"I, I was asleep. I'd been out."

"Out where?"

"Out. I got home late. I had work. We had a felony stop when I was on the way home. Thought the guy was a GLA suspect." Kelly mistook her glare for incomprehension. "That's a stolen car. I was close and . . ."

She rolled her eyes. "I called you. I called you all night. I paged you. Is your beeper working? I needed you." Rachel's hands shook, and a splash of coffee topped the rim and ran down her arm like mud, unnoticed.

Kelly's hands, still lying across the table, took her napkin and blotted the coffee smear from her pale wrist. She flinched as if burned.

"See, that caffeine is bad for you, especially now." She saw his grin for the distraction technique it was. He went on. "You should lay off it for a while, Mom."

And Rachel's heart stopped. "I'm not, you're not my mom. And I'm not a mom, now." He didn't get it, of course. Stupid lug.

"Yeah, well, once people know, once we . . ." He looked around the restaurant, as if pointing out all the people in the world who didn't know yet that John Kelly and Rachel Cohen were together, with child. Like it was a simple thing. God, how hard was he going to make it? Harder than she expected it would be, than she had feared all night, than she had played and replayed, planned and anticipated and tried to find the best, clearest, and easiest way for them to share this horrible moment. But she had never divined a clear path all sleepless and painful night, and now she could only blurt it out.

"The baby is gone, John. I'm not pregnant anymore." Her cup was down, and she finally allowed her hands to come toward his. Just as his withdrew, pulling back to his sides, his right hand automatically drawing close to his gun out of subconscious fright.

"Gone. Gone? Our, you . . ." Kelly, red-faced before, paled like sudden snow. His fingers were now steepled, shielding hands touching in front of his chest, and he leaned back in the booth, gaining distance. "Gone? What did you do, Rachel?"

"Do? Oh, God, John. It was just, it's what they said had to happen. I mean . . ." Thinking of what the ER doctor and nurses had told her. Nonviable, permanent failure, inevitable, stress-related. Other terms too jarring and sharp to absorb much less share so soon, even with Kelly, and especially not here in some restaurant.

The clinks and muted bell tones of cutlery and coffee spoons rang around the clotting silence between them as Kelly sucked in her words and she threw her heart at him. His comprehension failed them.

"Who, what . . . Had to? Who was it told you to have an abortion?" Rachel gasped but John plowed on. "You told someone, you decided or someone got you to decide, told you what to do with a baby that was ours? You . . ." Coffee bubbled in his gut, hotter than when it went down. She saw his hands vibrating with pressure as Kelly pushed them together.

Rachel was silent, first unable to comprehend Kelly's assumption, then feeling its vicious bite. *Abortion!* It dizzied her like yesterday. Rachel did not speak.

She was silent so long, Kelly took her failure to respond as an admission. A confession. He looked at her with eyes clouded with distrust.

No, John, Rachel could only think, *I didn't. I never would. I love you.* Her mouth almost opened as the loving thought tried to slip out. Rachel crossed her arms across her abdomen and pressed tight against her agonized insides. She could not yet speak aloud, but said to herself, *We are going to be happy. We will get over this. There may be nothing wrong with me and we can try again.* She projected her silent words at John's mind. Maybe it was the shock of what she'd heard those cops saying. *What did they mean? What happened to you, John? What did you do? Are you in danger?* A million fears spin in Rachel's mind, thoughts floating and spinning and crashing like torn roofs in a hurricane. *I don't know why I lost our child, but I want to be with you as mother and father. Husband and wife. Your wife. We can have that. I love you, John,* she thought, *I love you.* She opened her mouth to say it, soft lips parting.

"You killed our baby," Kelly said.

CHAPTER 24

Magnetism
Thursday, November 3, 1988
1000–1300 HRS

COMMONWEALTH DAY OPENED at ten a.m. with hundreds of cops, lawyers, defendants, witnesses, victims, parents, babies, and reporters wandering back and forth between three courtrooms on the fourth floor of the squat brick courthouse. The courthouse, built at the beginning of the century, was never designed for the pace and density of legal activity it handled.

There was no rhyme, reason, order, or understandable pattern in the way cases were set or assigned to each of the three Circuit Court judges. All the cases were felonies, crimes punishable by sentences of one year or more. There were trials without juries, motions to suppress evidence or confessions, hearings to review completion of or performance during periods of probation (dirty urine tests were the common subject here). Drug possession and sale cases followed assaults and larcenies both petit and grand, stolen cars mixed with stolen bicycles, armed robberies abutted pilfered baby shampoo. Officers commonly, attorneys only slightly less, found themselves called simultaneously in two courtrooms by judges who held themselves far above the mundane conflictions of schedule created by careless, inconsiderate, or conniving clerks.

TAC Unit 511, Officer T.C. Sharpe, was on the stand in Courtroom Two. Courtrooms One and Four were at each end of the fourth floor, and each had windows on one side. Courtroom Two had none. There was a Courtroom Three, reserved for civil cases, but no one had ever seen it used.

511 was on the stand for the second time that day, of a scheduled six appearances. In the first, Sharpe had testified against a twenty-four-year-old male named Will Alberts, who had pleaded "Na Guilty, Your Judgeship" at the beginning of the trial. Sharpe was only one sentence into his testimony and the judge, as always, ruled he could testify in narration, instead of simply responding yes or no to questions from the prosecutor, questions that the defense always challenged as leading the witness and that the judge allowed just to move things on. Always the same.

"Your Honor, on the date in question"—Sharpe took a quick glance at a report in his stack of files—"which was a Friday, I was on duty in plain clothes, assigned to the tactical unit of the Alexandria Police Department. I was in a concealed location within sight of the 800 block of North Alfred Street. I was using a Garmin twenty-power spotting telescope to observe behavior visible on the street. At approximately," glance, "4:15 p.m. I observed a subject whom I later determined to be Mr. Alberts, the defendant who is sitting there." Sharpe pointed across the courtroom. "I . . ."

"Let the record show that the officer has identified the defendant in this case, Mr. Alberts," the prosecutor said, standing to address the judge but more pointedly the court reporter, who was rapidly pressing buttons on her tripod-mounted device.

"Yes, yes. Proceed, um, Officer," the judge said, not even looking up. *Probably forgot my name*, 511 decided.

"Your Honor, at that time I observed," another glance down, "Mr. Alberts reached his right hand into the front pants pocket of his jeans and removed it. He then opened that hand, and I observed several small, light-colored, irregularly shaped objects in the palm of his hand. He reached his left hand up and with a finger appeared to move the objects around slightly. After a moment, another individual approached and stood in front of him. This individual did not block my view. This individual reached up his right hand and removed an item from Mr. Albert's palm. I then saw him hold that item in the palm of his right hand. This individual then handed Mr. Alberts a bill of US currency, and Mr. Alberts—"

The defense attorney stood up and said, "Objection to the characterization of the passing of currency, Your Honor." The defense attorney, one of the public defenders Sharpe knew, was trying hard. They all did. Shoveling against the tide, but that was their job. Over a fourth beer last night, this guy had bitched about how all these cases ended up the same. Convictions, with minor sentences and a rapid return of defendants to the community and to old criminal patterns. "Job security for the defense bar," Sharpe had told him.

The judge held a hand to stop the prosecutor who was rising from his seat and nodded toward the witness stand. "Officer Sharpe," he said and flicked his fingers in a proceed motion.

"Your Honor, the item in question was small, maybe five inches by three, whitish with greenish writing, and patterns on the side I could see. Mr. Albert placed that item in his left front pocket. After I advised officers to move in to take Mr. Alberts into custody, I continued to observe and saw Officer

Barstow remove an identical item from Mr. Alberts's left front pocket. Officer Barstow advised me by radio that the item, a twenty-dollar bill, was the only item in Mr. Alberts's left front pocket."

Sharpe paused for the ruling on the objection, and the judge allowed the currency testimony, as he always had. He continued with the narrative, describing how an officer stopped the buyer based on Sharpe's description and also in Sharpe's confirming sight and recovered a small, light-colored, irregularly shaped object in the pocket where Sharpe said it would be. They also recovered several small, light-colored objects from the area behind Alberts, where Sharpe had seen him throw the unsold items as the Jump-Outs rolled up. TAC didn't charge Alberts with the items on the ground—because this was the fifth arrest on the same block within two hours and because every jump forced dealers to dump their stuff whether they were the jump-out target or not. There were usually dozens of discarded crack rocks on the ground. Sharpe and others would watch later, after arrests ceased, for the users who crouched and duckwalked the sidewalks, checking and pecking for discards. The cops called them chickens.

On and on. When Sharpe finished testifying and was released from the witness stand, he walked to the prosecution table and picked up his pile of evidence envelopes and files, then left the courtroom. The Rule on Witnesses meant that persons testifying in a case had to leave the courtroom so as not to hear and be influenced by others' testimony. Sharpe whispered to the prosecutor, who asked the judge if Sharpe was dismissed from the case. Sharpe wanted to be free to go to Courtroom One, where the senior Circuit Court judge had more of his cases. "Yes." Sharpe skedaddled to his next court. He got there just in time and heard his name called. He passed through the gate, again piled his evidence on the prosecution table, and stood before the judge with his right hand raised.

"Do you solemnly swear or affirm that you will tell the truth in this case to the best of your knowledge and recollection?" No Bible to palm—they never did that up here.

"Yes, ma'am." And he took the stand. A quick glance at the next file, and off he went.

"Your Honor, on the date in question, which was a Saturday, I was on duty in plain clothes, assigned to the tactical unit of the Alexandria Police Department. I was in a concealed location within sight of the 900 block of North Alfred Street. I was using a Garmin twenty-power spotting telescope to observe behavior visible on the street. At approximately," glance, "6:30 p.m. I observed a subject whom I later determined to be Mr. Alb—er, Mr. Feeney, the defendant who is sitting there, um, at the defense table wearing the jail overalls." This public defender stood up and sat back down.

"Your Honor, at that time I observed Mr. um," another glance, "Feeney reach his right hand into the front pants pocket of his jeans and remove it. He then opened that hand, and I observed several small, light-colored, irregularly shaped objects in the palm of his hand. He reached his left hand up and with a finger appeared to move the objects around slightly. After a moment, another individual approached and stood in front of him. This individual did not block my view. This individual reached up his right hand and removed an item from Mr. Feeney's palm. I then saw him hold that item in the palm of his right hand. This individual then handed Mr. Feeney a bill of US currency . . ." He paused for the objection and glanced at the defense attorney, who didn't bother. "Which I could tell because it was small, maybe five inches by three, whitish with greenish writing, and patterns on the side I could see. Mr. Feeney placed that item in his left front pocket. After I advised officers to move in to take Mr. Feeney into custody, I continued to observe and saw, um," a glance, "Officer Hooper remove an identical item from Mr. Albert's, I mean, Feeney's left front pocket. Officer Hooper advised me by radio that the item, a twenty-dollar bill, was the only item she had found in Mr. Feeney's left front pocket." And so on.

Leaving the stand but before he got to the prosecution table, 511 turned to face the judge while the request was made to dismiss him, freeing him to go testify in his next three cases somewhere else. As he stood, TAC Unit 513, Charlene Hooper, entered the courtroom. She was the arresting officer, the one who put the grab on the suspect and found the money, which was now in an envelope that she carried in a bulky pile identical to Sharpe's. But when she dropped her pile on the table, it slipped from her hands and hit with a bang. The table vibrated. The judge stopped talking and swiveled her head toward the noise just as two of the bulkier envelopes, one from each of the TAC officers' piles, began to pivot untouched and slide toward each other, in slow motion but increasing speed until they clacked together at mid table like train cars coupling.

Sharpe and Hooper began to yank the envelopes apart when the judge said, "Stop," the authoritative equivalent of a shout, though she didn't raise her voice. She raised her eyebrows, however, and made a come-here motion with her hand.

"Bailiff, please take possession of those, um, items from the officers and hand them to me." The bailiff, a sheriff's deputy, had his back turned to the judge, who couldn't see his eyes brighten first with alarm, then fear for the officers, then fear for himself as he began to clamp his jaw down, face reddening in the effort to stifle his giggle. Failing, he began to cough to mask the sounds he couldn't stop. The cops made stone faces and held out the still magnetically locked envelopes, watching them handed over to the judge. Her face was now red, except for the area around her angrily pursed lips, pressed tight and white and bereft of blood. She took the odd package, hefted it, squeezed each half along its lumpy sides, cursorily checked the identifying markings, and said to the prosecutor, "This case is dismissed. Mr. Feeney, you are free to go."

She turned to the prosecutor had risen from his chair to protest the dismissal but stood mute. "You, and these two . . . officers, will see me in chambers at the end of the docket today. To discuss these." She held up the pair of evidence envelopes. "This." To her clerk, she said, "Miss Higgenbotham, make note that the case against Mr. Feeney was dismissed, and not nol prossed. Now please call the next case."

The prosecutor tried one last gambit. "Your Honor, that may be evidence needed in other cases later today."

"Mr. Prosecutor. It *is* evidence, in a case that will begin this afternoon, in my chambers."

Sharpe walked out past the bar, stunned, embarrassed, and in fear of what awaited him and his career at the end of the day. He was watched by the gallery of officers and others awaiting their cases. Most of the civilians in the courtroom sat quietly, having missed the drama. The seated mass of officers had caught some of the action, missed the specific details but not the ominous significance of the judge's orders, and none spoke or made eye contact as he passed.

CHAPTER 25

Flowers
Thursday, November 3, 1988
9:45 a.m.–1 p.m.

PUBLIC DEFENDER RACHEL Cohen hadn't been able to walk the seven blocks from the restaurant back to downtown Old Town where her office and the courthouse were, so she asked the cashier to call her a cab. Despite the time spent in meeting with John, awaiting the cab, and riding back, she still made it to her office in time to pick up files before the long day of court.

She was in agony when she left the car and trudged up the stairs to enter the Office of the Alexandria Public Defender. She was greeted by a smirk from Abby, the secretary/receptionist/file clerk/legal researcher whom they underpaid to hold down the front desk and everything else. Rachel tilted her head at Abby's cryptic expression.

"Look in your office," Abby said and giggled.

Rachel walked down the hall and found, on her desk, a huge bouquet of red and pink roses. Pleased, happy, lifted by the gesture from someone, Rachel felt buoyed above her gloom of a moment ago. Till she opened the card and read, in an immature, childlike, nearly illegible scrawl:

To Long Lives.
—John

Sucker punched, she closed her office door just as Abby crept up to share in the thrill of delivered flowers. Abby gasped, but Rachel was at her limit. She collapsed into her desk chair, leaned forward, and put her cheek on her blotter. *Time to cry,* she thought, but didn't. Couldn't. She was deflated, dead inside. Dead as the child she had lost just hours before. Dead as the future she had feared lost when Kelly accused her in restaurant. A future she now truly knew was lost with this, John Kelly's last shot at her.

Not even his writing, the bastard. How could he? How had he? How did he have time?

He'd fled the restaurant, but she was only minutes behind him. He had his cop car instantly available while she waited for a ride. She always thought he could accomplish anything, her image of him not yet degraded so, still her habit to think the world of the man she loved so much. She stared across her desk at the telephone. A pile of black pens lay next to it, some red ones intermingled. *Why, John? Why couldn't you let me explain? I can explain. I couldn't speak. Can you listen?* She clutched the handwritten florist's card. *To Long Lives.* She had mere minutes before she had to be in court. She'd left the emergency room so she could be in court for this case today. Only today. A continuance would lose her the edge she needed to win this one. Finally, a win. So many cases she and her office had lost, not

from poor performance on her part. No, from poor performance on the part of her client base. Sell drugs on the street in
plain sight, steal from stores with cameras, punch out people
who know you by name; the decks were always stacked against
the defense bar from the start. But today she had a chance to
win. Not because her client was innocent, but because he was
not guilty. There was a difference.

And her worry about what she would have to do to John
in court to win, the hesitation to hurt him that challenged her
duty to her client, vanished in the heat of his obvious anger.

Rachel's focus returned and her resolve reformed. She had
given up a lot to be ready for today. She had given up easy,
open access to Kelly, hiding her emotions and their connection to avoid the appearance of impropriety or bias. A defense
attorney dating a cop. More than dating. Less than that, now.

She tried to go, get out of the office, but she was consumed
by a need to strike back, to get up, to object. She looked at the
phone again and had an idea. It was a cheap shot, a thousand
times weaker than what she really had to say. But it was all she
could do. Rachel thought a bit, turned things around in her
mind, and picked up the phone. She punched in some numbers, waited for a beep, then punched in four digits, pause, one
more, pause, then two. She hung up and left for court.

Her two cases were both in Courtroom One, in front of the
judge she needed most today, a stickler for detail and precise
legal definitions. She hoped she wouldn't have to chase down
her clients, both of whom were on bond pending trial.

Cedric Stibble, forty-two, a California native now living
in Alexandria, father of an eight-year-old son whom he was
accused of failing to return to his mother—Stibble's divorced
wife—after a court-ordered visitation. The key to winning this
case, her first win since coming to Alexandria, would be in the
boilerplate. And in crushing Kelly.

And Stick, nineteen, a.k.a. Antonio Planter, the name listed on the docket, charged with possession with intent to distribute cocaine. A slam dunk for the prosecution, an unshakeable TAC case, from her view unwinnable. Crack rocks in his pocket and judges disinterested in how the cops got in there to check. This case was a loser, so why was Stick so certain it was going away? *He* was going away.

Actually, he was in front of the courtroom door when she got there. Stick chewed something, leaning against the wall next to the window at the end of the hall outside Courtroom One. "Hey, Mizz Rachel, how you doin'?" he said around a wad of brown gum showing in his teeth when he grinned.

"Spit that out, Mr. Planter. You can't chew gum in court. There's ashtrays out by the elevators."

"Nah, I'm good," Stick said and swallowed, to Rachel's surprise. She drew him to a relatively quiet corner, mostly away from the crowds and definitely away from the cops who roamed while waiting for sprinted to get to upcoming cases. "You know what we talked about. You know you won't have to testify in this motion, just the officers who say they found the crack rocks on you. You don't talk, you just sit next to me."

"I ain't talkin' at all, Mizz Rachel. I told you, this is gone. You ain't got to worry about it. I got stuff for it. Professor Vulture took care a' me." Stick patted a pocket, which drooped down low below his waistline, another track suit, a white band of underpants showing above. A style called "jailing," meant to evoke the hardcore look of a prisoner confined without a belt as a suicide prevention measure. Rachel knew from her law school internship with the state correctional system that inside prison, it signified a willingness to accommodate the sexual needs of more dominant males. So cops laughed at the look, which only made the street kids more willing to adopt it.

"Best not be anything the deputies will be concerned with, Antonio." Spoken like a mom. "No rocks, right?"

"Nah, Mizz Rachel. It a root. Wanna see?" He took a dried stick from his pocket and waved it at her.

"You think . . . It doesn't matter what you think right now. You go in and sit and wait for your name to be called. You might be early, or you might be after a trial I have to do. But for now we're going in and we sit. You sit, and you stay." *Golly, Rachel,* she thought, *pat him on the head, why don't you.* "You stay till I tell you that you can leave."

"Copacetic, boss lady." *How'd he get so cocky?*

He led the way in and sat at the last open seat in the gallery, on the right side. Something interesting was happening up front. She stopped and stood at the back of the courtroom as he sat down, and she saw him double-take toward a girl on the other side of the courtroom. Woman really, older than Stick, maybe as old as Rachel was. *So now I'm old,* Rachel thought, hollowly, still wounded physically from the loss last night and mentally from Kelly's vicious accusation just this morning. But despite herself, she lost track of her personal feelings as she tried to catch what the judge was saying to an officer and the prosecutor. Hard, because the voices were low. And she was intrigued by the sight of this woman reacting to Stick, not a come-on but definite interest. How does he do it?

Maybe it's the root.

Another attorney sidled up next to her, an older woman who took cases on the court-appointed list, cases like co-defendants of clients assigned to the PD's office whose defense would represent a conflict of interest. "You catch that?" she whispered.

At Rachel's negative, she said, "Cops were using magnets on the stand. Probably to erase tape recordings. Did you have any cases with that guy?" She pointed at Officer T.C. Sharpe as he walked from the prosecution table.

She had. TAC! She took out her tape recorder as he passed her leaving the courtroom, his face reddening, and looked at the small device as if she could divine its performance by sight. She moved to chase the cop, but the judge called the next case, and it was hers.

CHAPTER 26

Attraction
It's Thursday, right?
I just got here.

AFTER ANTONIO "STICK" Planter met with his public defender, he walked through the doors into Courtroom One. She followed. He walked like he knew where he was going, though this was his first time in the upper court. The downstairs court, what Mizz Rachel called Gentle District Court or something, was just for when you got arrested. You ended up here when you might go to prison. But he wasn't gonna.

He sat at the last open seat in the gallery, on the right side, trying to be quiet because the judge in front was talking all angry about something. For him the right side, because too many cops in gray shirts sat on the left. Some cop walking out as he came in, and Mizz Rachel behind him, saying sumpin' like, Um, um. Dumbass kike bitch. Cop in plain clothes but had a badge on his belt, looking all mad and stuff. One of them

Jump-Outs, but not the one who got him. Stick noticed how people looked. He paid attention.

As he sat, Stick glanced around the room and locked eyes with a beautiful fox. Fine, fine woman, older and a little lighter than he was but oh, my. Sitting over on the other side. And she was into him, he could tell, staring at him and nudging her friend next to her. *Hey, baby*, he said with his eyes and the waving tip of his tongue. *I knows you want some of this.* He made a mental note to get with her when they were all done with the court today. Maybe he'd seen her before, but he'd sure be seeing her now.

S'all good.

CHAPTER 27

Exhumation
Thursday, November 3, 1988
1300–1500 HRS

FTO JACKSON DIDN'T see Kelly anywhere on the fourth floor of the courthouse. The FTO Jackson with Higgins trailing behind peeked into each of the three active courtrooms but couldn't enter because they were still armed, not having taken the time to lock up their pistols. When he spotted Detective Ashby sitting next to a woman and child, he sent a nearby waiting patrolman in to get him. Ashby didn't know where Kelly was, and Ashby was pissed.

"You find him, Herb. You get his ass in here pronto. He was supposed to pick up the vic and his mom this morning, then he calls me saying he can't get there in time and I have to go do it. His fuckin' case. I'm just a babysitter. He . . ."

"What did he say to you?"

"He said he was gonna be late. We were supposed to meet at nine and go get the kid from his case and his mom up in the

New Projects. Calls me at my desk at nine-oh-five. I'm ducking so the sergeant doesn't see I'm still up there 'cause we're
supposed to be on the way already. Kelly says to me, go get
them and I'll meet you at Courtroom Four. Well, he isn't here."
Ashby waved around. "This's Four, right?"

"What did he sound like?"

"Sound? Like Kelly sounds all the time now. Like he was
dead. Snippy. Like he was sick but he sounds that way anyway.
Hungover. I don't know. But if he doesn't make it by the time
they need him, he's toast."

"What's the case?" The FTO and Ashby were doing the cop
dance. They looked like Rockem Sockem Robots.

"Parental abduction. Mom'll go first, tell about a visitation
where dad didn't bring kiddo home. Then the kid. Then Kelly
tells how he got 'im. So even if it starts now, Kell's got a little
bit before he's missed. But he better get here. He's got enough
troubles as it is without his getting jammed for missing court.
Missing a trial."

"What troubles?" Jackson wanted to see if Ashby really
knew.

"You know they're digging up Pickett today, the guy who
killed his niece. You know he was there when she . . . well, right?
Of course you know that. Piece of shit. He's being exhumed
today in my old case."

"Yeah, I know about it. I'm assigned to it. We're in early for
it. We're doing chain of custody 'cause you can't 'cause you're
here."

"Well, Kelly's freaked about it," Ashby said.

"Freaked?"

"Yeah. Digging up that monster. Gotta be freakin' him out,
having that POS above ground again." Ashby shivered theatri-
cally. "But we need his jaw to match some bites on an old case,

maybe clear a kid, his parents thought he was raping his sister. No end to ugly, all the way around."

You don't know the half of it, brother, the FTO thought.

"Send him up here, you see him," Ashby said as the FTO left to find Kelly. But he never did. The FTO had met with Lieutenant Ramirez earlier. Ramirez had a plan, and Jackson wanted to share it with Kelly, maybe take some of the pressure off. Lord, Kelly needed it, Jackson knew.

Two hours later, FTO Jackson and Recruit Higgins stood on the grass of the public cemetery off South Payne Street in the southwest corner of Old Town. There was no foot traffic on the sidewalk a dozen yards away and no mourners among the old and tilted tombstones of the historic burial ground shared by half the churches in the city. Cold rain that could have been snow fell thin from dark clouds. A backhoe was parked nearby. To fill time, the FTO was explaining standard field sobriety tests for drunk driving stops. Every day is a training day.

"Using the same tests saves you always trying to remember what to tell them to do or what you told them to do. You use the same thing every time, you get good at it. Makes it easier to take notes, too, 'cause you are familiar with what's gonna happen.

"Say you stop a guy, he's doing forty-four in a thirty-five. Not enough to make you stop them usually but it's a violation. Then he weaves across the double-yellow twice. Now you got something that'll sound good in court, reason to think he might be driving impaired. You get him stopped. License and registration, and you're sniffing in the window, see if you can smell booze. Remember, alcohol has no smell, in and of itself, so your notes and your testimony eventually are gonna say, you detected the *odor of an alcoholic beverage*. Just like that, you use those words, 'cause they work. Okay, here they are."

The FTO stopped the lecture as two city workers clumped up in work boots and snowmobile suits, hardhats mandated but unnecessary on their heads. The letters TES were embossed on the plastic helmets, for Transportation and Environmental Services. *Almost anything labor-intensive in the city is TES. Almost everything shitty is APD*, Jackson thought. *Like this.*

The FTO had the recruit make note of the names of both workmen and their time of arrival on the scene for his report. They watched as the men confirmed the name on the small white concrete marker, with the identical (they hoped!) name on a city form and a signed court order. Then one of the men fired up the yellow backhoe and reversed it to the foot of the grave. The claw began scraping up the ground in a line away from the tombstone. Around the grave was sparse grass giving way to brown, loose, and muddy earth, not yet frozen here at the beginning of winter. There was an unusual amount of broken glass here. The bucket bit deeply at the start, then took softer rips as it went lower into the trench.

Watching, the FTO resumed speaking. "So you pull him over, you smell something, you get him out of the car, and you decide you're gonna do field sobriety tests. Alphabet, counting, touching fingers, all that. But you gotta ask him some questions first so you can tell the judge the guy should have been able to do all these things, except he was impaired. You paying attention to me?" The recruit was looking intently at the scooping bucket and the rough, crumbling edge of the opening hole, but turned back to the FTO. Unconsciously he lifted his hands up in the field interview stance, mimicking his teacher. The pile of dirt next to the grave grew larger as the digging bucket, gray metal with protruding teeth, bit into the hole at the head end, nearest the stone, and pulled back toward the feet where the tractor bucked powerfully at each wet, grinding, drawn-out chomp.

"You say, and you're making notes on all this as you say, you say, 'Sir, how far did you get in school? Are you a high school graduate? Did you go to college? What college was that?' Note it down. Then you ask, 'So you can read and write, right? You know the alphabet? You do? Good. I want you to say the alphabet for me, but I want you to start at the letter M and go to Z, and I don't want you to sing it. Do you understand what I am asking you to do?' And of course he says he does. Nobody says they don't, so you write 'Alphabet Yes' on your pad. You don't have to write all the questions, because it's always the same questions. It's what you will always do. You just write the answers. He says yeah. You say go ahead. He just looks at you, because he doesn't have any idea what he is supposed to do. And you write . . . ?"

The kid answered quickly. "Nothing. I mean, I write he did nothing."

"Yup. Then you ask him, 'Did you understand what I asked?' He says no this time. You explain it again, and you note that you explained it again. He says he got it and he starts singing A, B, C, D, E, F, G, and so on. And you're just writing it down. It's even better if he can't even do that, because everyone can do that, even the judge can do that. But you make it even better when you testify, because the prosecutor is gonna ask you, 'Did you perform field sobriety tests on Mr. Whastsisnames here?' And you simply say, 'Yes, he failed.' Then it's the defense attorney who asks you, 'Well, what tests did you administer?' So it's the bad guy's lawyer who asks the question that zings his client. That's always fun.

"Then you ask, 'You went to college, so you can count, do your numbers, right, Mr. Whosis? You can? Good. I want you to count backwards for me, start with sixty-seven and end at forty-nine. You can use any numbers but always use the same ones, ones you can remember all the time. Keep 'em simple, because it's gotta be a test that a real person can actually do. But this cracker's gonna mess it up, gonna not start when you tell him to, and you write that down. Then he's gonna start with the right number but he's gonna either fluff it at the turn or never stop. And you're writing it all down.

"Lemme show you." The FTO reached into one of his front shirt pockets and pulled out an old notebook, rubber-banded to hold it open to a certain page. "Here's one I did last summer. Listen. 'Sixty-seven, sixty-six, sixty-five, six . . . pause.' See, I write in the pause if he pauses. 'Sixty-five, sixty-four, sixty-three, sixty-two, sixty, fifty, forty-nine, forty-eight, forty-seven.' And this guy went all the way to zero. Sounds great in court." The FTO raised his hand to gain the attention of the backhoe operator, who stopped so the FTO and the recruit could move up and look down into the deepening hole. Almost four feet down, the FTO estimated based on the disappearing length of the scoop arm.

"When you get to the coffin, stop, and I'll do some more with the shovel," Jackson told the operator, who was puzzled but put it down to police business. Jackson spun his hand to signal the operator to continue.

"So all you have to do is read from your notes. You've written down everything the guy said, and you just read it back to the judge. They ask you, 'Could he count?' You say no. They almost have to ask, they can't resist, 'What do you mean he couldn't count?' You just tell them what he said, all that sixty-seven, sixty-six, all the way to wherever he messes up. Judges eat that up. And . . ."

At that moment, the scoop bucket hit hard at the bottom with a hollow crunching *boomp*.

"Eureka," the FTO told the recruit. "Note the time."

CHAPTER 28

Trial
Thursday, November 3, 1988
1330–1530 HRS

DETECTIVE JOHN KELLY forced his mind not to wander. He'd been bashed around by the waves and rocks at the top of the day, but now Kelly was in control, sailing straight, on course, and doing what he knew he could do well. *I've got this now*, he thought, the morning's horror suppressed and behind him. Even as Rachel Cohen stood right in front of him.

He'd been able to avoid looking at her during all of his direct testimony, responding first with simple yesses and noes to questions from Assistant Commonwealth's Attorney Myron Duckworth, then expanding his answers to long narratives of investigative procedure and findings. Duckworth was competent, and Kelly was now glad he hadn't beaten him to death with the typewriter two days ago. Everybody had been ready just after ten a.m. when Commonwealth Day started, so of course Kelly's case wasn't called until what should have been after lunch, if the judge had paused so anyone could actually have lunch. No one was happy at the delay. Kelly stood next to Jumari and his mom as they were recognized by the judge. As they walked out together, Ashby, looming protectively alongside Jumari, looked maddest but only to Kelly's attuned eye. Ashby didn't speak of it in the hour before Kelly took the stand.

"State your name for the court."

"John Michael Kelly." *Jeez, Judge, don't yell,* Kelly thought, his ears sensitized by overindulgence the night before.

"And how are you employed, Mr. Kelly?" *Was that a dig? Dig! Oh, my God, that's happening right now. Focus.*

"Detective for the City of Alexandria Police Department."

"And how long have you been so employed?"

"Five years as a detective, and I have been on the Department for a total of eight years."

Boilerplate, setting the foundations of the case and his experience and expertise. Establishing the framework for the web of details that comprised a criminal case. Who did what? Where and when did they do that? Sometimes how. Rarely why.

As Kelly took the stand, much of the trial was already done, and it would have been possible to complete the prosecution case without Kelly testifying at all. First on the stand had been Dora Stibble, who had been angry but steadfast when she left Kelly behind in the lobby to take the stand. Kelly stayed out with Jumari while his mom told the court about her son, her ex-husband, and their divorce leading to court-ordered custody agreements and visitation orders. Cedric Stibble was permitted to have custody of his son only one month a year: June each year. He had picked up Jumari at the townhouse in the Andrew Adkins Homes at seven in the morning on June 1. Mom sending her boy out in new sneakers with a backpack full of peanut butter snacks and a little suitcase crammed with clean T-shirts, socks, and pajamas. She's had no contact with the father during the entire month, no calls answered, no sightings of her son near the dad's West End apartment nor anywhere in the city. Her worry cooked to terror the closer the clock spun to midnight on June 30. She called the cops at three the next morning.

Mrs. Stibble's eyes popped when Duckworth told the judge he had no further questions for Mrs. Stibble. She looked wildly back and forth between Duckworth and the judge and started to say, "You ain't asked me about—" but was cut off by Duckworth.

"Mrs. Stibble, please. Thank you for answering my questions. Please don't offer anything more, now. You should answer any questions Miss Cohen has for you." Duckworth held her stare for nearly half a minute, until Rachel stood and interposed herself to gain Mrs. Stibble's attention for her very few questions.

"Mrs. Stibble, after my client picked up his son for the visit, you didn't have any contact with him or see him for that month, did you?" Leading, but Duckworth let it go.

Another long pause, then Jumari's mother said, "Client? No, I didn't see that . . . him or Jumari until Kelly, Detective Kelly brought my Jumari home. That was after six weeks. Six weeks I didn't have no calls or . . ."

"Thank you, Mrs. Stibble. That will be all I have, Your Honor."

"Thank you, Ms. Cohen. Mrs. Stibble, you are free to leave or you may remain in the courtroom since your testimony has concluded." The judge lifted a hand toward the seats and doors at the rear of the room. Mrs. Stibble saw the room become brighter and its angles softer in the wetness over her eyes. She stood quickly but moved slowly down from the raised witness stand. She made it out the door before she broke. She sputtered when she emerged from the courtroom, and Kelly took her aside to avoid her being heard by her son, who was called in as she left and passed her at the door, shuffled forward gently by Ashby's hands at his shoulders.

While Jumari testified about the visit with his dad and their trip to San Francisco, Kelly tried to shush Mrs. Stibble outside in the lobby, finally walking away and leaving her in Ashby's company so when he was called, he would be able to truthfully answer another boilerplate question: did you discuss your testimony with any other witness today?

"No, Your Honor," Kelly testified.

"Tell the court what led you to Mr. Stibble."

"I received information that Cedric Stibble was at an address in San Francisco, California, and notified US Marshals there that I had a warrant for his arrest. They proceeded—"

"Objection, Your Honor." Rachel stood up to argue, and Kelly looked straight ahead from the raised witness stand next to the judge's bench, above eye level of the attorneys who stood as they spoke. He locked his eyes on a smudge high on the wall at the back of the court. Willing himself not to even glance at her, fearing he might. Wondering what he'd see. Lover? Destroyer? *Which Rachel was she now?* Her image danced in his peripheral vision. She went on.

"The basis of this information has not been offered to the court, and the actions taken by other police employees in another state are only hearsay from this witness and I ask that his answer be stricken from the record." Kelly could not stop himself from hearing her voice, now so biting and cold. Once so playful, warm, whispering . . . *Stop it. Now.*

"Your Honor, I will withdraw the question," Duckworth interjected. "It isn't necessary to demonstrate how Mr. Stibble was brought into custody, merely that he was in fact arrested on a lawful warrant and returned to Alexandria to face this charge. Is that true, Detective?"

"Objection. Leading the witness."

The judge stifled a sigh. "Miss Cohen, at some point the witness, any witness, must be allowed to state a series of facts that come together into information that will be heard and reviewed by the court," she chided. The judge had been looking curiously at Rachel, who was speaking in unusually clipped and bitter tones, obviously wrapped tightly over this case. "Overruled."

"Mr. Stibble was returned to Alexandria by me, after an extradition hearing in San Francisco, on the warrant that has already been admitted into evidence, issued by an Alexandria magistrate."

"And that arrest occurred on July 9 of this year, Detective, nine days after he failed to return his son?" Rachel just stood up, and the judge just waved her down before she could say "objection" again. Kelly's eyes moved across her, but he forced them past and looked instead at Cedric Stibble, seated at the defense table next to her. Stibble wore a blue suit with a thick pinstripe over a pink shirt and red tie. He was thin and clothes looked good on him. At the start of the trial, Kelly had watched Stibble turn and wave at a man behind him in the gallery, also thin, also well-dressed. Kelly knew this to be the man in Frisco at whose house the marshals and SFPD had grabbed Cedric and rescued Jumari. The man, Kelly believed, who would have been given free rein to molest Jumari had not Kelly found them in time, an involvement Kelly could not bring up in court because of Duckworth's wimpy decision. In prior motions the man had been listed as a defense witness, but Ashby, who kept moving in and out of court, informed Kelly that Cohen told the judge he would not testify today. *Shit!* Another opportunity to sneak in the pics and the letter was gone.

"Yes." And gutless Duckworth took Kelly through the interview that followed, with Stibble admitting he understood the court order describing visitation, understood the ending date was the end of June, and admitting that he had admitted to Kelly that he kept Jumari with him beyond the mandated return date. No questions about the photos and the letter, so no way to finesse them into evidence, but Kelly held out hope.

Then some last-minute boilerplate to end the prosecution case. "You were on duty with your badge of authority displayed?"

"Yes."

"Mr. Stibble understood his rights as you explained them to him?" Duckworth asked.

"Yes, we have his signed rights-waiver form already entered into evidence."

"All these events occurred in the City of Alexandria?"

"Yes." Kelly jerked. *Wait,* he thought, *there is something . . .*

"I have no further questions of this witness, Your Honor. That concludes the Commonwealth's case. May the witness be dismissed?"

"Hold up, Mr. Duckworth." The judge almost laughed. "The defense gets the opportunity to question the witness, doesn't she?"

"Um. Yes, Your Honor." The *oops!* was silent. "Detective Kelly, please answer any questions Miss Cohen has for you." Duckworth sat down, and Rachel stood up. Kelly looked at her, finally, had no choice, couldn't resist the pull of her face, his need to see her. Whether he hated or loved her, he had to see her eyes and listen to her voice. The morning was not forgotten but was muffled under the thick layer of duty, commitment, and detail that Kelly brought to his work. He always forgot his troubles at work.

But he'd forgotten something else.

"I have no questions for this witness, and I ask that he be dismissed." *Wow, that was . . . quick,* Kelly thought. *And wrong.*

He forced himself to look at her even more closely. He thought he saw nervousness or maybe hope. For what? Really, Rachel? Her eyes were wide but not direct, and Kelly couldn't make out their message.

"Really, Miss Cohen? All right. Detective Kelly, you are free to go. Since you cannot be recalled, you are free to remain in the courtroom. Miss Cohen, you may proceed with your defense."

The prosecutor watched Cohen carefully. The judge faced her in bored expectation. Kelly gazed at Rachel like a prisoner facing a one-woman firing squad—entranced, furious, repelled, devoted. He watched her take a deep breath as he stepped more slowly than usual down off the stand and across the floor where the attorneys' tables faced the judge. He passed within four feet of her, the table between them, the morning between them, last night between them. He could have smelled her hair. Then Rachel spoke loud and clear, moving very slowly to stand and address the judge. She drew herself up to her full five-feet-four in low heels and spoke as Kelly cleared the bar.

"Your Honor, the defense moves to strike the prosecution's case in chief based on jurisdiction. The Commonwealth has failed to meet its burden and demonstrate that the City of Alexandria has jurisdiction over the charge made against my client. Mr. Stibble and I request that the charge be dismissed and my client be free to go."

And Kelly knew, understood the tickle he'd felt at the end of his testimony, perceived the fatal flaw he and Duckworth had missed. He closed the gate of the bar and slid into a front-row pew, eyes loose in his slackening face as he realized his failure. Her words were hammers. His pulse pounded the back of his red eyes, and his ears were full of roaring so he could barely make out the clear words of the judge right in front of him. *Oh, my God.*

"Miss Cohen, you will need to explain yourself. I do not yet—"

"Your Honor," interrupted Rachel, her impudence a measure of her urgency to get this out, get this over with, win this one, for once. And her breathless rush was in part because she felt the hot eyes of her lover fixed on the back of her red head as she continued. "Your Honor, Detective Kelly has testified that Mr. Stibble was seized in California on or about July 9 of this year. Detective Kelly's testimony, and Mrs. Stibble's, and her son Jumari's all fail to state definitively the location of Mr. Stibble at midnight on June 30, going into the morning of July 1. Code Section 18.2-47 states, if I may, Your Honor." She lifted out a large bound codebook from her briefcase, opened it to a marked page, and didn't wait for the judge's assent to go on. "States in part, 'Any person who knowingly and willfully fails or refuses to return a child to a listed and identified parent or guardian as delineated in a court-approved custody agreement at the time of the expiration of a court-ordered period of visitation shall be guilty of a class five felony, to wit: parental abduction.'"

"Well, Miss Cohen, your client, at least according to the evidence presented by Mrs. Stibble and uncontroverted by any offered defense testimony, did fail to return the boy to his mother at the appointed time." And Kelly heard the judge reveal that she, too, had missed what Rachel had not. He could no longer look at her and didn't dare look around in fear of sighting Dora Stibble or, worse, Jumari, through the glass panels in the courtroom entry doors. Kelly, forced to silence when not under questioning, had no chance to speak to fix the case, and he had nothing to say were he allowed to.

"Without admitting to that set of facts, Your Honor, I assert that the law as written clearly states that the crime of parental abduction occurs at the moment that the child is not returned. At that precise moment, Your Honor. And no evidence has been offered to show where my client was at that moment." As the judge leaned back and looked away from her to squint at the silent, flummoxed prosecutor, Rachel knew she had a winner. Next year, when the legislature rewrote 18.2-47 to allow whatever court had issued the custody agreement to bring charges, regardless of the precise location at the moment of offense, she would lose this case. Next week, when word of the impending wording change would prompt cops to close holes in their cases by pinning down suspect locations, she would lose. Today, and only today, would Rachel win. She concluded, "Cedric Stibble has not been shown to have been in the jurisdiction of the City of Alexandria, so this court has no jurisdiction to hear this charge. And so it must be dismissed."

And so it was.

Kelly was blind, dumb, and deafened by the roar in his ears. He barely heard her going on to tell the judge that no further charge could be brought since trial had begun and double jeopardy would obtain. The bang of the gavel didn't even make him flinch.

She'd got him, got him good.

CHAPTER 29

Bust
Thursday—It's 1988, Right?
3:30 p.m.–5 p.m.

YEAH, STICK THOUGHT, *she's down for me. Maybe down on* me, *by the time we get all up in each other.* His excitement was now more than mental.

Stick sat through some trial or something; some man took his kid on a trip and came home late. His lawyer, Mizz Cohen, beat them all up, she did. Stick didn't get what had happened but he could read her eyes and her head and how she sat and stuff and could tell she was getting over on them all, the judge and the cop and the other lawyer. *Damn, my lawyer be good.*

And all the while Stick was watching the girl, more like woman, who had made eyes at him at the start of the day. She wasn't fat but wasn't thin either, and it was hard to tell, she sitting there, way down the other side of his pew, but she did seem to have legs that were thick and rounded in the muscles, like he could grip at the right time and go. Had her some titties too.

She was still reacting to him. Every time he looked at her, she was looking at him. He would look at her bust, then up into her eyes, imagining he was sending her a message. He'd seen her before, maybe on the block, maybe at T.C. He'd spent some extra years at T.C. Williams High School, the city's only one, and this fine girl maybe had come up alongside him in a class or two. He didn't know, but he would find out.

He was going to follow her when she left, whether Mizz Cohen said he could or not. He'd seen folks come and go all day in this room. Nobody sat still. Cops and normal folks getting up and leaving. Lady sitting up front calling names—never his yet—and folks with those names walking up to the front to tell their stories, or in from the side door, from the holding cells that Mizz Cohen had told him about. They guilty, they not guilty. They in jail clothes, and street clothes, and fine clothes like he was, all Fila'd out in his best sweats, shiny white sneakers on his big feet. He looked good, just right to go get at that good-looking trim over there.

But it was hours. Going on till late in the day, and they still hadn't called his name. He rubbed the root through his pants and thought, *Wish that Professor Vulture had told me how it worked. Was it all done now?* Stick wondered, *And all I have to do is wait? Or will it only be done when I chewed up that last root?* He didn't know.

Mizz Cohen had come back and sat next to him on the pew. She didn't say anything. A couple of times she held her hands up over her eyes, like she was crying but not letting tears come out. He knew she had won her case with the big cop, but she didn't seem all that happy about it. She rubbed her hands together, holding her elbows in tight to her sides like she was cold.

Another case finished up. Neither Stick nor Rachel was looking when the clerk spoke softly to the judge, who said something to the bailiff, who spoke loudly. "All rise, Circuit Court for the City of Alexandria is adjourned." Stick looked at Mizz Rachel, who sighed and said, "They never called your case, Stick. I don't know why. It just disappeared. I'm not going to try to track it down. It's missing, gone. Don't worry about it. If it comes up again, I'll get in contact with you." She sighed again, shook her head, and stood up. "You can go. Don't come back." Lady seemed so sad.

On his way out, Stick looked toward the girl. And she was coming out too, coming after him. She sidled up close as they hit the door, side by side. She smiled at him.

"Hey, boy. I been looking for you." Her voice was low, deep like she was excited to see him. He knew she was, knew he didn't have to lift a finger to get her. Side by side, they pushed through the double doors of the courtroom, but she turned right, toward the windows at the end of the hallway and away from the lobby, the elevators, and the outside, where he wanted to be with this fine girl. She turned and lit him up with those round, brown eyes, looking him up and down, checking him out. *Yeah, baby, you check my package. It'll be just . . . Wait, what she say?*

"You remember me, boy?"

Huh? "Nah, I ain't remember you, but you gon' remember me when we go out. I give you all you need to—"

"You really don't remember me? This summer, you 'n' me met up on the block. I was driving, you came up. You were selling. But you didn't sell to me." Her soft voice was getting harder. He had been hard but was getting soft. There was a crowd in the hall, and two big people were pressing up close behind him as he stood in front of her. He peered closer. *She knows me. How come I don't know her? For real, I seen her but . . . in summer?*

"Make it easier for you. I was sitting in a little red Mazda when you waved and I stopped on the corner, Alfred at Madison. You came up to the car, and I had a twenty in my hand. You said, 'Bitch, go home.' You remember that now, little boy? You remember what else you did?" She was standing right in front of him now, her hands up between them, fingers of one hand touching the fingers of the other, almost like she praying. Stick's slow mind raced. *Why she so mad? She . . . Fuck, this be the bitch I stuck up, stoled her through the window, took her twenty bill. She think she know me. I know her. Why she all being hard on me now, standing there all hands up front?*

Like she a police.

Exactly like a cartoon, Stick's frown popped open into surprise, recognition, alarm, and fright, all in the time it took for the two large TAC unit members behind him to each grab a wrist and push forward on the elbow to lever the joint into pain compliance, propelling Stick forward past the beautiful girl and chest first against the wall. Two big hairy voices yelled in his ears, "Police, don't move! You're under arrest." Handcuffs were ratcheted tight to hold his wrists behind his back, and when he tried to pull free, their big hands wrapped around the closed handcuff rings and clicked them painfully tighter. Stick swung his head around, trying to look at the police who held him against the wall and ran hands up and down his clothing, quickly at first for large objects like weapons, then more carefully for smaller items like contraband or drugs. His identification, a T.C. Williams High School student ID, was removed from his pocket by the cops behind, and he heard a police voice mutter his name, and a radio buzz. The ID was handed over his shoulder to the lady cop.

"Fuck, man. What . . ."

A hand reached into his front pants pocket and removed a short length of greenish-brown material, which was later secured in a lock-seal evidence envelope for submission to the state police laboratory for drug analysis. Their search finished, the unseen cops pulled Stick away from the wall and he faced the girl. Her eyes angry but cool, she reached into her purse and pulled out a police badge different and more ornate than the Alexandria shield, held it at his eye level, and said, "Police Officer Two Adrienne Carter, Manassas City Police Department. Antonio Planter, you are under arrest for robbery. Of me."

Stick looked over this female officer's shoulder and saw his attorney as she left the courtroom, looked at him, and widened her eyes. "Hey, Mizz Cohen, hey, look here, some bitch popo puttin' a charge on me. I . . ." Rachel kept walking away.

Officer Carter grabbed his chin. "Shut up, little man. You got nothing to say to nobody. Look at yo'self. Boy, you such a hard man. Are you handcuffed or you got flowers behind your back for me?" A cop behind Stick laughed. "You should'a just stayed a dealer, nobody cares about that. But you a big-time robber now. Gonna serve big time."

"Wait, no, bitch, what, I, you, we can, you know I . . . Hey Mizz Cohen, you gotta stop 'em. These cuffs too tight. Police brutality! Police—"

"You know that right you got to remain silent," the female officer said, up close to him, almost a whisper in his ear. "Use it."

During pretrial discovery two months later, Antonio "Stick" Planter's defense attorney would learn that the vegetable material seized during Stick's robbery arrest was tested and found to contain no perceivable narcotic levels and was a root of undetermined origin. That attorney was not Rachel Cohen.

CHAPTER 30

Searches
Thursday, November 3, 1988
1700–1800 HRS

RECRUIT HIGGINS WAS surprised when FTO Jackson said, "Let me out in front of the courthouse and go park the car." They were supposed to be a team, and he was not to be left alone until certified for solo patrol. On the other hand, he was flattered to be trusted to be set free even for only a few moments until he could catch up with his FTO inside.

His black jump boots left muddy footprints on the tile of the elevator lobby on four, matching those just left by his partner. He caught up to FTO Jackson outside Courtroom One, which had just closed at the end of its afternoon docket. The other two courtrooms were still in session, crammed with cops both uniform and plainclothes, vics, wits, watchers, criers. He watched the FTO peer through the glass panels in the doors of each, unable to enter because of his gun. No Kelly among the lumpy tweed jackets and dark suits of the police sides of the rooms.

They took the stairs to the Commonwealth Attorney's Office. The receptionist looked at their muddy shoes and pants and started to say something but was preempted by the FTO's question. "Kelly here lately?"

"John Kelly? He was, earlier. I think he signed out. Check the sheet."

The FTO checked the sign-in/out sheet on a clipboard hanging next to the gun lockers and saw that Kelly had left only five minutes before. He noticed another name on the list. The FTO unclipped his radio, listened a moment, and keyed the mic.

"Unit 224 to Unit 60?"

Silence and static. He tried it again ten seconds later, with no response. Other units began talking now that it was clear he was done. Okay, one errand on hold, but another had presented itself. They went back upstairs and checked Courtroom One, but it was closed, cases completed for the day. Then they stood outside Courtroom Four, where the FTO had peeked in the door and spotted an officer with whom he needed to make contact. They were still armed, so they had to wait outside a while till she exited. The FTO told the recruit to stand on the other side of the lobby while he talked with Pammie Martinson, his secondary target for this trip. The recruit was insulted at being shunned but did as told. "I'll explain later," the FTO said and pulled Pammie down the hall, out of earshot but still in sight, and the recruit watched them speak together softly, facing each other. The FTO looked over Pammie's shoulder occasionally as people emerged from the courtroom, assessing and dismissing them. Pammie still looked mad at, or despondent over, her beating in court the day before and the release of her shooter. And the FTO had learned she had to be back in the same courtroom tomorrow for her advisement on the reckless driving summons she'd received after the pursuit on the 14th Street Bridge.

The recruit watched Pammie, thumbs hooked in a gun belt still heavy with handcuffs and speed-loaders despite the absence of her gun. First through clenched teeth then an open-mouthed holler, Pammie let the FTO have it. He took it, nodding gently or heavily depending, till she wound down. When she dropped her chin, he slowly reached up and used a gentle fist to bring her face back up and began his own speech, too softly for the recruit to hear. She brightened, her back straightened, and her eyes softened. She looked past the FTO at the recruit and said, "You promise?" At Jackson's nod, she walked away past the recruit and down the stairs, treading lightly.

"C'mon."

"You gonna tell me?" the recruit asked as they rode down the elevator to street level.

"Which part?"

"Part? Whaddya mean, part? There's parts?"

"Yeah, part that happens tonight, and part that happens tomorrow."

"Tell me both parts."

"Wait till we're in the car. Where are we?"

The recruit led to where he'd left the cruiser, on a corner one block away off the main street, and watched in surprise when the FTO slid in behind the wheel, using his own key. "I just want to drive for a bit," he said in response to the recruit's look. "So . . . Pammie," the FTO began after marking back in service with Headquarters.

"I don't like not knowing what's going on," the recruit sniffed.

"You never know what's going on, all of what's going on, around here. Always something happening. You'll learn to pay attention, and how to pay attention, and to whom to pay attention. Half the guys around here are fluff. They come in and just put in the time. They're good cops, but that's just it, that's all they are. Good. Wanna be great? You gotta work harder, watch more. Pammie? She'll be a good example for you."

"Example?" The recruit had by now mastered the habit of talking in the car without looking at his partner, focusing his attention on scanning his surroundings.

"Pammie got in pursuit, got shot at, and got the bad guy without getting herself killed or having to kill anyone. That's pretty good work," Jackson said.

"But she got slammed. She got a VUS for reckless. That's ridiculous," Higgins said.

"Looks that way, doesn't it? Look closer." He glanced at the recruit, who caught the glance in his peripheral vision but didn't return it.

"A cruiser got crashed. Somebody gets in trouble when that happens. Always. Immutable law. And the way the written directives lay it out, they can either get a Virginia Uniform Summons for the traffic violation that caused the crash, or they can get a '67 for the same thing. One or the other, and they can't get both, and the watch commander has discretion over which they get. The lieutenant chose to make the sarge write Pammie a VUS. That means she can't get a '67. Believe me, the '67 is worse. It counts as discipline, goes in your squad file. And stays there, so whatever punishment she gets, 'cause we have progressive discipline, it means her next ding has to carry higher punishment. So you want to stay off that ladder if at all possible."

"But she's not off the hook. She still gets the VUS and has to go to court, right?" Higgins asked.

"Yes. But let's pretend you're a recruit in training and I'm your field training officer, so I can ask you some instructional questions." The recruit looked at him like he was from Mars.

"Recruit, answer this: what are the jurisdictional limits of police in the Commonwealth of Virginia?"

"You mean like where we can arrest people?" At the FTO's nod, he continued. "City police may arrest up to one mile outside the jurisdictional boundaries of their city. County police have jurisdiction one hundred yards outside their jurisdictional border."

"And so . . . ?"

"Huh?"

"Where'd Pammie crash?"

"On the 14th Street Bridge."

"Where's that?"

The recruit glared at the FTO for asking such a dumb question, but he knew he had to give some answer. "It's right there, down the parkway. It's over the Potomac, goes from the Arlington County side near the Pentagon side to D.C."

"And?"

"And what?" the recruit asked in exasperation.

"And the 14th Street Bridge is one-point-nine miles northeast of the jurisdictional boundary of the City of Alexandria. The crash location is in Arlington County, or maybe D.C. depending on how far across she got. Meaning a summons written by an Alexandria Police sergeant on the bridge is not legal. The shooting scene was point-eight beyond the border, so that's ours, but the bridge was further out. Meaning when Pammie goes to court tomorrow and the trial begins, she can strike the summons on jurisdiction and it can't be brought back because of double jeopardy, even if the bosses wanted to go get a new, correct ticket from an Arlington County or D.C. magistrate."

"Meaning she skates."

"Yup. Just like Lieutenant Ramirez wanted her to." The FTO pulled the cruiser to the curb so he could face the recruit for this. "Pammie's not a *good* cop. She's an *outstanding* cop. Makes quality arrests and doesn't generate citizen complaints. She thinks her way through situations, doesn't push people around, isn't badge-heavy. Has a college degree, not a requirement around here and maybe it should be, but it shows she can apply herself to bettering herself, and maybe to bettering us too. She is going somewhere on this department, and we need her to. We need smart, sharp cops to take us forward. We're always gonna need good cops to do the job, the basic job. Plus, I trained her, so she started off above average. All my kids do.

"So, do we watch out for and help out certain cops? Yes, sure. Who could blame anyone for trying to help? It's why we became cops in the first place. Yeah, we say it's to drive fast and carry guns, and we get shy when we look inward at the real reason we're here. But it is truly so we can help people. And if the lieutenant sees a way he can help someone, he will. But it's gotta be in a way that works in the system. He's gotta do something as a commander, gotta be seen as keeping his thumb on the team."

"So he dings her, in a way she can get out of?"

"Yup."

"Doesn't the third floor catch on?" The Chief of Police and high-level command staff occupied offices on the third floor of Headquarters.

"They never come out to see. All they know, she got dinged. If she skates, it's 'cause the courts let her off. Ramirez did his job, she keeps going, he keeps going, we keep going. Everybody's happy."

"So, today . . . ?"

"Today I told her what to do tomorrow. Go into court for her advisement, let the commonwealth's attorney get started. Then ask for immediate trial. You can do that, and the sergeant who wrote her will just happen to be there, so they'll find they've got everybody they need to go forward. Judge starts the case, Sarge testifies, then it's Pammie's turn. She asks the judge to strike the summons for jurisdiction. Judge does, double jeopardy obtains, Pammie's good to go."

"Long way to go just to let Pammie not get in trouble."

"That's just it. Pammie's got to get in trouble. Has to happen, she dinged a cruiser. LT's gotta ding her, he's a commander, it's his job. He's a scorpion."

"Scorpion?"

"D'you forget that story I told you about the scorpion and the turtle? Tell you again later. So, the lieutenant's got a job to do, and he'll do it. But the right way, no harm no foul. Keep your eyes open, Higgins. This goes on all the time. You may not ever see it, and God forbid you ever need it. But do a good, no, a great job, work hard and be smart, it'll be available for you too. We may not tell you when we do it, but we'll do it."

Recruit Higgins watched FTO Jackson's eyes focus out beyond the streets he drove down. Jackson drifted back ten years, to the night he needed a thin blue safety net. He'd fallen asleep in a moving cruiser, lulled out by the soft rustle of a falling snow on a quiet, white night, crashing off the street and blowing two tires on the high curb. His huge Dodge Monaco patrol car carried only one spare. As a rookie, his career would have been hurt or ended by the discipline that followed an accident investigation. Jackson's former FTO saved him, donating his own cruiser's spare to get Jackson back on the road without notifying the sergeant. The flats were hidden that night, fixed the next day, and returned to their correct car locations. So Jackson was introduced to, and protected by, the web of hidden help that some senior officers spread over the department. Senior officers like Jackon's savior, then-FTO Walter Ramirez, now Lieutenant Ramirez.

Higgins got impatient with FTO Jackson's reverie. "So why not tell her when you do it, or the sergeant or lieutenant does it, so she doesn't worry for days?"

"Worry's good for you. No, really, she might'a slipped, told a friend, big-mouthed it so the bosses could fix it before she pushed the case of the cliff."

"That's one part. The tomorrow part. You said there were two."

"Oh yeah. Tonight. The guy that walked yesterday, the shooter, when judge got pissed at Pammie and set him free? Lemme tell you what's going on there. There's a lot going on." It only took a minute.

The FTO looked at the recruit for a moment, then pulled out into traffic. They drove for a while, a rare few minutes when they were not on a call, en route to a call, or writing up a call. Down time.

"So, you told me that now. You gonna tell me the rest?" Higgins said.

"Huh?" Jackson said.

"Are you going to tell me what the secret thing going on with Kelly is?"

"'Chu mean?"

"I mean all this *Secret Squirrel* shit. Kelly and the coffin. And why we hadda be the ones handling the digging-up part today, the report, coming in early so it was us." Higgins dropped a hand to his calf and scraped off a lump of mud, holding it up like evidence. "Was there something there that helps Kelly?" The recruit looked at the FTO like he expected a full answer.

They drove another ten blocks before the FTO reached for the mic, called Headquarters to take them out of service on a training detail, and pulled the car behind a warehouse. He looked at the recruit for a minute or two, as if reviewing a set of conclusions he wanted to reach and hoping his observations matched the needed parameters. He switched his gaze to the rearview mirror for a moment, saw himself, and shrugged in acceptance, or prayer.

"This'll take some time."

CHAPTER 31

Clobbered
Thursday, November 3, 1988
1630–1700 HRS

KELLY LET ASHBY drive. He slumped in the front seat of the unmarked sedan with the Stibbles in the rear. Light snow further dimmed the overcast skies. Jumari was happy because he got to be with his dad again soon but sad because his mom was so sad. Or mad. Hard to tell the difference when you're ten.

Kelly could tell, however. She was both. Kelly was the cause of Dora Stibble's sadness and the focus of the anger she had spewed out at him when the trial ended. As they rode the two miles to the Stibble townhouse in the New Projects, Kelly's pager beeped again. He clicked it off his belt, stared at the read-out a while, and reattached it silently on his belt, in front next to his badge. Another county heard from, more crap pouring on his head. As it had for the past hour, in the courthouse after the dismissal.

When he first told her the case had evaporated, in the hall outside Courtroom One, Mrs. Stibble screamed. Literally screamed, bringing bailiffs and cops and a newspaper reporter running to see. They stood back, tensed and ready to intervene if she went beyond verbal to physical in her attack on Kelly, the reporter scribbling on a little pad. She lashed him for his "stupid, motherfucking, no-account useless, worthless, nothing cop job" in letting her "slimy, motherfucking, no-account, useless rapist" of an ex-husband get away with stealing her baby. With amused eyes the crowd watched Kelly maneuver her onto the elevator down to a conference room in the CA's office. He hoped she would tire of her tirade, or at least slow down her litany of complaints. But she didn't.

"What you mean, judge dropped the charge?" Dora Stibble was truly spitting mad, but Kelly could not move out of droplet range in the small gap between conference table and bookcases. As a cop, he'd been spit on before, and she wasn't thinking, didn't mean it. But if she were thinking, she'd probably mean it.

Her voice rose. "He did it, he admitted he did it. He told you he did it. Court visitation papers say he did it. He did it." Mother Stibble could not be pacified. Ashby had taken Jumari downstairs for a candy bar while Kelly moved Mom to a closed conference room in the prosecutors' office suite and let her flay him with her bitter anger. She focused on Kelly like sunlight magnified onto an ant, Kelly who had lost the case and so lost her son.

She marched around and around the long table, Kelly seated at one side, and screamed, barked, cursed. "He did it. And that man he was gonna give my Jumari to, there right there in the room with him. The courtroom! Right near Jumari! How come he's not in jail? What did the judge say about him, huh?" Kelly finally had to walk through a door he'd prayed he could keep closed. But she needed to know.

"The judge didn't say anything because we didn't tell him," Kelly said. He hadn't told Dora Stibble that the evidence from California, the seized photographs and letters, had been deemed inadmissible by the prosecutor. He didn't think he could make her understand. He didn't understand himself. "We never brought it up, didn't introduce the photographs and Cedric's letter. The judge never considered them."

"Didn't tell him? Didn't tell him! You didn't tell him, what the fuck else didn't you do too? Didn't consider . . . Fucking miserable, fucking . . ." She went on and on, with Kelly sitting at the conference room table from her, taking it. Once, the heavy door opened and a lieutenant in uniform stuck his head in, checking on the shouting and withdrawing at a small wave of okay from Kelly. It was Lieutenant Ramirez, not in his chain of command.

Kelly let her vent her fury, disgust, and protective motherly scorn on him, beating him senseless, burying him in contempt, finally breaking down into sobs and a long, low moan as she sat. He stood and reached to her, but she threw his hand off her shoulder, so he left her in the conference room alone.

The lieutenant was waiting for him. "She okay?"

"Define 'okay.' She has to let her son go off with his pervert dad who maybe's gonna sell him to a man. We lied to her that we'd get a judge to lock up Daddy and Daddy's friend, and they got to smile and walk out when the judge tanked the charge. I promised to protect her son, and I didn't. Sure, LT, ignore all that, and she's okay."

Lieutenant Ramirez paused before he spoke. "So you did a pretty incompetent job with this one, huh?" His accusation slapped Kelly. It was not totally out of the blue: Kelly had been telling himself that a lot recently. But it was from an unexpected direction and his armor was down, so it sank deep.

"What's it to you, Lieutenant? You're Patrol, not CID. Since when do lieutenants come to court anyway?"

The lieutenant drew himself up to his full five-foot-eight, pulling eye to chin with Kelly, smaller and thinner, but carrying more weight than the detective. Kelly tried to walk away, down the hall and into the receptionists' lobby, but the lieutenant stayed with him. "Things to do here. Beyond just cases. Things like seeing what you are up to, what you've done. What've you done here, Kelly? Is Mrs. Stibble going to file a complaint against you?"

How'd he know her name?

"Because I talked with Duckworth after she started screaming," Lieutenant Ramirez said, anticipating Kelly's question. "What's her issue?"

"Her kid has to go back to a dad we think is gonna molest him, or let someone else molest him."

"You know this how?"

"We've got pics of the other guy with kids. Not porn but stuff like they don't have shirts on, they look like they're in his bed. We got a letter from Dad to this guy, saying he'd introduce Jumari to him. Hinting at some kind of payoff. But we can't use the pics or the letter—Duckworth says they were illegally seized by California, so he wouldn't introduce them."

"Where are they now?"

"Case file," Kelly said.

"In the CA's file? Or the court file in the clerk's office?"

"Probably the CA's file. Duckworth would have them. We didn't introduce them, so they're not in the public file. Fuckin' Duckworth didn't want to risk his batting average by trying to bring them in."

"Duckworth wants to write you up for incompetency," Ramirez said.

"Me? Him!"

"You. You didn't know the law. You failed to analyze the needs of the case, see the gaps in your investigation, and fill them before trial. Where was Stibble at midnight? You didn't find out. He might have been right here in the city, you don't know, and we can't bring the case back."

"It's Duckworth's job to know the law. He's the goddamn lawyer."

"No, it's your job to know everything you need to make your case. You, you're the cop, you make the case yourself, you don't depend on anyone else to do it for you. You are responsible for yourself, your work, your people, your safety. We can help you, on our side, not anyone else. We cover each other and our own asses on this department, not wait for or blame others. But he's blaming you."

"Duckworth?"

"He wants to file charges against you for dereliction of duty. I told him not to."

"Thanks."

"Because *I* would."

"What! You, you're gonna . . ."

"Somebody has to, Kelly. You're not in control of your cases lately or yourself. You're becoming incompetent. Missing things, like this case. You didn't even read the law you charged the guy with."

"Well, then, neither did the magistrate, or Duckworth, or the judge at prelim, or the grand jury."

"Not their case. Your case. You blew it, Kelly. Look for a '67 when you get in tomorrow. Failure to demonstrate knowledge and procedures. You don't need any more charges than that, do you?"

Kelly looked closely at the lieutenant because that sounded like a real question and not the posturing snap of a martinet. "For what? For this? I lost a case? We lose fucking cases all the time, and we don't get written up for it. Sure you don't have any felonies you could charge me with?" *I could tell you all about a big one*, Kelly thought. Kelly was out on the edge, but the detective in him instinctively probed, pushed, and interrogated. From the lieutenant's straight face, Kelly decided he didn't know anything more. "Fuck you, LT. I don't know why the fuck you gotta stick your face into CID business. You're not my lieutenant."

"Voice down, Detective." His eyes were cast upward to meet Kelly's, but he still looked down on him. "You're out of control. Don't make it worse for yourself."

"You cocksucker," Kelly spat the words and walked out the office door, colliding with the newspaper reporter. The lieutenant's face went white, but he didn't speak further.

Not in front of witnesses.

The reporter followed Kelly down the hall. "Heard you lost a big one just now, John. Wanna give me a quote about it?" John, huh? Not Detective Kelly anymore. *I owed him for helping when Emma was . . . and I paid that off. I helped him with that story about the car thief girl.* Not an equal repayment but the best he could do. "How'd you lose the trial, John?"

"You were there in court? You got everything I want to say."

"No, I wasn't there. Wasn't in the courtroom. I don't have to be. I can't be everywhere. But the prosecutor told me all about it, and I got the file from the clerk to fill in the blanks. You charged an *innocent* dad with nothing."

"Innocent, huh?" Kelly had heard the reporter's emphasis. "What do you know about his innocence?" Kelly punched the elevator button, again and again.

"Heard Mama too, outside the court. She's pretty pissed. Something more's going on. She'll tell me later. I got her address off the file. Should be good for a story for tomorrow. Your chance now to tell your side."

As the elevator door opened, Kelly stepped in and immediately spun to face the reporter who was following him in. In his command voice, Kelly barked, "Back up!" The reporter stopped, and the powered doors gently slid against his shoulders and reopened. Kelly brought the flat of his hand up to the reporter's chest, fingers at the base of his throat, and shoved him firmly back. "I don't have a side. I don't have anything," Kelly said as the doors closed.

He found Ashby and Jumari outside the building, Jumari with an ice cream cone despite the November cold. He sent Ashby back in to gather up Mrs. Stibble where Kelly had abandoned her in the CA's conference room while he and Jumari retrieved the unmarked and parked in the courthouse loading zone. Ashby loaded the Stibble family in the back seat, Mom fuming but silent next to her son, her angry eyes Kelly felt boring into the back of his skull. Not a word all the way home, even when the detectives walked them to the door. Which slammed in their faces. He made to toss his keys to Ashby, but his partner held up his matching set and started the car.

Riding with Ashby back to HQ, Kelly took off his pager and looked again at messages. Two phone numbers had appeared on the pager since the important message. They appeared to be department exchanges, but he didn't recognize them, so didn't wish to call them back. Couldn't be good news today, with the case, the upcoming newspaper article, the exhumation, God knew what else. He looked at an earlier message, knowing Rachel had sent it from its structure. From its anger, too. He read the numbers: "7734 2 09." Turned upside down, the block letters read: "GO 2 HELL."

Kelly leaned forward, rolled the side window partly open, and tossed the pager out. He thought he heard it clatter along the pavement, but he wasn't sure.

CHAPTER 32

Management
Thursday, November 3, 1988
1730–1800 HRS

THE VILE EPITHET burned the lieutenant's brain but he didn't let on. Too many people around for him to push Kelly further now. Did he know? Lieutenant Ramirez watched Kelly stomp down the hall, nearly colliding with a reporter for the *Alexandria Gazette* who buttonholed the angry detective at the elevator. The lieutenant recognized him as the one in blue shirt and clipboard who'd bluffed his way through the perimeter on the 14th Street Bridge scene two days ago. Dressed that way, he could have been a bridge inspector, someone from the fire department, somebody who belonged there, so he wasn't challenged when he walked past officers sealing off the huge crime scene. Cute trick.

The lieutenant leaned a shoulder against the wall and listened to the reporter try to get a rise out of Kelly. He watched as the reporter stumbled back as the doors closed. He looked with contempt as the reporter approached him to complain about one of his officers pushing him around.

"I heard the detective give you a clear, firm command to step back. I don't know the reason for it, but you failed to obey instructions. Are you injured?"

"Injured? No, I'm not injured. But he can't just push people around."

"No, we can't do that. I'll have a talk with him." Not enough, the lieutenant saw that the reporter wasn't mollified, so he went into a full police public relations schtick.

"I understand your concerns, sir. As a member of the police command and one of Detective Kelly's superiors, I need to be made aware of issues involving our staff, and I thank you for bringing this to my attention. This is the kind of information and feedback we need to ensure the highest . . ." And he stopped listening to himself at that point, but went on for a few more sentences until this complaining citizen was fully assured that the problem with John Kelly would be dealt with most severely. Which, of course, was not what the lieutenant had said at all. ". . . level of professionalism and public service can be provided. I will review this incident and ensure that the proper discipline or retraining is instituted against Detective Kelly." *So back the fuck off, you little pissant*, Ramirez thought, his eyes reflecting nothing but concern and attention.

"Yeah, you do that," the reporter said, pausing to look closer at Ramirez's uniform. He didn't know how to differentiate the collar pins, but the badge had "Lieutenant" on it. "Lieutenant. And tell him to look for his name in print tomorrow."

"Really? A story about a child custody case? Big news for your readers?"

"Hey, it happened. And the story isn't the kid; it's the failure of the police to do their job. Duckworth says Kelly muffed it."

"And you're going to quote Duckworth on that? Those words?"

"I have it, he said it.   So, yeah, I can use it. It's what happened."

"Were you even there? Were you in the room when it happened? Do you really think you know the truth of what happened there?" The lieutenant stopped and took a mental step back. The reporter had also stopped, taken out a small spiral notebook and applied pen to same. "What was your name, Lieutenant? Can I quote you?" Like an instinct, an autonomic response, muscle memory.

Often in explaining the vagaries of police-public-political-press dealings in Alexandria, the lieutenant used a story to illustrate why people in general and politicians in particular always fell back on self-interest in making decisions, no matter the issue. One day, he would say, a scorpion walked up to a turtle by a river and said, "Turtle, carry me across the river." The turtle said, "You're a scorpion. You will sting me and kill me." "Why would I do that? It would kill us both." Turtle says, "Okay." Halfway across, the scorpion stung the turtle. Turtle said, "Why'd you do that?" Scorpion said, "I'm a scorpion."

The lieutenant looked at the reporter and imagined him saying, "I'm a reporter."

The lieutenant handed over a business card and said, "Call PIO for any quote," and walked away, back to the CA's office. He'd told FTO Jackson to meet him there to talk, sheesh, about Kelly's felonies. But first, Ramirez had to find Duckworth again. *Another ass to save, this time not Kelly's but Jumari's*, he thought wryly. He shouldn't be so concerned about asses.

People would talk.

CHAPTER 33

Alone
Thursday, November 3, 1988
3:30 p.m.–3:45 p.m.

ASSISTANT PUBLIC DEFENDER Rachel Cohen walked slowly from Courtroom One. She had paused to watch Stick's arrest but didn't care about it one way or another. She hadn't won his case. Or lost it either. It had disappeared. *Counts as a win*, she guessed.

She had won the other, setting a rapist free as her job required her to do. Or rather, required her to give the best legal defense she knew how to do. If the guilty . . . No, can't call them guilty here in the courthouse. If the ones who on the street commit crimes, even heinous crimes, are arrested by cops too incompetent or overworked to convict, then it was her job to exploit case weaknesses. No matter who walked. No matter who was hurt. Like Kelly. Kelly, distracted, worn out, worn down, stressed to the max. Grieving, as she'd learned. Why hadn't he ever told her about Emma?

Kelly, who had hurt her to her core. But she didn't feel she had gotten even. She couldn't feel anything except horror at their last talk, sorrow at her physical loss, and aching pain. It almost crippled her here, in the still-crowded but emptying courthouse. Somewhere she heard shouting. Sounded like her client's wife, whom Rachel had cross-examined but lightly. Nothing Mrs. Stibble could say would in any way help her client, so Rachel left her alone. Rachel had concentrated on Kelly, focusing on case details and seeming to gloss over the boilerplate in which her sole line of defense lay, or hid. She sure fooled Kelly. She sure got him.

Rachel stood in front of the elevator bank but let two go before finding an empty one to enter alone. Riding down, after a few seconds, she reached out tentatively and pressed the stop button. The box lurched, causing her more pain, and she doubled over, then sat back. Her rump rode down the slick paneled wall till she was sitting on the floor at the back.

She cried her eyes out for five minutes. Then Rachel stood up, pressed other buttons to resume her travel away from Circuit Court. Toward what, she was not sure anymore. Not toward Kelly.

CHAPTER 34

Visitation
Thursday, November 3, 1988
7:30 p.m.–8 p.m.

JANET PAULSON KELLY heard a car door slam and noise outside her old house, but she was folding clothes and didn't look right away. She heard voices.

"Can I help you?" Tony's voice, a little higher than usual, and she paused.

"Don't know. I'm looking for John Kelly." A voice she'd heard before but couldn't place.

"He's not here," Tony said.

"Okay, is Janet here?"

"Yes, she is. Why you want to know?"

"Who are you, her brother?"

"No, what's it to you?" Tony's aggressiveness, unusual for him, made her move to the window and look out into the deepening darkness. She saw a white unmarked Alexandria Police cruiser. And her heart stopped.

She'd been a cop's wife for enough years to know that cruisers showing up unannounced meant bad things. Whether she loved John Kelly anymore, a big part of her still cared in a damaged and overturned way. When she rushed downstairs to the door, she found a police commander there, a lieutenant in a white shirt talking with Tony. Tony had told Janet he would not come inside the house his new girlfriend once shared with her soon-to-be ex. *Not soon enough*, she kept thinking, though after this morning *sooner* was closing in rapidly.

"Hello, Janet. Don't panic, nothing's wrong, John's not hurt or anything." There, all bases touched, bringing him around to . . . "I was hoping he was here."

"No, John's not here," she said, squinting to read the nameplate on this man's white uniformed chest, hard to make out in the fading light of early evening. *W. Ramirez.* She knew him from work events but didn't know if John had ever worked with him, or for him.

"Can I . . ." The lieutenant paused, looking from her to Tony, who was six inches taller than he. "Can we talk, maybe inside?" Leaves were blowing around their feet as November asserted itself here in Kelly's quiet neighborhood.

"Outside's fine," Tony interjected, stepping next to Janet. He tried to loom menacingly over Ramirez but failed, and the lieutenant ignored him. "Like I said, what's this about?"

"'Asked,'" the lieutenant said.

"Huh?"

"If that was a question, then you asked it, not said it. Never mind. Janet, I just want to find John. He had a pretty bad day, I've got some news that might change things for him. I want to talk with him pronto."

"Well, I don't know where he is. He doesn't call me back when I page him anymore, and sometimes he doesn't even answer the phone when he's here."

"I know, for us too. But I'm . . . worried about him," Ramirez said.

"And I'm supposed to care?"

"You don't?"

"Don't you know? John and I are separated. I don't live here anymore. He—we want a divorce. Been half a year. Guess he doesn't talk to you much."

"Doesn't talk to anyone much lately. But his partner says he was pretty knocked down after today. He lost a big case, he's getting written up, and even the newspaper's gonna clobber him for it. And . . ." When he stopped, Janet saw something else in his eyes but didn't want to bring it out. She was done with John Kelly, or was trying to be.

"We're getting a divorce. He can deal with all that himself," Janet Kelly said.

"You guys were married for, what, ten years?"

Jeez, she thought, *who is this guy? I don't know him, but he knows so much.*

"Why did you break up?

"That's none of your business."

"Of course it's my business. He needs help right now, Janet. What's going on with you?"

"He . . . we, about a year ago was when it got bad. Or worse, I guess. It was already bad for a while." Janet turned to address Tony and touched his arm a moment. "I'm all right, Tony, I can talk with him about it. John's not getting back with me no matter what." Tony, his tenuous place reassured, took a step back, and Janet resumed.

"You know John, right? Always in control, all you guys are that way. You're calm, no matter what." Janet almost smiled. "You've got it, hard stuff, sad stuff, bloody stuff, whatever—it's always your call and we handle it your way. You tell me, tell us non-cops what to do, say, sit, even wear sometimes." *Well, maybe that was strong, but John had always made it clear what he liked me to wear, how I should look. He was happier when I looked that way, so I tried to, for a while.* While it worked. Until it stopped working. Janet was going too far, farther than she'd ever gotten in trying to explain or understand John's way.

"But he got too, I don't know, too *John* all the time. He would sit around and if I wanted to do something, he'd snap. He yelled a lot. He was like, frantic, most of the time. Drank a lot, drank beer so he could say it didn't count. And we, we weren't the same together. He was just there, just . . . So I left him alone as much as I could. Not that I drifted away from him, but it was like he pushed off fast. I couldn't keep up with where he was going, and we just weren't married people anymore."

"So he changed? He was a good man, Janet. You married him."

"Who do you think you . . . Yeah, yeah. Kell was a great cop. Won awards. But he changed into a dick. No time for me. Self-important. Maybe he always was, but he got so full of himself when he got on the department, like he felt good only because he was a cop. But less lately, the last year or so."

"So for years it was getting bad? And a year ago, it gets worse? Janet, what happened last year?" A pointed question. He already knew.

"I don't—you mean Emma's death? John was fine with that. Well, not fine, nobody was fine, but he wasn't worse than his brother or Brenda or his mom. Kell kept it together. Kept us together. Tough guy. He was strong."

"Not so strong. Not now." Again, Janet watched the man pause, considering something. Something he might say? Apparently he decided, no.

She continued. "Yeah, he got like manic lately. We didn't, we were never . . . We could never get anything happy to happen. I guess I didn't put Emma as a start to things, 'cause they'd maybe been bad before that happened. Too late now to fix it, and I don't want to try. Neither does he, I don't think."

"Janet, if you see him . . . What are you doing here anyway, if you all are separated? Is he living here or you?"

"Oh, it's his house. I came here to get some stuff. We only made the decision to go ahead with the divorce for sure this morning." Tony turned to gape at Janet, surprised, not even looming over her now. She shrugged at him.

"This morning?"

"I came for some stuff, some kitchen stuff. John was passed out on the floor. He'd been drinking. A lot. He's been doing that a lot recently. Fucking lush."

The lieutenant could only stare at her.

"Tell him to call me if you see him." He turned and walked back to the cruiser, turned, and came back to her. Again he glanced at Tony, again dismissed him, and asked, "Janet, other than his service weapon, does John keep any other guns in the house?"

"Guns?"

CHAPTER 35

Destruction
Thursday, November 3, 1988
2200–2330 HRS

IF ONLY THE tire had blown when John Kelly plowed it into the curb on quiet South Payne Street near the cemetery. Should have flattened and disabled the car and kept Kelly off the road any more that night. But it did not.

Hours ago, Kelly's failing Irish luck made him decline Ashby's offer of a post-court beer. They'd driven back to the parking lot behind APD headquarters and walked to their personal cars. He wanted a beer, desperately. But not with Ashby. Not with anyone. Well, he would have wanted it with Rachel, but they'd destroyed that option.

He'd driven for hours. First to his home in Falls Church, where to his disgust and fear he spotted not only his wife's car in the driveway but a white unmarked police car at the curb. *Jeez, they had to come for me at home?* And what was Janet doing there now? She'd been home this morning. Wow, was it just this morning, the same day as today? A long day. He was more than a block away when he saw the telltale cars, so he was able to turn away on a side street without coming close enough to be spotted. All they'd see was his headlights. *And now, my tail-lights, baby. Search for me? Search this!* And he gave the finger to his rearview mirror, recognizing the impotence of the failed gesture as he sped off. To where?

To nowhere, really. He stopped to buy some beers at a convenience store and opened them as he drove. Sipped the second, third, and fourth. The first, he guzzled. The fifth, he drank standing by the emptied grave of Edward Pickett in the Payne Street potters' field. Lumpy, freshly churned dirt failed to refill the coffin-less hole up to ground level in front of the small, concrete marker. Maybe the same backhoe parked nearby. Why'd they fill it back in? Maybe so kids couldn't fall in, a hole hard to see in the winter gloom.

Kelly's boozed brain skittered back and forth. He'd been back many times in the year since Pickett was buried, but he'd never seen any kids around, even though this had been his childhood playground. Such a year, this last one. Emma and Pickett, then Rachel. Emma died, Pickett should have died but didn't, then did all on his own. Death, then life with Rachel. Now death again. Thought after thought, in line but discon-nected. He threw the empty beer bottle at the marker but missed and wobbled back to the car to drive away.

Out of the city.

Where they're looking for me.

They would know by now. They'd dug up Pickett's grave and found the evidence. Seven months since Kelly had, well . . . since he'd not killed Pickett, but had done the next best thing he could.

CHAPTER 36

Loaded
Seven Months Ago

APRIL RAINS HAD drenched the cemeteries along South Payne Street, and mourners walking to new graves or popular stones had kneaded muddy paths into the grass. A renewed downpour was keeping visitors away, save for a marked police cruiser following a plain white van. FTO Herbert Jackson drove over the curb cut on South Payne Street and parked down a rough access road marked by parallel stone and gravel lines near a recently opened hole, its removed dirt usually discreetly covered by tarps but unconcealed from the eyes of the only attendants today, the professionals. A backhoe stood by, closer than propriety usually allowed.

As the driver and assistant exited the van and opened the swinging back doors, the FTO popped the trunk, got out, and grabbed his thick winter galoshes. He perched on the edge of the open trunk and pulled the heavy rubber boots on over his shiny shoes. He absently noted that his recruit's equipment bag still lay in the trunk, that the new kid forgot to transfer it to the other officer's cruiser in which he rode for this shift. FTO Jackson didn't want him along this afternoon. He had a bad feeling about Kelly.

The funeral home employees from the van already had their boots on and were sliding the plain wooden coffin off the van floor onto a platform with large but narrow wheels. They struggled in the soft muddy ground until Jackson stepped up to lift and push with them. At the side of the grave, they all paused.

The FTO pulled a small notebook from a chest pocket under his thick plastic raincoat, removed a pen, considered its unlikely chances of legibility in the wet, and traded it for a short pencil. He spoke to the men. "Gentlemen, can I confirm this is the body of Edward Pickett, fifty-three, of no fixed address, born in Richmond. Deceased in the Alexandria Adult Detention Center on March 15, four days ago?"

One of the men, respectful in a black suit, thin black tie, and white shirt, elaborately checked papers on a clipboard on a shelf under the coffin and said, "Yup. Technically, pronounced dead at Alexandria Hospital, but yup. Y'all already know this, you followed us from the hospital and you checked him there. Y'all even opened up the box. Now you asking us?" He tapped the head of the coffin and said, "You even checked the face with the photo you got. Hope that's enough for you."

"Gotta ask the questions, sir. My job."

Pickett had died earlier in the week in the Alexandria Hospital emergency room, taken there from jail after complaining of a severe headache after what might have been a fall. He'd been awaiting trial on capital murder, abduction with intent to defile, and weapons charges in the death of Emma Louise Kelly, age eight. Autopsy found a ruptured cerebral artery. He was also found to have suffered a rupture of his large intestine, apparently due to a congenital defect and not related to the regular beatings that a rapist received often in jail. The rupture was also well outside the range of any intrusions that might also befall a locked-up sex offender, or so the medical examiner's report showed. He had no family, no permanent address, no one to speak for him or bury him. So the City of Alexandria did. And any movement of the deceased under city jurisdiction since his arrest had to be monitored and documented for the official record. By the police.

More precisely, by FTO Jackson, stepping back in the rain as a cemetery worker fired up the backhoe and moved it close to the coffin. Heavy canvas straps were wrapped under the head and toe of the cheap, unfinished wooden box and hooked over the teeth of the backhoe scoop. As the scoop arm began to take up slack and lift the coffin, the cortege turned at the sound of a car skidding on the wet to park oddly angled at the curb where the cemetery path left the road. It was an unmarked cruiser, and they heard a clink of glass as the driver opened the door and stepped out, his suit instantly soaked in the downpour.

"Fuck," muttered the FTO. He intercepted the man. "Kelly, you don't need to be here for this. I got it." Jackson tried to step into Kelly's way, but the drunk detective staggered around him, steps splashing on the wet ground as he closed on the tableau: light pine coffin swinging slowly over the gaping hole, mud all around on the boots of the attendants, the burbling roar of the backhoe engine now idling, now accelerating as the arm took the coffin's weight and began extending. All glowing red momentarily in the taillights of the departing funeral home van.

Kelly almost ran to the head of the coffin, past the FTO and the immobile crew, and lifted his arms. Kelly's whiskey breath left steam puffs in the chill air. He took a boxer's stance close to the cheap white concrete marker and delivered a roundhouse right against the hard wood of the suspended coffin, then a left jab, then another right which missed, its unspent momentum propelling Kelly off-balance and dropping forward to be caught by the ready FTO before falling into the muddy hole, the coffin spinning like a dead piñata above him as he now knelt in the dirt, hands on knees. The work crew stopped the rotation and steadied the coffin, realigning it with the hole as Jackson pulled the blubbering detective out from under it and away. As it lowered, Kelly threw off Jackson and turned to watch, eyes wet with more than rain, his slurred words almost inaudible against the chug of the backhoe diesel and the wet wind.

"He did it. You know what he did. You know he killed Emma. You know that, right? He killed her."

The FTO heard. "Yes, John. I know that. I know. You did all you could. You tried to save her, you were there. Nobody could'a stopped it. Nobody knew he was going to do that. You did your best."

"I did nothing."

They both spoke, but Kelly never heard. When the coffin was fully lowered into the grave, the workman unsnapped the straps on one side, then lifted the scoop to slide the straps out from underneath, the heavy canvas thickened with clinging mud. He drove the tractor around to reposition the scoop by the dirt pile, then stopped it and got out. The other workman, rain dripping off the white hardhat his regulations required, picked up a shovel and walked toward the two cops with it.

"Either of y'all want to throw the first earth onto the coffin? It's the respectable thing to do."

Kelly exploded. From a position leaning back against the parked cruiser, he rushed forward, arms again raising but caught this time by Jackson before he could connect, his fists bloody from the first assault on the pine coffin.

"Respect! Respectable? You think that filthy piece of shit deserves respect? He's nothing." Kelly stomped one foot in the mud with his words. "Nothing! He's not a person, he's seized property."

But just that quickly, a switch was thrown and Kelly subsided. Spellbound, his arms relaxed under the grip of FTO Jackson's hands, his back curved loosely and he shrank. He spoke softly to his former FTO, who looked over at the workmen. "Why don't you guys take a walk, go get some coffee? Give us a bit," the FTO said. He pulled a twenty out of his wallet and gave it to the backhoe driver. "Coffee's on me. Come back in half an hour."

"We gotta see that he's planted," said the one with the shovel.

"I gotta cover him up," said the backhoe operator.

"You will. We'll be here. Just take off for a few."

"But we—"

"NOW."

After they were gone, Jackson and Kelly stood at the foot of the grave. Jackson's rubber boots sank to the ankles in the raised mud. Kelly's unprotected shoes were ruined. Kelly began to pace alongside the grave, stopping to mutter at the head a few times. The FTO said to Kelly, "Long as you need." He expected Kelly would piss on the grave, which seemed reasonable.

Kelly's wanderings got wider. He walked around the hole, wide past the dirt pile, ranging toward the cruiser stopped on the path. Rain dripped off the hard, shiny black brim of the FTO's uniform eight-point hat, and in the dim of late afternoon, it was becoming hard to see, so he didn't watch Kelly all the time. So he missed the moment when Kelly walked to the driver's side door of the cruiser, opened it, and used his fleet key to start the car, release the electric lock, and remove the shotgun from the rack along the seat. He only noticed when Kelly racked and loaded it.

The FTO dove to one side toward the cover of the backhoe. He drew his gun, instinctively aiming at the man with the shotgun, knowing a threat but confused, unwilling to accept that threat from a fellow cop.

"JOHN, DROP THE GUN! DROP IT NOW!" ordered the FTO. He covered Kelly as he marched toward the grave. If Kelly faced toward him, focused any attention on him, Jackson would shoot. But Kelly looked only at the hole.

"JOHN, DROP THE GUN! DROP IT! JOHN, DROP IT," the FTO continued. He touched his radio but paused. *Maybe later, but not if I don't have to. Not yet.*

Kelly stamped through the mud and stopped at the head of the grave, left foot against the marker, and pointed the dull black shotgun down into the hole. The FTO heard him sob, "All I can do," as he fired straight down into the coffin at the head of the grave. The powerful blast jerked Kelly as the black plastic butt slammed upward into his shoulder, ears stunned by the roaring bang, the orange muzzle blast outlining Kelly over the hold. *Clack-caclack* as Kelly pumped the gun to eject the spent shell and fired again, barely aiming but unable to miss at point-blank range, the twelve-gauge blowing pellets down that spread out in the scant feet between muzzle and pine, Kelly's cry slurring to an inarticulate wail as he pumped the gun again, propped it under his arm and fired a third time downward, ripping apart another section of the upper end of the coffin, lead smashing completely through the box and its loathed contents. After a fourth pump and a trigger pull that loosed another blast that deafened Kelly as it reverberated back up out of the hole, the shotgun was empty. Kelly, too.

The FTO had counted the shots, so he holstered his pistol and slowly walked out from behind cover to take control of

Kelly's smoking gun, its hot barrel steaming as the rain fell and sizzled on it. The FTO racked the long gun to eject the last spent casing and looked down at the wreckage of the top end of the coffin. Saw splinters spread out from the destroyed end closest to the tombstone, mixing with the mud and rising rainwater. Light-colored chunks. Shattered bits of wood. Bones? Teeth? He walked Kelly deeper into the cemetery and away from the defiled grave.

As they walked, the police radio squawked. "Unit 224, we have a report of possible shots fired in the area of the 800 block of South Payne Street, confirm you are still on the scene there, and can you handle? Will have backup en route."

"224, copy. That's negative on shots fired. Truck backfiring. Clear the call unfounded."

"Direct, 224. All units, disregard shots fired. Unit 324 on the scene. Unit 324? Will you be out much longer on your detail?"

"Affirmative, Headquarters. Gonna be a while."

He sat Kelly in the front passenger seat of the cruiser. Gently, unfelt by the stricken detective, the FTO plucked Kelly's handgun with the gentle skill of a pickpocket and dropped it into the pocket of his own raincoat. *Just in case*, he thought. He secured the empty shotgun in the car lock. He walked back to the hole, picked up the shovel, and began covering the coffin with dirt from the pile, concentrating on the damaged end. When the workmen returned, the cops left.

The FTO drove Kelly home and gave Kelly his gun back, with the cartridges removed. *At least Kelly will have to concentrate on loading it before he does anything else*, the FTO thought. Kelly would have to think, if only for the moment it would take him to reload.

Maybe that would be long enough.

CHAPTER 37

Count to Ten
Thursday, November 3, 1988
2345 HRS–Midnight

SHAKING OFF THE booze-blurred memory of Pickett's burial, Kelly drove in the dark and falling snow away from the Payne Street Cemetery and onto the Capital Beltway, the ring highway around Washington, D.C., and its closest suburbs. The inner loop of the Beltway ran in a clockwise circle and was three or four lanes at various spots. Here, it served as the border between Alexandria and neighboring Fairfax County. Both municipalities had jurisdiction, although patrol on this highway was generally left to the Virginia State Police. Kelly thought, *I can stay away from my guys for now.*

A metal lip on the dashboard by the radio served as a bottle opener and was well-scarred from continued service. He opened the sixth and last beer on it and sipped. Dropping the bottle into a holder by the shift lever, he turned on the radio. It searched and stopped on a station that was recommended to him by the young kid that his old FTO was training now, WHFS. It was a weak station in Maryland that didn't always come in on this side of the Potomac. A weird station that played odd rock called alternative and singer-songwriters that sounded good but of whom he'd never heard. He never stayed on WHFS long enough to catch the disc jockeys back-announcing the names of the songs. Here was a singer he'd heard before, droning about how the dreams in which he's dying are the best he's ever had. It stuck with him.

Kelly had never really thought about the meaning of death, or not more than any cop did—the moments and eons after death, that is, the permanence. He had imagined the moments before it a thousand times, all the ways that death could come to him, all the bank robbers who could shoot him or the beaten wives who could stab him or the cop-hating snipers who could pick him off. Burning in a wrecked patrol car. Failing to save a suicide, or suicide itself. Death was known to Kelly—he confronted it every day at work. As a patrol officer, he had worn a bullet-resistant (not bullet*proof*) vest and openly carried a pistol. Protections from deliberate attack, and pretty bizarre accessories for members of a civilized society, really. But the world was full of bad guys and girls, and they didn't look like they were ready to kill you. But they were. All the time. So you had to be ready. It wore on you.

And the job was filled with dead people. Sick and beaten and dying people. People in crashed cars. Burnt in home fires. Shot to death right in front of you. DRT. It wasn't that you got used to death, but you got to a point where it didn't surprise you anymore. You got comfortable with it.

He drove along the highway, high-speed lanes that first aimed west, then north, then began to turn back east as they rounded the circle. Almost midnight now, and few others out here in the rain. This was bad because it left him more visible to the troopers, but it was okay too because he wasn't drunk enough to need to cover one eye yet to see only one set of lane markers instead of a blurred convergence of double-visioned lines. A good thing, that, because he needed both hands: one to steer, the other to hold the last beer bottle.

And if they caught him, so what? Not that a cop would charge another cop, but what if they did? A weekend in the clink, with nobody coming at him? Nothing, compared to what was circling him. Maybe not so bad. No graves, no wives, no Rachel.

No baby.

The car weaved more as Kelly's vision blurred in tears. *Maybe I could get popped out here in Fairfax County and not in Alexandria City—then I wouldn't have to worry about things like messing up Ashby's old case by destroying the face of the prime suspect and the evidence they needed to clear the kid. I never knew that kid anyway. Who cares if he's cleared? He's not in jail. He's free. Jumari isn't free. He has to go with his dad. The bad dad. I could be in jail for a while. I need a break. I can't go to jail. I'm a cop for at least tonight. A last night.* Too many thoughts, none that lined up.

I need just a moment where it all gets quiet, Kelly thought at sixty-five miles per hour in the rain. A stretch of highway lay open in front of him as he crested a hill and saw no cars at all for more than a mile. No headlights, no taillights, dead, and Kelly thought, *I'm alone here, right now. I wish I could close my eyes and see the future. Or not have to see it.*

On the radio a band Timbuk 3 sang a new song called "Count to Ten." So Kelly did.

Hands steady on the wheel, he pressed his foot down on the gas pedal and shut his eyes. He would count to ten, he thought, and at the end . . . *something* would happen. He would open his eyes and move forward with his life, or he'd crash alone and be out of it all. He would be saved, by accident or by God. Or not. So he held his eyes shut, and it wasn't hard.

And he counted aloud and alone.

"ONE." *My day was shit, the worst day of my life since Emma died. Since all the bad began small and piled on today, big and all at once . . .*

"TWO." *I failed Jumari and now he goes back into danger, from his own dad and the creeps dad brings with him . . .*

"THREE." *I failed Dora Stibble and she thinks I'm shit, a mom trying to protect her kid and now she can't and it's my fault . . .*

"FOUR." *The newspaper's gonna rip me up and the department both. I look stupid, and the APD does too . . .*

"FIVE." *The LT's gonna rip me a new one with a '67 for, what? For incompetence, or knowledge of laws and procedures. Both . . . ?*

The tires sang, and the wind's song doubled in volume as the small car accelerated. The needle passed eighty and eighty-five, unseen on the speedometer before Kelly's closed eyes as the car rushed unguided down the empty highway.

"SIX." *I pushed Janet away, or just ran away. Maybe we were in a hole anyway but I dug it . . .*

"SEVEN." *Ashby can't prove Pickett did the little sister, so the brother stays on the hook, a freak to his family who'll never know for sure who did their kid . . .*

"EIGHT." *I'll get indicted and lose my job, probably go to jail. Destruction of evidence, interference with the administration of justice, abuse of a corpse. Pick a card . . .*

"NINE." *Rachel killed my baby. Our baby. Ours. Us . . .*

"TEN." *I've lost Rachel . . .*

"Oh, Rachel," he finally sobbed, his voice lost under the scream of the speeding car.

And with that, with ten, having received no answer from God or chance, Kelly spun the steering wheel, throwing the small sedan hard to the right across whatever lanes still separated it from whatever, guardrails or trees or ditches, consciously forcing a squint to hold his panicking eyes shut, left-side tires roaring with purchase on the pavement, wind rush changing as the car swung, then a hard jounce of tires bumping over something and a screeching impact with the rail.

Kelly bounced against his seat belts as the car shot through a hole in the guardrail between the main travel lanes and a parallel set for the Merrifield exit at Route 50, the road surface uneven in the gap left for emergency and service vehicles to pass. He flopped back, and his clenched hands were pounded with twisting right-left shocks sent through the steering wheel by the tires hitting the uneven paving as the car angled through the hole with feet to spare and in line with the curving exit ramp but offset just enough to let the front fender scrape hard against the curving steel rail, crushing in and shattering the left headlight and turn signal, their structures noisily buckling and throwing bright sparks unseen to Kelly's closed eyes. The curved rail guided the speeding car in a long right turn along the ramp, screeching, peeling the fender back, crumpling the driver's-side door and shattering the window by his ear. Bits of glass struck his head and face like buckshot as the car ground fast, then slower and slower around the turn, its exposed left front tire blowing out with a solid concussive bang that whammed through Kelly's chest and down his throat as he screamed in terror and finality and fury and opened his eyes as the ruined car . . .

Stopped.

And his life did not.

A few minutes later, blue lights strobed through the still-intact back window and reflected onto Kelly's red eyes from the rearview mirror. A white light suddenly illuminated the entire interior from the state police cruiser's spotlight, and a wavering beam intruded from the passenger side as the trooper approached with flashlight in hand. His flat hat deflecting the sleet, the trooper opened the passenger-side door and surveyed Kelly, still belted but leaning forward now against the wheel, rivulets of blood from his glass-cut scalp coursing down his pale face, ticks and pings sounding from the cooling engine and torn bodywork.

Kelly turned to the trooper, whose dark face was lost in the night but whose eyes shone with professional care, and slurred, "Would it make any difference if I told you I was a police officer?"

CHAPTER 38

Contract
Friday, November 4, 1988
0730–0900 HRS

KELLY WOKE UP dead. Or wishing he were. Before he could open his eyes, he had to pull the blanket over his head to block the daylight, weak though it was from cloud cover and the drawn curtains. In his own bedroom, he noticed. How? He clasped his hands to each side of his throbbing skull, but the fingers caused sharp pains of their own, touching crust in his hair, and he pulled them away, slowly, his eyes opening to note fresh blood and shiny bits on his fingertips. Everything was done slowly, movement triggering vast increases in pain in his head and his gut.

After an hour, or the true five minutes it was, Kelly was able to push himself sideways then up in the bed, swinging his sock feet off the mattress and onto the cold wood floor. He was wearing yesterday's T-shirt and slacks, but his belt, badge clip, and empty holster had been removed and lay on his bureau. He stared at them a minute.

Kelly accepted his state of dress even though he could not account for it, unable to devote much higher processing to such confusing matters. The internal hangover hurt he could account for, having much experience with it in recent years, but the surface scarring and sharp pain were new. His presence home was a surprise, though, as he remembered blurred images of the night before. His car? His freedom? His life? Mysteries.

Movement was a challenge worth meeting only to get to something that would help alleviate the agony. Coffee in the kitchen, Advil in the bathroom, booze somewhere. Not in that order. Kelly kept it simple. The bathroom was first because it was closest. The childproof cap fought back, but Kelly won and swallowed three painkillers dry through much practice. Next, down the stairs to the kitchen and coffee, but a sharp smell of alcoholic beverage there hit and surrounded him like an ocean wave, overcoming him with both the relief of meeting an old friend and the nauseating flood of recognized poison. He focused and saw a dozen assorted bottles lined up along the kitchen counter next to the sink. *All empty. Jeez, what did I do last night?* Kelly could not summon an answer.

Among the mist of smells, Kelly localized that of brewed coffee, spotted the drip pot steaming, and finally came to his senses. He walked past the kitchen and into the dining room, where Lieutenant Walter Ramirez sat reading a newspaper and sipping from his own fresh mug. At the sight of Kelly, the lieutenant checked his wristwatch, rose, and walked to the kitchen phone.

"Hi, Jane, let me talk with the sarge." After a moment he identified himself and said, "I'm with John Kelly. I'm over his house and he's sick. He won't be in today. Yeah. I'd put him on the phone but I think he needs to stay in bed . . . We'll talk about it later. Later. Yes, I'll have him call you if he needs another day, but I don't think he will. Sure thing." He hung up and said to Kelly, "Good, that gives us some time."

"Time for what? What are you doing here?" Kelly leaned forward, arms crossed and elbows propped on the back of a dining room chair

"You don't remember? Not surprised. Let's try questions and answers, John. Siddown, let me get you some coffee and you tell me some things, like where your car is. Can you remember that?"

Kelly did dimly, generally. He had crashed his car. As he sipped his coffee and the caffeine and Advil began loosening the pliers on his brain, more specific and bright flashes of memory illustrated other little parts: blue lights in the mirror, stinging pain on top of his head, and the smell of antiseptic, an ambulance crew talking with him. A stew of disjointed images that congealed into a series of events that he traced in reverse. Riding home with his old FTO, Jackson. Signing a form for a paramedic. Sitting with a trooper in a VSP cruiser and how tight it is in the back of a cop car. Crashing his car. Counting to ten. Killing himself.

He had tried to kill himself.

Kelly dashed into the kitchen to throw up in the sink, which already reeked of booze, the smell triggering a second internal explosion. His elbows jostled a lineup of empty bottles on the counter. Done, spent, he turned and sat on the floor of the kitchen, sock feet out, hands in his lap.

The lieutenant came in and sat down on the floor across from him. "Your car?"

"I, I wrecked it."

"How'd you do that, John?"

"I don't remember."

"I think you do, John. I don't think you wrecked accidentally."

"You . . . why . . . why are my bottles all up there, and why are they empty? Did we drink them last night?"

Ramirez almost laughed. "You could have. You didn't. I poured them all out for you. Focus, John. Where's your car?"

"You know. Don't play lieutenant games. You tell me."

"Okay, I'll tell you. You wrecked on the Beltway at Route 50. State Police handled it and called us when they figured out who you were. I came and got you and brought you home. And now we're gonna talk about the rest of your life. Pay attention."

The lieutenant got up and retrieved a steel trash can from just outside Kelly's back door, brought it into the kitchen, and placed it next to Kelly by the sink. One by one, Ramirez picked up and threw the empty bottles into the can, where they shattered. Kelly leaned away from the crashing sounds to lie on the floor and twitch hard with each smash. Irish whiskey, vodka, wine, vermouth, gin, bourbon, beer times eleven, emptied cans clanking or dry, bottle after bottle breaking to bits against the bottom of the can and Kelly's eardrums. Kelly held his palms against his hears till Ramirez finished, then pushed back to a sitting position and looked at his hands, on which fresh blood was again spotted. He looked at Ramirez with dawning understanding.

"Trooper saw what you are and called the watch commander. Me. I sent Jackson to get you. We'd been chasing you all day."

"Huh?"

"You had a pretty big day yesterday, didn't you? And you don't know the half of it. You still haven't answered my question. Where's your car?"

"Fuck do I know, where's my car. Why didn't I get arrested?"

"Should have. But the trooper's a friend of mine. We've been to schools together, and he and Jackson are both in Black Law Enforcement Officers of Virginia. He got the paramedics to treat you for the cuts on your head, from the window glass?" The lieutenant's voice slipped into the singsong stilted lilt of a police report or courtroom testimony. "When he noted they were using alcohol swabs, he recognized that he could not obtain a proper blood-alcohol level on you, so he could not in fairness bring drunk driving charges against you. Or at least, that's what he'll tell his II guys if they ever ask why you weren't charged. By the way, you know what they call Internal Investigations in the State Police? The Office of Professional Standards. OOPS. "

"Yeah, that's funny. Why would he do that? I don't even work for VSP."

"Because it's what I asked him to do. We do it all the time."

"What?"

"Watch out for you, guys like you. This is a tough job. You can't make it alone. We are a team and we make things happen for us."

"Team?"

"Not all of us. The ones who deserve it, the ones we think are worth working for. That's you, Kelly. You deserve a break or two. You work hard, and you've had some tough things happen. Emma, for one."

"Emma? What do you know about how tough things? Emma? I never talked about her."

"You think you gotta talk about something for us to know something? You should have talked with me. Everybody knows what happened with Emma, right in front of you. Everybody knows what that meant to you."

"No you don't."

"Yes, we do, because we would go through the same thing. And we'd do things for others like you."

"Like what?"

"Pammie Martinson, for example. We're taking care of her."

"Sure, taking care of her. Screwing her more likely . . . No, I don't mean *screwing* her, but you're sure beating her up. I mean, writing her up for no badge? And a traffic summons for a pursuit crash during a gunfight?"

"You don't get it. Maybe that's good, we're not obvious." Ramirez told Kelly about the flawed traffic ticket that Pammie would beat in court. "And the badge thing, we only went ahead with writing her up because the newspaper caught that the judge dropped the charges on the shooter because of it."

"The judge . . ."

"Is an asshole, but it doesn't matter. The charges were nol prossed, not dismissed. Nol prossed means they can be refiled. Were refiled, in fact, last night, and TAC went out and picked up Goodell. He had crack in his pockets, so a bonus charge. He's going down double."

"But her statement, Pammie gave it at advisement. He confessed shooting at her, and the judge threw it out."

"So what? We got civilian witnesses who saw him shoot at her, we got D.C. cops who saw him with the gun that matches slugs in her car, we got the gun dropped on the ground on the bridge in plain sight. *We don't need no stinkin' confession.*"

"But double jeopardy?"

"Doesn't obtain. Trial never started."

"So why the rigamarole? Why write her up if she's gonna skate? Why do that to her?"

"Because that's the system. We gotta write people up. We've got so many written directives they filled two big ring notebooks, like two thousand pages. You think anybody can move without violating one or two or three of them? She gets slammed, but in a way that doesn't hurt her, but the bosses see she got written up and they are satisfied. Good cover for me and the sergeant, too."

"Huh? Why do you need cover?"

"So I can keep doing it, can stay where I am and not get demoted or fired. Hard enough to do the job the way I am and not get the big bosses to come down on me."

"The way you are? What, Latino, you mean?"

"Nah. Different than that. I gotta be seen as a tough guy, all the time." Ramirez paused as he made a decision about how far to take this, how much to reveal, how important it was to show Kelly that secrets could be overcome and covered. "Got to be the one to be a hardass. Gotta keep that reputation, otherwise they think I'm a pansy."

"Why?"

"Because I'm gay, and the chief and deputy chiefs know it, and they don't like it because they're old style and prejudiced, and if a gay lieutenant gave them an excuse, they'd can him in a heartbeat."

"Gay? You're gay? You mean, like with guys? Really? I didn't know. But so what, who cares if you're gay?"

"Old cops do. The ones around long enough to be in charge, and who still equate homosexuality with femininity and weakness. Old-school bosses. If it got out, they'd fire me. They'd almost have to. By their reasoning, nobody'd work for me. Sucks, but that's how it is in a paramilitary organization."

"That's bullshit."

"That's the way it is, with them."

"So, what's that got to do with me?"

"I'm watch commander a lot, especially on Nights and Midnights. Lotta stuff happens that I can keep an eye on. Plus since I'm working till morning, I can set stuff up to happen on Days, like making sure the exhumation call got assigned to Jackson."

Kelly paled. Until then he'd forgotten they had dug up the coffin and thus revealed Kelly's drunken shotgun attack. So that all came flooding back, and the Stibble case, and the lieutenant's threat to write him up. Jeez, how many '67s can a guy get? If Kelly hadn't been empty, he'd have barfed again.

"I lost the case in court, yesterday, the abduction case. You said you . . ."

"Yeah, I'm gonna write you up for that, but it's only because it was in the paper today and the chief cares about that kind of press. Bigger case from yesterday is TAC and the magnets." The lieutenant told Kelly the events surrounding the tactical unit's use of industrial magnets to fuzz out defense attorneys' tape recordings and the surprise revelation in court in front of everyone.

"The press missed the TAC thing, but the newspaper's already out on you. It actually doesn't make you look too bad. More like it shows the judge as a bleeding heart, which around here shouldn't be newsworthy. The reporter took the tack that it was a bad law, enforced by a judge with no heart. That's the quote from the CA anyway. Duckworth. He's a good guy."

"He's a prick."

"He's saving the kid. I talked with him. He gave me the name of a good private attorney, gonna help Momma Stibble with the custody thing for free."

"What good's that gonna do?"

"Duckworth filed the photos and the letter in the court file. Jeez, they were gross." Ramirez would have shuddered if he weren't a twenty-year cop. "This way they are public. Fourth Amendment doesn't keep evidence out of a civil action. Illegally seized evidence is still evidence. It still exists, it just can't be used by the government in a criminal case. Now, civil? Bring it on. No judge in hell's gonna let that kid go with that man, dad or no dad."

Kelly, against all odds, felt a lifting in his chest. One weight removed. But many others still pressed down.

The lieutenant continued. "For TAC, Judge wants an internal investigation, but we're on that too. Turns out that the Public Defender's Office never established that they had a legal right to record testimony in General District Court. Circuit Court is a court of record and is always recorded. But there might not be controlling legislation that allows tape recording in the lower court. We're looking into it. It may be that the PDs were in violation in doing so. It clouds the issue."

At the mention of the Public Defenders' Office, Kelly's brain and heart filled with thoughts of Rachel. He felt sick again but confused. He rubbed his left hand where the pale trench from a wedding ring remained, and the lieutenant noticed. "John, no one told me about Janet. When did you split up?"

"Months ago. I don't tell people everything."

"Or anything. Janet told me yesterday you were getting a divorce."

"Yesterday? You saw . . ."

"I came here, looking for you. She had a guy with her. Didn't take her long. I guess maybe he's helping her. Help, you need help like that. All the help you can get, John. Someone . . ." Ramirez stopped when he saw Kelly's sick frown shift to despair. "You need help. And you're gonna get it."

"Get it? Get what, get clobbered? II's gonna zap me. I'm gonna get indicted for Pickett. You do know now about what I did with Pickett, last year in the graveyard." At Ramirez's nod, Kelly drooped even more. "What kinda help is gonna *help* me?" Almost a whine.

"You need help getting your head out of your ass. You gotta straighten yourself out, here, in this room first, then outside this room, then at work."

"What's in this room?"

"I'll tell you what's not. No booze. I poured it out, all I could find, while you were sleeping." The lieutenant kicked the steel trash can, which tinkled with broken bottle glass. "You're gonna get straight. You're gonna go to AA, and you're gonna go to EAP."

"You can't force me to go to Employee Assistance."

"We can if it's part of an II case."

"For a charge of violating knowledge of laws and procedures? Not big enough to warrant EAP."

"Oh yeah? How's this, John? How about something bigger. Something unforgiveable." Ramirez let his eyes show only a slight glimmer, like a professional poker player laying out a flush. "Where's your gun?"

Kelly reflexively brought his hand to his right hip where his pistol could have been but wasn't. He stared at the lieutenant in confusion.

"You lost your gun in the crash. Worst '67 in the world, a cop loses his service weapon." Ramirez didn't think Kelly could have turned paler, but he did.

The lieutenant continued. "In about," he checked his wrist-watch, "two hours, the state trooper who worked your crash is gonna call me, tell me he found it just now at the crash site. Nothing worse than losing your gun, John. Can be grounds for termination, but in this case, it's going to be a thirty-day suspension. Enough time for you to start getting your head together, get started with AA, go to the Employee Assistance Program for counseling."

"Wait. How do you know thirty days?"

"Because that's what I'm is going to recommend you get for losing your service weapon. When I finish writing you up for it. I came in this morning from Baltimore to do it."

"Baltimore?"

"Yeah, I live there. With Tracy. My significant other."

"I've never met her."

"Tracy isn't a her. Don't you listen? Tracy's a guy. That's why we live in Baltimore. Right on the edge of the maximum allowed distance from HQ, but far enough away we don't bump into APD much. My husband and I bumped into Jackson at an art festival once a few years ago and I introduced them. Tracy said, 'I don't get to meet Walter's coworkers much.' We all understood why. Too bad."

"But no, wait. How come you're writing me up already? And how do you know the trooper's gonna find my gun?"

"Because he already did. It's in my trunk. Jackson gave it to me this morning. I'll write a supplement that says the trooper turned it over to me later today. FTO Jackson and I talked this through on the phone last night after he picked you up out on the highway, John."

Kelly tried to think, but it was hard right then. "You got me, I guess," he said, softly.

"I don't want to get you, John. But I need you to do something, and getting you is the only way I can make you. I care about you, John, but you have to care about yourself. I can hold this over you, but it's all up to you. Get it? You gotta go with the flow. It's what's best. We got it worked out."

"You work out the Pickett thing?"

"What Pickett thing, John?" Kelly had woken up enough now to notice the lieutenant's eyes crinkle in a controlled smile.

"I destroyed Pickett. You know that. You have to know that by now. Jackson was there when I shot him up. Was all I could do to that bastard." Kelly's voice rose. "He gave up so fast after,

after he shot Emma, we didn't have time to kill him. Then he went and died, so no trial. You know what I did then."

"You shot up his coffin," Ramirez said.

"I blew up his head."

"You blew up his feet."

"Feet?"

"Yeah, dummy. You shot the end of the coffin with his feet in it. His skull is intact, I looked at it yesterday. Had the medical examiner's team open the coffin at the exam room. Jackson told them he had to see it to write the report, or his recruit did. Skull's fine. Teeth are fine. In good shape and ready for forensic examination. The report notes significant damage to the lower end of the coffin, though. Feet were at the end closest to the tombstone. Not usually how it's done, but it was. Guess they planted him wrong way around. Damage to the feet end was reportedly due to the mishandling of the backhoe scoop during disinterment.

"Or so the official report will state." The lieutenant's entire face was smiling now.

Kelly tried to catch up with all the changes, shaking his head and putting his hands up to the lieutenant. "My head's full."

"Yeah, you need a dump truck to unload your head, John."

"That sounds poetic."

"It is. It's a Dylan song called 'From a Buick 6.'" With a deep breath, the lieutenant unfolded himself, stood up, and became the center of the room.

"You get a big break, John. But it's time to call you on it. Last night was, well, you are going to have to admit what it was. To an EAP counselor or at an AA meeting. Or your family. But we both know what it was. Trooper walked Jackson through the scene, still some tire marks in the slush. Clear enough. You didn't crash accidentally."

Kelly didn't hang his head but let his eyes unfocus past Ramirez's face.

The lieutenant continued. "I got your gun, and I know you don't have any others. Janet told me that last night, but I checked this morning anyway. It'll be thirty days till you get it back, maybe more than that, the *investigation continues* and it starts now. Now, you can go buy one, just like you can go buy more alcohol. I found your hidden bottles. But I don't want you to and you better not. I'm not going to make you swear. It's juvenile. But you are going to make me this promise."

From the counter, Ramirez picked up an aluminum ticket case, with summonses inside an inner compartment and a notepad clipped to the outside front. "You're going to write this down, here on this paper. Start writing." Kelly took the case and a proffered gold Cross pen as the lieutenant dictated:

I, John Kelly, promise that I will not make any attempt to take my own life for the next two weeks. I make this promise to Lieutenant Walter Ramirez.

"Now, date it and sign it, John."

The lieutenant folded the handwritten contract and put it into his wallet. "This is between you and me. But I will be back to you in two weeks, and you will write another one. And another one, until I don't think you need to anymore. No one's gonna know, except me and Jackson. No one's gonna know about what you did last night except us, too. And my friend the trooper, but he won't tell. Who you tell is your business, but it better be someone. EAP, AA, if you can learn to believe in them. You got to talk about this. We all got too much going on not to talk about stuff. And there's a lot going on. And now you know some of it." He sipped his cold coffee and looked over the cup at Kelly.

Kelly thought, *I could have talked with Rachel. I would have. But I ruined that now. Did I? I want her to be happy.* His brain spun in a circle. From down on the kitchen floor, Kelly looked up at the lieutenant, then further up as if seeing the sky through the ceiling. *I want her to be with someone who makes her happy.* He remembered her eyes and her smile, her little fingers, and the way she made him happy and excited and thrilled about his future. Their future. Together? *I want what's best for her.*

Ramirez watched Kelly's face light up, an unexpected smile twitching his cheeks and crinkling the sides of his bloodshot eyes. He was suspicious of the change, but knew euphoria sometimes followed depression. Rarely so quickly in his experience, but he decided Kelly could think anything he wanted right now. He'd been through the worst.

"Who is she, Kelly? Who are you with, now?"

"I haven't told you about her."

"Like I said . . . So tell me now. When am I gonna meet her?"

"Probably never. Turns out, we were . . ." Kelly sighed and let it flow. "We were gonna have a child, but she . . . Yesterday, she told me we weren't. She aborted it." Kelly turned away from the lieutenant.

"Aborted. You know this, for sure?"

"She told me yesterday, before we were in court."

"We? What, is she a cop? A prosecutor?"

"Worse. Defense attorney. A public defender."

"Which one?" the lieutenant asked with pointed interest.

"Rachel Cohen."

The lieutenant slid forward on the kitchen floor to grab Kelly's chin and pull his face around. "Rachel Cohen didn't have an abortion. She had a miscarriage. Yesterday. On King Street. I was there."

Kelly gaped at Jackson. "King Street? You . . . How . . ."

"She collapsed. We were there, we called the ambulance. She had a miscarriage, not an abortion.

"Kelly, you fucking idiot. What did you do?"

CHAPTER 39

Bricks
One Week Later

KELLY'S BUTT WAS numb from the four-hour stakeout, but his eyes and mind were sharper than they had been lately, and he spotted his target several blocks out. The rain had stopped, and he had clicked the wipers to clear the windshield. From habit he called out a description, albeit silently; white, late twenties, dark coat or raincoat, dark pants. Shoulder-length dark red hair. Short to medium height, for a woman.

He got out to cross the street in front of her while she was still at a distance, wanting not to startle her by a sudden appearance. His hand swung down toward the console to reach the mic, but none hung there, in this car, his own new used car and not a department unmarked. Which he'd get back at the end of a month, he thought. It felt odd to have to find legal parking. Odder still to walk around downtown without a gun, which sat with his badge and credentials in a drawer in II.

She stopped a moment when she saw him, then continued, closing with him until a few feet away. She stood there and examined him, staring into his face.

"Hi, Rachel."

"John." And nothing more, letting the silence lengthen and the pressure build. It was his move, but he was unsure of her. Sure of how he felt but unwilling to force a response after his despicable behavior when they last spoke alone. His hands hung mute as he began to talk to her. Fallen rain dripped from sodden trees, thumping on car hoods.

"Rachel, there's . . . I . . ." His breath clouded around him and his slick, rehearsed speech vanished. "I know what happened, what it . . . It wasn't what I thought it was. What I accused you of. That you—" and John stopped as Rachel's chin snapped up.

"How . . . could . . . you, John? How could you say, how could you even think I, I would? I love, loved you, John." Her words barely above a hiss. He saw her little, dimpled chin begin to tremble as she spoke. She held her briefcase in both hands in front of her. "Do you have any idea what that meant to me? What that did to me? Do you? I love you. Do you? Do . . ."

And the tremble overcame her voice as her tears began, matching those now on his face. He lifted his hands and moved forward to hug her, but she stepped back.

"The fuck do you think you're doing? You think you're gonna hug me, just *hug* me? And that'll be okay, make everything right? You sent me flowers, John. Flowers? With a note, you cruel fuck. What were you, making fun of me with that note?"

John recoiled in confusion. "Note? What note? With the flowers? I sent flowers the day before the trial. After you told me about . . . our baby. The note, I don't know, the note said a life, an old life ends and a new life starts. Or something. The note was cruel? I was cruel? I thought . . ."

"That's not what you said. You said, 'To life.' Life." Rachel's trembling tears morphed into fury. "When you thought I'd killed our baby. To life. You rotten bastard."

"I didn't think that. Well, I thought that when you told me, but I didn't say it, didn't put it in a note. And I was wrong. I know I was wrong, now. I know what happened to you. And I'm so sorry, Rachel. God, I'm sorry. I found out later, I heard it from one of the guys who were there."

"Oh, yeah, the guys who were there. The guys who said you were going to get fired, or sent to prison. What . . ." Rachel paused, and her voice hesitated as if she were surprised at her words. "What were they talking about, John? Are you in trouble?"

"It's a long story, something I was going to tell you about. From a year ago, before you. But I'm okay, or I'm gonna be okay. We, um, we can—"

Rachel interrupted. "We? There's a we here? There's no *we*, John. You, when you . . . when you didn't believe in me, that's when *we* ended." She sniffed. John wiped away his tears, needing but not daring to reach for hers. A streetlight buzzed into life, first orange, then a pale white over them. "We aren't anything, John. I'm glad you're so fucking okay." She looked down to his side and blinked hard, setting up to begin walking around him and away.

John stepped slightly to that side and said, "Rach, please. You gotta hear me out. Please listen. I . . . I was wrong. I can't, I want to explain what I was, what was happening. I never would have thought you would . . . do that. But I was messed up. I shouldn't've been, I should have been able to be tough about it all, but it just hit hard. That week. It's not fair to you."

"Oh, you got that right, boy." But John was encouraged that she hadn't started walking, yet. He pushed on.

"Rach, can we go somewhere and talk? Can we sit somewhere? I need to tell you something, a lot."

"I don't know if there's anything you can tell me that I'm gonna care about. I . . ." Rachel seemed to try for anger, but sorrow took control.

"Please, let's just sit down. Let me talk to you. Come with me."

"No. I'm not going anywhere. I'm not going." Her voice softened and faded out, devolving into sobs.

When John set out that afternoon to find Rachel, he had searched the blocks near her office till he found her parked car, then posted himself between it and her office to catch her walking to it after work. No real plan. Now she didn't resist as he reached his arms and took her elbow, gently pulling her over and down to sit at the curb between a parked car and the corner. He sat next to her, his nearest hand twitching as he kept it from taking hers as her sobs subsided. She held her briefcase on her lap and turned her head to look at him as he hesitantly spoke.

"First, Rach, I can't tell you how wrong I was to say what I did. I, I know you didn't kill, didn't abort our baby. I know you better than that, even though I didn't say it, even though it's only been, what, a little while we've been together. Three months. And it's been the best time of my life." His voice pushed past the stammer he had started with and became stronger. He turned his body on the curb to face her, holding his hands in front, grasping his right fist with his left hand between them. "My time with you, I've never known what it was like to be so happy with someone. Never. Time with my wi—with Janet, was never as good as with you. But, this year was really tough. A year ago, um, my niece was killed. Right in front of me. And I couldn't do anything to stop it. And my brother . . ." Kelly stopped, willing his new flood of tears to stop and almost succeeding. Rachel moved forward and her hands came closer to his.

She prompted him. "The cops who helped me, they were talking about Emma. Was that your niece? And something else. They said you were in trouble." Kelly sighed and shook his head. Rachel remained sad, but the confrontational fire at her defense attorney core sparked. "You stopped me, John. You brought us here. Talk."

John began telling Rachel what had transpired in the past year, starting with Emma's death and the death of her killer. "Emma was . . . taken. Right after school. We found them. The guy killed her. Right in front of me. I couldn't kill him." Kelly sobbed, bit it back. "But I wanted to. Kill him. It was too quick." Kelly tried to take a deep breath, fought a moment, and went on. "When they buried him, I just found myself there."

Slowly, sentence by sentence, each heavy as bricks, he took down the wall between her and what he'd hidden. His drunken attempt to achieve some victory over or punishment of Pickett by shotgunning his corpse. His brother's righteous, awful hatred at Kelly's failure. His growing, final distance from Janet, the disappearance of their love and the recognition of the collapse of their marriage. A reluctant admission of the solace and shield of alcohol. Losing Jumari's case and surrendering the poor child to his father. His hands were still clenched on his knee, but Rachel's thin fingers had crept forward unnoticed and now wrapped around one of his corded wrists.

Rachel winced when Kelly talked of Stibble's acquittal, but Kelly said, "No, not your fault. You did what you were supposed to, and I didn't. I haven't been doing a lot I am supposed to do." Kelly refocused. "I got suspended, you know."

"No; I didn't, John. For how long?"

"Thirty days. The most you can get without being fired. It's so, well, so they can keep an eye on me."

Kelly explained about EAP, but not about the real reason for his crash. He hoped he wouldn't have to tell her about that today. Maybe never. He recognized that concealing this was a failure but just added it to the list. It was still a big brick in their wall, but he could step over it till later.

"So what are you doing now?" Rachel asked, as if she had forgotten her anger at him and still cared. He told her he kept busy down at the high school boathouse, cleaning and refurbishing the crew team's racing shells and regularly taking out a single.

"Rowing, and keeping up the boats, a little woodwork, tightening up the riggers, that sort of stuff. They call them shells but nobody knows what you're talking about when you say racing shells. I used to row, in school. In fact, I have the same name as a famous rower from Philadelphia." His grandfather had taught him to work with his hands, and other things. It was little nips at the Jameson bottle with Grampop in the backyard that gave him his first taste of whiskey. So good but maybe a bad thing. Maybe not the thing he'd do to his own kids.

And with a bang, his mind flooded anew. Kids. The miscarriage. Rachel's anger. They all crashed back into his head. He looked down and noticed she was holding his hand.

"You row? So that's why your legs look lumpy like that," she said. And of course that made him think of her legs, covered now in black slacks, her low-heeled work pumps wet from puddles, and their narrow taper. Kelly loved them, and wondered if he would ever caress them again. He'd wondered as he sat hoping and praying for her to walk by if she would look thinner from her illness or loss, or fatter from being away from him and happier, or sadder. He didn't know, and knowing was the most desperately important thing he had ever known. He kept mumbling on, and she kept leaning toward him in infinitesimally small measures without realizing.

In the hour they cried together on the curb, patrol officers twice slowed to check on them but disengaged when they recognized Kelly. A white unmarked parked at the far end of the block, almost out of Kelly's view but not quite. The rain resumed and masked their tears.

THE END

AFTERWORD

The trauma of a suicide or a suicide attempt does not dissipate as quickly as the foregoing novel portrays. I write fiction. The facts are these:

In my twenty-eight years with the Alexandria, Virginia Police Department serving as a patrol officer, narcotics "jumpout," field training officer, PIO, squad sergeant, lieutenant, and unit commander, we lost one officer to hostile gunfire and none to accidental death. But we lost three police officers to self-inflicted gunshots, with only one case ruled "accidental." During that time, our sister agency, the Alexandria Sheriff's Office, lost two of their deputies to suicide. All in all, five dead by their own hands.

These numbers reflect proportions nationwide. Far more members of law enforcement take their own lives than are lost to criminals, or to accidents like car crashes or falls, or to duty-related illnesses like heart attacks or stroke.

Law enforcement officers face crushing stress daily, stress incomprehensible to those outside the police field and often unseen or unaddressed by those inside. Help has not often been easily accessible to officers trying to cope with the death of partners or victims, disregard and disdain from the general public, and the hostility of suspects, arrestees, their families or other groups angry with law enforcement. Told to "toughen up," unable to access mental health assistance because of their fears of ostracism or career damage, cops bite down on stress—or choose to numb it with cigarettes, pills, booze bottles, inappropriate romantic partners—and show up to work the next day and the day after that, until they reach the end of their careers.

Even absent critical events, officers, deputies, agents, detectives, street supervisors, commanders, and cops of all types work under constant awareness—if not fear—of their imminent death. This crushing, wary pressure is called "hypervigilance," and it generates reactive, protective caution and distance, the us-versus-them stiff arm with which so many in law enforcement push away the public. It thickens the so-called "thin blue line" that some of us hide under or gather behind.

Police stress is unrelenting and builds over the years. Sometimes its effects on our body can be obvious, visible in the gasping of a red-faced patrol officer trying to catch her breath at the end of a foot pursuit or a detective's shaky writing hand over a notebook. Or it can be insidious and invisible like the arterial blockages that caused my two heart attacks on the same day, ending my career. But worst of all, stress can simmer, bubble, and boil over to overwhelm our most basic personal survival instincts and push us to embrace the unthinkable—the release of death at our own hand—as our only option.

Many agencies across the country have been working to provide counseling, stress relief, and help for their members to lead healthier lives. Many agencies (not Alexandria, at the time I write this) permit officers to work out on duty and set up exercise regimens and support programs. Suicide prevention programs and mental health services lag, however, and need help.

But you, in purchasing this book, have helped. Fifty percent of my profit from sales of this novel will be donated to law enforcement suicide prevention.

Thank you for working with me to protect our men and women in blue—or brown, green, tan, gray, black, or white. Whatever color their uniform, if they pin a badge to it, they are risking their lives to protect you.

Mark Bergin
Alexandria, Virginia & Kitty Hawk, North Carolina

ABOUT THE AUTHOR

Mark Bergin graduated from Boston University with a degree in journalism, then worked four years as a newspaper reporter, winning the Virginia Press Association Award for general news reporting before joining the Alexandria, Virginia, Police Department in 1986. Twice named Police Officer of the Year for narcotics and robbery investigations, he served in most of the posts described in *Apprehension* and rose to the rank of lieutenant.

Bergin lives in Alexandria and Kitty Hawk, North Carolina, with his wife Ruth, an attorney and former public defender. They have two children.

Write him at berginwriter@gmail.com or follow his blog at markberginwriter.com.

ACKNOWLEDGMENTS

With inspired respect and thanks to Alistair MacLean, Desmond Bagley, Adam Hall, Dashiell Hammett, Raymond Chandler, John D. McDonald, Ross Thomas, Jack D. Hunter, Donald Hamilton, and George V. Higgins. And to my editor, Chris Murray, and my writing partner, Paul M. Day, author of *Keepers of the River*, couldna'done it widdout cha.

GRAND PATRONS

INKSHARES

INKSHARES is a reader-driven publisher and producer based in Oakland, California. Our books are selected not by a group of editors, but by readers worldwide.

While we've published books by established writers like *Big Fish* author Daniel Wallace and *Star Wars: Rogue One* scribe Gary Whitta, our aim remains surfacing and developing the new author voices of tomorrow.

Previously unknown Inkshares authors have received starred reviews and been featured in the *New York Times*. Their books are on the front tables of Barnes & Noble and hundreds of independents nationwide, and many have been licensed by publishers in other major markets. They are also being adapted by Oscar-winning screenwriters at the biggest studios and networks.

Interested in making your own story a reality? Visit Inkshares.com to start your own project or find other great books.

CPSIA information can be obtained
at www.ICGtesting.com
Printed in the USA
FSHW011906030819
60670FS